Lucky in Love

NEW YORK TIMES & USA TODAY BESTSELLING AUTHOR

KELLY ELLIOTT

Lucky in Love
Book 4 Southern Bride Copyright © 2020 by Kelly Elliott
ISBN EBook 978-1-94363364-7
ISBN PAPERBACK 978-1-943633-65-4

Cover photo by: Shannon Cain
Photography by Shannon Cain
Cover Design by: RBA Designs, www.rbadesigns.com
Interior Design & Formatting by: Elaine York, www.
allusiongraphics.com
Developmental Editor: Elaine York, www.allusiongraphics.com
Content Editor: Cori McCarthy, Yellow Bird Editing
Proofing Editor: AmyRose Capetta, Yellow Bird Editing

For more information on Kelly and her books, please visit her website www.kellyelliottauthor.com.

Lucky in Love

You can't blame gravity for falling in love.

—Albert Einstein

Chapter 1

Truitt

THE NURSE LOOKED at me with a stunned expression as she asked for the second time, "What did you say you think you broke?"

I sighed while my brother Roger leaned forward and cleared his throat. "His dick. Is it even possible to break a dick?"

After a glare directed at my brother, I turned back to the nurse. "There was a bit of an accident while we were hiking. I'm not going to lie, I'm in a lot of pain, so if we could make sure it's not severely injured and figure out why my balls...I mean, my testicles, feel like they're in the pit of my stomach, I would be forever grateful."

Her eyes went from mine directly down to my junk. When she bit into her lip, I fought to roll my eyes. My looks were not something I was ignorant of. I knew women thought I was good looking. I had a mirror, I saw what I looked like. Good genes and a healthy regimen of food and exercise was the cause of said good looks and a body I was damn proud of. I fucking worked hard enough for it.

Most men would relish the attention of a beautiful woman, but I had grown tired of it early on. The idea that a woman wanted to sleep with me because I had a nice body and a pretty face wasn't something that interested me anymore, or honestly, maybe ever. Unlike my older brother, who played his cards all the damn time.

"Are you asking me to examine you?" the nurse asked as a flush crept up her neck to her cheeks.

Roger laughed, and that caused her to focus on him instead of my throbbing dick. "That could either make his pain worse, or better, depending on if the idiot actually broke it."

The nurse cleared her throat and tried to look me in the eyes as she spoke. "Well, you can't break your di...I mean, your penis. You can, however, have a blunt force trauma to an erect penis where you could get a condition known as penile fracture. It's not really a fracture, but it's as painful as one. Was your..."

Her eyes drifted down again before they snapped back up. "Was your penis erect at the time of the...um...accident?"

Roger hit me on the arm. "Dude, if you had a woody while we were hiking, we need to seriously have a talk. How long as it been since you've, you know?"

Shooting my brother a look that said I was going to kill him if he didn't shut up, I pulled in a slow, deep breath. "I wasn't hard when it was hit by the branch."

Her brows rose. "Are you sure?"

I felt my jaw open some. "Yes, I'm sure!"

"I don't know, dude, wood seems to get you all hot and bothered." Roger looked at the nurse. "He's a builder, likes working with wood and his hands."

She nodded. "Oh, I see."

I shook my head at her. "Wait, what do you mean, you see? What's that supposed to mean?"

The nurse shrugged and looked between me and Roger.

"Oh, for fuck's sake, I wasn't hard, hiking doesn't make me hard. Wood doesn't make me hard. Women make me hard. Women, only women."

She started to chew on her lip again before she said, "Well, with a penile fracture you'll hear a popping or a crack. It will swell, enough that you'll notice it's swollen."

I looked down at my junk, then glanced up to see Roger and the nurse staring at it.

With a smirk, I replied, "That's normal, it's not swollen."

"Oh!" the nurse said, with a slight lift at the corner of her mouth. "Is it black and blue?"

"Do you want me to pull my shorts down and look?" I asked.

A nervous laugh slipped from her lips. "No. I mean, yes. No, wait. We can certainly do a quick examination, so I can let the doctor know."

Roger used his feet to push the stool he was sitting on closer to me. I looked at him blankly. When his eyes met mine, I could see the corners of them crinkle up. He was attempting to hold back a smile, or a big ass laugh.

"What are you doing?" I asked.

"I want to see what a dick looks like when it's bruised."

I placed my hand on his forehead and pushed him back, causing the stool to roll away from me. "Get the hell out of here!"

The curtain pulled back and another woman walked in. A stunningly beautiful woman.

With a frustrated sigh, I said, "I'm sorry, when will the doctor be over here, I don't think I need another nurse."

The new woman gave a humorless laugh. "I *am* the doctor."

This time my brother let out a roar of laughter as I closed my eyes and cursed inwardly.

The nurse cleared her throat and said, "Mr. Carter has had trauma to his erect penis. He's in pain and believes he might have a penile fracture."

Roger leaned forward and smiled at the nurse. "I have to ask, are you single? Because the way you use the word penile is kind of hot."

The nurse nodded and blushed as I let out a frustrated groan. "For fuck's sake, dude! My dick is throbbing and my balls feel like they're about to fall off, will you stop flirting with the nurse!"

I looked at the doctor and added, "I wasn't erect, by the way."

She nodded, and I had to give her credit, she didn't falter with all the nonsense in the room. She kept her expression neutral. "Let's take a look. Put on the gown while we step out."

The nurse quickly turned and held the curtain open as the doctor handed me a hospital gown.

"You're going to look at it?" I asked, my voice shaking more than I wanted it to.

The doctor gave me a stern look. "Mr. Carter, trust me when I say I've examined a penis or two in my time."

Roger cleared his throat again and pushed the stool back some.

My eyes went to her name tag. "Doctor Turner."

"Yes?" she asked.

"No, I was just reading your name. Um, just take off my shorts?"

"And underwear."

I smiled. "I'm not wearing any."

This time she smiled while one brow rose ever so slightly. I saw her cheeks color just a bit. "I'll be back in a moment."

She pulled the curtain shut and Roger laughed. "Dude, you're fucking flirting with the doctor before she examines your cock. You think that's wise?"

"Get the hell out of here, you idiot."

"Hell to the no, this is classic. Of all the times I've had to sit with you in an emergency room for bullshit stuff, I am not missing the cock examination."

I stood and glared at him. "I hate you."

"Strip, little brother."

"Turn around."

He laughed. "Dude, I've seen your dick before. We grew up together, remember? Not to mention all the times I had to see it in the shower after football practice in high school."

I felt my face constrict. "Why in the hell were you looking at my dick in the shower?"

"How could you not? All of our dicks were out, at some point you're gonna see the dicks."

With a sigh of defeat, I pulled my pants down, causing Roger to close his eyes and spin around in the chair. "Jesus, give a guy some warning before you flash him!"

After I put on the gown, I sat slowly and carefully on the table. I had to admit, the pain was starting to slowly go away. I was beginning to think the trip to the ER for a sore cock was a bad idea.

"It feels like it's getting better...we could probably skip all of this."

"Your voice doesn't seem to be so high anymore," Roger stated as he looked at a poster about flu shots on the wall.

I started to reply to him with a few curse words I saved only for him when the curtain opened again.

Why in the hell can't I be in a regular room for this?

"I'm actually feeling a bit better," I said to the doctor as she stepped into the small exam room.

Roger chuckled and mumbled under his breath. "I think you're about to for sure."

Dr. Turner glanced over to Roger. "Did you want your partner to stay for the exam?"

"Partner!" Roger and I said at the same time.

"Okay, hold up, I'm his brother, first off, so yeah, we're not partners. And I'm staying for this entertainment because I'm sure to become the favorite son once I tell our father about all this."

Dr. Turner looked at me. "Would you like for your *brother* to step out?"

"No, he can stay because I don't want the story to *grow* more than it needs to. Get it, dude...*grow*?"

I stared at my brother in disbelief. The doctor pulled up a stool and sat down.

"Go ahead and stand while you hold your gown up," Dr. Turner stated.

I stood, lifted my gown, and looked at Roger. Cold hands took one of my balls and I glanced down. My breath caught in my throat as I watched her gently roll my ball around in her hands. Her damn face was an inch from my junk. My eyes widened, and I shot a look over at Roger.

He was attempting to hold his laughter in while he pressed his fist to his mouth. As he looked up at me he said, "Dude, I think the story is most definitely fixin' to grow."

I closed my eyes and tried to think of anything other than the fact that a beautiful woman had her mouth inches from my cock. "I'm checking for lumps or any abnormalities," she said.

I nodded, unable to say anything. It really had been a long ass time since I'd had sex.

Then she moved to the other ball, her face now millimeters from my cock.

"Dude!" Roger whisper-shouted, like the doctor wouldn't be able to hear him.

She paused for a moment and then looked up at me and smiled. "I don't believe you have a penile fracture, Mr. Carter. Your penis seems to be working just fine."

My entire body heated as I looked down and saw my cock stiff as a rod.

Betraying bastard!

"That's...um...that's good to know," I whispered as I tried to think of anything that would make the hard-on go away. The sound of Roger laughing quietly in the corner should have done it, but not when I felt the gorgeous doctor's warm breath on my freaking balls!

I jerked when she rolled my ball in her hand.

"Mmm," she softly said, rolling it and causing me to jerk again. "Does your penis hurt now that it's erect again?"

"Again? It wasn't erect when I hurt it!" I grumbled.

She nodded. "That's right. Well, is it tender?"

For a moment I thought for sure she was going to grab it. "No. It's not. Just my..."

"Testicles?"

I nodded.

"Okay, Mr. Carter, I'm going to order an ultrasound of your testicles, just to be sure."

With a groan, I dropped my head back.

"You can lower your gown now," Doctor Turner said.

She walked over to the sink and washed her hands, then grabbed my chart. She wrote something in it and then pulled out a notepad. She scribbled something down and ripped the page off.

"I'll have Lucy, the nurse, call down and get you in right away for the ultrasound."

Lucy walked into the small room and the doctor turned to her. "Lucy, put it in as STAT so we can have it read, and if all is well, let the Carter brothers go about their day."

Lucy nodded and left the room again, but not before she stole a glimpse of Roger.

"Thank you, doctor," I managed to say as I silently willed my cock to go down. It wasn't helping that the doc was now looking at me with a look I'd seen a hundred times in women's eyes.

"I think everything is okay, but better safe than sorry," she said, handing me the paper and then walking out of the small ER room.

Glancing down at the paper she'd handed me, I smiled.

If the ultrasound comes back with no issues, my number is 555-727-1111. I'll examine you closer later this evening if you're free.

Becca

"I've seen that smile before," Roger said with a laugh.

Reaching for my shorts, I replied, "She gave me her number."

"And why wouldn't she, your cock was bobbing in her face like a hungry bastard. If I wasn't in the room, I don't even want to think what might have happened. Christ, how is it you get all the women? They feel sorry for your ass or something?"

I shrugged. "I guess she liked what she saw."

He rolled his eyes and huffed. "Well, I can tell you one thing, I'm bigger."

Shaking my head, I stared at him. "Is it a contest?"

Roger smirked. "Do I really need to answer that?"

Lucy walked back into the small room with a wheelchair. "I need to take you for your ultrasound, Mr. Carter."

Roger stood, and I pointed to him. "No, you are *not* coming."

"Dude, I think I've seen enough of your penis to last me another thirty-four years." Then he faced Lucy. "You never did tell me if you were single."

Her cheeks turned red. "I am."

A smirk appeared on my brother's face. "Then let me give you this."

He pulled out his business card and handed it to her. Her brows rose slightly when she read the card.

"What kind of lawyer are you, Mr. Carter?"

He winked. "The kind that makes a lot of money."

She giggled as she pulled the curtain back and proceeded to take me toward the elevator.

"I'll be waiting for your return!" Roger called out. "Oh, and I'll be waiting for you too, Truitt."

When the elevator doors closed, I turned to Lucy. "Don't call him, Lucy."

She chuckled. "And why not, Mr. Carter?"

"He will wine and dine you with one goal only."

"What's that?"

"To sleep with you."

The doors to the elevator opened as she leaned down and whispered into my ear, "I'm totally okay with that."

I smiled and shook my head. If there was one thing my brother and I were good at, it was picking up women. Neither of us had ever had a serious relationship, much to my parents' dismay. Our mother constantly nagged us about how old she was getting and how she wanted grandkids. The irony is that she was hardly around when we were kids and was still busy all the time. I found it hard to believe grandkids would change that.

For some reason, my mother thought my brother and I were getting too old. I was thirty-two and Roger was thirty-four. Both still in our prime, if you asked us. Besides, I never could find anyone who would measure up to the one girl I compared every woman to. The one girl I let get away.

The moment I was pushed into the room and saw the tech who would be doing the ultrasound, I wanted to cry.

"Does this hospital not believe in hiring men?" I snapped as the tech smiled and motioned for me to change into yet another fucking gown. After I changed, I stepped out of the small changing room and she told me to lie on the table.

"I'll make this quick and easy for you, Mr. Carter."

"I've heard that before."

She chuckled.

"Honestly, the pain is going away. I don't think this is needed."

The tech gave me a reassuring grin. "Doctor Turner thinks it is needed."

With a sigh, I waited as she got everything ready. Warm liquid was spread over my balls. I stared up at the ceiling and tried to think of anything that wouldn't turn me on.

My grandmother in a bathing suit. Puppies. Roger. My dad when he falls asleep after Thanksgiving lunch. The pain I felt when the branch hit me in the balls and dick.

The way she was moving that damn thing around was not helping. I jerked my head up and looked down at her. Did she just touch my cock?

"Are you almost done?" I asked, while I watched her look at the machine, her brows pulled in slightly.

"Yes, almost," she said, looking back at me and then down at my stiff cock again. I really needed to get laid and soon. It hadn't been that long, had it? A month? Maybe two? Maybe six?

The tech cleared her throat and I closed my eyes. "Do you have to move it around so much?"

"Almost done."

The room was dark, and I tried to focus on the machine. Maybe looking at my balls on there would make my dick realize he wasn't about to have any fun.

Finally, she was done.

"All finished. I'll get this sent over to the radiologist right now to read the results." She turned on the light and started to wipe off my balls. I nearly choked on my tongue.

Her eyes lifted and met mine. A blush hit her cheeks and she softly said, "For what it's worth, I think you're okay."

I forced a smile. "In my defense, you were all over my junk."

She nodded and gave me grin. "You're not the only man who has been turned on during an ultrasound, Mr. Carter. You don't need to be embarrassed."

I scrubbed my hands down my face and groaned. "What I need is for this day to be over."

Chapter 2

Saryn

I STEPPED UP onto the massive covered porch and smiled.

Home. Why had I ever wanted to leave?

The large oak door opened, and my mother rushed outside. "They're here! Will, they're here!"

With a smile, I set Liliana down. My mother rushed forward and scooped my three-year-old daughter up into her arms. Liliana squealed in delight and laughed as Mom covered her in kisses. Daddy walked up and took me into his arms and held me tight.

"I always said he was a bastard."

With a chuckle, I drew back and looked up at him. "Yes, you did."

He shrugged. "I don't want to say I told you so, but, I did. Even when walking you down the aisle, I told you so."

"You did, Daddy. And I didn't listen because I thought I was in love, but what I was really doing was running away. I took the easiest way out."

Daddy gave me a nod. "You said it, not me."

He turned and looked at my mother and Liliana. "Well, we got something amazing out of the jerk, at least."

"The only good thing about him it seems," I replied.

"Oh, Saryn, sweetheart!" my mother said as she handed Liliana to Daddy and then wrapped me up in a warm, tight hug.

"I told you he was an asshole," she whispered.

Laughing, I gave her a squeeze and then let her go. "Can we all just agree that I was wrong and married him for all the wrong reasons?"

My mother pressed her lips together tightly and regarded me for a moment before she smiled and said, "Let me grab my phone so I can record that. I think I'm going to need it in the future."

With a roll of my eyes, I shook my head. "I'm starved, and I know Liliana is, too."

"I've got lunch waiting for the two of you! Let's go in," Mom said as she wrapped her arm in mine and we followed my father and Liliana into the house.

"How did Liliana do on the drive?" Daddy asked.

"Great! I was honestly surprised. I only had to stop two times, once for gas and once for us to get out of the car and stretch our legs. We stopped at a park, and after that Liliana was exhausted. She slept for the last two hours of the drive."

With an exasperated sigh, my mother said, "That drive from Dallas is awful. I hate it."

I let out a humorless laugh and said, "Me, too, and knowing I'll never be making it again makes me happier than you know."

She looked at me with a serious face. "And he gave up all rights to her?"

I nodded. "Yep, which really shouldn't surprise me, but I have to admit it did."

Mom shook her head. "I never did like that boy."

"I'm beginning to think I didn't either. Maybe I was in love with the idea of love." I lowered my voice, so Liliana couldn't hear me. "Tim is in love with his dick and how many women he can put it in."

With wide eyes, my mother pointed her finger at me. "A well-bred southern lady doesn't say that sort of thing." She leaned closer and whispered, "Unless we're alone and out of earshot of kids and men. I taught you better, Saryn."

Laughing, I kissed her on the cheek. "Yes, you did, Momma. He brings out the worst in me."

Daddy was slipping Liliana into her highchair as Momma quickly started cutting up the lasagna she had made. She pointed to the refrigerator and said, "Get out the salad and dressing, will you, honey?"

"Yep."

My father walked up to me and kissed me on the forehead. "You and Liliana are better off without him, sweetheart. You're home now and it's a brand-new start."

I smiled and gave him a reassuring nod. It wasn't like I was sad. Far from it. Six months after we got married, I'd caught Tim in a lie. He'd told me he was working late, and I had seen him sitting in the window of restaurant with a pretty blonde who couldn't have been more than twenty-one. He said it was a work thing, and he'd been nervous that if he told me he had to wine and dine some young executive I would worry. I wanted to believe him, but a small part of me knew he was lying. My heart had been broken by a boy in high school, one of my brother's friends, and Tim had been there to help mend my broken heart. The whole reason I'd followed him was to avoid staying in Boerne. To avoid the heartache I truly never did get over. Deep down inside, I think Tim knew I never got over the hurt Truitt Carter caused me.

Tim and I had dated since high school. We dated through college, both of us going to Texas A&M: me getting my degree in nursing, and Tim getting a degree in marketing. He'd gotten a job in Dallas, and the moment we graduated, we moved five hours away from our home town. In my mind it was a good thing. There was nothing in Boerne for me anymore.

But I ended up more miserable than I thought I would. I hated Dallas, while Tim thrived in the big city. We lived in a nice house in the suburbs, did the whole neighborhood potlucks and fancy business dinners when Tim's job required it. I worked at one of the hospitals as a labor and delivery nurse, then moved to the NICU. I thought I could make our relationship work. I fought for us to be happy, but, at some point, it became clear to me we were far from happy together.

After living in Dallas for two years, I told Tim I didn't think things were working and that I was going to move back to Boerne. He dropped down on one knee and asked me to marry him. My first thought was to say no...boy, how I should have gone with my gut. I didn't though, and we got married at twenty-five. Two years later, I was pregnant with Liliana.

To be honest, we hadn't meant to get pregnant. We went on a trip to Ireland, a last-ditch attempt on my part to see if things would work out. We both knew our marriage was failing. Tim worked all the time and I found myself living practically alone.

Then the rumors of his roaming eyes, hands, and dick, eventually made their way back to me. I told Tim we needed to separate, he said we needed a vacation. I ended up getting pregnant in Ireland when I stupidly forgot my birth control pills. I thought it would be okay. It was the first time we'd had sex in months, and the sad part was, we only made love once in Ireland. Both of us drunk. Talk about luck of the Irish.

I was scared to death when I found out I was pregnant. I was having a baby with a man I could hardly stand to be around. I was angry with myself for always letting Tim talk me into giving our marriage one more chance.

I knew the real reason it wasn't working. There was a ghost between us. I was in love with someone I fell for at fourteen years of age. Someone I dreamed of having a life with. Someone I dreamed of while still married to my husband. Deep down inside I felt like I was cheating on Tim. It was probably the reason I ignored all the signs that he was the one *actually* cheating.

I tried for two-and-a-half years to make it work, for Liliana's sake. But when I came home early from a girls' trip and caught Tim in our bed with his secretary while our daughter was in her room napping, that was the end. I filed for divorce. Tim didn't argue, said he didn't want the life of a husband and father, especially with a woman who never gave him her heart. I, of course, threw it back at him, saying he never gave me his. That was when he told me he couldn't give his heart to someone who pined for an old high school crush.

Tim really was an asshole. When he signed away his parental rights, I had to admit it felt like a punch in the gut. How in the world would I explain to my daughter that her dirty, rotten, low-life, cheating father didn't want her?

I sighed as I let the memory of that day filter back in. Sitting in the law office, the papers slid over to me to sign. I had given eleven years to him. And he signed it all away without a single hesitation.

After I signed, our eyes met.

"You realize what you're doing, right?" I asked.

He stared at me for a moment before he replied, "Yes."

"From this moment on, you'll never see Liliana."

Something washed over his face: panic, regret, doubt, maybe?

"It's for the best," he said.

Once I packed up our things and had a mover bring the few possessions I was taking to my parents', I loaded up my daughter in the car and set off for Boerne, Texas. A part of me couldn't help feeling that Tim had signed Liliana away for a deeper reason.

What man walks away from his own child?

My father's voice brought me back to the present. "Hey, you okay?"

"Yeah, I'm still trying to figure out how Tim could give up his daughter so easily."

Momma looked up, and my parents exchanged a brief look.

"What do y'all know?" I asked, placing the salad in the bowls Momma had set out, and then setting the large bowl on the table and crossing my arms.

"Well," my mother said, giving Liliana a small piece of lasagna she had cut up into small pieces.

She handed Liliana a spoon, but my daughter's fingers dove into the food instead. She shoved a handful of her favorite meal into her mouth, raised her brows and said, "Mmm."

Momma smiled proudly, then focused back on putting slices of lasagna on each plate.

"Momma?" I repeated, my voice a bit more intense.

"Fine, I spoke with LouAnne when I was at my monthly quilting meeting."

I rolled my eyes. "LouAnne? Tim's cousin?"

"She's some relation to the Ackermans. I never did like that last name, by the way. I'm so glad you went back to your maiden name."

With my hands, I motioned for her to keep going.

"She told me that Tim was fixin' to come into a large inheritance once his granddaddy died. He's very sick and not likely to live more than a few months. By large, I mean, at least a million dollars. He was in oil and all."

My mouth dropped open. "That bastard!"

"Told you so," Daddy said as he poured all of us, except for Liliana, a glass of sweet tea.

"He didn't want her to get any of it," I said.

Momma gave a humorless laugh. "Baby girl, he didn't want either one of y'all getting your hands on it. Little does he know, you're to inherit a lot more money than that."

My folks were well known and loved in Boerne. My granddaddy's granddaddy founded one of the largest cattle ranches in the county. Daddy still runs it, although he does more than ranch the land. There is a small vineyard on the west side of the land, a pecan orchard on the south side, and cattle that roam the rest of it. My brother Ryan works the ranch, but also does a dude ranch in the fall. When we were younger, my father started the dude ranch as a favor for a few of his business friends in Austin and San Antonio. They wanted some place different for their team building retreats, and Daddy joked about having them come out and work our ranch for two weeks. And work it they did, along with having a bit of fun in the process as they pretended to be cowboys. In all, our family owned close to ten-thousand acres. The Ciblo Creek ran throughout the entire ranch, making it one of the prettiest places on Earth. One of my favorite spots was up on a hill that overlooked a pasture that had the creek running through it.

"I didn't want his money, and Liliana doesn't need it either!" I spat out.

"Tim probably thinks the ranch will go to your brother Ryan. That you won't have any part in it."

"What about the store?" I asked. "I know Tim hadn't forgotten about your store."

My mother owns a boutique in town. The small area of shopping that runs through Boerne is known as the Hill Country Mile: a mile of locally owned stores that run down Main Street and attract tons of tourists to town.

"Maybe he doesn't realize how much money gets pulled in from that little shop, or the other two storefronts that people rent from us," Momma said, giving me a wink.

"He can have his money. I wouldn't have wanted it anyway. I'm just glad it's over and done with. My heart breaks for Liliana, though."

The three of us turned and looked at my daughter. The entire lower half of her face was covered in sauce. She smiled and shoved more lasagna into her mouth, oblivious to the conversation.

"She'll be fine," Daddy said, taking a bite of food and chewing. Once he swallowed, he went on. "You'll meet another fine young man who will love you and Liliana like you deserve to be loved. I mean, look at her, she looks like she doesn't give two shits about her low-life of a father."

"Daddy! Do not curse in front of her," I said with a chuckle.

He rolled his eyes. "She has no idea what I'm saying."

"She does, and she will repeat it. She's three, not three months."

"Bullshit," Daddy mumbled.

Liliana shoved more food into her mouth and said, "Bullchit."

Giving me father a glare, I pointed to her. "See!"

Both my mother and father laughed hysterically, which only made Liliana keep saying the word.

"Bullchit! Bullchit!"

"That's enough, Liliana, that's a bad word. We don't say bad words!" I reprimanded.

My daughter laughed and pushed her hands through her brown, curly hair. I groaned.

I focused back on my father. "I have no intention of looking for a replacement anytime soon. The only things men care about are themselves, and they only think with their D.I.C.K.S."

With a wink in my direction, my mother said, "Spoken from a scorned woman who needs time to heal."

"I'm healed, Momma. Trust me. My heart is not broken; I'm not crying myself to sleep at night. As a matter of fact, I plan on opening a bottle of your best wine after Liliana goes to sleep tonight and celebrating."

A wide smile crossed Momma's face. "I like the sound of that! Should I invite some people over?"

I lifted a brow. "You already have, haven't you?"

"A small group of friends. Nothing big."

Daddy laughed, and I tried not to smile but lost the battle. God, it was good to be home.

Chapter 3

Truitt

THE DOOR TO my brother's house opened and he looked at me with an expression that should have dropped me to my knees.

"Why in the hell are you at my house at...what time is it?"

"Seven," I replied, pushing past him and walking into his house. "I brought you an egg, bacon, and potato breakfast taco."

"No cheese?" he asked, walking behind me.

"I thought you gave up cheese," I said as I glanced back at him over my shoulder. He looked like he hadn't slept all night. I knew that look. I'd seen it on him a dozen or more times. I stopped and turned to face him. "Dear God, tell me you didn't."

He shrugged. "I did. I figured you'd be hooking up with Doc Turner. Your dick *must* be sore if you didn't hit that last night."

Scoffing, I pushed the bag of tacos into his chest. "You're a manwhore."

"I can't help it if you've had a dry spell, or that your cock isn't working. There are other ways to play you know."

"The nurse?" I asked.

He smiled. "She's taking a shower."

"Jesus, Roger. How many nurses have you banged in the last five years?"

My brother walked into his kitchen, opened the bag, and dumped the tacos out on the island.

"Let's see," he said while he looked up and thought about it. "I'm going to say six? You get hurt, I get screwed. It's a win-win."

The next thing I knew, Lucy, the nurse from yesterday, walked into the kitchen with nothing on but underwear and one of Roger's tank tops. She stopped when she saw me, and her face turned fifty shades of red.

"Want a taco?" Roger asked, handing her a foil-wrapped taco.

"No, I should probably be heading on out."

"You sure?"

I looked at Roger, stunned. He always pushed the women he hooked up with out the door, but for some reason, he wanted this one to stay.

"Yes, thanks for the fun night," Lucy said in a soft voice as she smiled at Roger.

"No, thank you. I learned a new position last night."

Lucy blushed and then made her way out of the kitchen.

Roger looked at me and smiled.

"You liked this one?" I asked with one raised brow.

He shrugged. "She was...different. Fun."

I laughed. "Listen, I've got a consult today. It's actually here in Boerne."

Roger lifted his brow. "Really? Who?"

"The Nights. Their daughter, Saryn, got divorced and is moving back with her three-year-old daughter. They want a playhouse to rival no other. Evie's words."

Laughing, Roger rubbed the back of his neck. "Evie Night. You know the reason she's most likely hiring you?"

I nodded.

"What is Saryn, two or three years behind you and Ryan?"

Ryan was Saryn's older brother and one of my good friends from high school. We were still friends.

"She's a year younger."

"She moved to Dallas after she married Tim Ackerman," Roger said, looking at me with an expression I hadn't ever seen before. Almost as if he was waiting for my reaction.

I snarled my lip. "Who in their right mind would marry that prick?"

"Who knows. She was pretty, if I remember."

My mind drifted back to high school. To Saryn, her light brown hair in a ponytail, those coffee-colored eyes sparkling as she rode her horse around the arena. Ryan never had to ask me twice if I wanted to go with him and watch his sister barrel race. Any excuse to see Saryn. I'd never told Ryan how much I liked his sister. Growing up, she was always just Ryan's little sister. Until high school, when Saryn became the beautiful young woman who looked at me with eyes that hinted at something I could never figure out.

"Yeah, she was pretty."

Roger gave me a quick glance, then looked away.

I drew in a deep breath, then let it out. "Well, anyway, I'm heading out to the Night's ranch later this afternoon. I'm going to text Ryan, see if he's around."

"Tell him I said hey if you do see him. And be prepared, Evie Night likes things big and showy."

"Big and showy is all I know."

Lucy walked into the kitchen, now dressed in her own clothes, grabbed a wrapped taco, and waved to both of us. "See ya around, Roger?"

Roger gave her a grin that didn't really reach his eyes, causing Lucy's smile to fade slightly. "Yeah, see ya around."

And like that, she walked out without so much as looking back.

Roger and I stared at the empty doorway until we heard the door shut.

I couldn't help but notice my brother looked a bit disappointed.

After pulling down the long gravel driveway, I saw the Night house in front of me. The large, two-story ranch had a wraparound porch with rocking chairs and other comfortable seating areas. I'd spent many a night on that porch.

I pulled up and parked to the side and got out of the truck. Glancing around, I took in the beautiful sight before me. There was nothing like the Texas Hill Country, and the Nights owned one of the prettiest ranches in the county. Not that I would ever let my father hear me say that.

Large, live oak trees towered over the driveway and house. The front pasture was short and fenced off, to keep their cattle away from the house. Two horses grazed lazily as one of them lifted its head to give me a quizzical look. When she saw I wasn't coming with food, she went back to eating the pasture grass. I couldn't help but smile. Horses always reminded me of Saryn.

I shook the thought away and headed toward the house.

"Truitt Carter! My goodness, look at you!"

I turned to see Evie Night walking toward me. The older woman had to be in her upper fifties, but she was still drop-dead gorgeous. Once upon a time, she'd been the rodeo queen who snagged the heart of the local football hero. Will Night had given up his chance to play pro ball in order to go to college, get the mandated degree for ranchers—whatever the hell that was—and come home to take over the family ranch.

"Mrs. Night, it's good to see you again."

She waved off my words. "Truitt, how many times do I have to tell you to call me Evie. Look at you. Good Lord, if they don't breed them good here in Boerne. Son, how are you still not married?"

I laughed. "Probably the same reason Ryan isn't."

Evie raised a brow. "You just haven't met the woman who wants to make you settle down. Now Ryan, I feel there's no hope for that son of mine."

I tipped my cowboy hat at her. "I won't argue with you on that last point."

Will walked toward us, a wide grin on his face.

"Truitt, how are your momma and daddy doing?"

"Mr. Night, they're doing well. Thank you for asking."

"Call me Will, son."

I nodded. "Yes, sir."

It was the same conversation each time I saw Evie and Will. Being raised in the south, it was hard to break the habit of addressing older folks with respect.

Will clapped me on the back. "You've made a name for yourself, son. Ryan tells us you're starting to build playhouses for folks in other states. I'm sure your daddy is proud."

My hand went to my neck where, out of habit, I rubbed at the ache that always seemed to appear anytime someone said those words to me.

Will pulled his brows in, then nodded in understanding. "It's hard when you're raised as a rancher and your kin don't want to follow in those footsteps. He'll move on someday, you'll see."

"Roger and I keep our hands in the family business, just not to the extent our father wants. He thinks I need to be working next to him, not building playhouses."

Evie waved her hands about her. "Psh, you're known all over Texas for those playhouses. I don't see your daddy's picture in *People* magazine after building that playhouse for...what was the actress's name in Austin?"

I laughed. "It was a country singer, Lisa Walker."

She nodded and said, "That's right. Anyway, let's walk around the house to the backyard and I'll show you where I was thinking I want the playhouse."

Will fell in step next to me and started firing off questions as the three of us walked to the back of their house.

"Who designs the houses?" he asked.

"I draw them up, then I have an architect do the plans, then an engineer signs off so that the customer knows they're structurally secure and safe."

"I have no doubt you do sturdy work," Will stated.

"Thank you, sir."

"How long does it take to build one?" Evie asked.

"Depends on what the customer wants. The more intricate the design, the longer it will be. An average playhouse takes about two months, but I've had one take a year to make, only because the customer changed their mind as often as the wind."

They both laughed.

"The materials?" Will asked.

"Mostly cedar. We use foam, hard siding, stone. It's really anything you want."

Evie stopped and faced us. "And each one is custom?"

I nodded. "Yes. No two are the same."

She smiled. "Perfect. Our daughter, Saryn, I'm sure you remember her from high school…?"

My chest squeezed slightly at the mention of Saryn's name. After twelve years, I couldn't believe she still had an affect on me. "Of course."

Evie grinned. "Well, she has just moved back home with our granddaughter, Liliana. She's three and I want her to be able to play in the playhouse now, but also grow into it and use it as she gets older. And of course, expand for other grandkids."

"That can easily be done. Most of it will be how it's decorated inside. As Liliana grows older, you simply change the design. Some people keep the outside simple, others go all out. The choice is yours."

"Who does the decorating?" Evie asked, giving me a skeptical look.

I lifted my hands and laughed. "Not me, I can promise you that. My cousin Lee, she's an interior designer. She handles all of that for me."

"I like the idea of making it grow with Liliana. As far as the slides and swings go, can you make them separate from the house?" Will asked.

With a smile, I looked at them both. "It's been my experience that even adults like to slide down the slides and swing on the swings. If it were me, I'd have at least one slide attached to the house. Maybe something coming from a window or tower, something along those lines."

Evie grinned. "I like the way you think, Truitt. I have a picture that I'd like it to be modeled after."

I nodded. "I can draw up a few different ideas for you after I see the picture. Once we get it narrowed down, then we can figure out what types of things you want to include in the playhouse."

"This is going to cost me a fortune," Will mumbled.

I laughed then placed my hand on his shoulder and gave it a squeeze. "I'm not going to lie to you, sir, but it probably will."

He rolled his eyes and let out a sigh as Evie clapped her hands and turned to look out over the massive backyard. "Anything for these women in my life, right?"

"Now that that's settled, let's start planning!"

I cleared my throat. "What about Saryn? Is this going to be a surprise for her and Liliana? Does she want any input in it?"

Evie looked directly at me, and the way she smiled made me think she was up to something other than just planning a playhouse.

"Oh, for right now it will be a surprise, but I'm sure she'll want input. She's a nurse and is going to be starting a new job, so for right now, I'll take the lead. We are paying for it, after all."

Another tip of my cowboy hat and I replied, "Sounds good. Why don't we head on back to the house and you tell me what you're envisioning so I can start on some plans for you."

Evie gave me a wide, satisfied grin.

"Son, I have a feeling this isn't going to turn out like either one of us plan," Will said, slapping me on the back and heading toward the house.

Chapter 4

Saryn

"**Y**OU HAVE GOT to be kidding me."

I stared down at the flat tire on my car and cursed inwardly. After I pulled out my phone and saw I had no signal, I debated what to do. It had been years since I changed a tire. At sixteen, my father and I were driving down the road and he yelled out, BANG! Then told me I had a flat tire and had to get out and change it. Of course, it wasn't flat, but I still had to learn how to do it...just in case. It had been a nightmare then, and I knew this was going to be a repeat.

With a sigh, I pulled out my phone again and checked for a signal, just in case.

"Shit!" I was going to have to break down and send my brother a text. "I'll never hear the end of this."

Me: Ryan, I'm on highway 23 with a flat. If you get this text, please can you come change it for me?

The moment I hit send, I heard a truck coming down the road. I stood back and debated whether I wanted them to stop or keep driving. This wasn't Dallas, but I knew dangerous people were also out in the country.

The Ford F-250 was headed in the opposite direction. He passed me, made a U-turn and then pulled up behind me and stopped. The driver's side door opened, and my breath caught in my throat. My stomach did a somersault at the sight of the man I had once had a thing for.

Holy hell.

Truitt Carter shut his truck door and made his way over to me. I hadn't seen him in a number of years, except for a few photos on Ryan's Facebook page. Truitt was still...good looking. No, that wasn't the word to describe him.

He smiled and tipped his cowboy hat as he said, "Howdy, looks like you need some help."

My heart felt like it jumped in my chest at the sound of that voice.

Oh, Saryn. You are in so much trouble.

I opened my mouth to speak, but nothing came out. When he stopped in front of me, I had to blink a few times. His eyes were the bluest I'd ever seen. Bluer than the sky after a spring rain, and the black ring around them made the blue stand out even more.

He tilted his head and smiled even bigger. "Did you need me to change that flat tire for you?"

I shook my head and broke the strange trance the man had put me in. He hadn't said my name, which led me to believe he didn't even know who I was. The memory of that day came back in a rush and inflated the anger once again.

Lifting my chin, I took in a deep breath. "I'm fine. I've got this, but thank you."

He glanced down at the tire, then back at me. I was suddenly aware of how I looked. I was dressed in white pants and a light pink top. I'd had an interview earlier, and was lucky enough to be offered a nursing position at the Methodist Hospital in town, working in the emergency room. The idea of working in the ER again wasn't a thrill, but until they had an opening in the labor and delivery or NICU, it was back to the grind in the ER.

"You've got this?" Truitt asked, a bit of snark in his voice. I looked at him a bit more carefully. Did he really not remember me?

"Yes, I've got this," I said, my own voice sounding not nearly as confident as I'd hoped.

Truitt slipped his hands into his pockets and looked at me. His piercing blue eyes made me feel hot. There was something about the way he stared that made me question every decision I'd ever made since that day he showed up on my front porch. I swallowed hard and forced a smile.

With a slight chuckle, he rubbed the back of his neck. "Okay, then why are you just standing here? Shouldn't you be changing the tire?"

My mouth dropped slightly open before I clenched my jaw together. "I was about to, thank you very much. Then you showed up and threw my plan of action all off."

He simply stood there, looking at the flat tire and then at me. "Your plan of action?"

I nodded and we stared at each other once again. Was it just me, or was there a crackle of energy between us? I cleared my throat. "Are you actually going to wait for me to change the tire?"

He shrugged, and the way the right side of his mouth curved slightly made my insides do something they hadn't done in a very long time.

Okay, clearly it had been awhile since my poor, neglected body had felt any sort of attraction. I couldn't honestly blame her for reacting. Truitt was good looking. He was built, with a broad chest that filled out his button-down long sleeve shirt perfectly. His jeans showcased his thick muscular thighs in all the right ways, and to top it off, he had on a black cowboy hat that made those baby blues seem like they were bolts of light sent straight from heaven. The boy I remembered from high school was ten times better looking now and his body...Lord, his body.

No. No. Don't look down his body, Saryn. Don't do it!

My eyes ignored my brain.

"Are you done?" he said, making me lift my eyes back to his.

"I'm sorry?" I asked.

"You just eye-fucked the hell out of me, Saryn."

I took a step back and laughed in surprise. *Okay, he does remember me, and he caught me checking him out.* "I'm sorry, I did what?"

He shrugged again, this time his smile appearing full on, revealing a dimple in his right cheek. Lord. Have. Mercy. I wasn't ready for the dimple.

No. No. No. Life was not going to be so cruel to me. I looked away. How in the hell did my body simply pick up where it left off at seventeen? I turned back and looked at him again.

Still smiling. Dimple still there.

"Please don't stand there and smile."

"Why not?"

"Because you obviously think I was checking you out and I wasn't."

His brow rose. "You weren't?"

"No!" I practically shouted. I cleared my throat and looked past him, then behind me. Not another car or truck was coming in either direction.

"Fine, you weren't checking me out. Now, let's get back to the tire business. I know you were going to change it, but since you're dressed so nice, maybe you should let me do it, so you don't..."

This time he was checking me out and he made no attempt to hide it. Slowly and in a way that said he didn't give two shits about me noticing. The heated look in his eyes made my entire body shiver. I hoped like hell he didn't notice.

"...Get dirty."

My mouth went dry. *Oh God, please say that again.*

I forced myself to speak. "Thank you, that's very kind of you, Truitt. I think I'll actually take you up on that."

His eyes sparkled when I mentioned his name. I wonder if he thought I didn't remember him. He winked and I quickly looked away. "The spare is in the trunk."

"Yep, I've got it," Truitt said, making his way to the trunk of my car. "Pop the trunk, will you?" he asked as he unbuttoned and rolled up his shirt-sleeves.

"Sure," I said, keeping my voice calm and unaffected.

I watched as he moved about easily, getting everything set up and barely using any effort to loosen the lug nuts and remove the flat tire. Good grief, that would have taken me an hour to do, I'm sure.

"You've got a full-size spare, so that's good. I'd make sure you get this one fixed right away, though. You don't want to get stuck without a spare."

I licked my dry lips and tried not to stare at the way his forearms flexed as he picked up the tire and put it onto the car.

"I will, thank you," I somehow managed to say without drooling on myself.

He glanced up at me and gifted me another smile. I hadn't forgotten how breathtaking Truitt really was.

"You have the bluest eyes I've ever seen, but they look black sometimes." I slammed my hand over my mouth, shocked I'd said anything about his eyes.

Truitt laughed lightly and then started to tighten the lug nuts. My insides turned to jelly as I watched him.

"I think you were giving me a compliment. I've got my father's eyes. My brother has them, too."

With a tilt of my head, I watched him finish up. "Do they have that black rim around the iris as well?"

He nodded. "Sure do."

I stared at him as he stood. Our eyes met and the strangest feeling seemed to come over me. Where had I seen those eyes before? He frowned slightly, as did I.

Slowly, I shook my head. "Thank you, Truitt."

He smiled, and there was no way a girl could ignore how sexy that smile truly was.

My phone rang just as he was about to say something.

"Hello?"

"Hey, it's Ryan. Where are you? I'll come change your tire. But you realize I'm telling Dad."

I let out a nervous chuckle. "Ha! I'm good, I don't need you to come anymore."

"You changed it by yourself? Damn, there goes all my fun."

Truitt put everything back into my trunk, shut it, and then lifted his hand at me. "You're good to go!"

"Oh...um...thank you! Do I...um...I appreciate it!"

He glanced back over his shoulder and called out, "No problem."

After he jumped up into his truck, he sat there, staring at me.

"Hello? Who are you talking to? You didn't change your tire yourself, did you!" Ryan said.

"Shut up, Ryan! I'm looking at Truitt Carter sitting in his truck looking at me."

"Been that long since you've had sex, huh?"

"I hate you. Why is he just sitting in his truck staring at me?"

My brother let out a sigh. "Well, if it were me, I would probably be waiting for you to get back into your car and safely pull away."

"Do you think that's what he's doing?" I asked.

"You could stand there and look like an idiot, or get in your car and save yourself anymore embarrassment."

I growled and made my way to the driver's door, slipped in, and started the car. I put the signal on and pulled out.

When I glanced into the rearview mirror, Truitt had pulled out, done a U-turn, and headed the opposite way.

"Yep. That's what he was doing."

"True gentleman that he is."

"Thanks for calling me back. I'm surprised you got through, I didn't have a signal at all."

"Yeah, it goes in and out sometimes. How did the interview go?"

I smiled. "I got the job, but I'll be working in the ER until they have an opening in the L & D or NICU."

"That sucks."

"Well, it's a job, and I won't feel like I'm living off of Mom and Dad."

"Saryn, you know they wouldn't care. They're more than over the moon you're back home and they get to see Liliana more."

I nodded, even though he couldn't see me. "I know, it's just, I don't want to rely on them. You know what I mean. I want to provide for Liliana myself."

He chuckled. "I know exactly what you mean. That's why I don't live in the main house."

"Hey, speaking of. Do you think I could move into one of the cabins that's set off from the dude ranch?"

"Why don't you move into the guest house?"

I chewed on my lip and remained silent.

"Oh, I see. Someone wants more privacy, so Mom and Dad won't see you getting on with your life."

Laughing, I shook my head. "Isn't that why you didn't move into the guest house?"

Ryan laughed. "You've got me on that one. I wouldn't get too excited about dating anytime soon. I'm sure half the guys our age remember the warning I put out to stay away from you in high school."

I rolled my eyes. "Tim never got the warning," I pointed out.

"Tim was an asshole. He didn't care that I wanted to pound his face in because all he thought about was his dick."

"Amen to that. Listen, Ryan, I appreciate the fact that you think you need to protect me and all, but now that I'm back, let's not put out that warning again. I really don't want guys afraid to take me out on a date because my brother threatened to castrate them."

"I only said that to one guy."

"Yeah, my date for homecoming my junior year. He was nice."

Ryan made some sort of grunting sound. "Damn, I shouldn't have said anything. You wouldn't have ended up with dickhead if I hadn't scared off that guy."

With a giggle, I replied, "You're probably right. But then we wouldn't have Liliana right now."

"That's true. Listen, you can stay at any of the cabins if that's what you want. I think you'll be more comfortable at the guest house, though."

I let out a sigh. "It's still close to Mom and Dad. I mean, I love them and I'm happy to be home, but I need privacy. Maybe I should just look at renting a house."

"If you do that it will hurt their feelings. The guest house is still a good ways from the main house. With the way the trees have grown up between the two, you really are blocked. Besides, Mom and Dad want to see you happy, Saryn. Just take your time jumping back into the pond. The right guy is out there. I promise."

"It's not like I plan on entertaining guys any time soon." My mind flashed to Truitt changing my tire and I ignored the pull in my lower stomach. "It's just, do you think Mom will still respect my privacy, being in walking distance and all?"

He laughed. "Yes. Just tell her, Saryn. If she starts to but in on your privacy, set it straight. Our folks have always been straight shooters."

"I just have this weird feeling Mom is going to try and start poking into my life."

"Isn't that what all mothers do? She didn't tell you not to marry Tim, when the rest of us did."

Laughing, I replied, "That's where you're wrong. Both Mom and Dad told me not to marry him."

"Let's not deny the fact that they're right sometimes. Listen, I've got to run. I'll see you at the house tonight for dinner."

"Is Miranda going to be joining us?"

There was a moment of silence before he replied, "Yes. She'll be there."

"Is everything okay with y'all?"

"Yep. I've got to go."

Wow, okay. Something was clearly wrong in paradise. The fact that my brother had dated Miranda as long as he had was a surprise.

"Okay, see ya tonight. Love ya!"

"Love ya, too, sis. Kiss Liliana for me."

The line went dead. I made a mental note to ask my mother if Ryan and Miranda were having problems. I may not want her meddling in my life, but my brother's life was a different story!

As I walked into the kitchen, I glanced back over my shoulder at Ryan and Miranda. Something was for sure off with those two.

I reached for the pitcher of tea, then faced my mother. "Is something going on with Ryan and Miranda?"

She stopped mixing the salad and looked at me with wide eyes. "Why? What did you hear?"

I almost laughed at how excited she looked when she thought I had a bit of information.

"Nothing, they just seem...off."

Mom looked past me and through the kitchen door. She nodded. "They've been that way for the last month or so. I think she's tired of waiting for the ring."

My brows shot up. "Oh. He's still not ready, huh?"

She shook her head. "Not anywhere near it. I hate to say it, but I don't think she's the one."

"Well, for both of their sakes, if she isn't and he knows it, he needs to break things off."

With a huff, she replied, "Maybe you should tell him that. From what some of the ranch hands have said, they argue a lot."

I frowned and looked back out at them. Ryan had just said something that made our father laugh, and I couldn't help but notice that Miranda rolled her eyes. She acted as if being here was a waste of her time.

"Do you think she's only with him for money?" I asked, chewing on my lip and hating that the thought had crossed my mind. My brother and I did get a monthly trust from our grandparents. It was enough that if I wanted to, I could rent a small house and only work part time, which was something I had considered. I really wanted to be able to do things with Liliana as she grew up, like my own mother did with us. Yes, she owned a store and helped on the ranch, but I don't think she ever missed a single school function or class party. Not one.

"Honestly?" my mother asked.

"I wouldn't except anything less from you, Momma."

"Yes. I do. I think your brother knows it, as well, but deep down he cares for her. The girl hates it here on the ranch, though. I think we've all known that from day one."

I exhaled. "I'll see if I can talk to him later. If I learned anything from marrying Tim, it's always go with your gut."

"Amen to that," Momma said with a chuckle.

The rest of the evening had an awkward feel to it. Miranda seemed to be in a piss poor mood and jumped at Ryan every chance she got. She was cold toward Liliana, and hardly spoke two words to me throughout dinner. I'd met her once before, last year when I had come home for a visit with Liliana. Even then she seemed distant.

Once dessert was cleared from the table, Miranda stood. "Thank you for dinner, Ryan and I need to be heading off."

Ryan jerked his head up and glared at her.

"Is that so?" he asked.

She glanced at him with a look that dared him to defy her. I was honestly tired of seeing her treat my brother like this, and was two seconds from telling her to sit her little ass down and knock off the diva attitude. I didn't have to, though. It appeared my brother had had enough by the way he was glaring at her.

"Miranda, Ryan offered to help me get the guest house set up for me and Liliana to move in," I said.

"The guest house! How lovely!" my mother gushed.

I looked at her and raised a brow. Instantly, she lifted her hands.

"Like I told your daddy, I promise to respect your privacy, just like I do your brother's."

Then she motioned with her index finger over her heart, making an x to signify her promise.

"You didn't tell me that, Ryan," Miranda bit out, causing all of us to look at her once again.

"It must have slipped my mind."

She huffed. "Well, I have things to do. We need to get back to the house."

"Why don't you take my truck, and Saryn can drop me off later."

Miranda looked at me, frowned, then rolled her eyes. "I'll see you at home. Thank you for dinner, Evie, Will."

And like a leaf on a breeze, she rushed out of the room as everyone stared after her. The fact that she hadn't said goodbye to me or Liliana hadn't gone unnoticed.

"I don't remember her being so charming," I softly said as my mother pressed her mouth into a tight line to keep from either saying something herself, or from laughing at my comment.

"Lord Almighty, that girl needs to remember her place," Daddy said. "She was downright rude this evening."

Ryan sighed and scrubbed his hands down his face, let out a few sounds that made Liliana laugh, then focused on me. "Thanks, Saryn. I really didn't want to leave with her."

I winked at him. "Don't get too excited, I really do need your help over there. I want to make sure everything is working okay before Liliana and I move in."

He nodded. "Yeah, sure. No problem."

After Ryan and I helped our mother clean up, our folks took Liliana on a stroll in her wagon while Ryan and I headed over to the guest house, which would soon be my new home. It was a two-bedroom, two-bath ranch-style cottage. It had been remodeled a few years back. It was the second house built on the ranch. The first was a log cabin that was now part of the dude ranch cabins.

"What's going on with you and Miranda?" I asked, unlocking and stepping into the cottage. I smiled when I looked around at the pristine house. "Lord, she had it cleaned. It's like she knew!"

"Had it cleaned?" Ryan said with a laugh. "Hell, she's been in here for a week getting it ready for you."

I shook my head and made my way over to the kitchen. The cottage was adorable and had always been one of my favorite places on the ranch. The open floorplan was my favorite part of the place. The living room sat to the right side when you walked in. A wood-burning fireplace sat in the corner with the large black metal pipe jutting up to the ceiling. To the left was the dining area, big enough for a table of six. The large wooden table had been made by my father years ago. On the other side of the house was the kitchen. It was an L-shape that went along the walls of the cabin. I gasped when I saw there was now a farm sink with updated faucets.

"This is amazing!" I said, looking at the freshly painted white cabinets. Along the back corner was a built-in bar with four stools. The floors were made of large oak planks that had been repurposed when my grandfather tore apart a barn that had collapsed in a storm.

"What made Mom paint the cabinets white?" I asked.

Ryan shrugged and I leaned against the counter.

"So? Miranda?"

He pulled out a stool and sat down. "She wants to get married. I don't."

"Is there a reason you don't want to?"

His eyes turned serious. "Yes. I honestly can't see myself having a future with her. Things were great when we first started dating. Now, well, now she's talking about moving to New York. She hates the ranch. She hates my job."

"New York!" I gasped.

Ryan rolled his eyes. "Yeah, some marketing firm wants to hire her. It's great for her and I'm happy, but I have no interest in going. She hates it here, this isn't the life she wants, so honestly, I don't see a future for us. She won't accept it, though, and lately she's been bossing me the fuck around and I'm getting really tired of it."

I nodded. "If it's over, then tell her it is. Let her move on with her life and you move on with yours."

He sighed. "I was going to. Tonight."

"Ah, so you're using me as an excuse to put it off."

The corners of his mouth twitched. "Pretty much. Just so you know, I've already been through the cottage, everything is working fine."

"I know, Daddy told me you had. I figured you needed an excuse to talk to someone."

"Thanks. I was going to tell her before dinner, but didn't get the chance."

"Take it from me, don't settle, ever. If your gut is telling you something is off, listen to it. I sure as hell wished I'd listened to mine. I simply saw someone whom I thought could..."

I let my words fade away. I had never told anyone about how Truitt had broken my heart. My entire senior year I planned how I would escape Boerne. Each time Truitt came back from college and I'd run into him or see him somewhere, I attempted to ignore him, the ache in my chest never truly fading. The way he would look at me, though...it confused me. So in my mind, Tim had been my knight in shining armor. The man who would sweep me away from my first broken heart.

"Who you thought could what?" Ryan asked.

I shrugged. "Heal a broken heart."

With that, my brother frowned but didn't say anything else.

"You ever going to want to get married again?" he finally asked.

With a soft smile, I nodded. "Of course. Maybe not anytime soon. I want to enjoy my time with Liliana."

"Mom will be upset about that."

I rolled my eyes. "Truthfully, I need a break from guys. Tim wore me out with his lies and games. It's going to be hard for me to trust again."

Ryan slipped off the stool and made his way over to me. He placed his hands on my upper arms and smiled. "Saryn, not all guys are dickheads."

"I know, but most are."

He chuckled. "I won't argue with that. Listen, don't let one guy ruin it for someone else. He wasn't the one, but you got Liliana out of the deal."

"That's the only good thing about that."

"Give yourself time. What about Truitt?"

My brother's words hit me like a cast iron pot to the head. I looked at him with what I was sure was a stunned expression.

Then I forced a laugh. "Truitt? The man has a reputation for being a player. Not to mention, he seems to get hurt an awful lot. Bad luck seems to follow him around."

Ryan laughed. "True, he has been known to visit the ER often. We actually have a running bet among our group of friends on how many times Truitt will have to go to the ER before he turns thirty."

I laughed. "And the rumor about his player ways?" I asked the question more for myself than anything. A part of me needed to know if Truitt really was the womanizer he was portrayed to be.

"Truitt, a player? Nah, that's his brother Roger. Don't get me wrong, the women line up for his attention, but Truitt really is a good guy. Hasn't seemed to find anyone he's interested in settling down with, though."

That piqued my attention. "Really? He hasn't been in any kind of serious relationship?"

Ryan looked at me, a smirk on his face. "No. None."

My stomach did a little flip. Why did that make me feel so happy? So...relieved?

I returned his grin with a smile of my own. I could tell myself I wasn't interested in dating until I was blue in the face. Truth be told, the entire drive from Dallas to Boerne, one thing had weighed on my mind.

Was Truitt Carter still single.

Chapter 5

Truitt

I ROLLED THE window down and spit out my gum, only to have it blow right back and land somewhere in my hair.

"Motherfucker!" I shouted. Jack, one of the guys who'd been working for me since I started Imaginations Unlimited, started laughing. We'd gone to high school together, so he was familiar with my...incidents.

"Dude, stop trying to figure out where the gum is, it's going to get stuck in your hair and you'll have to buzz cut it...again. It's just now grown back out."

I rolled my eyes. *What in the hell did I do in my life to be so damn accident prone?*

"When we get there, just get it out of my hair," I bit out.

As much as he tried not to, he laughed.

Before he could remind me of the last time this happened, I started off in a new direction. "We've got a new build. Ryan's folks, Mr. and Mrs. Night?"

"Ryan Night's folks, huh. They want a playhouse?" he asked with a chuckle. "Is it for Ryan since he's so pussy whipped with that girlfriend of his?"

I shook my head. "I don't know anything about that, but no, it's for their granddaughter."

Jack snapped his head to me. "Ryan's sister is back home?"

"Yes." I decided not to mention that I'd stopped and changed her flat tire. The moment I got out of the truck, all those old familiar feelings for her rushed back, nearly knocking me to the ground.

Over the years I'd gotten the scoop from Ryan about how unhappy Saryn had been in her marriage to that dickhead of a husband. Why she'd ever dated him was beyond me. I tried not to think of that day on her front porch. The day that changed everything, or at least felt like it had.

Whatever had happened between us, I could never figure out how Ryan Night had let his little sister get mixed up with a douche like Tim.

"I heard she finally left that jerk," Jack said. "What she saw in him was beyond me."

I let out a scoff. "I'm pretty sure it was beyond all of us."

Once I pulled into the driveway of one of the houses that we were delivering a playhouse to, all talk of Saryn came to a stop. And thank God. I didn't like the way my body still reacted to her. I thought it had just been seeing her, but talking about her nearly had my cock coming to attention.

My mind couldn't help but go back to the way she'd been slowly checking out my body.

"Truitt! Thank goodness you're here. They're doing it all wrong!" Pattie Lovesong stated as she rushed up to me.

"Ma'am?" I asked, tipping my cowboy hat to her.

"The swings were supposed to be on the right side of the playhouse and they're putting them on the left. I want them on the right."

Mr. Lovesong walked up, then, a look of utter defeat on his face. Their six kids, ages two to ten, were nowhere to be seen.

"The kids?" I asked as he walked up and wearily reached his hand out for mine.

"My sister has them so we can get it all set up and surprise them."

I nodded. Then I focused back on Mrs. Lovesong, who was still bitching, though she had turned her focus onto Jack now. He looked at me with utter panic. Jack was my master carpenter. His hands were magical. The things he could do to wood even made me envious. Dealing with customers, though? That was something he never did. His eyes pleaded with me to help him. A part of me wanted to leave him to deal with this, but I stepped between them and held up my hand to Mrs. Lovesong.

"Mrs. Lovesong, on the plans that you approved, the swings were on the right side of the playhouse to allow for the open window over the little kitchen to look out on the pasture."

She pursed her lips.

"I've been trying to tell her that," Mr. Lovesong said. "She insisted the swings were on the left."

"The plans are in my truck, let me go get them."

That was when she sighed, deeply. "No. No. You don't have to go get them, Truitt. I seem to recall now. I had forgotten about the little window. The girls will love that."

"The monkey bars are on the left, which you had wanted for the boys. It's up and out of the way of the window."

She beamed up at me. "That's right! I remember now. You're so amazing!"

Mr. Lovesong mumbled something about her being ridiculous, but she ignored him and gave me a flirty smile.

"Truitt, it looks like they're having an issue with the crane and the upper deck of the playhouse," Jack said.

We quickly took off toward the house. Climbing up on the ladder, I helped to guide the structure into place. Then I felt the ladder move slightly and looked down to see only Mrs. Lovesong standing there.

"You're going to get hurt, Truitt! Please, get down. Let my husband do that!"

"What the hell? I have no idea what he's even doing. Will you let the man do his job?" Mr. Lovesong said.

"Truitt, darling, please come on down, let my husband climb on up there."

"You do realize I'm standing right the fuck here," Mr. Lovesong said.

"Your language, Garth!"

"Is warranted in this situation. Holy shit, Marge. You're shamelessly flirting, with your husband—who happens to be paying for this—standing right here."

"I am not flirting!" she hissed, then glanced up at me and smiled. I shook my head and focused back on what I was doing. Once the upper piece was in place, Jack and I secured it to the bottom. I started back down the ladder and heard Mrs. Lovesong start going on about safety. Why in the hell she hadn't cared about Jack's safety, I had no idea.

"I've got the ladder!" Mrs. Lovesong stated.

"Get away from there. They've already told you that you're in the way and it's dangerous!" Mr. Lovesong shouted.

"Why must you shout!" she said, turning and somehow pushing her hand off with ungodly strength, sending the ladder over, with me still on it.

"Oh, shit." I attempted to jump off and land like a graceful cat. Instead, I heard something pop in my ankle as I rolled onto the ground and a few more curse words spilled from my mouth.

"I know what a broken ankle feels like, Jack. This is not one," I said, my jaw clenched tight. It might not have been broken, but Jesus H, it hurt like a bitch.

"Roger told me to bring you to the ER to be sure. He also told me to make sure you asked for the hot doctor again."

I rolled my eyes.

As we walked, or I limped, up to the check in, I caught a glimpse of the nurse Roger had slept with. Lucy was her name. At least, I thought that was her name. She lifted her hand and waved.

"Wow! Back two times in one week. Hate to tell you this, but Dr. Turner isn't here today."

I let out a humorless laugh. She chuckled and then leaned down to whisper something to another nurse. The girl who was checking me in spoke, drawing my attention back to her.

"Rose?" I asked with a smile.

"Close, June."

I frowned and tilted my head, then looked at Jack. He was attempting to keep from laughing.

"We're going to have to start giving you frequent flyer miles as much as you come visit us, Mr. Turner," June said.

"Ha! Wouldn't that be something," I replied.

After she checked me in and took my copayment, I was whisked away to have my ankle X-rayed.

"No vitals?" I asked the guy who was pushing me.

"They're a nurse short. A new nurse started today. She's normally labor and delivery, so she's running a bit slow. You'd think they would remember working in the ER. Or, maybe it's that they try to forget."

"And you are?" I asked.

"I'm your X-ray tech, dude. You have a bit of a reputation here at the hospital."

"Is that so?" I said with a chuckle. "Good, I hope."

"Well, if you ask any of the nurses, they'll tell you they love it when you come in."

Another laugh escaped.

After they twisted and positioned my ankle in ways that nearly had me tearing up, they brought me back to one of the dreaded little ER rooms with the curtains. I was going to have to make a hefty donation to the hospital simply so I could have a private room.

Yes. I was here that much.

"The nurse will be right in," the X-ray tech said. "Hopefully you get the new one." He leaned in closer. "She's hot as hell."

I smiled and gave him a nod.

Then I waited. And waited. And waited.

Finally, I hopped off the table, wobbled to the curtain and jerked it back. I was about to call for Lucy when someone small ran smack into me. The warmth of her body instantly had mine coming to attention. Her smell was familiar, and it made the little hairs on the back of my neck instantly rise. She looked up at me as I looked down at her.

And there went my dick. He decided to show up for the party, ready to have a good time.

A slow smile spread over Saryn Night's face.

"Truitt Carter." She let her gaze sweep over me, a little quicker this time, but the same heat was there. "Seems like you have a reputation at this place. I'm told our Christmas bonus will come solely from the amount of times you've visited the ER."

I snarled at her. "No one likes a snarky nurse, Ms. Ackerman."

"Night. My last name is back to Night."

"Glad to see you didn't simply get rid of the husband, but his name, as well."

Her eyes widened in shock, then narrowed as she gave me a sweet yet sexy smile. "Will you get back into the room."

"Please."

"Please what?" she asked.

"No, you demanded. You should ask me nicely, to please get back into the room. After all, I am providing part of your bonus. I was even thinking of making a donation to the hospital. Maybe they can give me a private room."

Her eyes rolled. She motioned for me to step back into the room as she tried not to smile and failed. I did as she commanded.

"I'm going to take your vitals, then the doctor will be in to tell you what your X-rays say."

"I just need an ice pack."

A perfectly arched brow slowly rose. "You sound so sure."

"I am sure. I've broken my ankle before. Twice. I know what it feels like. I think I simply pulled a tendon. I heard a pop. I'm only here to appease my pain-in-the-ass brother, Roger. If you could just get the doc in here to sign me off, I can get back to the job site."

She nodded, then pushed a thermometer under my tongue.

"You need to have it elevated with ice on it. Not go back to work."

My words sounded muffled as I replied, "I need to get back to work."

"You need to stay off your ankle," she insisted.

The thermometer beeped and she took it out. "No fever."

I sighed. Then the doctor walked in. Thank God it was Pete.

"Thank fuck you're working," I said.

Pete laughed and reached for my hand. Saryn folded her arms over her chest and I tried not to focus on how it made her breasts look even more incredible. Never in my wildest imagination would I think breasts could look good under a nurse's uniform.

Shit. I needed to get laid. Preferably with the pretty nurse standing to my right.

Ugh. Knock it off, Truitt.

"You really are here a lot," Saryn stated.

Pete shook his head. "Truitt and I went to college together. Met in our frat house. This guy talked me into moving to Boerne, Texas, instead of going somewhere amazing, like New York City. Or Denver."

Saryn's brows pulled in tight. "Denver?" she asked with a chuckle.

Pete laughed. "I'm from Denver. It's a joke," he said before focusing back on me. "It's not broken."

"I knew it wasn't."

"Roger texted me. Offered me three-hundred bucks to tell you it was broken and another three if I put a cast on it."

My jaw dropped. "That rat bastard."

"I thought about it, but the last time I put a cast on you it only lasted three days and you cut it off."

"You cut it off!" Saryn gasped.

My gaze swung over to her. "Roger offered him a thousand that time."

Saryn swung her gaze back to Pete.

"It was too good to pass up," Pete said.

Saryn looked like she wasn't sure what to say. "Um."

We both focused on her, waiting.

"Was it broken, at least?" she asked.

Pete barked out a laugh. "Slight fracture."

She shook her head. "So it's true, you are accident prone."

I shrugged. "I like to call them small incidents of unfortunate luck."

"Heard about your broken penis," Pete said, writing on a pad of paper.

Saryn's cheeks turned pink as she looked from me to Pete.

"It didn't break, because it wasn't hard when the branch hit it. Besides, my balls took most of the hit and it sorta grazed the...the, um...my...penis."

That made her eyes jerk down to my junk, then back up. "I'll go get his discharge papers ready," Saryn said and quickly spun around and walked out.

I laughed as I rubbed the back of my neck. "Thanks for that."

Pete smiled. "She is so out of your league, dude. She's nice, and if I wasn't engaged I would ask her out. Although she's been asked out six times so far today by five different guys and one woman."

My jaw dropped open some.

"She turned them all down," he went on.

"I know she just got divorced. She was married to a real dick," I said.

The curtain moved back and Saryn strolled in. "You do know it's just a curtain, not a door, right?" she asked while she pushed the papers in my direction.

I pointed to Pete. "He was the one who brought it all up."

Saryn looked at him. "Doctor, is that true?"

He looked up at the ceiling. "Was I just paged?"

With a look that could have pinned him to the wall, Saryn cleared her throat and said, "No. My shift is over. Lucy will take over from here."

Pete watched her walk away, then turned back and glared at me. "Thanks a lot, asshole. I have to work with her."

I laughed. "Well, I have to build her little girl a playhouse."

He handed me a prescription. "For the pain."

I shook my head. "I'm fine."

"Truitt, look at your damn ankle. It's swollen three times its normal size. You need to stay off it. That's an anti-inflammatory, as well. Just fill the prescription, please. You'll only need it a few days."

I took the prescription. "I don't have time to stay off of it."

He looked at me with one of those looks you get from your father when you've nearly pushed him to the edge and he's about to lose his shit.

With a very exaggerated sigh, I replied, "Fine. I'll take a day off."

"Take two."

"Can I go to the office, at least?"

He gave me a thoughtful look and nodded. "Keep it elevated and iced."

I sighed. "Damn. You drive a hard bargain."

He smiled in triumph.

Standing, I grabbed the discharge papers and prescription, then walked through the curtain Pete had pulled open.

"Hey, Truitt, can you let Roger know he needs to pay me the hundred bucks on Friday night?"

I turned and faced him. "Why does he owe you a hundred bucks?"

He smiled. "I won the betting pool. We all picked dates for when you'd be back into the emergency room and I won."

My mouth slacked in shock. Then I snapped it shut and glared at him. "I hate all of y'all. And I'm not hosting card night next week!"

Pete let out a roar of laughter as I limped my way out of the ER.

Chapter 6

Saryn

LILIANA JUMPED FOR joy as my mother and father stood there, smiles on both of their faces. I stared down at the drawing in front of me, then looked back up at them.

"This is a joke, right?" I asked, looking to my father first, then my mother.

Her smile faded slightly. "No, it is not a joke. We're having a playhouse built for Liliana."

I shook my head slightly in disbelief. "Mom, this is not a playhouse. A playhouse is what Daddy made me and Ryan. Some wood nailed together up in a tree with a ladder to climb up it. This is...this is..."

My eyes jerked back down to the drawing in my hand.

"Fine, it's a play-castle. But nothing but the best for our grandchild," Momma said.

"It's...it's...it's bigger than the cottage we live in!" I nearly shouted.

"Oh, it is not."

I gave her a look.

"Well, we can scale it back a bit if you'd like."

"A bit? Mom, there's a drawbridge!"

My father laughed. "That one was my idea."

I rolled my eyes.

"I can't afford something like this," I stated, my hands shaking as I held onto the drawing. It looked oddly familiar, but I couldn't place where I had seen it before.

"That's why your mother and I are paying for it."

"Daddy, I don't want Liliana getting spoiled right off the bat."

My mother took a step forward, her arms crossed over her chest. "Excuse me, but we haven't gotten to properly spoil our only grandchild at all yet. A few trips up to visit her and go to an amusement park is nothing. This isn't just for Liliana, someday Ryan will have kids, and you'll have more."

"That is the last thing on my mind, Mom."

"Then let's focus on little Liliana. Look how happy she is!" my mother said. The three of us looked down at my daughter who was standing there, staring up at us with a wide smile on her face. She hadn't seen the drawing, but as soon as she heard the word playhouse, she wanted to go to it right that moment.

"Paygound! Where is my paygound, Mommy?"

When I glanced up and saw the triumphant grin on my mother's face, I felt a bit of anger returning. I already knew the answer, but I had to ask. "Who's set to build this?" When I glanced back down, I saw a stamp. Imaginations Unlimited. Slowly, I lifted my gaze to my mother. She had that look on her face. She was up to something.

I smiled softly, but of course I already knew it was Truitt's company. I will admit I had looked him up on Facebook after I separated from Tim. "What is Imaginations Unlimited?"

"A local company that builds custom playgrounds. Honey, you should see what they can do!" my mother gushed.

With a nod, I pressed for more. "Who's the owner? If they're local, I'm sure I know them."

The woman never flinched; she even smiled brighter. "Of course you know him! He's a friend of your brother. Y'all went to school together. Well, he was a year older, like Ryan."

"You hired Truitt Carter to build Liliana's playhouse?"

She widened her smile. It was a full-on grin, ear to ear.

My father cleared his throat and glanced over to my mother.

Momma nodded and then had the nerve to go on about like nothing in the world was wrong with this picture. "Yes. He's very well-known and has won many awards. Not to mention, he does so many wonderful things for the community."

"That is true," Daddy added. "He built the community playground free of charge."

My eyes bounced back and forth between the two of them. "Did you also know that he's in the ER all the time because he's accident prone! I don't want that type of man building my daughter's playhouse!" Not to mention that having Truitt build something damn near in my backyard, showing off those muscles, would make me go insane. I might lose my mind and jump him.

"You snob!" my mother said, folding her arms over her chest. "You're going to judge the man's work because he's had a few... incidents? His work is top notch! I made sure."

I already knew Truitt's reputation at his job. It was exactly like my mother said. He was good. Very good. He'd even made a few playhouses for famous people. But there was more to this. I knew what my mother was up to. This wasn't simply about the playhouse. She was butting her nose in already. "Fine, so he does good work. But why him? Why not just find some contractor to build a simple playhouse?"

My father chuckled. "Saryn, this is your mother we're talking about and our only grandchild. You can't blame her for wanting to give Liliana something amazing."

I sighed. "I understand that. But look at this thing! It probably costs more than my car!"

Momma waved her hand at me, brushing off my comment. "It's our money and this is what we want to do. Let us spoil her this one time! I promise to rein it in with all the other gifts we give her in the future."

I looked down at the playhouse. I had to admit, my heart jumped at the sight at it. When I was Liliana's age, I would have died to have a playhouse like this. It looked like a medieval castle with three turrets and bridges connecting them all to the main keep. Off one of the towers was a swing set. It looked adorable. And expensive. The drawbridge led to another small area that was set up like a little patio.

Before I had the chance to tell my mother I could be on board only if we scaled it back a bit, she spoke.

"Now, Truitt is a delight to work with. I knew you would want to meet with him to discuss the finer details. I didn't want to be the deciding factor on the interior. No one knows your daughter better than you, sweetheart. So, I arranged for the two of you to meet for dinner tonight."

And there it was, my mother meddling in my love life, or lack thereof. "Excuse me?"

My father rubbed the back of his neck. "Oh, hell. We were almost in the clear."

"What? Would you rather I have the entire say?" Momma asked, acting as if she was truly giving me a say in any of this.

I forced myself to take in a slow, deep breath. After I exhaled and pushed the anger back down, I looked directly at my mother.

"You made dinner plans without consulting me?"

She smiled, and I had to keep my hands fisted at my side.

"You need a night out, sweetheart."

Daddy shook his head and stepped closer to my mother. "Evie, wrong thing to say," he said with a roll of his eyes.

"Now it's a night out? Momma, I don't *need* a night out, especially with Truitt Carter! I thought it was business. If it is business, I can speak with him over the phone, or he can come here."

"Or, you could go to his office on Main Street," my brother Ryan said as he walked in and made his way to my mother. After he kissed her on the cheek, he took the drawing out of my hands and whistled. "Wow, fancy AF."

"A F?" my mother asked with a confused look.

Ryan whispered, "As fuck."

Liliana was too busy playing with her toy dogs to be paying any attention to the adult conversation going on around her.

I pointed to my brother. "See, if Ryan thinks it's too much…"

"Wait, is this for Liliana?" he asked, then laughed when my mother smiled and nodded.

With a sigh, I grabbed the paper back from him, reached down, and picked up my daughter.

"Where are you going?" my mother asked, following close on my heels.

"To Imaginations Unlimited. I'm going to nip this in the bud right now," I stated as I spun on my heels. "You are playing games, Momma."

She scoffed. "I am not. I merely wanted my granddaughter to have the best possible playhouse available. Can I help it if the man who builds those happens to be your age? Handsome, I might add. And rich. And single."

"Ugh! You're impossible!" I yelled before stomping out of the house like a child.

I walked straight to my car, put Liliana in her car seat and then pulled up Truitt's business on my phone. After I put the address in my maps, I set off to let Mr. Carter know he would not be building my daughter's playhouse.

Thirty minutes later, I was walking down Main with Liliana on my hip. I stopped outside a larger, newer building. It appeared there were a few different businesses, all of them with the same last name.

Carter.

My pulse quickened as I read each sign.

Ryan Carter, Esquire.

Nick Carter, Southwest Land and Cattle Company.

Truitt Carter, Imaginations Unlimited.

I pulled in a deep breath and walked into the main door. To my left was the law office. On my right was the Land and Cattle Company, and straight ahead, Imaginations Unlimited.

"Okay, Liliana, we can do this."

"Payhouwse!" Liliana screamed as we walked toward the door. On the wall outside the office was a picture of the cutest playhouse I'd ever seen. It looked like a gingerbread house. For a moment my heart melted.

"Mommy! Look!" Liliana exclaimed.

"Yes, Mommy sees the playhouse."

I walked in. Sitting to the right was an older woman. I smiled and she returned the gesture.

"Hello, may I help you?"

"Um, yes, I was wondering if Truitt, I mean, if Mr. Carter was in?"

She looked me over slowly and raised a brow. "Do you have an appointment with...*Mr. Carter*?"

"No. But I need to talk to him about this." I handed her the architectural drawing of the over-the-top castle.

The older woman smiled. "Well, Mr. Carter is in the office today, which is rare, but he doesn't like people to show up without an appointment."

I wanted to roll my eyes. "Please, Ms....?"

"Townsend."

"Ms. Townsend, I'm supposed to meet with Mr. Carter this evening to discuss this project, and..."

Her eyes lit up. "*You're* Evie's daughter!"

My stomach dropped. Oh Lord, what was my mother up to? She had inside help on this one.

"Yes, I am."

Before I got the words out, she picked up the phone. "Mr. Carter, Saryn Night is here to see you."

Her smile disappeared as she listened to him speak. "Oh...well... yes, but wouldn't you rather...yes. Of course, Mr. Carter."

She hung up the phone and this time her smile was forced. "He is unable to see you right now, and he also wanted to tell you that he will not be able to join you and your family for dinner tonight."

I frowned. "My family?"

Her gaze dropped away from mine. What in the hell was going on here?

"I need to speak with him. Now."

Ms. Townsend opened her mouth, then closed it. Then opened it again, only to snap it shut.

"This is insane," I said, turning and walking down the hall. "Which office is his?"

I didn't need to wait for her to reply, although she was now up and trying to walk in front of me.

"Mrs. Night!"

"Ms.," I corrected.

"Ms. Night! You can't go into his office!"

Ha! Watch me, lady.

The large oak door at the end of the hall had the cowboy's name on it. Truitt Carter. I reached for it and pushed it open, only to come to a halt. My eyes nearly popped out of my head at the sight before me.

Standing before me was Truitt Carter, wearing next to nothing. My insides melted like butter on a hot biscuit. Slowly, I let my gaze move over his body.

His almost naked body.

Chapter 7

Truitt

THE DOOR TO my office flew open as I pulled up my boxers. One of the things I loved about my office was that I had my own private bathroom, shower and all. After working out in the gym doing upper body—since my ankle was still a bit swollen—I had jumped into the shower and was in the process of re-dressing.

"Oh my gosh, you're naked!" Saryn nearly shouted.

"I'm so sorry, Mr. Carter, she just walked back here on her own!" Ms. Townsend said, panic etched in her voice.

I smiled. "It's okay, Ms. Townsend."

Three sets of female eyes were now on me. Saryn's daughter was in her arms. I nodded to my assistant and said, "I'll see Ms. Night since she's already shown herself in." With a nod, Ms. Townsend quickly shut the door.

I swung my eyes back to the other two. Bright blue eyes locked on mine, and I couldn't help but smile. Brown curls bounced as Saryn's daughter fought to get out of her mother's arms.

"And I'm not naked," I said as Saryn went to speak but closed her mouth, instead.

"Down pwease! Down, Momma, down, pwease!"

Reaching for my jeans, I quickly slipped them on, then pulled my black T-shirt over my head. Saryn watched my every move, her eyes filled with something I hadn't ever seen in a woman's gaze before. It wasn't lust. Or desire... It was confusion. Most likely because she had walked into my office and I had been wearing nothing but my boxer briefs. Five seconds earlier and she'd have seen a hell of a lot more.

"You must be Liliana!" I said to the little girl who was now making her way to me. I bent down to her level and took the little bear she was holding out for me.

"Is this your bear?" I asked.

Liliana nodded. "Muke!"

"Muke?" I asked, glancing over toward Saryn who was still standing in the same spot. "I'm sorry, I just finished working out and took a shower. That's why I couldn't really see you right now."

"A shower?" she asked, still confused and with a dazed look in her eyes.

"Yes, we have a gym in the building. I have a bathroom with a shower over there." I pointed toward the door that led to the private bathroom. "Since my father and brother also have offices here, Dad thought it would be easier to have a gym in the building."

Liliana reached up and touched my damp hair. Then she giggled and a strange sensation rushed through me. It was something I'd never experienced before, so it took me by surprise. I stilled, and that caused Saryn to rush over and take her daughter's hand.

"I'm so sorry. Normally she has boundaries, but I guess she liked what she saw, too."

My eyes snapped up to her.

"No, I mean, I liked what I saw...no, wait. Hold on a second. I came in here with the intention of firing you, and you have me all flustered. Since you were naked."

The corners of my mouth lifted slightly. "I wasn't naked."

Her throat bobbed with a hard swallow. "You might as well have been. I saw everything!"

"Everything?" I asked, mock shock in my voice.

"Not everything," she mused, "but it was...shocking."

"Yes, that's obvious from the way you're stumbling on your words."

Her eyes narrowed. "I'm not stumbling on my words, Mr. Carter."

"Call me Truitt."

"No, thank you."

Liliana reached up and took my hand, then led me over to the small play area I had set up in my office. All of my clients had children, for obvious reasons, and when I met with them, I liked having a place for the kids to be entertained while the grown-ups talked business.

"You have a playground in your office?" Saryn asked.

"Don't make it sound like it's a bad thing. When I meet with my clients here, they most always bring their kids."

"Oh, that makes sense," she said. I held Liliana's hand while she climbed up the steps to the slide.

"I'm going to be frank, Mr. Carter. We don't need you to build Liliana's playhouse."

I gave her a puzzled look over my shoulder. "Did you find someone else?"

Her eyes widened in panic. "No! It's just. Well, you see..."

Her voice trailed off. Liliana giggled and shrieked as she slid down the slide.

"I see she likes slides. I'll make sure to incorporate two: a straight slide, and every princess has to have a twisty-turny slide."

Liliana looked up at me, those blue eyes sparkling with sheer bliss, before she raced over to the little swing.

"Push me, pwease!" she said as she ran back and grabbed my hand, tugging me over to the swing.

"My goodness, I've never seen her take to someone like she has to you," Saryn said, trying not to smile.

"I have that effect on women."

She snarled her lip at me and seemed to come back to her senses. "As I was saying, we don't need such a fancy playhouse, and my mother's motivations may not have been one-hundred percent in the right place."

My brow rose. "Meaning?"

Saryn twisted her fingers together nervously. "When you said you had to cancel dinner with my family this evening, you weren't expecting to have dinner with just me?"

"Your mother said it would be the whole family."

She nodded. "Well, she told me it was just going to be you and me."

"Ah, I see," I said, trying not to show the amusement on my face. "So your mom wants the playhouse, and is also hoping for something more."

Her cheeks went red. "Which is exactly why you're not doing the playhouse."

"That's where you're wrong, Ms. Night, because I am most certainly doing the playhouse."

When her eyes flashed with something that looked like heat, I noted it. It quickly faded away to anger. Pure anger, and it was hot as hell.

"Excuse me?" she said, her hands going to her hips. I let my gaze take her in quickly. Not as slow as I did when she was standing on the side of the road last week.

"I'm building your daughter's playhouse."

"No, you are not."

"Yes, I am."

Her mouth fell open, and she let out a disbelieving laugh. "You're incredible. I'm firing you, Mr. Carter."

"With all due respect, Saryn—"

"Ms. Night."

This time it was me who crossed my arms over my chest. "Ms. Night, with all due respect, you are not the person who hired me. Your name is not on the contract I signed, nor is the property where the playhouse is to be built yours. So, you cannot fire me."

She laughed, but it was far from a happy laugh. "I can't?"

I shook my head. "No. So, I suggest we move forward and figure out what it is about the design you don't like."

"It's not that I don't like it, it's just a bit over the top."

"We can scale it back some, but I think once you hear my ideas for the interior, you'll want to keep the extra room."

I could tell that piqued her interest.

Then her eyes drifted down my body and she stared at...of all things...my bare feet. I glanced down at them, then back up at her.

Her eyes closed and she pressed her lips together tightly. "This isn't going to work, Truitt."

"Why not?" I asked.

Saryn's gaze jerked back to mine. There was something in her eyes that held me captive. "Truitt, my mother is trying to set us up."

I laughed. "First names now?"

She glared at me.

With a sigh, I went on. "That's a pretty expensive way of fixing up your daughter, don't you think? And why would she do that?"

She waved her hands in the air and let out a dramatic sigh. "God, you have no idea how my mother is. I'm recently out of a disastrous marriage. The last thing I'm looking for is to get involved. Especially with...um...a guy like you."

That caused me to jerk my head back in surprise. "A guy like me? I'm trying not to take offense to that, Ms. Night."

Saryn chewed on her lip as she looked down at her daughter who was stacking up blocks.

"I'm sorry, I didn't mean it that way, but let's be honest here, shall we," she said. "You're a player."

My eyes widened. "I am?"

"Yes. You're not the type of man I want in my daughter's life."

I leaned back against the swing set. "Wow. I don't think I've ever had someone judge me like that before. You know nothing about me, Ms. Night."

"Saryn, please."

"Fine, Saryn. I haven't seen you in...how many years? You followed that dickhead of a husband of yours straight out of town and never looked back."

Her mouth dropped open and she glared at me.

"I take pride in my work and believe me when I say that your mother isn't the first client who has tried to set me up with her daughter. Trust me, I'm not the least bit interested in you either."

My fists clenched as I said the lie, hoping like hell she believed it.

"As far as your comment about me being a player, I'm not. My number-one love in my life is my job. I live, eat, and breathe it. My goal is to make little kids—like your daughter—happy and safe with a playhouse they can use for years to come. So, we can do this two ways. We either work together, knowing that neither of us is interested in the other, and we ignore your mother's misguided intentions. Or, I work directly through your mother and you and I don't have any contact. I don't think that's a very good idea, since this is for *your* daughter. But I'll let you decide how you'd like to proceed."

"Wait, just hold on one second," Saryn said, her hands held up to stop me from walking to the other side of the room to put my socks and boots back on. "No matter what I say, you're not going to walk away from this job?"

"No. I'm not. Your mother signed the contract, I've already worked the project into my calendar, and I've purchased items for the playhouse. I'm financially invested in it now."

Her gaze grew hot, and holy hell did that make my body hum with desire.

"You've already bought things? I haven't signed off on the design!"

I walked over to my desk, looked for the file, and opened it. I pulled out a slip of paper and held it up for her to see.

"Your mother has. I'm guessing she didn't inform you of that either."

The steam was practically oozing out of Saryn's body. "She didn't!"

"Well, as far as I knew, everything was a go. Now, if you'll excuse me, I've got some work to do. I'll be in touch with your mother about the interior of the playhouse in the next week or so."

Saryn buried her face in her hands and groaned. The sounds vibrated straight to my cock. I had to look away from her. The moment I saw Liliana, I got my wits about me. I couldn't be thinking about her mother like that when she was in the room. What kind of asshole does that?

"This is not happening, Mr. Carter," Saryn said, her voice muffled by her hands.

I sat on the sofa on the other side of my office and slipped on my socks. When I tried to put the boot on over my sore ankle, I winced.

"Have you iced it, Truitt?" she asked.

"We're back to first names again?"

It came out harsher than I intended, and I watched as embarrassment washed over her face.

She sighed and sat in the chair across from me. Liliana was now playing with her bear on the table between us.

"I'm sorry I came in here acting like I did. I didn't mean the things I said. I'm sure you do amazing work; I was upset that my mother was meddling in my life. I took it out on you, and for that I'm sorry."

I nodded. "It's alright. I'm sorry your mother wasn't up front with you."

She smiled. "Don't force the boot on, you'll only make it worse. Have you iced and elevated it today?"

With a shake of my head, I replied, "No. I haven't."

Saryn stood. "Do you happen to have ice or an ice pack?"

I tilted my head. "Are you trying to nurse me, Ms. Night?"

"Yes I am. It's a habit."

Pointing past her, I said, "The small refrigerator has an ice pack in it. A few, actually. Ms. Townsend insists I keep them on hand."

A slight smile tugged at her mouth before she turned and walked over to it. She took out the ice pack and made her way back to me.

"May I use this?" she asked, pointing to the small towel I had used to dry off my hair.

"Sure."

She wrapped the ice pack with the towel, then pulled the table closer to me, grabbed a pillow, and motioned for me to put my foot on it. I did as she asked, keeping my gaze locked on her every move. She was stunningly beautiful.

"You really need to do this a few times a day. It will help with the swelling and the pain."

A strange tightness hit me in the middle of the chest. I replied with the only word I could manage. "Okay."

"How did you hurt it?" she asked as she sat down on the table and held the ice pack in place. She didn't need to: it could rest on top of my ankle easily, but I liked that she was still holding it. Liliana was now walking her bear up and down Saryn's body as she played make-believe and babbled. Most of what she said I couldn't even make out, but it was cute as hell.

"Would you believe me if I said a woman pushed a ladder and caused me to fall?"

She laughed. "Did you sleep with her and never call her back?"

It was my turn to chuckle. "No. She and her husband were arguing, and she pushed off the ladder I was climbing down on. I'm telling you, the woman had the strength of ten men. The ladder went over with me on it. I tried to jump, but my one foot caught on a rock and twisted my ankle. I knew it was just twisted, but my brother has a bet going with a few friends, hence the visit to the ER."

Her brow rose. "What kind of bet?"

"It's a pool, really. They all bet on different things. How many times in that quarter I'll get hurt, head to the ER, break a bone...you get the picture."

When her hand came up to hide her smile, I laughed. "It's okay, you can laugh. I've been blessed with a string of unfortunate events since I could remember."

"You think that's a blessing? To be accident prone?"

I chuckled. "No, but I'm a positive person, so I try to look at it that way."

She looked down at her daughter, then back to me. "I have a confession to make, Truitt."

I raised my brows.

"I read your medical file. I have to admit, the penile fracture made me laugh."

I rolled my eyes, dropped my head back, and let out a frustrated groan. "I need that stricken from my medical record."

"Would it be wrong of me to get in on this pool?" she asked.

My head jerked back up only to find her giving me the most breathtaking smile I'd ever seen in my life. Something inside me stirred with a longing I'd never experienced before.

"Yes. It would!" I said, tossing the pillow that was next to me, hitting her right square in the face, causing us both to laugh.

"Ohh, no! Momma get mad!" Liliana stated, her little hand on her hip as she gave me a look that would put any my mother used to give me to shame. It was obvious, she was her mother's mini.

"I'm so sorry, Liliana. Your momma had it coming."

When my eyes met Saryn's, our gazes locked for a few brief moments. A flush slowly crept up her neck, then filled her cheeks. I wanted to know what in the hell she was thinking that made her blush like that. And what I could do to make it happen again. I couldn't help but wonder if she remembered that day on her front porch. The day she told me she was dating Tim.

"You're blushing," I said.

Her hands went to her cheeks. "I'm hot, that's all."

I smiled and she rewarded me with another stomach-dropping grin. I felt like I'd just been dropped out of the sky and was free falling. I hadn't felt like this in years.

Maybe I just didn't want to admit that the last time I felt this way was when Saryn came to Boerne for a visit a few years ago. Just the sight of her had made me weak in the knees. I'd hated that she belonged to another man.

The need to touch her swept over me so fiercely I had to force myself to look away and then clear my throat. I felt like I was that awkward boy in middle school who was afraid his voice would pitch up the moment he talked to the girl he liked.

"So, since you're here and holding ice on my ankle, let's talk about the inside of Liliana's playhouse."

Her tongue came out quickly and wet her lips and I had to fight to keep myself in check. Jesus, this woman was going to drive me insane. In that moment, Liliana crawled up onto the loveseat and sat right next to me. All thoughts of playtime with her mommy vanished. She took my arm and with her free hand, pointed to my ankle.

"Ouchy. S'okay, Momma make it better."

I stared at the little girl with the striking blue eyes as she gazed up at me with a smile so innocent I was left speechless. No woman had ever won my heart before, and Liliana could now claim to have taken it straight from me without so much as a blink of her eyes.

Dear God, I am in so much trouble.

Chapter 8

Saryn

MY HEART RACED in my chest as I watched my daughter stare up at Truitt like he was her Prince Charming. I knew how she felt. The moment I had walked into his office and seen him standing there, dressed in nothing but his boxer briefs, my knees had nearly buckled out from under me.

This Truitt was so different from the one I had known when we were younger. I'd seen him play football, watched him run around the track on Saturday mornings, and stole glances of him at parties. He'd been the hot cowboy every girl in high school wanted, and it seemed things hadn't changed. The few nurses I had spoke with after he left the ER had commented on how Truitt was the one cowboy in town every single woman wanted to snag. He had the looks. He had the money, and from what I could tell, he had the charm. He'd always been charming, though. Even to me, one of his best friend's annoying little sister.

Truitt cleared his throat and looked from Liliana to me. "It already feels better."

Good Lord, why was his gaze so hot? Why was my lower stomach pulling with want?

Nope. No. Forget it. Not happening. Get it out of your head right now, Saryn.

"Liliana, tell me some of your favorite things to do," Truitt said, focusing back on her. I pulled my gaze from him and put it back on Liliana.

"Dwess up."

"Dress up, okay, like princess-type dress up?"

She nodded.

"What else?"

"Wead."

He looked at me. "Read?"

"Yes, she loves reading."

"Okay, so maybe a little reading nook."

My heart stuttered. Was he really attempting to find out what interested my three-year-old daughter by asking her? Why was that so refreshing? Her own father could not have cared less most of the time.

"What else do you like?"

She smiled. "Twirling!"

Truitt looked amused as he turned his attention to me. "Define that one, Mom."

I laughed. "She's in dance, and ballet is one of her favorites. And tap."

"Well, who wouldn't love tap."

"Right?" I said, feeling my cheeks ache. I realized I was smiling like a silly fool.

"Do you like to look at the stars, Liliana?"

She nodded.

"What's your favorite color, pink?"

Liliana scrunched up her nose and shook her head. "Gwoss."

"Gross?" Truitt gasped. "What color do you like, then?"

"Lellow!" Liliana declared.

Truitt rubbed at his chin and reflected on her answer. "Yellow. That's a fine color, I think I can work with that."

When he swung his gaze over to me, I couldn't keep myself from looking at his lips. Why my attention focused there was beyond me.

I quickly corrected myself and sat up a bit straighter. "Do you do all of your research like this?"

He laughed. "I do like to meet with the kids. They're the ones who usually give us ideas for what's best for the playhouses."

I tilted my head and regarded him for a moment. "I like that you make them feel like they're a part of this process."

"They are, as far as I'm concerned. The parents may be the ones paying me to build it, but the playhouse is for the kids. They're the ones I want to make happy with it."

I nodded. "The drawing had a swing, can you also add monkey bars?"

He lifted one of his brows. "Are you on board for this playhouse now?"

With a roll of my eyes, I nodded. "I guess I have no choice. But, like I said earlier, can we maybe scale it back just a tad?"

And there it was again. His smile. Big, bright, full of excitement, with a dimple that made my knees weak.

"Two turrets instead of three, then. I have ideas for both."

"Okay, what are they?"

"One tower could be her dress-up room. Where she can change into whatever she's feeling like that day. A princess, a superhero, a ballerina. The second tower I think should hold an art area, or maybe a little bedroom."

That made me take even more notice. "An art area?"

He winked. "Well, if she's anything like her mother, she probably likes to draw and paint."

I sat there, stunned. "How did you know I like to paint?"

Truitt shrugged. "I remembered from high school. Ryan mentioned it a time or two, and it must have stuck in my memory."

Staring at him, I opened my mouth to speak, but nothing came out. Finally, I got my wits about me. "Ryan was always supportive of my painting."

Truitt nodded, then rubbed the back of his neck and looked around his office. He suddenly seemed nervous.

"We've probably taken up too much of your time," I said. "I'm glad we're able to...um...get this all...you know."

He shook his head. Damn him.

"Well, since I can't fire you."

The way his mouth twitched with a hidden smile made my insides heat. Good Lord, I really needed a night out.

"No, you can't," he said.

"Yes, and because of that, I'm glad we were able to put our differences aside and make this work. For Liliana's sake. Purely."

"Of course," he said, a hint of something like seduction lacing his voice.

Nonsense, Saryn. You need to leave this office and now.

"Liliana, come on, sweetheart, we need to let Mr. Carter get back to work."

My daughter jumped up from playing on the floor and rushed over to Truitt. He instinctively bent down and she threw her arms around his neck. I nearly gasped at her show of affection.

"Tank you for letting me pway! See you later!" Liliana said, giving Truitt a hug and then coming back over to me. I wasn't sure who was more shocked.

Me...or Truitt.

Two weeks had passed since I'd walked out of Truitt's office. As much as I didn't want to think about the man, I seemed to always be thinking about him. Damn my mother.

With a sigh, I wrote my notes in a file and closed it. I was exhausted and ready to go home.

"Saryn, a few of us are going out tonight...want to join us?" Lucy asked.

God, a night out sounded like the perfect thing. What I really needed was a mindless hook up. Not full-on sex, but it would be so nice to feel my body against a man's. A little innocent flirting and a bit of male attention were very much needed. Maybe it would even break the spell Truitt seemed to have placed on me all over again.

"Who all is going?" I asked.

Lucy smiled. "Just a bunch of nurses. Linda, who works up in L & D will be there. You might want to get on her good side. She has some pretty big pull with who they hire up there."

That caught my attention. Not that I hated working in the ER, I had just done it enough in the beginning of my career, and my heart was with the babies.

"Where are y'all going?" I asked.

"Bricks Dance Hall. A local band is playing tonight and they're really good. Mostly do cover songs, but it makes for a fun night."

I chewed on my lip, thinking it over. Lucy had been so nice to me since I'd started. My best friend from high school, Linnzi, didn't live in Boerne anymore. I missed her terribly and made a note to myself to go visit her parents and see how they were doing.

"Saryn, give yourself a night out. Let loose and have some fun. Besides, there are always some good-looking cowboys who are more than willing to spin you around the dance floor."

With a smile, I said, "Okay. I need to make sure I can find someone to watch Liliana, and I'll meet y'all there?"

Lucy gave me a triumphant smile. "Don't even think about going home and taking your bra off, crawling into comfy clothes, and texting that you're not coming."

I laughed. "I promise, I really do need the night out."

With a beaming smile, Lucy waved her fingers at me. "See you soon!"

As promised, I went home, arranged for Liliana to stay with my folks, put on a pair of my favorite Wrangler jeans and a cute shirt that probably showed too much cleavage, and slipped on my favorite pair of boots.

When I opened the door, I let out a yelp. "Ryan! You scared the crap out of me."

He grinned. "Our mother called to inform me you were going out."

I raised a brow. "Tell me she didn't ask you to go along."

"She didn't. She invited me over for movie night. But I need a night out, too. I broke up with Miranda."

"You did it!" I gasped.

"Yes, and before you judge me, I intend on hooking up with a woman whom I hope has loose morals and is only interested in a one-night stand. So you're driving."

I snarled my lip. "Okay, first off, that was way too much information. And how do you know I didn't want to hook up with someone?"

Anger flashed through his eyes. "Saryn, you're not having a one-night stand."

"Ryan, you don't get to say what I can and cannot do. Sorry."

He rolled his eyes. "God, at least let me make sure I know the dude and he's not a douche or a serial killer, or a douchey serial killer."

I reached for the door and pulled it shut behind me. "If you're hanging out with serial killers, I think we have a bigger problem here."

Ryan laughed and draped his arm over my shoulder. "I never thought I'd say this, but let's go find some pussy...um...and dick."

"Yeah, you just made it really weird."

"I know, let's forget I even said anything."

The moment Ryan and I walked into Bricks Dance Hall, I felt like I'd stepped back in time. The music pulsed through my body and I had an incredible urge to dance.

"Who is the hottie walking toward us, tell me you know her!" Ryan said, nearly screaming it over the music. With one quick glance to where he was looking, I smiled.

"That's Lucy. She's a nurse I work with. And I'm pretty sure from the stories she tells us at work that she's your perfect rebound girl."

My brother let a charming smile play across his face. By the look on Lucy's, he wasn't going to have to work hard at this tonight.

"Who's your handsome friend, Saryn?" Lucy asked, somehow managing to make her voice sound seductive over the music.

"This is my brother, Ryan. Ryan, Lucy Hart."

He took Lucy's hand and kissed the back of it, causing me to roll my eyes. He said something to her, but I couldn't hear what it was since he leaned in and said it close to her ear. By the way she flushed, I was glad I hadn't heard it.

"Where have you been hiding your brother, Saryn?" Lucy asked, tearing her gaze from Ryan.

"In the woodshed," I replied.

She laughed then focused back on Ryan. "Care to dance?"

"Lead the way."

And like that, I was on my own. I didn't even know where Lucy was sitting with the other nurses. I looked around the bar in an attempt to find them, but it was packed with people.

"Shit."

I turned and headed to the bar. I'd order a beer and make my way around until I found them.

As I stood in line, I let my eyes wander. I didn't know anyone in the place. Boerne wasn't really the small town I'd grown up in any longer. More and more people were moving outside of San Antonio. Boerne still managed to keep its small-town appeal, but little local places like this clearly had attracted more city folk. Half of them weren't even two-stepping the right way.

With a sigh, I finally stepped up to the bar. The bartender gave me a smile, let his eyes drop to my chest, then snapped them back up. "What can I get you?"

"Bud, in a bottle, please."

He nodded and walked away to get my beer. After I paid and tipped him, I turned and froze in place. Standing not far from the bar was Truitt. My knees felt wobbly. Again. This time the man wasn't nearly naked. Oh, no. He was wearing tight jeans, a very snug blue T-shirt, and a black cowboy hat. Why, of all the men in Texas, did this one make my insides quiver with desire? The dull pulse between my legs was almost instant. As if he could sense I was staring at him, he turned and looked directly at me. He smiled. Good Lord up above. I actually let out a sigh.

"Look away, Saryn. Look away," I muttered to myself as I looked past him, attempting to make it seem like I was searching for someone. I walked in the opposite direction, quickly.

As I moved away from him, I spotted Natalie, one of the nurses I worked with.

"Thank God," I mumbled.

By the time I pushed through the crowd and made it to the table, I was positive I'd worked up a sweat.

"Natalie!" I nearly shouted.

She looked up and grinned. "It's about time you showed up!"

I glanced to her right to see her talking to a handsome cowboy. He tipped his hat at me as I sat down.

"Saryn, this is Luke. Luke, Saryn. She's the new nurse I was telling you about."

The way he looked at me made me glance at Natalie with a questioning look.

"He's my cousin."

Ahh...that explained the way he was eye-fucking me. "It's nice meeting you, Luke, was it?" I asked as I stretched my hand out to shake his.

"That's right. It's my pleasure."

I glanced over my shoulder to look in the general direction I'd just come from. A small part of me was disappointed Truitt hadn't followed. Quickly dismissing that thought, I focused back on the table.

"Is everyone dancing?" I asked, looking directly at Natalie. I didn't want Luke to think that was a hint for him to ask me.

"Yes. Luke and I just finished taking a spin and I needed a break."

I smiled and looked out at the dance floor. When I saw Truitt, I felt my entire body tense. He was dancing with a beautiful blonde. He had her tucked up nicely against his body, and the two of them moved across the floor like they'd done it a thousand times. I tried to ignore the instant pang in my chest. Holy hell, was that jealousy?

Nonsense.

"Do you know Truitt?"

Natalie's voice pulled my gaze away from the dance floor.

"What?" I asked, flustered by her question.

"Truitt Carter, do you know him?"

"Um, sort of. He's friends with my older brother, and he's building a playhouse for my parents."

Luke and Natalie both looked confused by that.

With an awkward laugh, I corrected, "Well, not for them, for my daughter. They hired him to build her a playhouse."

Natalie grinned. "He does amazing work and has a long waiting list of clients."

That little bit of information was interesting. How had my mother been able to get him to build Liliana's playhouse so quickly?

"I've heard he's amazing. At his work. With playhouses," I said like an idiot.

Luke stared at me, then tilted his head. Crap.

"I mean, I don't really know. My mother is handling most of it since it's on their property."

He smiled warmly, but there was a bit of lust in his eyes that caused an instant rush of heat to my cheeks.

"What do you do, Luke?" I asked, hoping to shift the subject off of Truitt.

"I'm a deputy sheriff for Kendall County."

A cop. There was something hot about that. "Well, thank you for your service, sir."

He winked, and I wanted it to make my stomach dip, but it didn't.

Damn it.

"Luke, you should really ask Saryn to dance," Natalie said. "I need a bit more time to recover. I'm so out of shape."

Turning to look my way, Luke raised his brow in question. "What do you say, like to take a spin around the dance floor?"

This was it. The moment I was officially moving on from my divorce. Could I honestly hook up with a guy for a night of meaningless sex? That I wasn't sure about, but a little bit of personal contact would be nice. And Luke was for sure giving me signs he was interested.

"I'd love to dance, thank you."

He stood, reached for my hand, and led me to the dance floor. A Chris Young song played as Luke expertly drew me close to him as we started to two-step. For the first time in a long time I felt a little reckless. Free. Like a girl who was finally able to enjoy herself.

And tonight, I had every intention of enjoying myself to the fullest.

Chapter 9

Truitt

LUKE BARNES WAS dancing with Saryn, and I didn't want that to bother me as much as it did. Why should I care who she was dancing with? But when I first looked over and saw her standing there, staring at me with a beer in her hand, that old familiar feeling of want and desire rushed through my body.

"Truitt, if you glare at Luke any harder, you're going to burn a hole right through him."

Shay's voice pulled my gaze off of Luke and Saryn. "Don't be ridiculous."

She raised a brow. Shay Barnes probably knew me better than I knew myself. We'd had a off and on friends-with-benefits thing going for the last couple of years. Neither of us were looking to settle down or get into any sort of relationship. I'd known Shay since high school, she was a friend and one of the few people who knew I had once upon a time had a thing for Saryn. She was someone I could trust. And someone I could fuck and walk away from the next morning knowing she wasn't after my money or a ring.

"She's a client and Ryan's sister."

Shay glanced back over. "No old feelings coming back?"

"Don't be ridiculous," I said, then spun Shay and did a little dip. When she came back up, she took another peek over at Saryn and Luke.

"She's a client. Is that all, Truitt?"

"Yes, that's all."

Shay left the subject alone, for which I was grateful. I wasn't exactly sure what my feelings were toward Saryn. She'd ignited something inside of me years ago that never fully died out. Hell, every woman I ever tried to date I compared to her. I'd woken up with my cock in my hand more than once, with her as the star in my dreams.

I was having a hard time trying to figure out what I was exactly feeling for Saryn. Hence the reason I called Shay earlier tonight. It had been way too long since I'd hooked up, and I wasn't in the mood for a one-night stand. I rarely did those any more, and honestly hadn't really had that many. Shay was a safe place to go. Both of us had an understanding that if either of us ever found ourselves in a relationship, this thing we had together was over and we would both walk away friends. We'd stayed true to it. Shay had met someone last year, dated him for a while, and when it turned out he was cheating on her, she found herself at my house in the middle of the night. We didn't have sex then, we simply talked. She was more than a fuck buddy, she was truly a friend.

After a few hours of dancing with Shay, talking to other friends, and trying not to pay attention to what Saryn was doing, I sat at a table and watched as Luke walked out of the dance hall, his hand on Saryn's lower back. She had stopped, said something to her brother, then left. The fact that Ryan didn't stop her from leaving with the guy pissed me off. I knew she wasn't a little girl anymore, but was he really going to let his sister just leave with someone?

I finished off my beer, looked around for Shay and found her dancing with some city slicker who didn't have the first clue on how to properly two-step. I rolled my eyes and decided it was time to cut in.

I made my way toward them and Shay caught my eyes. She almost looked relieved to see me coming their way.

"Darlin', you about ready to head on out?"

The guy turned and faced me. "Are you together?" he asked, looking slightly defeated.

"No, he's just going to take me home and give me a few orgasms, then we'll call it a night."

Now the poor bastard looked confused.

I tipped my hat and wrapped my arm around Shay's waist and guided her off the dance floor. "Why do you do that?" I asked with a chuckle.

"I like to see the look of shock on their face," Shay answered unapologetically.

"Some day a guy is going to catch your attention, Shay, and you're going to be screwed."

She tossed her head back and laughed. "And some day you'll realize why no woman has ever caught your eye."

I sat in my truck and ran my hand down my face. I'd had a long night with Shay and hadn't gotten home until almost four in the morning. A few hours of sleep and I was practically begging the girl in the drive-through to hand me my coffee.

"One large black coffee and an orange scone."

I took the coffee and the scone and gave her a polite smile. "Thank you."

She grinned and then promptly began taking another order.

By the time I got to the shop, I felt like I could at least keep my eyes open without force.

When I walked in, Jack, my right-hand man, was waiting for me. We didn't normally work on Sunday, but he had texted me with a problem. *A major problem* were the exact words he used.

"You better have a damn good reason to call me on a Sunday. It's the only day I take off, dude."

He rubbed the back of his neck. "The playhouse for the Nights..." he started, then trailed off.

I narrowed my eyes at him and asked, "What about it?"

"There's a tree that's going to be a problem."

"A tree?" I asked.

"Yes. A tree."

The next thing I knew, Jack, Evie, Will, and I were staring at a large Spanish Oak tree on the Night's property.

"What do you mean, they won't let us cut it down?" I asked, staring at Evie.

"Well, last night I had a dinner party and I was walking some of the folks around back here. I explained to them that we were having a playhouse built for our granddaughter. Well, one of our dinner guests noticed this tree, then went on to say it was some sort of trail tree that the Native Americans used to mark things like rivers and creeks."

I stared at her, not sure where it was all going.

"She informed me this morning that she contacted someone from the state to come out and see if this was a trail marker tree. If it is, we can't cut it down."

"Is it a law?" I asked, never having heard of such a thing.

"I don't know. It could be just this woman attempting to throw some weight around, or it could be something real."

My hand scrubbed along my jawline. "I think the easiest thing to do is move the playhouse to another location, so we don't even have to worry about this."

"Not worry about this! Some woman is trying to tell me which trees I can and cannot cut down on a ranch that has been in my family for generations. Who in the hell does she think she is?" Will practically shouted.

I glanced over to Jack, who raised his brows and gave me that look that said, *See what I mean. We have a problem.*

"Will, Evie, if I can give my advice to you both."

The couple stopped arguing and turned to face me. Both wore looks that said they would start this up again the moment Jack and I left.

"You have plenty of options for where to put the playhouse. If we're going to move it, now is the time to do it. I say, let's just take the tree out of the equation and move the playhouse."

Evie nodded. "I agree. Where would you suggest, Truitt?"

I looked around, trying to find a spot where we wouldn't really need to clear a lot of trees out. I hated cutting them down anyway and always tried to find the spots on folks' property where we would have to cut down as few trees as possible.

"Well, since Saryn and Liliana are staying in the guest cottage for the foreseeable future, I suggest putting it between the two buildings. What about in that little clearing right there?"

"Oh, that was where Grandma cleared years ago for a garden. I don't think we would have to cut any trees down if we put it there," Evie stated.

"Well, what happens when Saryn moves out of the guest house? Then the playhouse is farther away from our house," Will added.

"Will does have a point." Evie sighed.

Jack cleared his throat. "You could put it more toward the side of your house, rather than the back. If we went to the right side of the house, I think you'd only need to clear out that one cedar tree and the one live oak."

Everyone looked over to where Jack had suggested. The sound of a car pulling down the drive caused all eyes to swing over toward the guest house. Saryn pulled up and stopped. She got out of the car and paused as she realized everyone was looking at her.

She was clearly arriving home from her night out. She started toward us and I took a long drink of my now cold-as-ice coffee. Evie headed toward her and started to grumble.

"Oh, Lord. This ought to be good," Will said.

Before Saryn could say anything, Evie spoke first and didn't even attempt to keep her voice down.

"Really, Saryn? I was worried sick about you, out all night and coming home in the clothes you went out in."

Jack and I both turned and started to make our way over to the newly proposed building site.

As we got farther away, I glanced back over my shoulder to see the two women arguing.

"Looks like Saryn didn't waste any time moving on from the douche ex of hers," Jack said with a chuckle.

I took another drink of my coffee and tried to ignore the strange ache in my chest. Saryn had most likely spent the night with Luke and that bothered the fuck out of me. Hell, who was I to judge? I'd gone back to Shay's place last night. Still, the idea of her sleeping with Luke, him touching her, made a strange feeling rush through me.

"Guess not," I finally said before coming to a stop.

"Wonder who the lucky bastard was?"

"It's none of our business," I stated, harsher than I had intended.

Jack simply nodded and put his hands in his pockets as we waited for the three of them to walk our way. I had to admit, I was surprised Saryn hadn't turned and walked back to her place.

Evie cleared her throat. "I've filled Saryn in on what was happening and told her that we are going to relocate the playhouse."

Will kept walking and made his way toward the house. I glanced his way and Evie spoke again.

"Liliana spent the night with us last night and is watching a movie with Rose. Our housekeeper."

"Momma, I don't think they need to know all of that," Saryn snapped.

The two women exchanged a look I couldn't read, nor did I want to. Saryn avoided looking directly at me and kept her eyes on her mother, the ground, or occasionally, Jack.

"Well, anyway, are we good with this new spot?" I asked.

Evie nodded, then turned to Saryn. "Don't you think this will be a good spot? I think it actually works out better because we can see the playhouse from the kitchen."

Saryn wrapped her arms around her body, almost as if she was self-conscious about something. Finally, she answered her mother. "Yes, I think it works great, Momma."

A loud shriek had everyone turning to see Liliana rushing out and running toward her mother.

"Mommy!"

The smile that erupted on Saryn's face made me smile, as well. "Hey, baby girl!"

She bent down and scooped up the little girl, giving her a hug and then peppering her with kisses. Liliana turned and saw me, then promptly asked to be put down. She quickly made her way over to me and I bent down to greet her. What I wasn't expecting was for her to hug me.

"Twuitt! Pwayhouse!"

Everyone laughed, but when my gaze caught Saryn's, she was simply staring, a blank expression on her face.

"Hey there, Liliana. What do you think about this spot for your playhouse?" I asked, picking her up with one arm and turning her to look at the open area.

"Yes, pwease!" she said in the sweetest voice. My heart fell a little more for this girl.

Evie clapped her hands. "Then the whole tree debacle has been avoided. Come on, Liliana, let's go get your things."

As Evie reached for her granddaughter, I was caught off guard again when Liliana framed my face with her little hands and looked me directly in the eyes. She smiled and my goddamn knees went weak. She didn't even utter a word to me, but in that moment, that little girl wrapped me around her finger and I knew there wasn't anything I wouldn't do to make her happy.

"Twuitt."

"Liliana," I said in a serious reply, because I didn't know what else to say.

"Well, it appears you've made a friend, Truitt," Evie said.

I smiled back at Liliana. "Well, I hope I'm invited to the first tea party in her castle."

Liliana nodded happily, then let her grandmother take her from my arms.

As they walked off, I watched them go before swinging my gaze to Saryn. Her blank expression had disappeared, only to be replaced by another I couldn't read at all.

I faced Will. "We'll be back out tomorrow to survey everything and mark it all out. I'll give you a call before we head over."

He nodded, reached for my hand and shook it, then did the same with Jack. "Damn nosy people. Marker tree, my ass."

I attempted not to laugh as I watched Will stomp away toward his house.

Once he left, Jack and I both laughed, then faced Saryn. "Well, enjoy your Sunday, Saryn," I said.

"Um, thank you. Y'all, too."

Jack and I started toward my truck when Saryn called out my name. "Truitt, might I have a word with you, please?"

I stopped and walked back toward her. "Sure. Do you not like the new location?"

Her eyes swung over to the new spot, then to Jack's retreating back, then to her folks' house before finally settling back on me.

She looked down for a moment before piercing me with her brown eyes. "I don't want you to think I go out on the weekends and stay out all night. I realize how this looks, me coming home clearly after being out all night."

I held up my hand. "Saryn, you're a grown woman, you don't owe anyone, especially me, an explanation."

She chewed on her lip. "I know that, but I also know how it must look to you. I saw you last night and..."

"What you do in your private life is just that. Private. You won't be getting any judgment from me."

With a forced smile, and an uneasiness in her eyes, she nodded. "Thank you, but I know how people talk and...well...I'm not usually a one-night-stand kind of woman. It's just, I needed it, if that makes any sense whatsoever."

The fact that she had admitted to sleeping with Luke felt strangely like someone had stabbed a knife in my chest. Her eyes filled with something, not regret, but something foreign to me. Something that said she might have wished she hadn't stayed with Luke. Maybe if I had asked her to dance, it would have been me she spent the night with. Or maybe that was simply my wishful thinking.

I shook my head to clear my thoughts.

"Like I said, no judgment. I'm far from being innocent myself. If you'll excuse me, I need to get going." I pointed toward my truck where Jack was now waiting in the passenger seat. This conversation was turning more awkward as the seconds ticked on.

Her cheeks turned red with embarrassment. "Yes, of course. Right. Have, um, have a good Sunday, Truitt."

I tipped my cowboy hat to her and said, "You, too."

As I walked away, I felt her gaze practically boring a hole into my back. I had to force myself not to turn and glance back her way.

Chapter 10

Saryn

I'D SUCCESSFULLY GONE a week without anyone from work asking me about Luke. Not even Natalie, his cousin, asked about it. But today was the first day I'd be working with Lucy, and I knew she wasn't about to hold back.

I knew from talking with Ryan that he'd had his own night of fun with her. From what he'd filled me in on, she was very open about her escapades. I'd recently discovered she'd slept with Roger, Truitt's brother, the night of his ER visit.

"Good morning!" Lucy said, practically skipping into the break room.

I glanced up at her and gave her a polite smile. "Morning. How were your days off?"

Lucy winked. "Fun. It started off with your brother, who I might add is super nice."

With a roll of my eyes, I tried not to gag. "Please, don't even go there, Lucy. What the two of you did is your business."

She took a drink from her coffee, and I swear her eyes twinkled. "Natalie told me you and Luke hooked up."

I nearly choked on my tea. "What!"

With a wave of her hand, she moved closer to me. "Be quiet, Saryn. My gosh, the other nurses are dying for information."

My brow lifted and I gave her a look that said she was doing the very same thing.

"Listen, if there's one thing you should know about me, it's this. I like men, I like sex...a lot...and I have my fair share of fun. What I don't like is women who gossip about my sex life."

"Aren't you asking about mine?" I asked with what I was sure was a disbelieving look.

"Yes, but I'm not going to turn around and tell anyone else. I get the feeling that what happened that night is not something you do often." She gave me a once-over, then added, "Or ever, if I'm being honest."

My mouth fell open slightly.

"Oh, please, don't act like I've offended you. I don't blame you for wanting a mindless night out, especially after your divorce. I take it the marriage wasn't a happy one."

"No, it wasn't. He cheated, but we had pretty much checked out of our marriage long before I found out. And you're right. I've never had a one-night stand before. I mean, Luke was the second guy I've ever slept with."

Lucy stared at me like I had grown two heads.

"Shut up."

I nodded. "The worst part of it all is that my parents had to see my walk of shame."

Her eyes widened and she looked at her watch. "We've got ten minutes, tell me everything!"

When Lucy sat in the chair, I glanced at the door, then took a seat next to her. I closed my eyes and let out a long sigh before I focused back on her. "Lucy, it was humiliating. My folks were out in the yard with Truitt Carter and a guy who works for him."

Her brows raised. "Go on."

"Well, I pulled up and got out wearing the same thing I had on the night before, so it was plain and simple to everyone I was just then shagging my ass home."

Lucy attempted not to smile, but the corner of her mouth twitched up.

"I hate the idea of anyone thinking I..."

"Had sex? You're a grown woman, Saryn. If you want to spend the night with a man, that's your right."

"I know that, but my father was out there. He knows what I did! And my mother, she wasn't angry with me, but I could see the disappointment in her face. Lord knows what Truitt thinks about me, although he was super nice about it." I let a small smile play across my face.

"What do you mean?"

"Well, after my folks walked back into the house, I spoke with Truitt alone. I didn't want him to think I was—"

I stopped speaking abruptly.

"A whore?" "That's not what I was going to say, Lucy. More like...loose. Please don't think I think of you that way."

She laughed and waved her hand. "Like I said, I like sex. I don't sleep around like everyone thinks; I'm careful, and I'm always up front with the guys I'm with. Truth be told, most of them want the one night, as well. I'm not ashamed, so don't feel like you have to tiptoe. And you shouldn't feel guilty for having a night out. And who cares what Truitt thinks? From what I hear, he's no saint. Why care about his opinion?"

I shrugged. "He's building my daughter's playhouse and he's friends with Ryan. I just didn't want him to think I'm a bad mother."

Lucy rolled her eyes. "He's not going to think that. Okay, real talk. Did you enjoy your night with Luke?"

My face scrunched up and I made a little noise.

"No! He sucked? But he's so damn good looking and has a body to die for."

"That he does. The man is in shape, but he...oh God...I can't believe I'm talking about this. Promise not to say a word to Natalie!" I whispered.

Lucy crossed her heart with her finger, then made like she was zipping her lips.

With another quick look at the door, I said, "He came practically the moment he got inside me. I mean, it was like four, maybe five thrusts, and then he was groaning. He didn't even offer to, you know."

"Make you come?"

I groaned. "Oh God, someone is going to hear you."

"What? I'm a get-to-the-point kind of girl."

Sighing, I shook my head.

"I mean, he rolled off of me and I sort of laid there for a few minutes, and I think it finally dawned on him."

"His mouth?"

I was positive my eyes nearly popped out of my head. "You are direct, aren't you?"

"Are you a prude, Saryn?"

"A prude?" I asked with a humorless laugh.

"Yeah, I mean, if you need me to tone down my words, I can. It's okay if you're not into that sort of stuff. Not all women like it."

I could feel my cheeks heating. Then Lucy nearly dropped her mug.

"You've never had a guy go down on you, have you?" she whispered, a look of horror on her face. "Your husband? Never?"

With a shake of my head, she let out a sigh that said she needed to fix this and stat.

When she focused back on me, she asked, "Okay, so he used his fingers, did it feel good, at least?"

I nodded. "Yeah, nothing I couldn't do for myself, though."

She placed a hand over her chest and smiled. "You're not a total loss. I can work with this."

"Excuse me?" I asked, jerking my head back.

"Did you have sex with him again?"

"No. He fell asleep."

She motioned with her hands. "My gawd, what a dick!"

I leaned in and whispered, "After he made me orgasm, he literally rolled over and fell asleep. I laid there for about an hour trying to figure out if I should just leave! He woke up around seven and we had sex again. This time he made sure I…" My eyes darted to the door again, then back to Lucy. "He made sure I came first before he did his quick five or six pumps."

This time Lucy did laugh, and I finally let myself laugh, as well. It was nice having another woman to talk to. Most of my high school friends had moved away and were happily married. Linnzi had moved to France after her accident and we hardly got to talk.

Honestly, I hadn't really talked to any friends from high school. Tim had made sure I'd focused most of my time and attention on him, which cost me most of my friends.

"Note to self, never hook up with Luke," Lucy said as she pretended to type it on her phone.

I slapped at her hand and shook my head.

"Thank you for talking to me. I don't really have many friends here."

Her smile softened and she said, "I don't either. Most women are put off by me, which is fine. But if you ever want to talk or need to talk…or, hell, just need someone to hang out with, I'm your girl."

My heart was touched by her kindness. "Thank you, Lucy. You've made me feel at home since the day I met you, and I appreciate that. Not everyone has."

She nodded. "That's because they know you're a better nurse than them."

And there it was again: the woman shocked me into silence once more with her brutally honest words.

She smiled. "Come on, our shift is on, let's go heal people and shit like that."

Laughing, I turned and rinsed out my mug before setting it on the drying rack. It had felt good to talk to someone about what happened during my first attempt at moving on with my life. Even though a pretty big part of me regretted my night with Luke, another part was glad I did it. It had felt good to throw out caution and let my guard down.

An hour hadn't gone by when Lucy walked up to me and handed me a chart. "Can you see the guy in bay four? I've got to help Dr. Passel with a patient."

"Sure," I said, taking the chart and slipping it under my arm. "What's wrong with him?"

She shrugged and headed over to another bay. "I didn't get a chance to ask."

I turned and walked over to bay four. Before I opened the curtain, I froze as I read the name.

Luke Martin.

Shit. Shit. Shit.

I took in a deep breath and pulled the curtain back. Luke was sitting on the table, a smile on his face.

"Luke, is everything okay?" I asked, scanning him to make sure he hadn't been hurt in any way. He was dressed in his cop uniform.

"Everything is fine. Do you know how hard it was to bribe them into letting me come back here?"

I glanced back over to where Lucy was. She was indeed busy with a patient; I didn't think she even knew who was sitting in this bay.

"I was hoping I'd get you for a nurse; they couldn't promise me it would be you."

Focusing back on him, I forced a smile. "Why did you go to all this trouble?"

He shrugged. "You never gave me your number, but I remembered you worked here, so I thought I'd pay you a visit."

"And you couldn't just walk in and ask to speak to me?"

Luke looked confused for a moment before he forced a smile. "What fun would that be?"

Irritation rushed through me. I was busy, this was an ER, and he was a cop. He should know how wrong this was.

"I'm sorry, Luke, I'm really busy."

He nodded and slid off the table. "Right, I'm sorry. I wasn't thinking. I just really wanted to see you again. Ask you if you wanted to go to dinner or something."

Guilt wrapped around my heart and squeezed tight. He was a really nice guy, just not the type of guy I was interested in. And I felt terrible, but the first thing I had thought of when I left his apartment was that I wished it had been Truitt I'd spent the night with.

What a bitch I was.

Lucy's voice popped into my head and I lifted my chin some and stood up straight. Honesty was the only way to go here.

"Luke, I had a great time with you the other night, but I'm recently out of a marriage and I was only looking for a...a, um...a..."

He tilted his head. "A one-night stand."

My cheeks heated and I felt like I was starting to sweat. "I thought you were on the same page."

For a moment, he looked unsure of what to say before he rubbed at the back of his neck with his hand. "No, right. You didn't promise anything. I simply thought maybe you might like to go out again."

I chewed on my lip. "I'm sorry, but I was only interested in the one night. Please know that isn't something I normally do."

"Right, no. I get it. I was the guy you needed to move on with."

"I'm sorry if I misled you in any way."

He moved back and forth on his feet as if he was forcing himself not to bolt from the room.

"I understand. Thank you for being so honest with me, Saryn."

All I could do was smile and give him a nod.

"I need to get on back to my patrol. Have a great day," Luke said, reaching down and giving me a quick kiss on the cheek. Then he walked past me, and I let out the breath I hadn't even realized I had been holding in.

After a few deep breaths, I turned and walked out of the bay, looked around the ER, and noticed not a single person had been paying any attention to what had been going on with me and Luke. A sense of relief hit me, and I walked over to the front desk, handed the young administrative clerk the file and said, "Next time, please don't let anyone take up a bay that might be used for someone who truly needs it."

The young girl flushed with embarrassment and nodded as she took the file from me.

I spent the next four hours counting down until I could leave and get home. I wanted to see Liliana and just relax and not think of anyone or anything. An image of Truitt popped into my head as

I made my way back to the nurses' station. The man seemed to be invading my thoughts more and more.

"What's with the serious look on your face?" Lucy asked.

"What?" I asked.

"I can't tell if you're angry, excited or confused right now." Lucy chuckled.

Slowly, I shook my head and picked up another patient's chart. I tried to focus on it and couldn't. I had no idea if nursing was beginning to be something I wasn't interested in, if it was simply the ER, or if my problem was something different altogether.

I looked up at Lucy who was still giving me a questioning stare. "I can't tell either."

Chapter 11

Truitt

SARYN PULLED UP and parked. She sat in her car as she stared through the windshield at me. Liliana was running her toy car up and down my arms and back as Ryan sat on the porch steps next to me.

When Saryn's eyes narrowed, Ryan laughed. "She has that look on her face that says she thinks we're up to something."

I smiled, and she got out of the car and made her way over to us.

"What's going on? Why are you here, Truitt?"

Ouch. She sounds annoyed that I'm here.

"I've called and left you three messages on your phone regarding the paint color for Liliana's playhouse. Your mother keeps referring me to you, you keep ignoring me, so I had to make the time to come over and ask you in person. I wasn't sure of your work schedule, and Ryan told me you'd be home shortly, so I waited."

Saryn folded her arms over her chest and gave me an expression that said she was calling bullshit. "I sent you a text back, Truitt. You didn't get it?"

Pulling out my phone, I brought up my text messages and scrolled. It could be possible it had come through and I'd forgotten about it. But I didn't see anything from her.

"I don't have a text from you."

With a heavy sigh, Saryn pulled out her phone. "I sent it yesterday and I know..."

Her voice trailed off and her cheeks turned a bright red.

"Shoot," she whispered as Ryan laughed, causing Liliana to laugh for no reason other than mimicking her uncle. He pulled her into his arms and tickled her.

When I looked back at Saryn, she was chewing on her lip. "I'm so sorry, Truitt. I never hit send. I don't think I've ever done that before. I was at work and must have been distracted."

My phone buzzed in my hand and I glanced down to see her reply.

It wasn't like I had all the time in the world to be tracking down freaking paint colors, but it was hard to be annoyed with Saryn. She looked tired and slightly defeated by something. So I stood and gave her a smile.

"It's not a worry at all. I brought the swatches with me, if you could pick the one you like, then I'll get out of your hair and let you enjoy the rest of the evening with your daughter."

A flash of something moved over her face before she replaced it with a smile and then a nod. I walked to my truck and Saryn followed.

"Mommy!" Liliana cried out as she ran over to Saryn who picked her up and hugged her.

"You can come, too, and help Mommy pick the color for your playhouse."

A girlish giggle came from Liliana, and I glanced back over my shoulder at the two beautiful ladies following me.

With my eyes focused back on my truck, I pushed away the weird sensation in my chest and threw open the passenger-side door. These feelings I felt when I was around Saryn and her daughter annoyed me. As if a part of me was missing something. I was not missing anything. I was happy with my life, where it was going, and how I was living it.

Wasn't I?

Ever since Saryn came back into town and all those old feelings started bubbling up again, I found myself second-guessing everything.

For fuck's sake, get it out of your head, Carter.

I yanked the swatches out and handed them to Saryn. "Here you go. I narrowed the colors down to these six." My voice was clipped and an edge of annoyance came through.

She looked at me with a surprised expression and took them out of my hand before setting Liliana down. She began showing her daughter each color.

"This one, pwease!" Liliana said, pointing to the Fun Yellow color. I couldn't help but smile.

Saryn glanced up at me, a grin plastered on her face. "The girl knows how to pick out colors."

I nodded and took the swatch back from Saryn.

"Where will this color go?" she asked, almost timidly.

"Most of the exterior is going to be rock, but there will be a few areas that we'll need to paint. Since Liliana stated yellow was her favorite color, I figured we'd add that color to the exterior. The inside will be more princess-type colors."

A smile slowly moved across her face. "More princess-type colors? Such as?"

I lifted my shoulder in a half shrug. "Pinks, greens, the usual."

Saryn folded her arms across her chest and said, "You baffle me, Truitt Carter."

I laughed. "Why is that?"

"It's just surprising to see a man like you doing a job like this."

One of my brows lifted. "A man like me? Should I take offense at that?"

Liliana was currently wrapping her arms around my legs and asking me to walk like a monster, so I did.

"Liliana, sweetheart, let go of Mr. Carter."

I lifted my leg off the ground as Liliana squealed in delight. Saryn stared down at her daughter.

"I swear, she has never taken to anyone like this. I mean, anyone other than my brother and father. There's something about you she adores."

I glanced down at the little girl currently wrapped around my leg who was looking up at me with those blue eyes that would make anyone melt. I winked at her. "It was the little playground in my office that won her over."

Saryn quickly averted her eyes and turned back to Ryan who was standing on her porch watching this whole scene play out.

"I really do need to get going, though," I said, motioning at the small child still clinging to me. "I'd take her with me, but I'm afraid it's not the safest place for a three-year-old."

"Oh, my gosh, right. I'm so sorry," Saryn said, reaching for her daughter and peeling her off of me.

"I see even the young ones attach themselves to you still, Carter," Ryan shouted.

"Ha ha, I'll see you tomorrow night?" I asked as I put the swatch back on the passenger seat of my truck and made my way to the driver's side.

"Wouldn't miss it for the world," Ryan stated.

"Tomorrow night?" Saryn asked, glancing between the two of us.

"Bachelor party for one of our friends," Ryan said, taking Liliana out of Saryn's arms, then flying her around like an airplane.

One quick look at Saryn and I nodded, smiled, then slipped into my truck. "I'll give you an update on the playhouse in the next few weeks."

"Okay. Thank you, Truitt. And again, I'm sorry you had to come over here to track me down. I didn't mean to avoid your calls. Most of the time my phone is on silent."

"No worries."

"Well, I really am sorry you had to come over."

With a wink, I replied, "I'm not."

Before she could reply or I could see the look on her face, I started my truck and slowly turned around and headed down the driveway. I gripped the steering wheel as I attempted to slow my racing heart.

Paul sat down next to me and handed me a beer as Rus, my ten-month-old silver lab, looked up and then promptly laid back down when no signs of a ball could be found. "Thanks for coming, Truitt. I know how busy you are."

I took the beer from him and pulled a long drink from it. "Dude, it's not very often I get to take a day off, and no better reason to do it than a bachelor party."

He grinned like a fool, then looked out over the deck. Paul's family owned a house out on Lake Cannon, and he had asked a group of us to come celebrate the last few days of his freedom.

"You look happy," I said.

Turning to face me, he nodded. "I am happy. She makes me happy. I tell ya, Truitt, I never thought it would be me going down this path, you know? I figured I'd be like Roger, carefree and hooking up with women when and where I pleased."

At that moment I looked over and found my brother deep in conversation with Pete. They had hit it off when I first introduced them, back when Pete was new in town. The doctor and the lawyer. Perfect pair.

"Roger puts on a good show, but I think it's starting to weigh on him. That, or my mother's nagging for him to settle and give her grandbabies."

Paul looked out over the balcony, some intense expression on his face. Worry?

"You're not having second thoughts, are you, about getting married?" I asked.

He snapped his head and looked at me. "Hell no. I want to marry Lisa more than I want my next breath. It's just, we've had something unexpected come up."

"Something good or bad?" I asked.

Paul lifted the beer to his lips and took a long drink. Then he let out a breath and faced me. "Lisa's pregnant."

"What? Holy shit, dude, congratulations," I said, reaching my hand out to shake his, then pulling him in for a quick bro hug and slap on the back. "This is a good thing, right?"

He rubbed at the back of his neck. "Yeah, I mean, it's just faster than I had wanted. I want kids, don't get me wrong, but I was hoping to spend some time with Lisa first. You know, travel, go on last-minute trips, stay out as late as we wanted. All the things couples do when they don't have kids yet."

My eyes searched our group of friends and it hit me. Not one of us had kids yet. How had that possibly happened? Some friends of ours who did have kids had left our group not long after, stating that hanging out with a bunch of single guys wasn't going to go down well with their wives. Or they simply never got the time to get away.

"Paul, you and Lisa have dated what, three years now?"

"Yeah, almost four."

"And in those four years, you've traveled, stayed out and partied till all hours of the night, and did all those things that couples without kids do. Just because you're now going to have a piece of paper tying you together doesn't mean your life is any different."

He looked at me and a slow grin moved across his face. "Shit, man, you're right, we have been able to do all of that."

"Do you think y'all will miss the late nights?"

"Hell no. We hardly even do that anymore. As a matter of fact, the other night we went out and left at ten, both of us exhausted. We simply wanted to be home with each other."

A small part of me ached with jealousy. It must be nice sharing your life with someone in that way. Just to sit on the sofa each night, watching a movie together. A part of me deep inside longed for it, but I wasn't ready to admit why I had never searched for it. For now, I'd have to be content with Rus. He was my partner in crime.

"How is Lisa feeling about the baby?" I asked.

"She's over-the-moon happy but worried I'm not happy. I haven't actually been over the moon, dick move on my part, I guess. I've just been worried."

I nodded, then reached down and started to rub my dog on the head. His tail hit the wood deck in approval.

"Have you sent her flowers or anything?"

Paul looked at me once more, his brows pulled in tight. "Flowers?"

I shrugged. "Yeah. Maybe just send her some flowers that tell her you're excited about starting this new journey together and you can't wait to see what an amazing mother she'll be. Some shit like that."

When he didn't say anything, I looked at him. "What?"

"Since when did you become so knowledgeable on women and flowers and shit like that?"

I chuckled and took another drink of my beer. "Who the hell knows."

Roger came walking up to us, reached down, and rubbed Rus on the belly. "When are the strippers getting here, dude?"

Paul laughed and stood as he clapped Roger on the back. "Sorry, buddy, no strippers at this party."

As Paul walked away, Roger tossed up his hands and shouted as he followed Paul, "No fucking strippers? What kind of pussy-ass bachelor party is this!"

I looked out over the water and stared at the clouds reflecting off it. It was a beautiful fall day. A sense of melancholy moved over me and I closed my eyes. I tried not to think about what she was doing, or where she was, but those beautiful coffee-brown eyes popped into my head and I couldn't help but smile.

Chapter 12

Saryn

MY MOTHER SET the plate of pancakes down in the middle of the table. Ryan and my father were the first to dig in. I picked up Liliana's plate and put a pancake on it, then cut it up into slices for her. I poured the syrup into a bowl and set them both in front of her. She loved to dip her pancakes into the syrup and eat it that way. It had driven her father mad when she did it. He had wanted me to force her to eat them with a fork.

One more reason I was glad I had left him.

"Did you happen to check on that mare this morning, Ryan?" Daddy asked.

"Yes, sir, I did. She isn't ready to foal yet, but I think we're getting close." My brother looked at Liliana. "Liliana, are you ready to see a baby horse?"

"Yes!" she cried out in delight. "Can we see her now, pwease?"

Ryan chuckled. "She isn't born yet, princess. Soon, though."

I loved watching my brother with my daughter and wished he would find a girl to settle down with and have a family. He'd make such an amazing father. Truitt would make a great father, too.

I nearly gasped when I realized what I had just been thinking about.

"What if it's a little boy horse, Liliana?" Momma asked.

Liliana smiled and her little blue eyes sparked with excitement. "We can name it Twuitt!"

I jerked my head over and attempted not to look like I hadn't just been thinking of said man. My father groaned next to me as I waited for what he was going to say.

"Lord, the girl is obsessed with that man. She's going to make me gray, I can see it now."

"I'm still shocked by how open and affectionate she is with him. He's so good with her and patient," I stated.

"I think it's from working around kids," Ryan stated matter-of-factly. "I mean, look at his job. Kids are what keeps the man in business."

"No," I said, glaring at my mother. "It's grandparents who want to spoil their grandkids who keep the man in business."

She huffed. "Please, like it's only the grandparents who are paying. Plenty of parents are spoiling their own kids."

Ryan pointed to our mother. "Yeah, but they don't have a busybody mother trying to fix them up with the builder of said playhouse."

"Oh, son, you took it too far with the name calling," Daddy said as my mother shot daggers at Ryan.

"If you prefer me to move my attention to you, dear son, I'm more than happy to fix you up on a few blind dates," Momma said. "A number of women in my book club have single daughters."

"Did I say busybody? I meant, the most caring and amazing mother ever, who is simply looking out for her daughter's happiness."

I snarled my lip at my brother. "Kiss up."

He winked at me.

My phone rang and my mother glanced down at the same moment I did. "Speak of the devil."

Sliding my finger across the screen to answer it, I quickly put the phone to my ear and got up from the table to take the call. I could feel the heat of my mother's stare on my back.

"Hello?" I said, peeking back at her before I stepped out onto the sun porch.

"Hey, Saryn, this is Truitt."

My chest did a little flutter and I tried to sound casual. "How are you this morning, Truitt?"

"In a bit of a pickle. Listen, Lee is on vacation in England and fell and broke her leg in two spots. She's due to have surgery over there and won't be back for another few weeks, at the least. I really need to get some of the decorations down for the rooms in Liliana's playhouse, as well as the paint colors."

"Oh no, I'm so sorry to hear that. Mind if I ask who Lee is?"

"Shit, yeah sorry. She's my cousin, and she works for me, doing the interior decorating and paint for the playhouses. I can build them, but when it comes to decorating them, she's the go-to girl. I've got your playhouse and another one I'm making for a senator in Austin. That one is for a boy, Jack, and I can pretty much take care of that one, but Liliana's, yeah, I'm thrown for a loop. I have a few ideas, but I could really use some help, and who better to ask than her mother?"

I couldn't help the smile that spread across my face. When I looked up, I noticed my parents and Ryan were all staring at me. I dropped the smile and acted casual. "What do you need me to do?"

"I was hoping you and Liliana might go shopping with me today."

For a moment I was stunned into silence. I wasn't sure if it was from the anticipation of seeing him, which was crazy, or the fact that he had thought of Liliana in his invitation. Then again, the playhouse was for her, so of course he would invite her to come along. Or maybe he wanted her to come along so I wouldn't think it was a date.

"Um..."

"If you have plans I'll totally understand, I know it's last minute, but today is about my only free day to get this done."

"No, we don't have any plans. Should I meet you somewhere?"

"I was thinking I'd just pick y'all up, if you don't mind me driving with Liliana in the truck, that is."

Good Lord, my stomach dropped. I'd never met a man who put such thought into my child and my feelings regarding things. It was so damn refreshing. "I don't mind at all," I said, barely above a whisper.

"Perfect, I'll swing by in about an hour if that works for you. We can head to the Rim in San Antonio."

"Sounds good."

"See you soon, Saryn."

The line went dead and I stood for a few moments, trying to let what had happened sink in. I was going on a shopping date with Truitt. Truitt Carter. The guy I left Boerne because of. The guy who I was almost positive still had a piece of my heart whether he knew it or not. Broken as it may be.

And it means nothing, you fool. He's building your daughter's playhouse and he needs your advice. It's as simple as that.

Then why in the hell is my heart racing in my chest?

After taking a few deep breaths, I made my way back into my folks' kitchen.

"Tell me that wasn't the hospital calling you to work today," my father said. I quickly looked over at my mother. She'd seen Truitt's name on my phone and I was surprised she hadn't said anything.

"No, that was Truitt. His cousin who normally does all the interior decorating for the playhouses is in England and she won't be back for a number of weeks because she broke her leg. He asked if Liliana and I wouldn't mind going shopping with him today to pick out some things for her playhouse and for another one he's building."

"Pwayhouse! Yes!" Liliana cried out from her place at the table. Ryan and my father laughed as my mother simply kept her back to me while she cleaned dishes. I knew she was still upset with me regarding the whole one-night-stand thing with Luke. She might not have said it, but she thought it looked bad in front of Truitt.

"What did you say?" Ryan asked before stuffing pancakes into his mouth.

I walked up to Liliana and leaned down to kiss her on the forehead, then wiped her face with a napkin I had quickly picked up without her seeing. She fussed, but I managed to get the syrup off her chin. "I told him we'd love to go. I mean, who better to pick out the things for her little castle than the princess herself."

Momma turned and wiped her hands down her jeans. The way she was looking at me made me feel uneasy. I pulled my brows in and tilted my head. "You look like you've got something on your mind, Momma."

She folded her hands across her chest. "Not at all. I think it's lovely he asked you."

"Why do you have sarcasm in your voice?"

"Oh, hell," Daddy and Ryan said at once.

"I have no such thing in my voice, Saryn. I believe that is in your imagination."

She pushed off the counter and headed out of the kitchen. I followed.

"Daddy, can you watch Liliana?" I called back, not waiting for him to answer.

As soon as I caught up with her, I said, "Momma, if you've got something to say, just say it."

Stopping, she turned and looked directly into my eyes. "I raised you better than that, Saryn. Do you have any idea how embarrassing it was for your father and me to be standing out there with those two men when you pulled up dressed in the same clothes you went out in? It was clear to all you had spent the night with a man."

"So what, I'm a grown woman," I said with a humorless laugh.

"Is this something you're going to be doing often?"

Anger boiled up inside of me and I shook my head. "Momma, I wanted one night out and yes, a good-looking man paid attention to me and it's been one hell of a long time since a man has looked at me like that. I wanted to let my hair down for once. I wanted to be reckless and do something all of my friends have done at one point in their lives. If that meant having a one-night stand, then so be it. And to answer you, no I don't plan on doing that, ever again."

Concern washed over her face. "Was he..."

"He was a gentleman. He even asked me out again, but I was up front and honest with him. I told him I wasn't looking for anything more than that night. I'm sorry if you're disappointed in me, but honestly, it's none of your business."

Her mouth opened to speak, then she shut it again.

"I'm sorry, Saryn, I didn't mean to judge you, sweetheart. It's just, I only want what's best for you and Liliana. People still talk in this town, no matter how much it's grown."

I nodded. "I know they do."

"It's still not the same for women like it is for men. I know for a fact your brother has been a little bit of a manwhore since he broke up with Miranda. Peggy down at the corner store informed me she saw Ryan with some girl and they looked like they had just rolled around in a hay loft."

I laughed. "They probably had."

She sighed. "I also know he hooked up with a nurse you work with."

With a stunned look, I asked, "How do you know that?"

"I have a lot of friends in this town. The gossip mill is as strong as ever."

I sighed. "Do you think people will be talking if they find out I'm going shopping with Truitt?"

She shook her head. "I don't think so. It's not like y'all are doing shopping on the mile. And for him to be coming over here wouldn't raise any eyebrows since he's building the playhouse."

With a nod, I replied, "Good. I don't really want the gossip mill filled with details about me. Ryan is another thing."

Momma winked and then pulled me in for a hug. "I just want what's best for you, sweetheart."

"I know, Momma. I know."

Truitt pulled up exactly an hour later. I had rushed around trying to get Liliana dressed and ready. A cold front was expected to push through today dropping temperatures, so I had to pack us both something in case it got colder, especially since the Rim was an outdoor mall.

When the doorbell rang, Liliana ran to the door calling out Truitt's name. She was beside herself with glee. I think she was even more excited to see Truitt than to go shopping. I was right there with her.

"Hold on, Liliana, there's no fire."

She jumped and clapped until I opened the door. My mouth gaped open when I saw Truitt standing there, a little bouquet of flowers in his hand. He bent down and Liliana threw herself at him.

"Okay, have you put some sort of spell on my child, Truitt? She has never acted this way before."

He laughed. "Nonsense, I've seen her with Ryan and your dad."

"Yes, but no other man. She's usually very shy."

"I told you, it was the playground that won her over." He handed the flowers to Liliana and said, "These are for you, Princess Liliana. Lilies for Liliana."

And there went my heart. And my legs. Nearly taking me to the ground. But a strange thought occurred to me. Was Truitt attempting to get to me through my daughter? If he was, I wasn't sure how I felt about that.

"Mommy, flowers! For me!" She jumped up and down and held them up for me to smell.

I smiled and reached for her hand. "Let's go put them in water, and then we can leave."

Truitt stepped inside and shut the door, following me and Liliana into the kitchen.

Before I had a chance to say anything, his phone rang.

"Excuse me," Truitt said. "This is Truitt. Hey, Shay."

I paused when I heard the name. I had asked Natalie and Lucy for the name of the woman Truitt had danced with nearly all night at the dance hall. Natalie had told me her name was Shay. I hadn't wanted to ask if she was a girlfriend since it might have looked weird to ask about Truitt while I had been shamelessly flirting with Luke.

"I would if I could, but I'm actually on my way to San Antonio," he said. "Want me to call Paul, or Roger?"

With a quick look his way, I tried not to listen to his conversation, but it was hard not to when he was standing right there. I placed the little flowers in a Mason jar then turned and put them on our small table. Liliana climbed up on a chair and smelled them. The gesture truly had been a sweet one, and not anything her own father would have ever thought of.

"Are you sure? I might be able to swing by and help," Truitt said into the phone.

That caught my attention. I felt like a silly fool, thinking Truitt had given Liliana the flowers as a means to get to me. He clearly was seeing this Shay.

"Call me later if you need anything, I should be back in a few hours."

He looked at me and mouthed he was sorry. I waved it off.

"Listen, I've got to go. Okay, talk soon."

Truitt ended the call and looked between me and Liliana. "Who's ready to do some shopping?"

Liliana jumped and shouted, "Me! Me, pwease!"

Truitt chuckled and motioned for us to lead the way.

As we walked out to his truck, I grabbed Liliana's car seat and Truitt took it from me. For a moment I was agitated, then quickly pushed it aside. I had no business feeling this way. Truitt didn't owe me anything.

"Do you know how to put one of those in?" I asked.

Truitt laughed. "Yes. Lee has a daughter. She's had to go a few times with us to pick up supplies or to run in on shopping trips. I've gotten really good at putting her car seat in my truck. She's about a year older than Liliana. I need to have Lee introduce her to Liliana."

"That would be nice. I'm planning on starting her in preschool next year."

"Well, if she's anything like Netty, she'll love it."

Truitt stepped back and put his hand out for me to inspect the seat. I did, and it passed with flying colors.

"Let's hit the road," Truitt said after we were all buckled up in the truck.

Liliana talked Truitt's ear off for the first twenty minutes. Then silence filled the truck and I looked back to see she had talked herself right into a nap.

"Wow, I guess that wore her out."

Truitt laughed. "Thank goodness you were here to help with half of what she said. I don't have my little person language down pat yet."

I giggled and looked over at him. He was rolling his window down. He spit out his gum and then cursed.

"Son of a...crap!"

"What's wrong?" I asked.

"The damn wind blew my gum back into the truck. Shit, it hit me in the eye, and I think it's in my hair now! Not again."

I covered my mouth with my hand. "Do you, um...need to pull over?"

"Dang, freaking, crap."

It was obvious Truitt wasn't used to keeping his words in check. He pulled over and put the truck into park. He pulled the visor down and looked in the small mirror.

"How in the heck did that come back and hit me right in the eye?"

I chewed on my lip to keep from laughing. When I was able to keep myself in check, I said, "Let me take a look at your eye."

He turned and I lost it laughing.

"What? What's so funny?"

"The gum, it's in your hair. How did you get it in your hair?"

"How did it hit me in the eye is the better question!"

With a quick glance back, I saw Liliana was still sound asleep. I unbuckled and leaned over to try and get it out of his hair. "Don't move or we might be cutting it out."

"I refuse to cut it again."

I looked at him and and asked, "Again? This has happened before?"

He nodded, and I covered my mouth to keep from waking up Liliana.

"What does my eye look like?" he asked.

I glanced down and was struck by how beautiful his eyes were. They were blue, but more of a deep dark blue. So dark they left me stunned for a moment.

"Well?" he asked.

"It's fine, a little red, but that could be because you keep rubbing it."

"It feels like there's something in there."

I placed my fingers on the top and bottom of his eye and looked closer. I had to crawl out of my seat to get close enough to look.

"Nothing is in your eye, but if you want me to pour water in it, I can."

I let go of his eye and noticed I was inches from his face. His mouth. Like a stupid idiot, I let my gaze go down to his lips. He licked them.

A moan almost slipped from my lips. What in the heck, Saryn? I jerked my eyes up to the gum again and Truitt cleared his throat.

"Hold on, let me get the gum out of your hair."

Carefully, I got it out and then tossed it out the still-open window and dropped back down into my seat.

"Thanks," Truitt said, his voice sounding strained.

"Sure. Did you want me to pour water in your eye?"

He shook his head. "No, I think it's okay now."

Rolling up his window, Truitt looked back and saw that Liliana had slept through the whole show.

"She's a heavy sleeper," I stated.

All he did was nod, then pull back out onto the road. It took a few moments before he broke the silence.

"You know, you can ask about the gum."

"Oh, thank goodness! How many times has it happened?"

"Twice. Well, now three times."

Trying with all my might not to laugh, I lost the battle. Soon, Truitt was laughing right along with me.

"Truitt, how?"

He shook his head. "I don't know. I don't think I spit it hard enough, or the wind gods hate me, and it blows back in."

I laughed again. In that moment he looked at me. Our eyes met and something sparked between us. I chuckled again and let out a sigh.

"Man, I needed that laugh."

"Glad to be of help."

There were so many things that just felt right. And right now, it felt amazing to just be in his company.

Chapter 13

Truitt

A S WE WALKED along the shops at La Cantera, I carried Liliana up on my shoulders. She'd given up on the idea of walking about thirty minutes ago after we left Pottery Barn Kids.

"Truitt, you don't have to carry her on your shoulders," Saryn argued, for the hundredth time.

"She's light as a feather, stop worrying so much, Saryn."

Chewing on her lip, she focused ahead of us. When she was unsure of something, or nervous, she nibbled on her lip, and I knew to look away because it did weird things to my body.

"Are you dating anyone?" she asked.

The question had just flown out of her mouth and the moment she asked it she seemed to regret it.

"No."

Her brows rose. "No?"

Laughing, I replied, "No. I haven't really ever seriously dated anyone."

That caused her eyes to go wide with shock. "Never?"

I shrugged. "I mean, I've dated one or two women, nothing that I would call serious."

"Why not?"

I looked straight ahead. "I have a bad habit of comparing them to someone I once cared a lot about."

Saryn's gaze felt like it was burning a hole into me.

"What happened? I mean, with this person."

With a slight smile, I looked down at her. "She started dating someone else."

Saryn looked like her breath had caught in her throat, then she looked as if a million questions were running through her mind.

Liliana gasped and let out an excited giggle. I looked to where she was pointing and said, "Build-A-Bear? What's that?"

"Someplace you don't want to go. Keep walking, Truitt, for your own good," Saryn stated.

"Pwease!" Liliana cried out and my heart melted on the spot. "Pooh Bear! Momma, pwease."

"Oh no, no! I see it in your eyes. Truitt..."

Turning to look at Saryn, I replied, "How can you be so cruel? Listen to that voice!"

She shook her head. "Trust me, she'll forget all about it."

Liliana bent forward and pulled my chin up to look at her. "Pooh Bear! Pwease!"

Oh, God. How could anyone say no that. Those baby blues pierced right into my soul and damn near brought me to my knees.

"There is no way I'm saying no to that." I walked straight over to the stuffed animal store. "Let's get you a Pooh Bear, baby girl."

Liliana bounced around on my shoulders. I reached up and took her down. She grabbed my hand and pulled me over to a bunch of bins.

"You caved, just like that," Saryn said, a smirk on her face.

"Do you not see those eyes? They were pleading, Saryn."

"Yes, I see them every day, and that is called manipulation, Truitt. You've just been had by a three-year-old."

"What's the harm in getting a little Pooh Bear?"

Her arms folded over her chest. "Okay, this is all on you, *Mr. I Can't Say No.*"

I smiled and then focused on Liliana. "What do we do first?"

"We gets Pooh!" Liliana exclaimed.

Once she picked out the unstuffed, almost scary version of Pooh, we made our way over to a machine where they stuffed the bear. There was a heart that had a whole procedure with it. When they said to make a wish, Liliana took it very seriously. She had to clutch her chest and say a prayer so long that a line started to form. When I looked at Saryn for help, she made no attempts to move. I'd remember that for the future when she needed my help.

"Okay, let's say amen and stick it on in there, Liliana," I said, prompting her to wrap up the prayer.

She kissed the heart and pushed it into Pooh Bear.

After Pooh was all stitched closed, we moved over to give him a bath. Liliana was very thorough in her bathing skills. From there, I quickly learned why Saryn wanted to avoid this place. It was time to shop for clothes.

"Doesn't Pooh just wear this shirt?" I asked, holding it up for Liliana to inspect.

"Yep!" she answered while she jumped up and down.

So we dressed him. Then she saw the outfit for Eeyore, then Piglet, and when I saw Tigger's outfit, we were done for. Back through the line for three more bears. This time I made Tigger, and when it came time to make a wish on the heart, I quickly glanced around and made my wish.

If any of my friends had seen me in that moment, I'd never live it down. Once the other three bears were bathed and dressed, we walked out of the store with nearly the entire Hundred Acre Woods in tow.

Saryn gave me a stern look. "You just spent a small fortune, all because of those blue eyes."

"And the way she says please, don't forget that," I added.

"Yeah, that one still gets me sometimes, too. Let me ask you something, is the Tigger for you?" Saryn asked, trying not to laugh.

I looked down at her. "Of course, he is!"

"Tigger!" Liliana said with a giggle. She was back up on my shoulders as I carried the stuffed animals and Saryn carried the other two.

After we dropped the stuffed animals off in the truck and explained to Liliana that it was their nap time, we headed back over to the shops and hit a few stores. Shopping had never been one of my favorite pastimes, but somehow being with Saryn and Liliana made it different. I actually enjoyed myself.

"I can't believe we stayed on budget and got all of this stuff," I said, manhandling the bags from Pottery Barn kids, Restoration Hardware, and Dillard's. "Liliana, you are the perfect woman to go shopping with. You absolutely know what you want and we are in and out."

Saryn chuckled. "She's her mother's daughter. I hate shopping. I go as fast I can."

I glanced her way. "I don't think I've ever met a woman who didn't like to shop."

She shrugged. "I mean, I enjoy shopping for other people, but for me, I hate it. If I could live in a pair of sweatpants and my old favorite T-shirt for the rest of my life, I'd do it."

"A girl after my own heart," I said as our eyes met. I gave her a wink, and I couldn't help but notice how her cheeks turned a soft shade of pink. I was quickly liking that look on her.

After a few moments of silence went by, we both went to speak at the same time.

"So what..."

"Why did..."

We both laughed.

"You go first," Saryn insisted.

"So what made you decide to come back to Boerne after the divorce?" I asked.

With a shrug, Saryn answered, "It's home. My family is here, and I want Liliana to be near my folks and brother."

"What about her dad?"

She laughed. "He didn't want a family, he made that very clear."

Anger boiled up inside of me. "So you mean to tell me he was willing to let y'all just walk away?"

She nodded. "Yep. He wants a different life."

"Then why the F. U. C. K. did he marry you?"

Saryn looked up at me and smiled with a twinkle in her eye. "You spelled that out."

"Of course, I did. I'm not going to swear in front of Liliana."

Something moved across her face. She looked away and chewed on her lip. "Thank you, for that, for thinking of her little ears."

"Comes with the job," I said.

She bumped against my arm and laughed. "Don't play it off, Truitt, you're different from any other guy I've ever met."

"Different good or different bad?" I asked with interest.

Saryn paused for a few moments before she replied, "Good."

Our gazes met and I swore my body heated from her intense stare. The feeling quickly vanished when her daughter cried out from on top of my shoulders.

"Ice Cweam!"

Smiling, I headed over to the yogurt shop.

"Can she have some?" I asked.

"I think some ice cream sounds good right about now," Saryn said.

After ordering Liliana a small chocolate yogurt with sprinkles on it, Saryn ordered a small peach and I ordered vanilla with crushed Heath on top.

"Mmm!" Liliana said when she took a bite. Her blue eyes sparkled with delight, and I swore I felt my heart beat a little harder and faster. This little girl was quickly winning a gigantic place in my heart. How in the hell could her own father just let her walk out of his life?

"Will Tim come and visit Liliana?" I asked, watching the little girl gobble up her ice cream, getting more of it on her face than in her stomach.

A look of sadness crossed over Saryn's face as she gazed down at her daughter. "I don't think so."

"How? I mean, why would he not want to be a part of her life?"

"Some men just don't care."

I watched her as she smiled and wiped yogurt off of her daughter's face.

"He's a D.A.M.N fool."

"Damn!" Liliana said, a proud look displayed on her face.

My eyes widened in shock. "Oh, my God, she can spell? She's a prodigy at three!"

Saryn lost it laughing. "No, she can't, but she's learned that word because I say it all the time, then correct myself by spelling it."

"So, basically, you taught her how to spell a bad word."

She nodded and then shrugged.

"You do realize she's putting two and two together. Your daughter is going to be brilliant."

"You're right, I didn't really think about her making the connection like that."

Pointing to Liliana and then back to Saryn, I chuckled. "You're screwed with this one."

With a roll of her eyes and a sigh, Saryn said, "Tell me about it."

We spent the drive back to Boerne singing some song that Liliana insisted we all sing. When I pulled up to drop them off, Evie scooped up Liliana and whisked her away, the little girl chatting her grandmother's ear off about how much fun she had as Will carried the three boxes of Build-A-Bears.

"Thanks for helping me out like that," I said, smiling down to Saryn.

"It was our pleasure. I had fun today, thank you."

Our eyes locked for a moment before she looked away.

"Yeah, me, too," I said. "I guess I should be heading on out."

She nodded, then took a few steps back.

"Hey, if you ever think nursing isn't your thing anymore, you can come work for me. You have a good eye for decorating."

I couldn't help but notice the way her eyes lit up for a quick moment before she let out a nervous laugh. "Well, if they don't get me out of the ER soon, I may take you up on that."

We stood there, simply looking into each other's eyes. I took a step closer to her, and that seemed to draw her out of whatever spell we had been under.

I leaned down to look at something she had stuck on her face. But before I could say anything, she took a giant step away from me.

"I'm not looking to start anything with you, Truitt. I mean, other than friendship."

And that felt like a five-gallon bucket of cold water pouring over my body. Before I had a chance to respond, her mother called out.

"Saryn!"

For a moment I swore I saw something like regret in Saryn's eyes, but it was gone as fast as it had appeared.

"Bye, Truitt."

The way my chest ached wasn't new to me. In fact, I'd felt it at the very young age of eighteen, the first time she rejected me.

The fact that I wanted to kiss her now and she didn't want to kiss me in return depressed the living hell out of me. This woman and her little girl had completely turned my entire world upside down since they swept back into town.

"See ya around, Saryn."

Even I could hear the disappointment in my voice.

I watched as she headed into her folks' house, not turning to get into my truck until the door shut and she was completely out of sight.

Chapter 14

Saryn

IMADE MY final notes in a patient's file, surprised I'd been able to focus at all. I hadn't been able to get the other day out of my mind.

No, I hadn't been able to get Truitt Carter out of my mind. The way he took to Liliana: laughed with her, played with her, sang that stupid little song at the top of his lungs in his truck just to make her happy.

The way he looked at me. I could have sworn he had wanted to kiss me. Or maybe he was going to ask me out. I'd freaked out when he stepped closer to me. The urge to have him kiss me and turn and run away had been a battle. Was he truly interested in me, or was it like last time? Did he simply want to sleep with me?

A part of me knew that wasn't true. That Tim had lied to me that day. I saw the look on Truitt's face, the hurt in his eyes when I said I was going out with Tim. But then he simply turned and walked away. If he had truly wanted to ask me out, why would he just walk away?

Glancing up when I heard a commotion at the main door of the ER, I nearly dropped the chart. My brother was in a mad rush to get over to me.

"Liliana?" I asked, my voice panicked.

"She's fine. It's Truitt."

A sense of dread washed over me, so intense it was almost shocking. "What about him?"

Looking past Ryan, I saw Phil, one of the male nurses, and Pete helping Truitt into a wheelchair. "Oh, my gosh, what happened?" I asked as I rushed over to help them.

Ryan came up next to me. "Well, I stopped by Truitt's place to check on the playhouse. I asked him if I could help with some of the framing, and we had a bit of an accident with the nail gun."

Sickness rushed through me. "The nail gun?"

Lucy rushed past me and made her way over to Truitt. "Get him into bay seven."

"My lucky bay!" Truitt said with a humorless chuckle.

Spinning back to face Ryan, I gave him a look that demanded he told me everything.

"Fine! Fine! I accidentally shot a nail into his foot."

My hand came up to my mouth as I gasped. "How in the world did you do that, Ryan?"

"It got jammed, and Truitt was trying to tell me what to do, and for some reason it went off."

"How far did it go in?"

He shrugged. "He had on some pretty thick boots, so hopefully it isn't in too deep. Although, he did let out a pretty long string of curse words after it happened and told me he was going to pull my balls through my throat, so I'm going to guess it hurt."

"For the love—!" I said, pushing past him as I made my way over to where they had taken Truitt. Pete and Lucy were both trying to see how far the nail had gone into Truitt's foot.

"Let's order an X-ray so I can see where the nail's path went. Then call and get me an orthopedic surgeon on the line to take a look at it."

Lucy glanced my way and smiled. "We've got this, you can head on home."

My eyes bounced from her to Truitt. Why was I not wanting to leave? My shift was over. Lucy was the attending nurse.

Truitt let out a soft groan, and I knew I wasn't leaving. I needed to make sure he was okay. It wasn't like Truitt's injury was life threatening; it wasn't, by any means. Unless an infection set in.

Lucy was now staring at me with a befuddled expression. "I haven't ever seen an injury like this before, I'd like to stay and observe," I said, quickly thinking on my feet.

With one brow raised, Lucy tried not to smile. I saw the twitch at the side of her mouth, though. "You want to observe?"

I nodded. "If that's okay with you, Doctor."

"Pete doesn't care if you observe, do you?" Truitt asked, a hint of pain laced between his words. He looked as if he was fighting with all his might to keep from crying out.

Pete simply smiled and shrugged. "I don't care, the more nurses the better."

Truitt closed his eyes and I knew he was in pain. Then he looked my way. "I think my brother paid yours off to get me into this place again. The odds weren't looking so good for Roger in the pool, I guess."

My mouth opened, then snapped shut. For once in my life, I was unsure of what to say. My gaze took in his entire body. I needed to see for myself that he was okay. Something deep inside me cared very much for the man lying on the table...and that confused the hell out of me.

"I'm kidding, Saryn. It was an accident."

"Something you're very familiar with," Pete said.

"Hey, I'm keeping you in business, Pete," Truitt replied.

"X-ray is ready," Lucy said.

While they took Truitt to get X-rays, I pulled Ryan off to the side.

"What in the hell happened?" I asked in a hushed voice.

"It's like I said, the stupid gun got jammed. I was trying to fix it, but Truitt got impatient and walked over to me. He went to take it, and I don't know, it went off."

I rolled my eyes, then chewed on my thumbnail as I looked around the ER.

"Don't worry, he isn't going to try and sue me," Ryan said with a chuckle. "That poor guy has the worst luck of anyone I know."

Hitting him in the chest, I let out a sigh.

"Wait, if you're worried he won't finish the playhouse on time, Truitt will get it done."

I was positive my mouth dropped to the floor. "What? You think I'm worried about the playhouse?"

"Yeah, he's been a hell of a lot worse off and has gotten projects done."

"You think I'm worried he won't be able to finish the stupid playhouse I didn't even want in the first place?"

I knew my voice sounded more upset than angry. I was pissed at myself for telling Truitt I wasn't interested in getting involved with him. I was angry he had just accepted it. He'd walked away... yet again.

Ryan pulled his brows down and stared at me. "Why are you so angry?"

"I'm not angry! I'm worried!"

"About Truitt?"

My mouth pressed into a thin line as I looked away.

"Holy shit, do you like him, Saryn?"

I snapped my head back so that my gaze hit his. "Don't be ridiculous. I do not like him, Ryan. My God, you shot a nail in the man's foot. How do we know he wouldn't try to...to do something?"

"Truitt? Do you have any idea how many times he's stuck, twisted, or hurt himself because of one of his friends? Or simply because he's...Truitt? You're overreacting. Why don't you just go on home, Saryn?"

With my hands on my hips, I glared at my brother. "Are you dismissing me, Ryan?"

"Yes, I am, because you're acting crazy. It was an accident, Saryn. I didn't do it on purpose and yes, we may have a pool going about Truitt's trips to the ER, but none of us would ever put him in any danger or try to hurt him. He knows that."

I shook my head and walked away from my brother.

So, what if I had spent one afternoon with Truitt. He was sweet to my daughter, and he was sweet to me. That didn't mean anything.

Pete walked by, and I turned to see where he was going. When I saw him walking into another bay in the ER, I followed. Ryan was on my heels.

Ryan came up to walk next to me. "Why are you suddenly interested in Truitt? I thought you were with Luke."

I stopped, causing Ryan to stop alongside me. "Why would you say that?"

He shrugged. "Because you hooked up with him. I heard he stopped by the ER to visit you not too long ago."

Heat instantly hit my cheeks. Before I had a chance to reply, Pete walked up to me. "If you want to watch this, let's go."

As I turned to follow Pete, I looked back at Ryan and whisper-shouted, "I am most certainly not with Luke. Or anyone, for that matter!"

He held up his hands in defense. "Fine. Whatever you say."

Once we were in the room with Pete and Lucy, I watched as they cut away at Truitt's jeans, then his sock. After cleaning the area, Pete injected a blocker into Truitt's ankle in a few different locations.

"Okay, so you want to tell me what happened?" Pete asked Ryan.

My brother shrugged. "It was stuck, the nail gun. Honestly, it was Truitt's fault for trying to take the damn thing from me. He didn't give me a chance to fix it."

Truitt opened his eyes and shot Ryan a dirty look. "So now it's my fault. You had your fucking finger on the trigger, you asshole!"

Ryan tried not to smile.

"Roger paid you, didn't he?" Truitt asked through gritted teeth. "I'll fucking kill him."

Pete and Ryan both chuckled.

"How do y'all find any of this funny?" I asked as Pete handed Lucy the last needle.

"Surgical pliers, please," Pete said.

Lucy handed them to Pete as I walked over to Truitt. "After they pull it out, they'll X-ray your foot again to make sure there are no bone fragments."

Truitt watched as Pete grabbed the nail and pulled it.

"Fuck!" Ryan and Truitt both said as Pete removed the nail in one swift movement.

Pete snapped his head and looked at Truitt. "Did you feel that?"

"No, but I feel dizzy now."

"Put your head back down," I softly said, grabbing Truitt's hand.

"I don't think we'll have any worries about infection, especially since it didn't go through the rubber part of the sole. But, just to be sure, I'll probably start you on a round of antibiotics. Let's also get him a tetanus shot, Lucy," Pete stated.

Truitt nodded but didn't say anything. He only took one steady breath after another.

"I'll wash it as best as I can. I can't say if any fibers got into the wound," Pete said.

After clearing his throat, Truitt spoke. "I'll be able to walk on it, right?"

Pete nodded. "It will be sore...isn't this the same ankle you twisted?"

Truitt looked over at Ryan and shot him a dirty look. "No, it's the other one."

Ryan tried not to laugh.

"I've never in my life met anyone as unlucky as you, Carter," Pete stated.

When I looked over at Lucy, I noticed her gaze was down on my hand. It was resting on top of Truitt's. I was rubbing my thumb over his skin. I instantly pulled my hand away, but not before she lifted a brow in a questioning look. I shook my head, then took a step back.

It was my turn to clear my throat. "Well, I guess I can add that to my list of crazy ER moments. I'm going to head on home. Thanks for letting me watch, Truitt."

He smirked. "Like I had any options."

His response stopped me for a moment. Had he not wanted me there? Maybe he was embarrassed to be back in the ER. Maybe the pain of having a nail shot through his foot made him cranky. Maybe I was overthinking this.

Without a word, I headed to my locker in the break room. After I grabbed my purse, I quickly made my way outside and to my car.

"Saryn! Wait."

The sound of Ryan's voice stopped me. I turned to face him.

He stopped in front of me and asked, "Hey, is everything okay?"

I forced a slight smile. "I'm tired. I didn't like working in the ER the first time I had to do it, and I hate it even more now. I'm ready to get back to babies. That's all."

He nodded and looked at me thoughtfully. "I didn't mean anything when I brought up that whole thing with Luke."

I waved him off. "It's fine. I knew what I was doing and figured the rumors would start eventually. It's not a big deal."

"Hey, it's okay if you have feelings for Truitt."

My mouth opened slightly, and for the briefest moment I wanted to tell Ryan exactly how I felt. But I didn't *know* exactly how I felt. "I'll see you later."

Ryan nodded, then leaned down and kissed me on the cheek. "Give Liliana a kiss for me."

This time my smile was genuine. "I will." I turned to get into my car before I faced him again. "Did you drive here? Do you need a ride home?"

"I drove Truitt here in my truck. I'll wait around until he's ready to head out, then take him home."

"Sounds good, Ryan. See ya."

"See ya."

As I watched my brother walk back into the ER, I pushed away any and all thoughts of Truitt Carter.

Chapter 15

Truitt

I LOOKED OUT over the pasture and stared at the sun slowly sinking into the western sky. The sound of something or someone walking up behind me made me go still. It wasn't a deer, so it had to be one of the other guys.

The slap on my back made me sputter out a cough.

"What the fuck?" I said as I jumped up and saw Roger standing there—a damn smile on his face. "I could have shot you! Stupid asshole."

He held up his hands, his rifle strung over his shoulder. "Damn, little brother, you're on edge. What's wrong, haven't gotten laid in awhile?"

A sinking feeling hit me in the chest. "Something like that."

"Call Shay."

I rolled my eyes. The night I went back to Shay's place we hadn't had sex. I made her come, simply because I wasn't an asshole and it was me who had asked her out, but we didn't have sex. I couldn't bring myself to want to. "I'm not interested in that."

Roger looked at me, then turned his gaze out over the open pasture. "See anything this afternoon?"

Relief washed over me that he'd dropped the subject of Shay.

"No. They probably smelled your damn men's perfume coming from a mile away," I mumbled.

He laughed, then bumped me on the arm. "Come on, let's go back to the cabin, grab some food."

I shook my head. "Nah, I'm going to hike on over to my tree stand, see if anything comes in."

"Truitt, the sun is fixin' to go down soon. Even if you do see something, it'll be too dark to shoot and then track it if you get lucky enough to hit it at all. Let's go, man."

Rubbing the back of my neck, I sighed. "Maybe I'll just head on home. I need to work on the Nights' playhouse."

Roger narrowed his eyes at me. "Truitt, what's going on with you? You haven't been yourself since we got up here."

My brother, Ryan, Pete, Jack, Paul, and I visited the deer lease my father had in Llano every year. First weekend of rifle season, the six of us came up here to go deer hunting. It was like clockwork. Hell, Paul had scheduled his damn wedding around this weekend.

"I've just got a lot on my mind, that's all."

Without taking his gaze off of me, Roger asked, "Business is doing good?"

I nodded. "Yeah, I've got a waiting list. Even some clients out in California are interested in a playhouse. One's an actor."

He smiled, the pride evident in his eyes. "That's great, so why the long face?"

I stared back out over the open land. "I don't really know, to be honest. I'm feeling...something. A void, a loss. A fucking sadness, I have no idea why. I don't know what in the fuck it is. Maybe I do need to get laid."

"That's what I'm thinking. I think we need to head into Llano tonight. Go out for a few beers?"

"Yeah. Maybe." Even though getting laid wasn't really what I wanted. At least not with some stranger.

The truth was, I hadn't been able to stop thinking of Saryn ever since that damn shopping trip. When she stayed in the ER with me the other day, she truly looked concerned, which I knew was insane.

She had even stated that she'd only stayed to see something new. It was clear she wasn't interested in anything other than friendship, and I needed to keep that in mind. She was fresh out of a divorce and told me she wasn't looking for anything more.

"Come on, dude, let's head back to the cabin."

After getting back, showering, and grabbing a bite to eat, everyone decided a night out would do us all some good. Paul, on the other hand, decided he was staying at the cabin and FaceTiming his wife. Roger teased him about having video phone sex, and a part of me wasn't sure my brother was that far off. Paul was in that lovesick stage still, fresh off his honeymoon and pining for his wife. He had almost called off coming on this trip, but Ryan had practically dragged him out of the house.

As we walked into the bar in Llano, it became clear that picking up women tonight wouldn't be an issue. All eyes turned to us as we walked in. I knew we were a good-looking bunch, and the way we were being eye-fucked, the ladies in the bar obviously agreed.

"Oh, hell yes. Look at the cowgirls in this place!" Ryan said. He was newly out of a long-term relationship and ready to pounce on the first person who showed interest. I hadn't informed him or Roger that they'd both slept with Lucy, not that I thought either of them would care, to be honest. I doubted it was the first time the two of them had slept with the same girl.

After ordering our beers, we took a seat at a table in the back corner. Ryan slid in next to me and pointed to a blonde dancing with two other women. A redhead and a brunette.

"You can have the blonde, I'll take the redhead, and Roger and Jack can fight for the brunette."

Roger laughed. "What makes you think I don't want the redhead?"

"What makes you think I want the blonde?" I asked with a smile.

"You like blondes."

"No, I don't."

"Shay's blonde," Ryan stated.

"She was a fuck buddy, that's all," I said.

"Was?" both Roger and Ryan asked at the same time.

"You got your eye on someone?" Ryan asked.

My gaze caught Roger's before I looked out over the dance floor.

"Anyone hear from Nolan lately?" Roger asked, purposely changing the subject. It seemed like my brother was actually on my side in some instances.

Nolan was one of our best friends from high school. He'd joined the Air Force straight after graduation and was now a test pilot stationed in Louisiana. He hardly ever came back home. Both of his parents had died and he had some pretty bad memories of Texas. Memories he was constantly attempting to drown out with the crazy-ass adrenaline rush shit he did all the time.

"Last I heard from him, he was in New Zealand and was going zorbing," I said.

Ryan furrowed his brows. "What the hell is zorbing?"

Jack pulled out his phone, typed something into it and then handed it to Ryan, who lost it laughing.

"He's a giant fucking gerbil in a plastic ball?" Ryan said, looking up from the phone and at each of us with a horrified expression. "What the fuck is the military doing to our friend?"

"At least he didn't ask us to go. The last trip we went on with him, I nearly shit my own pants bungee jumping off that damn bridge in Colorado," Roger said, his body visibly shaking at the memory of that day.

We all laughed.

After I took a drink from my beer, my smile faded. "I wish he'd come back."

Ryan handed Jack back his phone. "He will, someday. It will probably take *you* getting married in order for him to do it. He sure as shit didn't like Paul that much if he didn't come back for his wedding."

"In Paul's defense, Nolan was in England on some B-52 bomber training exercise," Jack said.

I nodded. We all knew the reason he wouldn't return to Boerne, and only Nolan could work those demons out for himself.

The three women on the dance floor made their way over to us, stopping and flashing smiles all around.

"Evening, gentleman. Feel like some company?" the blonde said, eyeing me, then Ryan. The way she was looking at us told me this woman probably wouldn't mind having us both. At the same time. That was a hard pass for me. No chance in hell I'd risk crossing swords with any other guy, not even if the woman was a fucking goddess.

"I think we're good, but thanks," Ryan quickly stated.

My gaze jerked over to Ryan. He was brushing off the very women he'd been talking about only minutes ago.

The blonde narrowed her eyes and looked around at each of us. "Y'all gay or something?"

"Yeah, sweetheart, that's it," Roger said smugly.

"We're just not interested, that's all."

That jab came from Ryan, which surprised me. He usually wasn't so blunt. Or rude.

"Fuck you, dick," the redhead said before turning and walking off. The other two quickly followed, but not before the blonde tilted her head and looked at me intently.

"You have no idea what you're missing out on."

I smiled. "I'll take my chances."

When she walked away, Jack sighed. "You three are killjoys. I'm going after them."

While Jack did just that, I looked at Ryan and Roger. "What happened? I thought you both wanted the redhead."

Roger shrugged. "Turns out I'm not in the mood for that tonight. For once I'd like a woman to not be so willing to just meet me in the bathroom for a quick fuck."

Ryan leaned back in his chair and took a long drink from his beer.

That I could understand. I'd been feeling that way for a while now. I jerked my head toward Ryan and asked, "And your excuse?"

"I don't really know. I just want to sit here and drink a beer. I wouldn't mind a dance or two with a pretty little thing, but I'm not interested in fucking some girl in the back of her car."

Leaning forward, I looked at them both. "You two are whores, do you know that? Bathrooms? Back seats?"

Ryan pointed at me. "This coming from the guy who fucked a girl up against a wall in the back of the dance club. In plain sight of anyone who wanted to watch."

"In my defense, it was dark. I was eighteen and...and..."

Roger lifted a brow.

"And an asshole. I wish I knew who she was so I could tell her I'm sorry. I used her because I was trying to..."

I almost said I was trying to forget Saryn's rejection.

"Pretty sure she was the one who asked you to have sex with her in public," Ryan said, laughing.

I smiled as I took a drink of my beer. "That's right, it was a dare from her friends. First and last time I had public sex."

As the night went on, the less I thought any of us wanted to be there. Jack had taken off with all three women. The rest of us placed bets on how that was going to turn out.

"Do we wait for his ass to show back up or leave?" Ryan asked as we made our way through the bar.

"We don't have to look for him, he's walking toward us," Roger said as he pointed to Jack.

"Holy hell, look at that smile. Someone got lucky!" I said with a chuckle.

Jack walked up to us. "Were y'all going to just leave me?"

"Yes," the three of us said at the same time.

When we got into my truck, Jack spilled the beans on his adventurous night. Turns out he had himself a little fun with both the blonde and the redhead.

By the time we got back to the cabin, I was in an even worse mood than before we had left. What in the hell was wrong with me?

"I'm gonna sit out on the porch for a bit," I said, taking a seat in one of the rocking chairs. I didn't even care that the temperature had dropped to around fifty-five. I needed the fresh air. Everyone walked into the cabin, except for Ryan. He sat next to me.

"You want to talk about it?" he asked.

I turned to look at him. "Talk about what?"

He smiled. "Truitt, we've been friends since what, sixth grade?"

"Fourth," I corrected.

His head dropped back as he laughed. "Right. Fourth grade, when we both liked that same girl. What was her name?"

"Linda."

"Linda. That's right. Good thing she moved away, we might not have become friends."

I grinned.

"Anyway, dude. I know when something is bothering you."

Ryan was the last person I needed to talk to about what was on my mind.

"I'm fine."

He nodded. We sat in silence for a good three minutes before he spoke again.

"Is it because she's my sister? Are you worried what I'll think?"

My head jerked around to look at him. "What in the hell are you talking about, Ryan?"

"I'm talking about Saryn. I know you liked her in high school but never did anything about it. One, because she was my sister, and two, because that dickhead got to her first. What's your excuse now?"

"Now? You think I like Saryn?"

"No."

"Good," I stated.

"I don't think, dude, I know it."

I stared at him, not sure if I should admit that I did indeed like his sister once upon a time and that maybe I still did.

No maybe. I for sure liked her, but she wasn't interested in me that way.

"Truitt, like I said a minute ago, I know you. I see the way you look at my sister, and I've never seen you smile at anyone like you smile at her."

I shook my head. "You've got it wrong, Ryan."

"Do I? Really? Because she's been moping around just like you are ever since the two of you went on that little shopping trip.

You don't think I notice you come around when you know she's not there? Or that she nearly punched me in the gut when she found out I'd accidentally hurt you?

I lifted a brow.

"Dude, you tried to grab the gun from my hand!"

"You had your finger on the trigger!"

Ryan rolled his eyes, then shook his head. "Listen, I don't know what's going on in my sister's head. She claims she isn't interested in dating anyone, and believe me when I say I was less than pleased when she hooked up with that cop after she came back to town. Maybe that's what she thought she wanted, or maybe she needed it to move on from Tim. I don't know. But I see the way she lights up when someone mentions your name. All I'm saying is, if you're worried about me, dude, I'm not going to be a problem. I wouldn't stand in your way. You know my folks wouldn't either. Hell, this has been my mother's plan all along, you know that, right?"

I looked out into the dark night and chuckled. "Honestly, Ryan, I'm not really sure about much of anything right now, least of all my feelings."

He didn't say anything for a few minutes before he spoke again. "I don't know if my sister ever really loved Tim. As a matter of fact, she told me she was going to leave him before they even got married. She wasn't happy with him. Then he asked her to marry him. She gave it a try, and when things weren't working, she told him she wanted a divorce. Then she found out she was pregnant, so she stayed. I think she hoped Liliana would bring them closer, when all it really did was push them further apart. He hurt her, I do know that, and she seems so happy to be out of the marriage. She claims she doesn't want to date, but the way she reacted at the hospital when you got hurt? I know my sister, and she has feelings for you. Maybe she's a bit confused like you are? I don't know. I don't want to see her hurt, and I sure as hell don't want to see her push someone away simply because she thinks all guys suck."

My gaze met his. I nodded, not really sure what to say. He clapped me on the back and laughed. "Women, they totally fuck with our heads, don't they?"

"Yeah," I said with a slight laugh. "They sure do."

Ryan stood and went to walk back into the cabin before he turned and spoke again.

"If there's anything I learned from my relationship with Miranda, it's that communication has to be there. Maybe Saryn isn't ready for a relationship. If not, you need to decide if being her friend is going to be enough for you, Truitt. If it's not, you need to tell her how you feel. Don't let her slip away like she did in high school. Especially since my niece has already fallen head over heels for you."

I pulled in a deep breath. "I would never want to hurt either one of them."

He nodded. "I know, dude. I know."

Chapter 16

Truitt

ANOTHER MONTH PASSED by, and I had hardly seen Saryn at all. Since most of the work on the playhouse was done at my workshop, I didn't really need to be onsite that much. We'd worked double time to get the playhouse finished before the cold weather really kicked in. It was the beginning of December, and even for Texas it was colder than normal. Evie had begged me to get it finished by Christmas, and a part of me truly did want Liliana to have it by then. The only problem was that Christmas was three weeks away. There wouldn't be any rest for any of us. We had a huge playhouse project for a client in Austin that had just come in a few days ago, one we were trying to finish up, as well as Liliana's.

"What do you think?" Jack asked, a look of pure happiness etched on his face.

"I think we performed a fucking miracle, but it's not finished yet."

He nodded and I swore. He puffed out his chest some.

"We're right on schedule, so maybe now you can stop riding everyone's ass. I had to talk two people into not quitting because of the iron hand you've been giving lately," he said.

"It was a big project, one of our biggest to date. I want it to be good and delivered on time. This project landed us the Austin one, don't forget."

"I know it did, and it'll be finished on time, dude. Now will you take a damn breath, Truitt. Are you going to Pete's dinner party tonight?"

I rolled my eyes. "Jesus Christ, do I have to?"

Jack nodded. "Yes. The man has saved your life on how many occasions?"

Staring at Jack, I laughed. "Saved my life? He's pulled a nail out of my foot, told me my ankle wasn't broken...wrote a prescription or two for pain...

"Got glass out of your eye when that bottle exploded."

I shivered at the memory of that accident. Not one of my finer moments.

"Well, it was far from saving my life."

"Still, he's a friend, and you're the one who talked him into moving to Boerne to practice medicine here. The least you can do is have dinner at his house."

My head dropped back. "Dude, you know I don't like the evil queen!"

He laughed. "None of us like her, but Pete does. He's going to marry her."

I shook my head as I looked at Jack. "Fine. I need to go home and change, though. Knowing the evil queen, I mean, Wendy, it will be formal."

"It's not. I asked Pete. He said it's going to be casual."

"Thank fuck. I don't think I could sit around another dinner table and listen to her tell us what freaking fork to start with."

"What's funny is that you probably make three times the amount of money Pete does. Please don't ever turn rich on me, dude, I really don't like all that fancy food rich people eat."

I slapped him on the back. "Last I saw when I signed your paycheck, you were making good money, as well."

He looked around and frowned. "Don't let that shit out."

"Why not?" I asked with a smirk.

"Women, gold-digging women. Example number one: Wendy. Do you know how many women in this town are trying to get into your pants with the hopes you'll get them knocked up simply so they can get at your money? I don't want that kind of attention. I like the fact that women like me purely for my body and big dick."

I snarled my lip. "You took it too far."

He shrugged. "Want me to pick you up?"

"No, I'll drive myself, in case you meet another dinner guest who simply can't ignore that body of yours."

He walked backwards and raked his hands up and down himself, as if showing off his body.

"And big cock...don't forget about my big cock!"

I rolled my eyes and turned my back to him. I took in the playhouse in front of me. Without a doubt, it was huge. Saryn had wanted it scaled back, and we had scaled it back...some. I couldn't help but smile. Liliana was going to love it, and I was almost fucking giddy at the idea of her seeing it for the first time.

"Hey, boss, the exterior is all painted. The plans for the transport should be here tomorrow. We can go over it all, and whenever you give the go-ahead, it'll be ready for delivery."

With a nod, I replied to Mark, one of our painters, "Thanks. You did a great job with the painting."

He smiled. "Yellow is a bitch to paint, but I think it looks good. Some little girl is going to be very happy."

I let out an uncertain sigh. Liliana would be happy, but would Saryn? "That's the plan. That's the plan."

The moment I walked into Pete's and saw her, my heart nearly stopped beating. Saryn was there, and she was with a guy. She laughed and looked up at him like he had said the funniest thing in the world, and boy did that feel like a kick in the gut for some reason. Was she dating again? She had made it clear she wasn't interested in that, or maybe she wasn't interested in me.

That idea left me feeling sick.

When she looked directly at me, I quickly turned and started to head back out the door, but stopped when Pete called out my name.

"Truitt! Where in the hell do you think you're going?"

I closed my eyes and cursed inwardly. I knew all eyes would be on me now. Slowly, I turned and pulled my phone out of my pocket in hopes that everyone would think I'd had it in my hands the entire time.

"Just got paged, there's a problem at the warehouse."

Even though I was trying not to look at her, I felt Saryn's eyes on me.

"What kind of problem?" Jack asked, pulling out his own phone. "I haven't gotten any calls."

When I looked at Jack, I caught a glimpse of Saryn. I had been right...her gaze was locked on me. Staring. Hard. Almost with an angry expression. I finally allowed myself to fully look at her.

God. She was beautiful. Her long dark hair was pulled up into a ponytail, and I let my eyes move down her body in one quick sweep, taking in the jeans and off-white sweater she had on. Brown cowboy boots finished it all off.

What in the hell was she doing here? Pete didn't normally invite people he worked with. Maybe some of the other doctors, only for the formal dinners. But something casual like this was reserved for friends only.

"I just got the call from Mark. Sorry, Pete, I need to take off."

"I'll go," Jack said.

"No!" I shouted, causing everyone to give me their full attention once again. "I mean, stay, you're already here. Have a drink. I've got it."

Turning, I headed for the door and quickly made my way out. I was almost to the safety of my truck and my new plan to get in, drive home, and crack open a six-pack, when I heard her call my name.

"Truitt? Truitt, wait!"

I paused before opening my truck door.

"Saryn, good to see you."

My voice sounded cold and distant. She frowned slightly, then gave me a soft smile.

"How are you? I mean, how is your foot and ankle, and all of that."

With a quick glance down toward my feet, I looked back at her. "I'm good. Thanks for asking."

She nodded, then wrung her hands together. "I got your email about the playhouse nearly being finished. Liliana will love getting it for Christmas."

"It turned out great, I think y'all will be happy with it. Listen, I've got to run."

Saryn stepped closer to me. "You're not leaving on my account, are you?"

"Why are you even here?" I asked, hating the way it sounded so harsh and realizing I hadn't answered her question.

Her brows lifted and she opened her mouth, then closed it. It looked like she was attempting to get her emotions in check. I had acted like a dick and I needed to stop.

"I was...um...invited by Wendy. We were friends in high school and she asked if I would come."

With a quick look back at the house, I saw the guy she had been talking to in the doorway.

"Saryn? Is everything okay?" the dickhead called out.

The way her whole body tensed was hard to ignore. I looked from her to the guy. I'd never seen him before, so I had no clue who he was.

"Your date is waiting for you."

Without waiting for her to reply, I climbed into the truck. Before I shut it, I looked back at her, hoping like hell she'd tell me that wasn't her date. Instead, she stood there and watched me go. This was starting to become all too familiar.

"I'll be in touch in the next few days to let you know when we expect to deliver the playhouse," I said.

"Okay, sounds good."

After I shut the truck door, I let out a rush of air, started my truck, and drove off. I only looked in the mirror once. Long enough to see Saryn walking back over to her date who wore a wide smile on his face.

Focusing back on the road, I decided home wasn't my destination after all.

Chapter 17

Saryn

WHY IN THE world had my heart dropped when I watched Truitt walk out of Pete's house? Maybe it was because when he saw me, he looked so taken aback. Or the fact that I hadn't seen him in a number of weeks and realized how much I had missed him when I looked over and saw him standing there.

My mind raced as I tried to think back to anything I might have said or done to have angered him. It was in the ER when Pete had removed the nail my brother had shot into Truitt's foot. He hadn't wanted me there, that had been clear. Then, I hadn't heard anything from him other than a couple of emails updating us on the progress of the playhouse. Even then he had copied my mother on them. It took everything out of me not to text and ask if we needed another shopping day, or ask him if he needed help decorating the playhouse. It had become clear to me over the last few weeks...I longed for something more with Truitt.

"You okay?" Abram asked.

With a forced smile, I made my way back into the house. When Truitt had assumed Abram was my date, I was conflicted if I should have corrected him or not. In the end, I stood there not saying a word, which seemed to be the wrong thing to do.

Truitt had looked upset. Not angry, but almost defeated. Maybe he had been tired. Jack said Truitt had been working non-stop to get the playhouse finished in time for Christmas. Jack had also mentioned Truitt never made promises to clients on delivery dates. He'd mentioned that this project had seemed to be more special to Truitt than his past projects. That little bit of information Jack had dropped only thirty minutes ago had been processing in my brain when I forced myself to laugh at one of Abram's stupid jokes.

That was when Truitt walked in. Right at the exact moment it appeared I was being entertained by another man. I let out a sigh.

The moment he walked in, the air in the room changed. I felt a sensation go down my spine that left me in a state of wanting. Just what I wanted wasn't very clear. But it most certainly involved Truitt Carter. I might have made a promise to myself to not get involved with anyone, but there was no denying I had feelings for Truitt, still. And a part of me thought he might have some for me, as well.

"I'm fine. You really didn't need to follow me out here, Abram." My voice sounded a bit like I was reprehending him, and a part of me felt guilty for that. When Wendy had invited me to this dinner, she hadn't told me she was attempting to set me and Abram up. The guy was nice, but he wasn't anyone I would normally be interested in. Some hotshot investor type who lived in Austin full time but had a place here in Boerne to visit on the weekends. Wendy had met him at a conference a number of years back and had dated him, only to find him boring as hell. Of course, she hadn't told me any of that before the dinner. Only when I got here and figured out she was trying to set this up like a blind date but out in the open, did I come to my own conclusions.

"Oh, I wasn't worried, just wanted to make sure all was well," he said.

"It's fine!" I said, attempting to make my voice sound chipper and less like I wanted to stab him for interrupting me with Truitt.

Truitt.

Good Lord, why was the man invading my thoughts so much? Not to mention my dreams. I had actually woken up recently so horny after a pretty intense dream staring Mr. Carter himself that I found myself slipping my hand into my panties and giving myself some much-needed relief. Something I rarely ever did.

"Abram, I'm really sorry, but I'm actually coming down with a massive headache. I'm going to find Wendy and Pete and let them know I'm leaving."

His face went into an almost pout. "You're leaving before we really had a chance to get to know one another."

"I'm sure you'll find plenty of other people to chat with. Wendy and Pete seem to know how to throw a dinner party," I replied.

With that, he finally got the hint that I wasn't interested.

"Do you need someone to drive you home?"

"No," I said, brushing that off with a wave of my hand. "It's been a long week, I'm simply tired is all."

He nodded and said, "Well, it was nice to finally meet you. Wendy has talked about you a lot the last few weeks."

I forced a smile. Wendy had very much neglected to tell me about him. "It was nice meeting you, as well. Enjoy the rest of the evening."

Before he had a chance to say anything else, I made my way over to Wendy who was starting to direct people onto the back patio.

"Wendy!" I called out, getting her attention before she made her way outside.

"Saryn! We haven't had a chance to chat since you got here!" Wendy said, a huge grin spread across her face.

There was an evil look in her eye. One that said she had been up to no good.

"You've been busy with your other guests, and besides, Abram kept me company."

Her brows lifted, and then in a low, seductive voice, she said, "He did? Good!"

"Yeah, not that kind of company. As much as I appreciate you trying to set me up without telling me, I'm not interested in dating him, Wendy."

She folded her arms over her chest and narrowed one eye at me. "Really? And why not?"

I shrugged, not feeling like I needed to go into why with her.

A perfect eyebrow arched. "Only interested in dating Truitt Carter?"

"What!" I said in a disbelieving laugh.

"Please, girl, I saw the way you went after him when he walked in and then turned right around and walked back out. I don't blame you. Most of the single women in Boerne are interested in Truitt. The man is rumored to have a lot of money. Not to mention, he's very easy on the eyes."

I wasn't even sure how to respond to that.

"Abram has money, too, and I feel he's handsome," she added. "Maybe not the kind of handsome that makes a girl want to drop her panties for him, but he would be a good match."

"For whom?"

"You, silly!" Wendy laughed.

"Wendy, you told me not even an hour ago you broke up with him because he was boring and you realized that he made a better friend than a boyfriend."

"Yes, I did, but the guy has a magical dick. No joke. After we broke up, I still hit him up for the occasional night of passionate sex. He does things with his hips and that dick that make your toes curl."

My mouth dropped open. "What?"

"Oh, honey, he's huge!" She fanned herself. "I'm getting hot thinking about it."

"You're engaged to another man!" I whisper-shouted.

"So? I'm not saying I'm going to jump in bed with Abram, I'm saying *you* should. He'll get Tim right out of your head."

I sighed. "Tim is out of my head. I'm not interested in a sex-only relationship."

She gave me a look that screamed she thought I was lying.

"Wendy, I'm serious. Please don't try and fix me up with anyone."

When her expression didn't change, I begged a little harder. "Please."

With a dramatic roll of her eyes, she sighed. "Fine. I won't. But please tell me you're not interested in Truitt Carter."

There was something about the way she had said that last statement that made me take pause.

"And why not? Only seconds ago, you said he was good looking."

She swallowed hard, then avoided looking me in the eyes as she stated, "He's just not your type, and I hear he sleeps around. A lot."

"Thank you for the gossip, but I think I've formed my own opinions on Truitt. I'm going to head on out, talk soon."

I kissed her on the cheek, then lifted my hand and gave Pete a wave. He was standing in the dining room, chatting while people lined up at the buffet table. The fresh flowers Wendy had put out everywhere masked the smell of the food. The odor was actually making me feel a bit nauseous, and I was positive I wasn't the only person feeling that way. To say she had gone over the top with this dinner would be an understatement.

"Lunch this week!" Wendy called out.

I gave her a quick nod on my way out. Lunch would not be on my list of things to do this week with Wendy.

As I drove home, I turned left on Walter Street instead of right. Right would have led me home. Left led me directly to Imaginations Unlimited. If Truitt really had gotten a call, I knew he'd be there. Otherwise, the aching feeling that he was avoiding me would become all too real.

It didn't take me long to pull up and find Truitt's truck in the parking lot. I felt a little bit better knowing he hadn't left the party because of me. There was only one other vehicle in the small parking lot. I made my way to the door, hoping it would be open. It was early evening, and I wouldn't have been surprised to find people still working. Especially if they were attempting to have Liliana's playground finished in time for Christmas.

With a quick twist of my wrist, I found the front door unlocked. I dragged in a deep breath and walked in.

"Hello?" I called out, hoping someone was in the offices. I was met by silence.

I'd come here only once since my first visit. My mother and I had dropped in when Truitt wanted us to see how a few different shades of yellow would look on the wood. The playhouse was in pieces then, so I had no real idea what it would look like.

I followed the path that led to the workshop space. The door was open, and I heard the faint sounds of music filtering through the hallway. It was a Waterloo Revival song. A two-member country group with original roots in Austin, and a band Truitt must have liked. He'd had them on in his truck when we went out on our little shopping trip.

Once I stepped inside the room, I froze. The playhouse in front of me was mostly in pieces still but laid out in a way that you could see what the finished result would be. The sight of it made my breath hitch in my throat. I tried to take every inch of it in. It was going to be massive, and I wanted to be angry, but it was so beautiful I couldn't feel anything negative if I tried.

Movement caught my eye and I saw Truitt. He hadn't seen or heard me yet, and with the music playing I wasn't surprised. I moved to the side of the large crate and simply watched him. He was walking around each piece of the playhouse, inspecting it, writing down notes on a notepad and singing his heart out to "Like I Miss You."

Something inside of me cracked open and I was flooded with a warmth I hadn't felt in years. Lord knows I never felt it with my husband, and for a moment that made me sad. But this feeling, the rush of tingles that raced through my body when I saw Truitt, was too good to stay sad for long. I loved to see him so carefree and singing. The man even had a good singing voice.

"Oh, my," I whispered as I watched him push his fingers through his brown hair. My fingers instantly itched to do the same thing.

With a shake of my head, I pulled myself together and pushed aside the warm feeling that had rushed through my body only seconds ago. I walked toward him, his back facing me. He leaned over, giving me a shot of his perfect ass in those Wrangler jeans.

Of course, in that moment I would trip over something and let out a yelp. Truitt spun around and saw me stumbling. He was by my side and grabbing me before I could even register I was actually about to fall.

"Are you okay?" he asked, his hands on my upper arms. His eyes were the color of the ocean when a storm was fixin' to move in. His deep blue gaze stared at me intently and left me feeling weak in the knees.

"You have a nice voice."

Oh. My. Gosh. Did I really say that?

"I mean, thank you for helping me not fall flat on my face. *And* you have a nice voice."

The corner of Truitt's mouth twitched with a slight smile.

"You're welcome, and thank you. What are you doing here?" he asked, his eyes flickering past me to see if I was with anyone.

"Turns out I wasn't in the mood for one of Wendy's little get-togethers after all. Especially when I found out she'd attempted to set me up on a blind date."

His brows rose, and I couldn't help but notice the heat from his hands that were still holding onto my arms. He let go, almost as if he had noticed it, as well. With one quick motion, he leaned over and lowered the volume on his Bose speaker.

We stood there and stared at one another before he asked again, "What brings you here?"

I snapped out of the daze his touch had thrown me into. There was something about this man that turned me into a young school girl again. Filled with hope that maybe I had been wrong that day when I thought Truitt only asked me out to use me. That Tim had manipulated me. That the look in Truitt's eyes, the look of defeat, was because maybe he felt something for me, as well.

"Oh, um, yeah…"

I chewed on my lip and almost shivered when his gaze went to my mouth. I'd never wanted a man to kiss me more than I wanted Truitt to kiss me in that moment. So maybe my brain was on board, as well.

"Have I made you angry?" I finally asked.

That made his gaze jerk back up to mine.

"What?" he asked, looking every bit as dazed and confused as I felt.

"You didn't seem to want to be at Pete's, and I thought it was because I was there. You didn't want me to be there in the room when you came into the ER last month, and you've been avoiding talking to me. I wanted to make sure I didn't do anything to make you mad."

The way Truitt was looking at me left me nervous as hell. What in the world was this man thinking? And why in the world had I just acted like a sixteen-year-old girl trying to figure out why her crush wasn't paying attention to her? I had hit a new low with this one. I instantly wanted to pull all the words back in that I had just spoken.

Then he laughed a disbelieving laugh and shook his head while he rubbed the back of his neck.

"You haven't done or said anything to make me mad at you." His brows pulled in and he honestly looked befuddled. "You said you weren't interested in a relationship, Saryn. I got the message loud and clear."

That made my eyes go wide.

"I'm sorry?"

"The day we went shopping, you made it clear you weren't interested in anything other than friendship."

I ignored the lump forming in my throat and forced myself to ask the question that was now burning into my mind. "Do you want something more than friendship? I mean, with me? Do you want... um...me?"

Good Lord, that came out all wrong. Where was the confident woman who had realized she deserved more in a man? The one who'd packed up and walked away from her life? The one who vowed she would never run away from anything ever again? If I wanted something, I was going to fight for it this time.

"Do you want more than friendship with me, Truitt?" I asked, my voice clear and strong.

His eyes lit with a fire that made my insides tremble.

Truitt looked away for a moment, as if he was thinking about how he wanted to answer my question. When his eyes met mine, I realized I had been holding my breath.

"Honestly, yes. I want to be friends with you, Saryn. I enjoy being around you and Liliana, but I'm not going to lie to you. I desperately want more of you. And right now, I want to kiss you."

I swallowed hard. "You do?" I whispered, barely loud enough to hear myself.

He lifted his hand and brushed a piece of my hair back from my face. When he tucked it behind my ear, I was pretty sure I sighed at the feel of his fingers touching me again.

"I do," he softly replied while the corners of his mouth lifted into a sexy grin.

"What happens after you kiss me?" I asked while my eyes searched his face.

"Well, I'm hoping like hell you like the kiss and want to kiss me back. A lot."

I giggled and rolled my eyes.

"To be honest, I don't know what's going to happen, Saryn. I hope the kiss leads to more, when you're ready."

I chewed on my lip for a moment before meeting his intense gaze.

"I used to have a crush on you, Truitt. Back in high school. When all the other boys used to flirt with me, I remember wishing you weren't friends with Ryan because you never so much as glanced my way."

That made him lift his brows in surprise. "You had a crush on me?"

With a nod, I went on. "I knew things were over between me and Tim long before I finally admitted it. I vowed I wasn't going to get into another relationship until I had time to just be me. Be a mom to Liliana, find the girl who seemed to slowly disappear as the months and years went by. Then you showed back up in my life and I feel something here." I pressed my hand to my chest. "It's a feeling I have never felt before, and I'll be honest with you, that scares me a little bit. I can't risk Liliana getting hurt. I won't risk it. When I do commit to someone, I want to go slow, I need it to be more than just sex, Truitt."

He smiled bigger. "I want that, too."

With a tilt of my head, I regarded him for a moment. This man whom everyone said was one of the most sought-after man in Boerne. Why had he not settled down yet? What was he looking for in a woman, and did he really want to be tied down to one who had a kid already?

"What exactly do you want, Truitt? I mean, with me who has a ready-made family?"

He drew in a deep breath and slowly let it out. He shook his head, almost as if he was debating how much to tell me. Then his eyes met mine and I felt the energy pulse between us. It was unlike anything I had ever experienced before in my life, and I knew by the look in his eyes, he felt it, too.

"I want to get to know you better. Spend time with you and Liliana. I want to kiss you. Take you out for ice cream. Hear Liliana laugh when I attempt to sing one of her silly songs. I don't want to just have sex with you, Saryn. It's always been more with you."

My heart felt like it jumped in my chest. What did he mean, it had always been more? Before I could ask, he went on.

"I also want someone to kiss goodnight every evening and make love to every morning. I want a best friend I can share all my dreams and fears with. I want to be a husband and a dad someday. I want to have someone whom I can trust and who can trust me."

Truitt looked away and let out a slight laugh. "Okay, I might have shared a bit too much of what I want."

I shook my head and placed my hand on the side of his cheek. Oh, where had this man been all my life? The fact that he could be so open and honest made the emotions inside of me feel raw and new.

"No, what you shared with me was perfect. How should we do this, Truitt? I've only ever been with Tim, well, with the exception of a terrible one-night stand."

Another brilliant smile appeared on his face, and I felt my knees wobble slightly.

He winked and said, "I think we should start with a kiss."

"That sounds like a solid plan."

Truitt cupped my face in his hands and looked at my mouth, then into my eyes. I had longed for this moment longer than I remembered. Needed it more than I ever dreamed. I needed this man's mouth on mine. Now.

"Kiss me, Truitt," I whispered.

He leaned down and did just that, and Lord help me. It was soft and slow. His lips felt like the softest things I'd ever felt in my life. And just like that, with one kiss, I'd let Truitt in and I had zero regrets.

Chapter 18

Truitt

WHEN MY LIPS pressed against Saryn's, I knew I was in trouble. One kiss and my body felt like it was tumbling over an edge, and nothing would ever be the same again. I didn't want it to be the same.

This kiss was amazing. Beyond amazing. Unlike any other kiss I'd ever experienced before. Every imagined moment of kissing Saryn was nothing like the actual thing. She let out a little moan when I pressed against her body, and I nearly lost my head. I wanted this woman desperately.

When we both needed to come up for air, we pulled our mouths apart. Our eyes locked and she smiled. My legs felt like someone had attempted to sweep me off my damn feet.

"Wow," Saryn whispered.

I smiled. "Wow, is right."

She slowly shook her head as she placed her hand on my chest, sending a bolt of heat instantly through my body.

Saryn lifted her eyes to mine. "I've never in my life been kissed like that before."

"That's because the wrong guy has been kissing you all these years."

Her teeth dug into her lip, and I groaned internally. Christ, if I didn't want to bury myself inside her right here and now.

Slow down, Truitt. Slow the hell down.

"You have no idea the restraint I'm using to keep from touching you."

Her brow lifted. "Touching me? Where?"

This time I growled and pulled her body against mine. "Don't," I warned. "You said you wanted to go slow, and asking me where I want to touch you is not going to lead to slow."

Saryn nodded. "You're right."

Her words said I was right, but the look in her eyes said something completely different. They screamed that she was in need of something from me, and I had a feeling I knew exactly what it was.

I watched as the pulse at her neck throbbed faster. The urge to touch her nearly drove me mad, but I was hell-bent on doing this right with her. There was no way I was going to spook her or make her regret any part of us.

"We should probably leave, or at least step away from each other," I managed to say as I took a step back from her.

"Why?"

Her voice sounded breathy. Full of the same need I knew I had. If we didn't put the brakes on, I was afraid I'd be fucking her right here in the shop. And the first time we were together, I didn't want to fuck. I wanted to make love to her.

Saryn laughed and looked away, her cheeks red with embarrassment. "I mean, I know why. It's just...wow. Okay, we need to slow down."

This time it was my turn to laugh. "I think so, sweetheart."

Her eyes sparkled at the endearment, and she nodded, seeming to confirm her own thoughts.

"Go out with me tomorrow night?" I asked, brushing away the same loose piece of hair from her face.

"What did you have in mind?" she asked, a soft smile on her face.

"Dinner. My house?"

Her brows went up. "Your house?"

I held up my hands in defense. "We can go out somewhere, but I really want to spend a bit of time getting to know you better before the town gossips come out swinging."

She smiled, and I swore it lit up the entire shop.

"I'll do you one better. I'm off tomorrow, and I know you're trying to finish up this playhouse." Her eyes swung over to her daughter's castle spread all over the shop in pieces. "Lord, that thing is huge."

"We did scale it back some, I promise," I stated with a sly grin.

Her gaze locked back on mine. "Ha. Anyway, I know Liliana would love to see you. Let me make you dinner, at my place. If you don't mind Liliana being there."

I couldn't help the way the corners of my mouth lifted. Saryn was offering to make me dinner at her house and wanted Liliana there, as well.

"What time should I be there?"

She thought for a moment before answering. "Liliana goes to bed around eight. If it's okay with you, I'd like to keep her dinner at the same time she's used to. Does five thirty work for you?"

"That works great."

"Good," she said, a hint of seduction laced in her words. "Then I'll see you tomorrow evening."

"Let me close up, and I'll walk you out."

After getting everything locked up, I walked with Saryn out to her car. She leaned against her door and looked up at me with eyes that seemed to plead for me to make some sort of contact between our bodies again. Lord knows I wanted to.

"What do you need me to bring tomorrow?" I asked, attempting to break the need to kiss her again.

A shocked look moved over her face before she quickly smiled. "A bottle of wine?"

"Red or white?"

A blush washed across her cheeks, and she chewed on her thumbnail before meeting my gaze. "I have a favorite wine, and if you could find it, I'll make it worth your while."

That caused me to raise my brows. "Is that so?"

She nodded.

"Tell me the name of this wine, Ms. Night, and it's yours."

"It's from Australia. It's called The Stump Jump. It's a shiraz."

"I love a good shiraz."

Her teeth dug into her lower lip, and I ached to pull it free with my own lips. "Me, too."

"Consider it done. Any certain year?"

She shook her head. I brought my finger to her chin and lifted her head so that her eyes met mine. "I'll see you tomorrow, Saryn."

Her throat bobbed with a hard swallow. "See you then, Truitt."

I leaned down and kissed her mouth softly. Saryn reached up and grabbed onto my shirt and moaned into my mouth. It caused a rush of desire to race straight to my damn cock. I was going to have to go home and jerk off in the shower, no question about it.

Quickly, I stepped back and broke the kiss. It left us both a little dazed. I tipped my cowboy hat at her as she opened the door to her car. As she slipped in, I leaned down and smiled.

Saryn rewarded me with a smile that made my chest feel tight. Then I shut the door and watched her drive away. I was positive I wouldn't be able to wipe the smile from my face if I tried.

"So, what happened last night?" Jack finally asked after bugging me about why I had come back to the shop the night before.

"Nothing."

"So it's just a coincidence that Saryn left the dinner party only minutes after you did. And you've had a damn smile on your face like you got...lucky last night."

My head turned to him. "Lucky?"

"Yeah, you remember that, don't you? Getting laid? Sleeping with a woman? Having sex. I haven't seen you this happy in a long time, so that leads me to believe you got lucky."

I chuckled. "Well, you would be wrong."

He looked shocked. "No shit? Did you see Saryn last night?"

If Jack had wanted to, he could check the security cameras and see exactly what happened, another reason I had to stop the kiss last night with Saryn. Or I'd be erasing part of the security recording before he took a notion to snoop.

"I saw her. She stopped by here, we talked."

"That's it?"

Turning on the saw, I cut a piece of wood. I could practically feel Jack's eyes burning into my back. The moment the saw went off, he was back at it.

"Nothing else happened? How long did she stay? What did she say about the playhouse? Is she liking it?"

"You really sound like a busybody, you know that, Jack? Are you taking lessons from Evie?" I said, picking up the piece of wood I'd cut and walking over to the window box I was making.

"Guilty as charged. I know she was here."

I stopped what I was doing and shot him a look. He laughed. "No, I didn't look at the security footage, but Lou told me she showed up last night."

Lou. We had hired him to keep an eye on the place at night. I'd forgotten all about him being here. He had either walked in on us and back out of the shop without making a sound, or had seen our vehicles out front. He was a good guy, so if he had seen anything, I knew he wouldn't be running his mouth all over town.

With a dramatic sigh, purely for effect, I faced Jack. His eyes lit up, and he looked as if he was about to get a birthday gift.

"Saryn stopped by. We talked, and I'm seeing her for dinner tonight. At her place. With...Liliana."

He grinned like a school boy. "Fucking finally."

"What's that supposed to mean?"

Jack rolled his eyes. "Dude, everyone can see how much you like her. You've always liked her. Even when we were in school."

My mouth dropped open. "How in the hell did you know that?"

A look of hurt moved over his face. "I'm sorry, have we not been friends since like fifth grade? Ryan's not your only best friend, jackass."

I laughed and shook my head. "I know, but I didn't realize it had been so obvious in high school that I liked Saryn."

"Dude, why do you think Tim went after her? The moment he knew you were interested, he did everything in his power to keep you away from her."

It felt like all the air in the shop suddenly got sucked out. I found myself not able to breathe, let alone think about what Jack had just said.

"What?" Was all I could get out.

"What?" Jack asked, confused.

"What do you mean, that's why Tim went after her?"

Jack looked around the shop and then back at me. He looked conflicted before he finally spoke again. "You've never, since I've known you, looked at a girl like you do Saryn. It's always been that way, Truitt. High school was no exception. I think it started when we were around sixteen."

"And you never thought to say something?"

He shrugged. "Ryan never said anything, I figured you stayed away because she was his sister."

It was true, that had been the main reason I kept myself away from Saryn back in high school.

"It doesn't matter, she wasn't interested in me then."

This time he looked at me like I was an idiot. "Dude, you didn't move fast enough in high school. If you hadn't been afraid of Ryan, that might have been you married to Saryn."

Now my head was spinning. I laughed. "Don't be ridiculous."

Jack pulled in a deep breath and then slowly let it out as he stepped closer to me, suddenly caring if anyone else heard his insane comments. "Why have you never dated anyone seriously, Truitt? I mean, seriously, like you thought maybe she was the one?"

I gave him a half shrug. "Probably because I haven't met the one yet."

That was a flat-out lie. I had already pictured what it would be like to marry Saryn. She and Liliana were the missing piece in my life, and deep down I knew that.

He lifted one single brow. "Oh, I think you have met the one. When you were too young to know it was her. It took her leaving and marrying some dick and then coming back for you to see. Face it, Truitt, you've never let yourself get close to any other woman."

"That's because all the women in this town are after my money, something you should know about, as well."

His head dropped back as he let out a round of laughter. "Ah, hell, I know it. Trust me." Jack rubbed the back of his neck and leaned onto a table that had been set up for cutting. "Truitt, I'm talking to you as your friend, your longtime friend who happens to be your business partner, as well. I see the way y'all look at each other. I'm pretty damn sure she feels the same way about you."

I looked away for a moment before glancing back his way and saying, "She told me she had a crush on me in high school."

He shook his head. "Fucking Tim."

I nodded in agreement. "Yeah. Fucking Tim."

"Truitt! You've got a call! It's Ms. Townsend."

The voice calling out to me belonged to Jack's younger sister, the shop manager. She pretty much handled everything coming and going from the shop.

"That can't be good. Let me go see what she needs," I said as I slapped Jack on the back. Before I walked away, I faced him again. "I don't want to mess this up with her. She wants to go slow and I'll go as slow as she wants, but I'm scared to death I'm going to screw this up like I do everything."

He smiled and then opened his arms and motioned around the shop. "Dude, you don't screw up everything. Look at this. Look at what you built."

"We built," I added.

Jack shook his head. "No, dude, you built this. This was your dream and you saw it through. Go see what the true boss wants."

With another chuckle, I headed out to the small office area where Renee worked. She handed me my cell phone.

"Hey, Ms. Townsend, what's going on?"

"I've been trying to reach you all morning, Truitt."

I had forgotten to charge my phone last night. Then I plugged it in this morning and forgot about it again.

"I'm sorry, my phone has been in Renee's office charging. What's wrong?"

"The trucking company is saying they can't make the deadline to deliver the Nights' playhouse."

It felt like a rock dropped straight into my stomach. "What do you mean? They're obligated to show up. We have a contract. I've paid them already."

"They know that, but there's been an accident. One of the rigs slid off the road in some winter weather up north and it's beyond repair."

"Is the driver okay?" I instantly asked.

"Yes. He was on his way back to Texas, was due to switch out with another driver in Oklahoma."

I let out a frustrated sigh.

"They do have another company they can refer us to. They're new, but Ricky says they're good and he wouldn't refer you over to them if he didn't have the utmost confidence they could get the house moved safely."

"Lynn..." I softly said.

"I know, Truitt. I know this one means something special to you. I've told Ricky and he gave me his word. I don't think he would ever lead you wrong."

An instant headache throbbed in my temples while I pressed my fingertips to the bridge of my nose.

"What's the company?" I asked, trying not to sound as frustrated as I was. This playhouse was one of the biggest we'd built, and now my normal trucking company wasn't going to be delivering it.

"Stein Brother Haulers. They're out of Austin."

"How many moves have they had?"

Lynn remained silent for a moment too long.

"Please tell me we're not their first."

"No, no, you're not the first. The first large load haul, but not the first haul."

"Cause that makes me feel loads better," I bit out.

"Truitt, accidents happen. You know this, we get thrown obstacles in life all the time. You have an amazing crew there, Ricky tells me these guys are amazing. It will get there safely."

I nodded, even though she couldn't see me. "You're right. As usual, you're right. Okay, is there anyway I can meet with them before the transport? Even if by video call."

"I've already scheduled a time for them to come by today. They'll be here at five."

"Five? That's not going to work for me, I have a date tonight."

I was met by silence on the phone and a shocked expression from Renee. Who then smiled and mouthed, *a date*?

With a smile, I nodded.

"Lynn?" I asked as Renee shook her head in wonder.

"You done killed her with that kind of news," Renee said with a chuckle.

Lynn cleared her throat. "I'm not dead, I was simply caught off guard. You normally share your...um...appointments with me."

"This isn't an appointment, Lynn. It's personal."

"Well, your date is at a bad time. Can you change it?"

I didn't even have to think twice. I grew up with a father who constantly put work before his family. Hell, he still did. Sure, he loved us, and we knew it, but it would have been nice for him to show up to our games, class parties, and plays, things that meant something to us. But he felt that his work was more important. And my mother, hell, she was never even in town half the time. I was not about to start off my relationship with Saryn and Liliana by putting work first.

"No, I can't. Let's just say from this point on, after five during the week I'll be on call for emergencies only. No more meetings."

"I see. Well, do I know her?"

"You know her momma. Evie Night."

"Saryn! You've got a date with Saryn!"

I pulled my cell phone away from my ear. "Shout it out to the world, Ms. Townsend."

I heard her chuckle and watched as Renee leaned in a bit closer as if she couldn't already hear the conversation.

"Let me see if I can move it up by a few hours. I'll call you back. Keep your phone on you."

"Thank you, Lynn, I appreciate it."

"You're welcome, Truitt."

The phone went black as my secretary disconnected our call. Renee stood there with a shit-eating grin on her face.

I pointed to her. "Not a word to anyone. We're going slow. This is our first date and I don't want the whole town gossiping about it."

She mocked surprise. "You're worried 'bout me? You might have given that little speech to Ms. Townsend. She's probably on her little Facebook group message board right now informing them all that Boerne's most eligible bachelor is off the market."

I shook my head and walked away. It was going to be a long-ass day.

Chapter 19

Saryn

I BUZZED AROUND the grocery store with my list in my hand. Liliana sat in the car, her eyes taking in the new book my mother had given her this morning.

The morning had been spent frantically cleaning my house, which wasn't even dirty. Or at least that was what Lucy had kept saying. I'd called her last night on the way home to tell her about the date with Truitt. I didn't know who else to call, and Lucy was the first person to pop up in my mind.

Lucy was still back at the ranch helping my mother make some weird pie made of rhubarb. That didn't even sound appealing, but if it kept my mother busy and out of my business I was okay with it.

"Momma?"

I glanced down to Liliana.

"Can we goes to da park today?"

"Oh, sweet girl, that sounds like fun, but Mommy has to buy food for dinner tonight." I leaned down and whispered, "Mr. Truitt is coming over to have dinner with us."

My daughter's eyes lit up like the Fourth of July. "Twuitt!"

I nodded. "Yes, so we have to hurry and buy all the yummy food so we can go home and cook it for him." And make sure I have at least three hours to figure out what I'm going to wear to a casual dinner at my house that is not going to lead to anything. No way was I going to sleep with Truitt with my daughter in the same house. At least I kept telling myself that. Lord knew what would happen when she went to bed, though.

My phone buzzed, and I reached into my purse and answered it without even looking.

"Hello?"

"Hey, how's it going?"

It felt like a buzz of energy raced straight from the phone and into my body. It was Truitt.

"Hi. It's going good. Liliana and I are at the grocery store getting everything for dinner tonight. I hope you like eggplant parmesan with homemade pasta and my grandmother's secret breading."

"I hate eggplant parmesan," Truitt replied, causing me to stop walking and stare down at all the ingredients in my cart for eggplant parmesan.

I had two choices: tell him tough cookies, that's what I was making, or quickly come up with another menu. Then he laughed.

"Saryn, I'm kidding. My mother is Italian, if she ever heard me utter those words, she would slap me from here to the border. Don't ever tell her I said that, it was a joke."

The breath I had been holding quickly whooshed out. "Truitt Carter! That was not funny. That was just plain mean!"

I couldn't hold back my smile, and I was positive he heard it in my voice.

"I'm sorry, I couldn't resist. Hey, do you mind if I bring Rus along? He's been stuck back at my place all day. It's been a crazy day at work."

"Please, bring him. Liliana will love playing with him."

"You're sure you don't mind?"

"Positive. I love dogs, so does Liliana."

"Goggy!" Liliana cried out with a huge smile.

Truitt laughed. "She sounds on board with this plan."

"Oh, trust me, she is. When I told her you were coming over, her face lit up. You have two Night women thrilled to see you and Rus, Mr. Carter."

"Well, a guy could certainly get used to that. Listen, I've got to run into a meeting, the guys drove here from Austin. I'll see you soon?"

"Okay, see you soon."

"Bye, sweetheart."

My heart fluttered in my chest and I hardly got my words out. "Bye, Truitt."

I hit End and looked at Liliana. I nearly swooned right there in the store. "Oh, Liliana, this man. This man is going to be dangerous, but oh so fun!"

She giggled, her little blue eyes dancing with excitement.

"I have a feeling it's going to be the kind of dangerous your mommy could get used to."

"Saryn! It's so good to see you!"

I spun around to see Tim's older cousin, LouAnne, standing there. Her eyes bounced from me to Liliana. "My goodness, I haven't seen y'all in forever! Tim told me you moved back to town and I kept meaning to call on y'all to say hi."

Forcing a smile, I replied, "Oh, no worries at all. We've been busy getting settled back in."

She looked me up and down. "So I've heard."

"What is that supposed to mean?"

With a half shrug, she said, "Nothin'. It don't mean nothin'. I'm sure you heard the family news."

"No, I'm afraid I don't know anything about Tim's family. They've pretty much decided to not have anything to do with Liliana."

That wiped the smile off her freaking face. Why hadn't I remembered LouAnne being such a...bitch? She glanced down to Liliana and sent her a wave before she focused back on me.

"Granddaddy died and we all inherited a little money, Tim, of course, got the brunt of it all, him being the only boy in the family on his momma's side."

The fact that she showed no grief over losing her grandfather made me question why I ever married into this family.

"I'm so sorry for your loss."

She sighed. "Yes, of course, it was hard losin' him. But he made sure we were all taken care of. You know he was in the oil business."

I wanted to roll my eyes hard. "Yes, I knew that. If you'll excuse me, LouAnne, I've got to get going. It was nice seeing you again."

"Oh, you, too. Maybe you'll even run into Tim while he's in town."

That made me freeze. Tim was in town? How long had he been in Boerne? Even though he had signed over his rights to Liliana, how could he not even want to see his daughter? Of course, I knew the answer to that, and I shouldn't have been surprised.

"I doubt it, I'll see you around."

"Twuitt!" Liliana said as she looked past LouAnne. My heart stopped, but it was another guy in a cowboy hat, and when he turned around, Liliana nearly sighed. Apparently my daughter had it just as bad as I did...

LouAnne looked back at me and raised a brow. "Did she say Truitt? As in Truitt Carter?"

"I'm late, LouAnne. It was nice seeing you."

With that, I dashed down an aisle and moved away from the woman as quickly as I could. Everything about that family was toxic.

"Come on, baby girl, let's get some stuff to make cookies tonight with Truitt."

Liliana smiled wide, and I knew exactly how she was feeling as the excitement of seeing Truitt kicked up another level.

The doorbell rang at four thirty, an hour earlier than Truitt was supposed to arrive. Thank goodness I had gotten ready while Liliana took a nap. I made my way to the door and opened it, a wide smile on my face, only to have it instantly fall.

"Tim. What are you doing here?"

He smiled, then looked past me. "Is that anyway to greet your husband?"

"Ex-husband. Who cheated on me. Signed his parental rights to his daughter away. The man who only cares about himself. You're that guy, nothing else."

His cocky smile faded. "Rumors are going around town, saying you're dating someone."

I rolled my eyes. "I don't believe that would be any of your concern."

"It is when you're raising my kid."

"Oh, she's your kid now? Should I expect child support checks to be coming in soon, then? I heard you just had a windfall."

Tim took a step back, a look of pure horror on his face. The thought that he might actually have to pay for his child seemed to be a painful thought. What a prick.

"What do you want, Tim?"

"Are you seeing Truitt Carter?"

My eyes widened in shock. *Holy hells bells.*

Boerne wasn't exactly a small town anymore, but clearly the rumor mill still worked like it had in the good ol' days.

"Excuse me?"

"You know he's a player, right? He wanted you back in high school. Bragged that he could get you to fuck him."

I glanced back into the house to make sure Liliana was still playing with Lucy. Then I stepped out onto the porch and shut the door.

"*My* daughter is inside, and I don't want her hearing the filth that comes out of your mouth."

He smirked. "It's true. Why do you think I even asked you out in the first place? I thought you were a nice girl. I was saving you from that manwhore."

My mouth nearly dropped to the ground. "What? You *saved* me? From Truitt?"

With a scoff, he said, "Yes, I did. Heard he was starting to sniff around you like the dog he is, so I moved in on you instead. I'm sure your brother was happy about that, saved you from his best friend who likes pussy too much."

I narrowed my eyes at him. That was when I smelled the alcohol on his breath. He'd been drinking. Tim only had a mouth on him when he was two sheets to the wind.

"Why don't you take your drunk ass and get off my property," I said, folding my arms across my chest. His eyes moved down to my breasts and caused me to drop my arms to my side. How had I ever been married to this guy? He made my skin crawl.

Tim lifted his hands up in defense. "I'm only trying to save you from making a mistake, that's all."

"The only mistake I ever made, Tim, was marrying you to try and get over Truitt in the first place."

That gave him a shot to his ego. "So you are dating him?"

"It's none of your business."

"Heard he's making our daughter one of his fancy overpriced playgrounds. How are you paying for it? By sleeping with him?"

Anger rumbled up inside of me, to the point where I really wanted to kick him in the balls. "She is *my* daughter, and yes, he is. My parents are giving it to her as a Christmas gift, if it's any of your business. Now, I'm going to ask you one more time, get off of my property before I call the cops."

From the corner of my eye I saw my daddy walking over. *Oh, Lord, please don't have a rifle.*

"I don't want him around you," Tim said, taking a step closer to me. I didn't move. Tim wasn't a threat to me, drunk or not. I could probably punch him right now and he'd run home crying to his momma.

"You don't get to have a say in who I date and who I don't date. Leave, Tim, now. Before something happens that you'll regret."

"You heard her, Tim. It's time for you to get on outta here," my father said. He didn't have a rifle, but he was holding a stick. I shook my head at him, and he gave me one nod, as if he knew as well as I did that Tim was mostly harmless.

"Mr. Night. Good seeing you, sir."

My father gave Tim a once-over before he spoke. "I wish I could say the same. Son, I'm giving you thirty seconds to get your ass back in that truck and get the hell off of my property before I give you the beating I've wanted to give you since the day you picked my daughter up for that first date."

Tim's eyes went wide. Ryan walked up next to my father and smiled as he rested his rifle on his shoulder. Tim took one look at Ryan and made his way back down the sidewalk to the waiting truck without saying another word. When I looked at the driver, I saw it was LouAnne's boyfriend.

Once the jerk was in the car and it was heading back down the driveaway, I let out a long breath.

"I cannot believe he had the nerve to show up here," I mumbled.

"What made him come?" Ryan asked as he watched the truck drive farther down the gravel road.

"Ran into LouAnne today. She must have told him she thought I was dating Truitt. He came to let me know how displeased he was by that."

My father and Ryan both laughed.

"What a dick," Ryan said, then looked at me. "What in the hell did you ever see in him, Saryn?"

My eyes jerked back to the gravel road where the truck turned and was lost from my view. "He was a way out when I thought all I wanted was out."

I looked down at the ground before I met my father's eyes. He nodded. "Grass isn't always greener in the other pastures."

With a forced smile, I nodded. "Lesson learned, Daddy. Lesson learned."

"So, is it true? You and Truitt?" Ryan asked.

"Does that bother you?" I asked.

He laughed. "Hell no. Couldn't think of a better guy for you, Saryn. He's one of the good ones. If you don't take into account that he's clumsy as all hell. Good thing you're a nurse, I guess."

"Seems to me he just has a bit of bad luck. I believe it was you who shot him in the foot with a nail gun."

Daddy turned to Ryan. "What!"

Ryan waved it off. "It was nothing. I'm going to, ah...go see if Mom needs any help with anything."

My father looked back at me for an explanation.

"I'll tell you another day, Daddy. I've got dinner to cook and Lucy's gonna be leaving soon, so I need to take advantage of her keeping Liliana occupied."

He pointed at me. "I'm going to hold you to it. No telling what those two boys were up to. Enjoy dinner and call me if that asshole comes back. Next time I'm going to grab Ryan's gun and shoot the man in the ass as I'm chasing him off my property."

I tried not to smile, but a small giggle slipped through. "He won't be back, he got what he needed to say off his chest."

"Hope you're right. I'll talk to you later, darlin'."

Once my father was headed back to the main house, I rushed into mine and started getting everything ready for dinner. Lucy walked into the kitchen and bumped my shoulder. "She's watching a Disney movie and glued to it. I actually checked to see if she had fallen asleep sitting up with her eyes open and a smile on her face."

I chuckled. "What's she watching?"

"*Frozen.*"

"Oh, one of her favorites."

"Do you have everything under control? It's five, so I should probably slip on out before Truitt gets here."

I glanced around the kitchen. I had the noodles ready to go, the eggplant was in the oven, and a freshly made peach cobbler was sitting on the kitchen island. I'd overheard Truitt back in high school say peach cobbler was his ultimate dessert.

Here's hoping I made it like he likes it.

"I think I'm good. Thank you so much."

We hugged and I checked on Liliana before walking Lucy out to her car. When we stepped out onto the porch, I heard a truck driving down the road. I held my breath until I saw that familiar Ford. I knew it belonged to the handsome cowboy I was having dinner with tonight. My stomach dipped in excitement.

"Look at him, showing up early," Lucy said, sliding into her car and waving goodbye to me. She waited for Truitt to park before she quickly started off down the drive. Maybe she thought I was nervous and would chase after her and beg her to stay. She'd be wrong on that. The moment Truitt stepped out of his truck and looked over at me, my body tingled. It really ought to be a crime for a man to look so gosh-darn handsome.

My cheeks felt hot as I thought about all the things I wanted to learn about his body.

Lord, Saryn, stop with all that silliness, girl.

I watched Truitt walk around the passenger side of his truck. He opened the door and a silver lab came bounding out and running toward me.

"Rus! No, heel!"

The dog skidded to a stop, ran around in a few circles and waited for his human to walk up to him.

"Wow! Did you train him or pay someone?" I called out.

Truitt placed his hand over his heart as if I had wounded him. "I trained him! As if I'd need someone to train my own dog."

At those words, the dog took off in a run and headed straight toward me. At full speed. Tongue flying out his mouth and not a care in the world.

"Oh, no," I whispered.

"Rus! Stay! Heel! Stop! No! Shit! Brace yourself, Saryn."

But before the silver lab could jump up and knock me down, he bounded up the steps, ran around me a few times and then sat. His tail thumped fast and hard, and his whole body seemed to vibrate with pure excitement. I bent down and quickly made a friend. By the way he licked all over me, I'd say we were best friends from the get-go.

"Jesus, this dog is going to be the death of me. I think he just likes to give me heart failure," Truitt mumbled as he held onto his side from the mad dash to try and stop his dog.

I lifted my eyes and my breath caught in my throat. Truitt was looking down at me with a smile on this face. It was in that moment that I knew exactly what I wanted.

Him.

Desperately.

Chapter 20

Truitt

SARYN WAS GAZING up at me with a look in her eyes that made my heart speed up and my cock twitch in my pants.

Shit.

"You keep looking at me like that, Saryn, and things are going to happen very quickly that will go against the slow rule we put into place."

Her teeth dug into her bottom lip, and her cheeks turned a soft shade of red.

"He's beautiful, Truitt. How old is he?"

"Still a pup, six months old. He's really good around kids, though, and I know he'll love Liliana."

"I'm sure she'll fall for him the moment she sees him. Let's head inside."

I paused for a moment. "He can stay out here."

Saryn looked shocked. "What? No! He's coming in. Come on, let's introduce him to Liliana."

When she turned and walked into the house, I couldn't help but take a quick look at her body. Damn. The woman was perfect in every single way. Those curves had a starring role in my dreams last night after sharing a few kisses with her.

She glanced back over her shoulder just in time to see me checking her out like an asshole. I smiled sheepishly.

When she winked at me, I nearly tripped.

"Liliana! I have someone for you to meet!" Saryn called out as I put the leash on Rus in an attempt to keep him under control.

We walked down a small hall and turned into the living room to find Liliana sitting on a white overstuffed cushion on the floor. Her eyes were focused on the TV.

"I see she's been a casualty of the *Frozen* movement."

Saryn turned to look at me. "You've seen *Frozen*."

I gave her my best wounded look for the second time in the last five minutes. "Excuse me, but Roger and I went and saw it the first day it came out."

Her jaw fell open slightly as she stared at me. Before she could say anything, I heard a little gasp, and then a scream of delight.

Liliana came running over and dropped to her knees in front of Rus. I was stunned by how well-behaved my dog was being. He'd been around little kids before, but I knew he could feel Liliana's excitement and he was nearly trembling with his own.

"She loves dogs," Saryn said as she knelt down next to Liliana. "Be nice to Rus, he's still a puppy."

Liliana looked up at her mother and smiled. "Wus? His name is Wus?"

I couldn't help but smile as I looked down at Liliana. Her face was lit up like Christmas morning.

The moment I leaned down and Liliana saw me, she gasped again and smiled the most brilliant smile I'd ever seen. My chest squeezed tight and I didn't want to admit that I loved the way she looked at me with such happiness.

"Twuitt!" She jumped up and ran over to me. When she threw her arms around me, there went another piece of my heart.

Saryn was watching with her own grin on her face, but I also saw a look of concern in her eyes. It had to be hard for her to watch her daughter grow so attached to me and so quickly. A man who wasn't her father. A man who sure as hell hoped he would be a part of their lives. I wasn't a hundred-percent sure what Saryn wanted, but I hoped we were on the same page.

When Liliana abandoned me for my dog again, I said, "You can give him a hug, just be gentle."

Little brown curls bounced as Liliana nodded and then very carefully gave Rus a hug. He thumped his tail in delight. Then Liliana reached for his leash in my hand. I gave it to her and watched as the two of them walked away and into the living room. Rus stayed on his best behavior as he walked next to his new best friend.

"Why do I feel like I just lost my best friend?" I asked with a slight frown.

Saryn chuckled next to me and asked, "Is that the same dog that just nearly plowed me down outside?"

"I think so."

"Truitt, that is the sweetest thing I think I've ever seen. He's such a good boy."

I smiled. "He's on his best behavior this evening."

We both looked at each other and grinned. "Is his daddy also on his best behavior?" Saryn asked, a slight bit of flirtation in her voice.

"He's sure as heck trying to be, but someone is making it sort of hard."

Her cheeks blushed, and she reached up and kissed me quickly on the lips. "You go in with the kids, I'll finish up dinner."

My heart felt like it skipped a couple beats when she mentioned kids. I hadn't ever realized how much I wanted to settle down and have a child of my own until Saryn showed back up in my life with Liliana in tow. I wanted to be a part of their little family, and now it appeared my dog did, as well.

As I walked into the living room, I came to a stop. Liliana was sitting in a giant plush beanbag with Rus snuggled up on it next to her, his head on her lap and her little hand playing with his ear while she watched *Frozen*. I had never seen anything so precious in my life. I was lost and I never wanted to be found.

"You like Rus, Liliana?" I asked, sitting down next to the two of them.

She nodded and gave him a kiss on the head. "I wuv him, Twuitt."

Okay. There went another piece of my heart. God, this girl was the cutest little thing. How in the hell would any father willingly give up this child?

"I'm glad you love him, Liliana. It looks like he loves you, too."

She giggled, then reached for my hand. I gave it to her, thinking she was going to have me pet Rus. Instead, she turned back and started watching *Frozen* again, one hand on Rus, the other holding my hand.

Oh, man. I am in so much trouble.

Rus was soon snoring while Liliana held onto my hand tightly. She giggled at the movie every so often. There was no way I was moving an inch, even though my foot had started to fall asleep. I glanced around the living room and noticed it was decorated in a chic sort of rustic way. It reminded me of Evie's store.

"Who's ready for dinner?" Saryn said from behind us. I turned to look at her and she froze in place, her eyes locked on Liliana's hand in mine.

Saryn looked at me, then over to Rus, then back at our hands again.

"You ready to go eat, little one?" I asked Liliana, withdrawing my hand from hers and reaching over to unclasp Rus's leash. He seemed calm enough around everyone that I felt like he could be trusted.

"Dinner!" Liliana cried out as she jumped up and bounded out of the room, Rus following her.

I stood and gave Saryn a slight smile. "I'm sorry if that was wrong to let her hold my hand."

"What?" she asked, looking a bit confused.

"Holding her hand. I wasn't really sure what to do when I realized what she was doing. I'm sorry if that was overstepping. I'm sorta in new territory here."

Saryn stared at me for a few moments before a stunning grin moved across her face. "I'm new in this area, too. I guess I shouldn't have been surprised by her showing affection toward you. She adores you, Truitt. I think she might have developed a crush when you took her to Build-A-Bear."

I laughed. "Well, I hope her mother feels the same way."

Her eyes turned dark with desire, and I forced myself to swallow. To breathe. To keep my thoughts rated PG.

"Yes, she does. I believe it's moved on from a crush, though."

Breathe, Truitt. Breathe.

"Slow," I whispered, not wanting to, but knowing the way the air was crackling with heat that I needed to.

She nodded, then reached for my hand. "Let's go eat dinner."

We walked into the kitchen, and I took off my cowboy hat and placed it on the counter. I couldn't help but laugh when I saw Liliana waiting there with Rus sitting next to her.

The kitchen was larger than I had expected with the guest house being a bit on the smaller side. It had plenty of counter space and felt bigger because of the white painted cabinets and white granite countertops.

"Truitt, would you mind helping Liliana into her booster seat, and I'll get her plate going?" Saryn asked, giving me a wink as she squeezed my hand.

"It would be my honor to help Princess Liliana into her seat."

Liliana giggled as she jumped up and down with her arms out for me to lift her up.

"Twuitt, can I keep Wus?"

After getting her all settled into her chair, I tapped her on the tip of her nose. "You like him, do you?"

She nodded hard and fast. "He wuvs me, too. You said so."

"I see that!" I said with a slight chuckle.

"Liliana, Rus is Truitt's puppy. He would be so sad if he had to leave him somewhere else and not be able to take him home with him."

Liliana looked down at Rus, then back at me, her little eyes so sad I nearly offered up my own dog just to see her smile again.

"I don't wants him to be sad. Twuitt should stay here wif us, too."

"Oh, gosh," I whispered as I nearly stumbled back.

"Stay strong, Carter," Saryn stated as she placed Liliana's dinner in front of her.

The only thing I could do was nod. It was clear that this little girl would have me wrapped around her finger and playing me like a puppet if I let her.

"I made eggplant parmesan with homemade noodles."

That turned my attention from the beautiful daughter to the even more stunning mother. "You had me at eggplant parmesan."

Saryn smiled as she placed a plate in front of me and motioned for me to sit.

"Rus is not bothering you, is he?" I asked, pointing to the dog sitting patiently by Liliana's plate in hopes of something falling to the floor.

"Nonsense. I love having him here. I've been thinking of getting a puppy for Liliana."

Liliana's face erupted in delight. "Puppy! I want a Wus!"

Both of us laughed at Liliana's declaration.

"Well, I am more than happy to let you borrow mine as much as you like. Of course, he is a package deal."

Saryn gave me a warm smile. "I like that package deal."

I winked at Liliana, causing her to blush, which I thought was precious.

"Okay, I'm starving," I said as I took a bite of food. The moment it hit my taste buds I let out a groan.

With a look that said she was pleased, Saryn asked, "Good?"

"My goodness, woman, you know how to cook."

I loved the happiness in her eyes and decided right then I would compliment her as often as I could, so I could see that look over and over again. I had a feeling her good-for-nothing ex never complimented her.

"Eggplant parmesan is one of our favorites. My grandmother taught me how to make it when I was about thirteen."

"So you've always liked cooking?" I asked before I shoveled more food into my mouth. Out of the corner of my eye I saw Liliana drop the smallest bit of food for Rus. I ignored it when I saw that Saryn had noticed, as well, and didn't say anything.

"I have. I honestly love to cook and bake. Be ready for an epic birthday cake, by the way." She paused. "When is your birthday?"

"December 26."

"The day after Christmas! That has to be a bummer."

I laughed. "Not really. It was like having Christmas two days in a row. At least, growing up it was. My mother never did the whole *I'll split your presents* thing. But to be fair, I usually got something big for my birthday. A truck when I was sixteen. My first shotgun. A dirt bike. Things like that."

"That makes sense, I guess. Do you still like to hunt?"

"Love it. What about you? I remember you going with your dad and Ryan a time or two."

She smiled and nodded. "Yes. Growing up with an older brother and a father who loves to hunt, they started dragging me along when I was about five. Daddy built me my own stand, and he would set up all my Barbie dolls in there. I'm pretty sure a few times I scared away the deer playing make-believe. Ryan used to get so mad at me. But I loved going with them and I do miss it."

I laughed. "Would you like to go with me? Maybe tomorrow if you're able to?"

Her teeth dug into her lip. "I'd love to go. Morning or evening hunt?"

I glanced over to Liliana. "Depends on what's easier for you."

She simply nodded.

The rest of dinner was filled with both of us asking each other questions. We avoided any topics that included Tim or her marriage. She told me about living in Dallas and how much she had thought she wanted out of Boerne when she was in high school, only to realize she missed it. How she had longed to be back home. I told her about my dreams of starting my own business when I realized I didn't want to run the ranch. How my father wasn't too happy with my brother or me when we picked careers that didn't involve ranching.

"Do you work the ranch at all?" Saryn asked as we cleared the plates from the table.

"Roger and I are still a big part of it, but my father does have a lot of hired ranch hands helping him. Roger plays a pretty big role in helping my father on the business side. I think Dad is waiting for me to step in as foreman."

"Will you ever take it over, do you think?"

I shrugged as I watched Saryn fill up the sink and begin washing the dinner dishes. "Probably, someday. It's in my blood. But I wanted to make my own name at something. When I was young I discovered I loved building things. It started when my father was attempting to mend a chicken coop and I made a comment about how he could make it better. He turned and faced me, handed me the hammer, and told me if I thought I knew more than he did, then it was up to me to fix it."

"Did you fix it?" Saryn asked, handing me a dish to dry. I glanced over my shoulder and saw Liliana sitting down at her little table, drawing, Rus laying right at her feet.

I focused back on Saryn. "Did I fix it? I built a new chicken coop."

She busted out laughing. "You did?"

With a nod, I chuckled. "I did. I was ticked off at my father, and it was more to prove a point than anything else. But from that moment on I found myself building anything and everything."

I placed the last dish in the cabinet and took another look at Liliana.

Saryn handed me a glass of wine. "Let me just say I'm impressed you found the wine I liked."

"I can be resourceful when I need to be."

Her cheeks turned a slight pink as she took a sip. Liliana was now in full-on story mode as she held up her picture and explained to Rus what it was all about. He was her captive audience and even appeared to be listening.

We sat down on a sofa in the living room as Liliana pulled out more paper to draw on. She informed Rus he needed to sit still so she could draw him, and the damn dog did just that.

"He really is such a good dog, Truitt," Saryn stated as we watched the two of them.

I scoffed. "Don't let him fool you. He's wants you to think he's a good dog."

Rus looked my way, thumped his tail a few times, then looked back at Liliana. We both laughed.

"So, tell me what got you into building playscapes."

I smiled as the memory came to me. "It started on a dare. A friend of mine was building a playground for his daughter. Mind you, she was only two months old at the time."

Laughing, Saryn took a sip of her wine.

"He really was just so happy to be a father. He was engaged to his high school sweetheart and was honestly madly in love with her. The baby wasn't planned, but both of them were over the moon. He was home on leave from the Air Force, he's a test pilot, and he wanted to make his little girl something. The guy can do anything, I swear...with the exception of build a playground. He was having a hard time of it, and I, of course, made a smart a-double-s comment about how I could do it better."

Saryn shook her head and grinned.

"So, Nolan challenged me. I drew up some plans and asked my father if I could use part of his shop back at the ranch. I designed that playground in the shape of a plane, since he was a pilot and had always loved flying. He used to help his daddy with crop dusting."

She gasped. "Nolan Byers?"

"Yeah. Did you know him?"

Slowly, she replied, "No, but I was friends with Linnzi. She was older than me, but we met at the stables."

I smiled. "Yeah. Linnzi loved her horses, just like you did."

Sadness quickly filled the room. "How is Nolan doing?"

With a shrug, I replied, "He never talks about it. Hasn't been back to Boerne since Linnzi moved."

She reached for my hand. "I'm so sorry, Truitt. I totally forgot about you being such good friends with Nolan. Ryan doesn't much talk about him."

I nodded. "Yeah, I miss him."

Her hand squeezed mine.

"Anyway," I said, "I built the playground and impressed a lot of people with it. It was actually Nolan who encouraged me to start a career in it. So that's how Imaginations Unlimited was born."

"From another dare."

I laughed. "Yep."

"You truly are talented, Truitt. It's clear you love what you do."

Liliana walked up to me, Rus following closely behind. "I dwew this for you, Twuitt."

She handed me a drawing that had a stick person on it and what looked like a dog next to him.

"Is this me and Rus?"

Liliana looked proud as all get out. "Yep!" she said, jumping in excitement.

"I love it, Liliana. I can't wait to hang it up in my house."

That statement earned me another brilliant smile.

"How about we go outside and let Rus run and fetch his favorite ball? Want to do that before it gets too dark out?" I stood and set my wine glass down, looking to Saryn to make sure it was okay.

"I think heading outside sounds like a great idea."

So the three of us, with Rus in tow, headed outside and played fetch. Saryn and I laughed as we watched Liliana run and chase Rus, rolling around on the ground while Rus attempted to do the same. By the time the sun was nearly gone, Liliana and the pup were both worn out and I realized I'd had the best evening I'd ever experienced in my life.

Saryn picked up a very exhausted little girl and started back toward the house. "Want to help me get her ready for bed? Then we can sit in the living room and have another glass of wine if you want."

"That sounds amazing," I said as I turned and whistled for Rus to come.

Chapter 21

Saryn

THE EVENING HAD been perfect, and I didn't want it to end. As I carried Liliana into the house and up the stairs to her room, I realized my little girl was falling asleep.

"Come on, princess, let's get you in your jammies and into bed."

Rus bounded up the steps ahead of me, causing me to smile. He waited at the top, unsure of where I was taking his new best friend.

As I walked into Liliana's room, Rus and Truitt followed me in.

"What can I do to help?" Truitt asked.

I pointed to the bookshelves as I grabbed Liliana's PJs. "Pick out a book, and I'm going to get her teeth brushed."

Truitt nodded and walked over to search for a book to read.

As I walked into the bathroom my mother and I had painted pink with white strips, Liliana giggled.

"What's so funny?" I asked as I sat her on the counter and began to take off her clothes and slip on her pajamas.

"Twuitt. He twipped and fell."

I smiled. Truitt had been playing fetch with Rus and had been running to chase the dog when he tripped over an exposed branch and did a pretty darn impressive tumble roll.

"That was sort of funny. I'm glad he didn't get hurt, though."

My daughter nodded.

"Do you like Truitt?"

She nodded again.

"I like him, too."

Liliana smiled.

"How would you feel if Mommy dated Truitt and he came over for dinner more?"

"Yes, pwease! Wus, too?"

I chuckled. "Yes. Rus, too."

Liliana clapped. "Will Twuitt wead to me tonight?"

"I'm sure he will if you ask him to."

"Okay!"

We brushed her teeth and were soon back in her room. Liliana ran over to Truitt and threw herself into his arms.

"Wead to me, Twuitt! Pwease!"

He glanced my way and I nodded. "She would really love for you to read to her if you don't mind."

"Mind? Are you kidding me? I picked out my most favorite book ever."

Liliana's eyes grew wide with excitement. "Show me!"

Truitt held up *Bears in the Night*.

Liliana jumped in delight and flew up onto her bed. Rus did the same. Truitt turned to look at me to silently ask if it was okay his dog had made himself right at home. I nodded and sat down in the chair across from the bed. Truitt helped Liliana under her covers and sat down on the bed. When I watched Liliana snuggle into his side, my heart melted on the spot.

Her own father had never read her a book once, and to see her take to Truitt like this both thrilled me and, of course, worried me. What if things didn't work out between us? Her little heart would be broken once again, and this time I feared even more, since she was clearly taken with Truitt and now Rus. The dog had laid across the bottom of Liliana's bed and was resting his head on her leg as Truitt started the story.

As I watched the three of them, my heart pounded so loudly I was positive it filled the room. Truitt fell into the story quickly, and I couldn't help but wonder if his own father had read stories like this to him. He was a natural with Liliana. It was painfully clear to me this man would make an amazing father.

Did he want to be a father? Did he truly want an instant family? He seemed like he did, he had said he did. Even Rus seemed to be settled into the idea of it. My stomach dipped as I watched my daughter look at the book and glance up to Truitt as he made his voice change while he read. Then she smiled at him, a smile I had never seen before. When Truitt smiled back down at her, my heart cracked wide open.

Oh, no.

No. No. No. No.

It wasn't possible. There was no way I was falling in love with this man already. Maybe a part of me had always been in love with him, and that was why it felt so right. So amazingly perfect.

Don't be silly, Saryn, it was a crush. That was all. A crush.

Yet, I had been almost devastated that day he walked away from me. It was honestly the first and only time in my life my heart had broken. Not even when I found out Tim had cheated on me had my heart hurt like it did that day.

Liliana laughed and broke me from my thoughts. I glanced over to the bed and couldn't help but smile.

I needed to be careful with Truitt Carter. He held the power to break my heart into a million pieces—and my daughter's, too.

His eyes lifted and met mine, and I felt the air in the room change. Something intense, yet beautiful, crackled between us. We both smiled, and I saw it in his eyes.

There was no doubt about it, I was falling in love with Truitt. I was almost positive he felt the same way about me.

Oh, help me.

Liliana fell asleep with Truitt reading her a book. Rus also fell asleep, and I was almost positive if I left him there, Truitt would have dozed off.

He handed me the book and carefully slipped from the bed. I tucked the covers around Liliana and kissed her gently on the forehead. She let out a contented sigh, which made Rus do the same. I almost laughed as I turned and saw Truitt glaring at his dog. When our gaze met, he shook his head.

"Can Rus spend the night?" I asked.

That made Truitt's brows jerk up before he rolled his eyes and nodded. When we got to the living room, I poured us both another glass of wine.

"I can't believe my dog gets to spend the night and I don't."

With a giggle, I sat down next to him on the sofa.

"Liliana adores you."

He placed his hand in mine and rubbed his thumb over my skin, causing a million little bolts of electricity to pulse through my body. I loved this feeling. It was all so new and so amazing.

"I adore her, too. I think I fell for her the moment y'all came bounding into my office. She stole my heart right then with Muke."

"Just her?"

He squeezed my hand tighter. "No, not just her. You stole my heart when I was sixteen years old."

I stilled but then looked up at him. "Really? Why didn't you ask me out, Truitt?"

With a laugh that sounded forced, he shrugged. "Ryan was my best friend. I thought you were off limits. Plus, I was older than you."

"Not by much!" I argued. "A whole year!"

He smiled. "When I got up the courage to ask you out, it was too late. Tim beat me to it."

Tim's words from earlier today came back to me. "He told me he found out you were going to ask me out and that's why he did it first."

That made Truitt's body go rigid. "What? When did he say that?"

I moved back some so I could look at him. "Today, he stopped by the house and asked me if we were seeing each other. I, of course, told him it was none of his business, but he went on to tell me he asked me out to save me from you because you only wanted..."

My voice trailed off.

"I only wanted what?"

"To have sex with me."

A look of pure anger flashed across Truitt's face. "So that was the reason he asked you out? What in the hell did you ever see in him, Saryn?"

I laughed. "I'm not sure, but I know what he said isn't true."

He lifted a brow. "Really? Because you don't seem like you believe that."

"Was it true? Did you see me as some sort of quest to conquer?"

He answered instantly. "No. I saw you as a girl I was extremely attracted to. One of my best friend's sisters, someone I was afraid would turn me down if I did ask her out."

"Turn you down? Why in the world would you think that?"

"You were...and you still are...very beautiful. You could have had your pick of any guy at our school. Of course, your brother threatened to kill anyone who looked at you the wrong way. Tim was the only one with enough guts to ask you out, so I guess I can't fault him for that. But I didn't just want in your pants, Saryn. I liked you. A lot."

I swallowed hard. "I liked you, too, and always thought you were out of my reach. You were, and still are, so very handsome. Truitt, you could have dated any girl at that school. I heard them talking about being with you. You never hid the fact that you were a bit of a player. It used to make me so insanely jealous. Are you still?"

His eyes locked with mine. "Most of those rumors you heard are not true. Half the girls in this town have said I've slept with them and I haven't. I'm not a saint, Saryn. I played the bachelor role in my early years, but I'm not that guy anymore and I haven't been in a long time."

"Why haven't you settled down and gotten married?" I asked before I took a sip of my wine. My heart suddenly felt like it was racing in my chest. I feared he would say he had fallen in love once. He had wanted to marry someone, but it hadn't worked out for some reason. I prayed Shay wasn't the woman he'd fallen for. A jealous energy rushed through my body and I knew I had no right to feel that way.

He gave me a half shrug. "I guess I never met the one. Or maybe I had met her, and she left town with an idiot for a husband, and I could never find another woman to fill her shoes."

Thud. There went my heart, straight to my stomach.

"Truitt, you honestly don't expect me to believe you're talking about me. You hardly ever noticed me."

"That's what you think, Saryn."

I was positive I gave him a skeptical look. He laughed and shook his head.

"In Spanish class when you couldn't figure out an answer on the test, you would tap your nose with your pencil until you came up with it. I'm pretty sure you still do it, because I saw you in the ER tapping your nose. When you played soccer you always stopped and helped up anyone who fell, even someone on the other team. You hate to eat your tacos in a soft shell, you don't like vanilla ice cream, and..."

His eyes met mine and locked. "And you have the most beautiful brown eyes I've ever seen."

I felt a tear slip free and make a slow trail down my cheek. I was too shocked to even attempt to hide it. To hide the fact that I was desperately trying not to cry. Truitt reached over and gently brushed it away with his thumb while I attempted to form words. Any words. At least one word.

Nothing would come. I stared at him in disbelief.

"You think I didn't notice you, sweetheart. I noticed, believe me...I noticed."

"Truitt."

It was the only word I could manage to say. I wanted desperately to kiss him. To pull him into my bed and beg him to make love to me. I wanted to know what having a man make love to me felt like, because suddenly every single moment I was with Tim felt like it wasn't real. None of it was real. The only good thing I received from Tim was sleeping upstairs with Truitt's dog guarding her like she was his greatest treasure.

"You're looking at me like you don't want this to go slow, and we need it to go slow."

I shook my head. "We don't need it to go slow."

"We don't?" he asked, a smirk appearing on his face.

"No," I replied with a shake of my head as I set my wine glass down, then took his glass from his hand and placed it next to mine. I stood and reached for his hands. "I need you to kiss me, while I'm naked, in my bed, with your body over mine."

Truitt moaned as he closed his eyes. "Saryn, you said—"

"I don't care what I said, Truitt. No man has ever made me feel like this before. Ever. Please don't deny me this, because I think we've wanted this for over ten years now."

"Don't deny you?" he repeated with a laugh. "You don't have to beg me, sweetheart, I wanted you the moment I pulled over to change your tire."

The smile on his face made my insides melt. A rush of heat sprinted through my body, making me ache everywhere, especially between my legs.

"Will you make love to me, Truitt?"

He reached down and picked me up, eliciting a small gasp followed by a giggle.

"Nothing would make me happier, sweetheart."

My mouth crushed against his and he started to walk. When he tripped over my rug, we both laughed.

"Maybe I should walk, and you follow me to the bedroom," I said as I looked down at the rug he'd tripped over.

"Are you saying you think I'll drop you?"

My gaze met his, and I loved how his eyes crinkled at the corners when he smiled at me. A true smile that screamed he was happy simply to be in my presence.

"I am very much saying that," I said. "If you drop me, we're both going to get hurt, and then I won't have the orgasm I am desperately needing from you."

In that moment he let my legs fall to the ground while he still held onto me with his hand. I busted out laughing, grabbed his hand,

and guided him into the master bedroom. One quick check of the front door and we were soon standing in my bedroom. I suddenly felt like that shy sixteen-year-old girl who used to admire Truitt from a distance. The girl who stood on the sidelines as he played football and cheered him on. Or watched him and my brother work the cattle on branding day, trying not to act like I'd been studying every single move Truitt made. Or the girl who laid in bed at night and wished that Truitt would notice me. Ask me out. Tell me he wanted me.

A part of me wanted to weep that we had lost so much time together, but the other part knew we had both gone on our journeys separately for a reason. I wouldn't regret it, not when I had Liliana.

Truitt walked up to me and cupped my face within his hands. "Are you sure about this?"

I nodded and whispered, "Yes, I'm sure."

He brushed his lips lightly across my forehead and mumbled, "You look nervous."

My eyes closed, and I told myself to be honest with him. I needed that from him, so I had to give it in return. "I'm scared to death and feel like this is my first time all over again."

He ran his thumbs over my cheeks and smiled so sweetly I felt my knees shake.

"Then we'll go slow."

When his mouth came to mine, it felt as if something inside my chest exploded in a fury of mad craziness. I had never felt this way before. I had only been with two men, and neither of them pulled out this feeling in me.

I needed to make sure I wasn't dreaming.

"Pinch me," I softly said against his mouth.

Truitt chuckled. "Getting kinky a little early on, aren't we?"

Smiling, I hit his chest and said, "Pinch me so I know this is really happening and I'm not dreaming."

He dropped his hand from my face, reached behind me, and gave my ass a good pinch.

"Ouch!" I cried out in a loud whisper.

"Sounds like you're awake to me."

"Thank God," I said with a smile as he picked me up and I wrapped my legs around him.

When he pushed me against the bedroom door, he moaned into my mouth, "Yes, thank God."

Chapter 22

Truitt

IWAS IN Saryn's bedroom. Her legs were wrapped around me as she pushed herself against my hard dick. She wanted me. My God, the woman I had dreamed about so many times wanted me.

Fuck, someone pinch me and make sure I'm not the one dreaming.

Our kiss deepened and something inside me ached with anticipation. Her hands pushed into my hair and she tugged slightly, which caused me to push into her core. She dropped her head back and gasped for air.

"Touch me. Truitt, I need you to touch me somewhere. Please."

Her begging only added fuel, and I had to force myself not to rip her shirt off. This woman deserved to be treated like a princess. A queen. Not to mention, her brother would kill me if he knew I fucked her like a madman against a door.

I spun us around, walked her over to her bed, and gently laid her down.

"Where do you want me to touch you, sweetheart?"

Her eyes burned with desire as she arched her back up toward me. "God, anywhere, everywhere. With your hands, your mouth, Truitt, please."

Holy fuck. "Jesus, I think I've died and gone to heaven."

She smiled as she sat up and pulled her shirt over her head, leaving me with a view of her in a white lace bra. Her nipples pressed hard against the fabric and caused me to let out yet another moan of delight. I had dreamed of this woman's body for so many years, and none of those dreams were even coming close to reality.

I reached behind my back and pulled my own shirt over my head and tossed it to the floor. Saryn's eyes moved over my body with an intensity that made me shiver.

"If you keep looking at me like that, I may come in my pants and embarrass the hell out of myself," I said.

She giggled, then crawled over to the end of the bed and reached for my belt. She quickly undid it, then went to work on unbuttoning and unzipping my jeans.

Deep breath, Carter. Deep breath. Don't come the moment she touches you, please don't lose your load.

Saryn looked up and met my gaze while she pushed my jeans down over my hips and freed my cock. Her eyes darted down and she licked her lips before meeting my gaze again.

"I'm telling you, if you want this to last, do not touch me."

Her teeth dug into her lower lip, and she batted her eyelashes at me.

"One taste, Truitt? Please."

"No," I said as I placed my finger on her chin and reached down to kiss her quickly. "Later, right now I want to taste you."

"Oh," she breathed out. "I've never…"

With a frown, I pulled back. "Tim never…?" I stopped my words because simply thinking of him touching her made me want to punch the living shit out of him.

She shook her head. "I've only ever been with two men. Tim and that stupid one-night stand, which was nothing to brag about."

I smiled and took a step back to kick off my boots and finish taking off my jeans. Saryn followed my lead and quickly got undressed.

"Lie back on the pillow, baby, I'm going to give you that orgasm you want."

She scrambled so quickly I had to force myself not to laugh. I crawled onto the bed, and she sat up with a jolt.

"Wait! We need to lock the bedroom door."

I nodded and quickly made my way over to the door. Stepping on something sharp, I covered my mouth to keep from crying out.

"What the fuck?" I said as I reached down and held up the smallest little shoe I'd ever seen. "I've just punctured my foot with a tiny high heel."

"Barbie doll shoe, toss it to the side."

Toss it to the side, my ass. If I knew myself, I'd step on it again. I placed it on a side table, then locked the door. I was headed back to the bed when Saryn said, "No, wait! What if she tries to open the door and can't and she panics? We'd better keep it unlocked."

"Okay," I replied, turning and unlocking the door.

When I faced her again, she smiled and sank back down on the pillows. "She won't wake up. Liliana is a heavy sleeper, always has been."

"Just make sure you're quiet," I warned as I crawled onto the bed and placed my hands on her hips. The feel of her body under my hands was the best thing I'd ever felt in my life.

"Let me touch you, feel you, for just a minute or two," I said, my hands running over her silky-smooth skin.

Saryn moaned softly, squirmed and arched her body as I ran my fingers over her. When I got to her breasts, I cupped them both and then took one nipple into my mouth. Her fingernails dug into my back as she arched her breasts closer to me. My other hand ran down her side and between her legs. She spread open, and I quickly slipped a finger inside her warm, wet body.

"Oh, my God. Truitt!"

She was wet, so fucking wet. I pulled my finger out and rubbed her desire over her clit while I continued to suck and nibble on her hard peak. Saryn jerked her hips and let out a soft, low moan. "Yes. That feels so good. Please don't stop."

I smiled and lifted my gaze to watch her. Eyes closed, hands gripped on the headboard, and her mouth open ever so slightly.

It was the hottest thing I'd ever seen in my life. I wanted to make her come in every way I possibly could. The plan had been to make her come with my hand, then my mouth, but I abandoned that and moved my mouth down her body.

"Truitt, I..."

"Shh, let me make you feel good, sweetheart."

She nodded while she chewed nervously on her lip.

I took my hands and spread her open wider, moaning at just the thought of tasting her. Being the first man to kiss her, taste her, make her come on my tongue. Shit, the thought of it nearly had me coming myself.

"God, you're fucking perfect," I whispered before I licked my way through her brown curls to the tight bud of nerves that desperately needed my attention. I loved that she wasn't shaved bare.

Saryn let out a gasp, then pushed her fingers into my hair.

"Oh, my...Truitt."

Her voice was soft with a slight shake to it. I went slow, taking my time as I savored her sweetness. Her legs trembled, and I knew it wouldn't take much to make her come. Being the selfish bastard I was, though, I wanted this to last a bit longer. I pulled back and kissed around her soft lips, pushing a finger, then two, inside of her.

"Wait. No. So close," she gasped out, attempting to push my mouth back to her clit.

I chuckled. "Not yet, I'm still playing."

"Truitt." Her head thrashed back and forth on the pillow and I nearly died when I saw her pinch one of her nipples.

"Does it feel good, baby?" I asked, pumping my fingers faster.

"Yes. More. Please."

The moment I pressed my mouth back to her clit I knew she was going to fall apart quickly. I licked, sucked, and stroked, until she covered her mouth to hide her moans of pleasure. I held onto her hips to keep her still, and I kept going until her body went limp.

I slowly crawled up her body and smiled when I saw her eyes closed and a very satisfied smile on my girl's face.

"How are you feeling?" I asked while I placed soft kisses around her neck.

"Can't speak. No words."

I laughed and rubbed my nose over hers. "May I kiss you after that?"

Her eyes opened and she nodded, a shy smile on her beautiful face.

When I kissed her and she opened her mouth to me, she let out a slight moan, and I swore my cock grew harder. I wanted to ask her if she liked the taste of herself on her tongue. I wanted to beg her to let me do that to her every single day for the rest of our lives.

She pulled back slightly and sheepishly asked, "Do you want me to...?"

"No. I want to be inside you, but we have to have the talk." "The one where we give each other a safe word?" she asked with a wink.

"You really are trying to make me come before I even feel you, aren't you? I was sort of thinking we'd hold off on the kinky stuff until at least the second date."

She gave me a fake pout. "Okay, fine. No kink. In all seriousness, I'm on the pill, and like I said earlier, I've only been with two men. The whole one-night stand disaster, he wore a condom. And Tim, I don't honestly think in the last five years we had sex more than twice."

The fact that she didn't enjoy that one-night stand made my chest feel a hell of a lot lighter.

"I wish I could say I've only had two partners, but I've had a bit more."

"Don't tell me a number, I don't care about your past. The only thing I care about is that we're exclusive. I don't think my heart could take it if you...I mean...I know this seems so soon and all, but I...ugh."

With a smile, I kissed her gently on the lips. "I have strong feelings for you, too, and I swear to you, Saryn, I will never cheat on you or do anything that would hurt you or Liliana. Not when I've waited for you all this time."

Her eyes widened and then glassed over as if she might cry. I pulled back, but she grabbed onto me.

"No, I'm okay. It's just, I've never met a man like you before. The way you not only think of me, but of Liliana, as well. It's so damn refreshing. Her own father never gave her much thought. Yet you take her into account with everything. Why is that?"

"She's a part of you. That makes her someone I care deeply for. Truth be told, that little girl already has me wrapped around her finger."

Saryn laughed. "She really does."

"So, back to the talk. I've never had sex with any partner without wearing a condom."

"Okay."

"Speaking of, do you have any?"

Her eyes widened in horror. "Why in the world would I have condoms, Truitt?"

I shrugged. "It was worth a try. I have some, but they're in my truck. Let me run out and get them."

When I went to move, she reached for my arm. "Wait. What if you trip and fall and break something? You do remember the penile fracture, don't you?"

With a frown, I stared at her. "Seriously? I wasn't hard when the branch hit me!"

She smiled but then turned serious. "Well, you do have a bit of bad luck when it comes to getting hurt. We're so close to making love, and I have this terrible feeling something is going to get in our way."

"Nothing is going to get in the way. I'll be right back." I quickly kissed her on the lips and then jumped out of bed. I reached for my boxers and slipped them on before I headed toward her door.

"You're going out in your boxers?" she asked, sitting up on her elbows.

"Yeah."

Shaking her head, she laughed. "Truitt, what if my parents see you, or worse yet, Ryan?"

That made me pause and think for a moment. "Wait!"

I reached into my pocket and pulled out my wallet. Reaching behind one of the folds, I found two condoms. I lifted it up and smiled.

"Emergency condoms."

This time it was her turn to frown. "I don't know how I should feel about you having emergency condoms in your wallet."

Laughing, I dropped my jeans and wallet and slipped out of the boxers.

"My father made us put them in our wallets the first time he ever had the talk with us. Told us to always keep one in there because you never know when the mood will strike."

She rolled her eyes and attempted to hide her smile.

"Now, where were we?" I asked while I kissed up her leg.

"I think you were about to take me to heaven again."

Laughing, I settled between her legs and used my mouth to do just that.

Chapter 23

Saryn

MY CHEST ROSE and fell as I gasped for air. The orgasm was building quickly, and I reached for the pillow next to me and pushed it against my face as I tumbled straight over into another freefall that had my entire body trembling with pleasure.

His mouth. His tongue. His fingers. Lord, the man was stimulating me everywhere all at once and it felt glorious. And something about Truitt being the only man to have ever given me oral sex made it seem even hotter.

My fingers pushed through his hair as I shamelessly rocked my hips against his face. I came so hard I nearly screamed. How was it possible the second orgasm was more intense then the first?

Oh, yes, I could get very used to this indeed.

I used my hand to push his mouth away when I felt like I couldn't take anymore. The orgasm seemed to go on forever, and if it didn't stop I was pretty sure I might die from it.

When he moved his body away, I tossed the pillow to the floor and looked at him. He was sitting on his knees, his very impressive dick in his hand as he rolled the condom on.

Lord up in heaven, I was finally going to be with him. The man who had starred in my fantasy the very first time I figured out how to make myself come with my fingers.

Real life was so much better than my dreams.

He looked up and our eyes met. When he smiled and the corners of his eyes crinkled and his dimples came out in full force, I swore I almost sighed. The man was beyond handsome. He was breathtaking. I was positive the angels sang the day Truitt was born.

"You okay?" he asked while he moved up my body and placed soft kisses along the way.

"I'm more than okay. I feel like I'm living out a fantasy."

He raised a brow and then chuckled. "Maybe I'm the one who might need that safe word."

With a chuckle, I shook my head. "I'll stow it away until our next date."

He settled between my body as I opened my legs and felt my lower stomach pull with anticipation as he pressed against me. He leaned down and gave each of my breasts attention while I arched into him, longing for more of him. More of the heat his mouth was providing. More of the pressure he was giving me between my legs. I had just had the orgasm to end all orgasms, and my body was craving more.

Then he looked up and our eyes met.

"You have no idea how long I've waited for this moment, Saryn."

Oh. My. There went the last wall around my heart. It crumbled and opened wide for this man and this man alone.

Please, please don't hurt me, Truitt.

"Truitt," I whispered as I laced my fingers into his thick, dark hair. His blue eyes seemed to look directly into my soul, asking for permission to own me, body and soul, and I gave it all to him. Willingly. "I want you desperately. All of you."

He smiled and reached between us, aligning himself with me, and then slowly pushed inside. I gasped at the feel of him, hard and thick. Goodness, he felt like heaven. When he stilled, I wrapped my legs around him, drawing him in deeper.

"Fuck, you're so goddamn tight."

"More," I panted right before he pressed his mouth to mine and he pushed in deeper.

"Jesus," he groaned. "I can't move...if I move I'm going to end this before it even begins."

With a huge smile on my face, I ran my fingers lightly over his back. The muscles this man had were insane. Each movement made them flex under my touch. A girl could get so used to this.

"As wonderful as this feels with you inside me, I have a feeling we could make it even better if you moved just a little," I whispered as I placed a kiss on his neck.

"Better? This is fucking amazing, Saryn. You're amazing."

My chest tightened with his words, and when he moved, I felt myself come alive even more.

"Yes," I gasped when he pulled out and pushed in harder.

"Fucking hell. Yous feel so good," he gasped as he moved faster. His hands slipped under my ass, pulling me even closer to him. "I can't get close enough. Deep enough."

My legs wrapped around him tighter, as did my arms. I needed him deeper.

"Truitt. I think...oh my...I'm going to come again," I softly cried out as he adjusted his hips and hit a spot that instantly sent me into a tailspin. Stars felt like they burst in front of my eyes, and I buried my face into his neck while I moaned in pleasure.

"Saryn, oh God, I'm going to come."

The feel of him swelling inside me sent me into another orgasm and we came together. His body moved fast and hard into mine and I held onto him with all my might.

When he slowed and our panting mixed together, I loosened my grip around his neck some, but not all the way. I was almost afraid to let him go. Fear instantly took a hold of my heart and squeezed, nearly throwing me into a panic attack. Now that I had Truitt, I never wanted to let him go.

"That was unlike anything I've ever experienced before in my life, sweetheart," he mumbled into my ear. "I hope you know that no other man will ever be making love to you again."

The tightness in my chest instantly faded away, and I relaxed my body. Truitt was still inside me, and it didn't appear he was in much of a hurry to withdraw, which was fine by me.

"I'm totally okay with that just as long as you know it works both ways."

He buried his face in my neck, and I felt my entire body shudder from the sweet kisses he gave me.

"Deal."

I had no idea how long we stayed there. Truitt balancing his weight over me, his body still joined with mine. It was a blissful peace I had never felt before, and I longed to feel it every single day.

"You know I'm going to have to go out to my truck and get more condoms. I can't just do this twice and then leave. I have a feeling I'll be sneaking out of here before dawn."

Laughing, I ran my fingers through his hair and let out a contented sigh.

"That was the best sex of my life, and that is not a lie," I said.

"I agree. Let me go get this condom off and show you what else I can do with my mouth."

He pulled out of me and I instantly felt the loss. When he rolled off of me, I reached for him. "Truitt, this is going to sound cheesy, maybe a little weird."

Truitt stopped moving and looked at me. "What?"

"I've always wanted to have sex in the shower."

His shoulders slumped. "How did you conceive your child? Immaculate conception? Does that asshole even know how to fuck?"

I covered my mouth with my hand as I gasped and then laughed. "Yes!" I said, hitting him on the chest. "He was just very boring in the bedroom."

"No wonder you had the one-night stand. You should have come to me for that, by the way."

With a roll of my eyes, I sat up and reached for his hand. "Would you mind making another fantasy come true?"

"Baby, you don't have to ask me twice. You're lucky I'm always doubly prepared. Can't complain about the two condoms now."

He stood up and pulled me to my feet, then reached for a tissue from the box on my nightstand. He pulled the condom off and wrapped it up.

"Grab the other one and I'll meet you in the bathroom."

He pulled me to him and kissed me quickly before he smacked my ass and told me to go start the shower.

I practically skipped into the bathroom. I was on a high that I never wanted to come down from. It was still early in the evening, so it wouldn't be strange for Truitt to still be over here. I was just glad my mother hadn't wandered over to stick her nose in.

After I turned the shower on and adjusted the temperature, I stepped inside. The hot water running over my still-sensitive skin caused me to groan in delight. Then I felt him behind me. His hands wrapped around me and cupped my breasts as he pushed me into the cold tile wall. I gasped from the cold, then nearly melted when I felt his hardness pressed against my body.

"You're hard already?" I asked, suddenly feeling shy again.

"I have a feeling me being hard around you is not going to be a problem for us."

I went to turn, but he pressed me harder against the wall.

"Tell me, Saryn. Did your fantasy about shower sex involve making love or being fucked?"

My eyes closed and I felt my stomach tumble at his words. I loved hearing him talk to me that way. I'd be able to check that off my Truitt Carter fantasy wish list.

Amazing in bed. Check.

Dirty talker. Check.

"Tell me what you want, baby."

I shivered from the anticipation of him taking me. Would he take me from behind? Just like this? God, I wanted him to so desperately.

With a deep breath, I told Truitt exactly what I wanted. "I want to be fucked. Like this, from behind."

He kissed along my neck, his hands moving up and down my arm. I was beginning to feel dizzy from his touch. "Have you ever been fucked from behind?"

I shook my head, and I heard him cuss softly and say something about another first for us. I smiled.

"Saryn, I need you to tell me if it becomes uncomfortable. If I hurt you. Promise me."

His hand slid down my stomach to play with my clit. I pressed back against him and tried to spread my legs apart for him.

"Promise me."

With a gasp of air, I said, "I promise! I swear I'll tell you."

In that moment I would have promised him anything just to feel him inside me once more.

Truitt lifted my leg and pressed his mouth against my ear. "Place your hands on the wall."

I did as he said. His one hand played with my clit while the other guided himself to my entrance.

"I've got you, baby," he whispered as he pushed slowly inside of me. The feeling was completely different. I honestly felt like I was having sex for the first time. He filled me to the core and I loved it. The hot water, the sting of him stretching me, the feel of the cold tiles against my body, and Truitt inside of me. It all made my head swirl and my knees tremble.

"You okay?"

I nodded.

He moved slowly at first, allowing me to adjust to the feel of him this way. I soon found myself pressing against him when he thrust into me.

"Christ, Saryn. You're so fucking sexy."

"Truitt!" I gasped, my head dropping back as he kissed along my neck and pulled out of me, only to push back in harder and faster each time. "Yes! Don't stop. It feels so good."

"I'm not going to last long, baby. Are you close?"

I groaned in frustration. Every delicious thrust pushed me closer, but my orgasm felt out of reach.

"Touch yourself, Saryn."

My eyes shot open, and I held my breath for a moment. Then I did as he said. It only took a few strokes of my fingers against my clit and I was coming hard. I could feel my body squeeze around him. Truitt pulled out and pushed into me harder.

"Saryn," he panted, his breath hot against my skin as the water rained down on us. "Fuck, you're squeezing me. God, I'm coming. It feels...fuck...so good."

I absolutely loved that Truitt talked to me during sex. I loved that he told me it felt good. That I was beautiful. And when he told me he was coming, it damn near made me come all over again.

After he stopped moving, he gently pulled out of me and then lowered my leg. I turned to face him, and before I could say a word, his mouth was on mine. He lifted me up, and I wrapped my leg around him. Then he was back inside me, moving ever so slowly. I could tell he was going down, but it still felt amazing.

He stopped moving and pressed his forehead to mine. The water cascaded down around us and relaxed me even more. "I'm sorry I lost control. Did I hurt you?"

"Hurt me?" I repeated with a laugh. "God, no. I wanted more. Needed more. That was ... that was something we will need to do often."

Truitt laughed and looked into my eyes. "I take pleasure in watching you fall apart when you come, because, trust me, it is the most beautiful thing ever to watch you have an orgasm."

My face felt hot and I pressed my lips together tightly.

"Let me clean you up."

Truitt lifted me up like I weighed nothing, then pulled out of me again. Like earlier, I missed the connection we shared when he was inside of me. He set me down and then froze. His body went rigid, and his face drained of all color.

"What's wrong?" I asked.

He looked up at me, something etched on his face that was unreadable.

"Truitt, what's wrong?" My voice was filled with worry.

His throat bobbed hard as he swallowed, and his brows pulled in tight. "The condom broke."

My eyes immediately went down, only to see that the end of the condom was indeed broken. For a moment I simply stood there, staring at it. How in the world had that happened?

Truitt turned and stepped out of the shower. I quickly turned off the water and followed him. He reached for a towel and wrapped me up in it, the broken condom still on. It touched my heart that he wanted to take care of me even when I knew he was most likely freaking out inside.

"That has never happened to me before. Never. I'm so sorry, Saryn. I...I don't know why that happened. It wasn't an old condom. Well, maybe it was older than I thought. Fuck." His fingers jerked through his hair.

I waited for him to remove it and wrap a towel around his waist before I walked over to him and placed my hands on his chest.

"Truitt, breathe. It's okay. I told you, I'm on the pill."

"But..."

My fingers pressed against his lips. "Shh...you're freaking out and it's starting to freak me out. Take a breath."

He did as I asked him to do.

"Listen to me, I'm on the pill. I know that isn't one-hundred percent effective, but it's better than me not being on the pill. It's going to be okay."

With a simple nod, he said, "I'm sorry. I'd never put you in a situation you didn't want to be in."

I placed my hand over his cheek and smiled. "We're both adults, and I'm pretty sure we both understand what sex can lead to. I'm not worried, and I need you to not be worried."

"I'm not worried. I want kids."

My mouth dropped open and I was pretty sure I was rapidly blinking at him in my state of shock.

"I mean, someday. Not right now. With you. I mean, I would love to have kids with you, not right now, unless it happened then I would be happy. I think. I don't know, I mean, I do, I would, but talking about that right now seems kind of weird since we're only on our first date and I've already unloaded my seed in you."

He closed his eyes and cursed. "Okay, that didn't come out right and sounded so unromantic. My mother would probably smack me if she ever heard me say I unloaded my seed in a woman. I just meant—"

"Truitt."

"Yeah?" he asked, his eyes meeting mine.

"Maybe you should stop talking now."

With a quick nod, he replied, "Okay. I will. Right now."

"Should we call it a night?" I asked, hating that our evening might end on a sour note like this.

"Do you want to?"

I chewed on my lip. "Well, you did promise to do naughty things to me with your mouth again."

He smiled, and I couldn't help the bubble of excitement that rose up in my chest.

"And I am a man of my word."

Truitt led me back into the bedroom and spent the rest of the night showing me all kinds of wonderful, naughty things he could do with his mouth and his hands. When I couldn't take anymore, I dropped onto the bed and sighed as I felt myself drift into euphoria with Truitt wrapping his arms around me and pulling me to him.

"Five minutes. I'm going to rest my eyes for five minutes," I whispered as I drifted off to sleep.

Chapter 24

Truitt

"TWUITT?"

"Mmm?"

"Twuitt, I had a baw dweam."

I stretched out my arms and let out a groan. "A bad dream?" I said as a yawn slipped out.

"Ah huh. Wus did, too, cause he was scared."

I smiled. I didn't want to wake up and ruin the dream I was clearly having.

"Can I sweep with you and Mommy?"

That made me open my eyes with a start. Standing right at eye level was a little blue-eyed, curly-brown-haired girl clutching a white rabbit. Next to her was Rus, his tongue out as he stood there and bounced his gaze from me to Liliana.

"Liliana?" I asked, squeezing my eyes shut and then opening them as I prayed this was all a dream.

When my eyes met hers again, she smiled. "Twuitt!"

Oh. Shit.

I looked over my shoulder and saw Saryn sleeping like a beautiful queen who had been given a dose of drugs that caused her to drift into a hard slumber. Why hadn't she heard Liliana talking? Weren't moms supposed to have some sort of super-hearing or some shit like that?

Facing Liliana again, I quickly took in the situation. There was no way she was getting up into this bed. For one, I was butt-ass naked. Two, I was completely naked. Three, I was naked.

"Um, how about I take you back up to your room with Rus, and we read another book?"

Even in the dark I could see her eyes light up. "Okay!" she said, bouncing up and down on her toes.

Okay, how do I get out of bed when I'm naked? I glanced around and saw a robe draped over the chair in the corner.

"Sweetheart, will you hand me that robe?" I asked as I pointed to it. Rus looked in the direction I was pointing, and then back at me. If I hadn't known any better, I would swear the bastard was smiling.

"This isn't funny!" I snapped at him.

Liliana rushed over and got the robe, and then rushed back to hand it to me.

"Turn around and close your eyes for me, okay?"

With a nod, she did as I asked. I slipped out of bed and put the robe on so fast I was positive I broke some world record. I turned and looked at Saryn. She looked so peaceful sleeping, and if I woke her up and she knew Liliana had walked in on us in bed together, she would freak out.

I took Liliana's hand and very quietly walked us out of the bedroom. Once I shut the door, I scooped her up and bounded up the steps with Rus on my heels.

Liliana giggled and wrapped her arms tightly around my neck. "I wuv you, Twuitt."

My God. There was no way my heart could take any more tonight. None. If I hadn't already given this little girl my heart, she fully owned it now.

After tucking her back into bed, I picked out another book and strained to read it by the nightlight in her room. It didn't take long before she drifted back to sleep, her head on my arm and her little hand clasping mine. I glanced at Rus who was sitting next to the bed, looking at me with pleading eyes.

"You woke her up, didn't you?"

He whined and looked down.

"You couldn't have come and just woken me up, could you?"

The sound of his tail thumping the floor caused me to roll my eyes.

After carefully slipping out of Liliana's bed, I motioned for Rus to follow me back downstairs. He ran to the front door and waited.

"You're gonna have to learn to hold your pee, buddy, if you want to spend the night here."

The moment I opened the door, Rus caught sight of a cat and took off running at full speed, barking. I had no idea what in the hell time it was, but there wasn't a light on at Evie and Will's house, which led me to believe it was late.

"No! Heel! Stop!" I whisper-shouted as I took off running after him. Before I knew it, I was jumping a hedge, running through the garden and chasing Rus, who was still chasing the cat, all through Saryn's front yard. Dressed in her robe, in my bare feet.

Finally, the cat ran up a tree and Rus stopped in front of it and decided to start barking. When I reached him and was about to grab onto his collar, he heard a noise to his left and took off running, pulling me with him, which caused me to lose my balance and fall. The moment I felt something in my knee tear, I cursed. I clutched my knee and let out a moan. I looked up and saw Ryan standing in front of me and instantly I knew I was fucked.

"Oh, hey there, Ryan," I said, attempting to stand and groaning in pain as a burning sensation ripped through my knee.

"Hey, Truitt."

He looked me up and down, and then slowly shook his head.

"I can explain," I said, trying to push away the pain in my knee. It was then I noticed Rus sitting next to Ryan, looking as innocent as could be.

Ryan folded his arms over his chest and smirked. "Oh, I cannot wait to hear this."

"Well, you're probably wondering why I'm dressed in your sister's robe," I said, attempting to laugh, only to stop when he raised one brow.

"That would be a good place to start."

"Well, I needed to wear something because Liliana woke up from a bad dream and…"

The moon was full and I could see Ryan almost perfectly, so when the muscle in his neck twitched, I stopped talking and took a few steps back, as best I could with the pain in my right knee.

"Um, Saryn was passed out sleeping and didn't hear Liliana, so I had to walk her back up to her room, and I couldn't very well let her see me naked."

"Naked."

My hand rubbed the back of my neck. "Yeah. Um."

I swallowed hard and glanced over my shoulder, willing Saryn to wake up. Damn me and my ability to make a woman pass out from sheer pleasure.

"I spilled something on myself."

He tilted his head and regarded me. "Want to try again?"

"I needed to do my laundry?"

Ryan shook his head.

"Your sister seduced me into a night of utter pleasure and I accidentally might have fallen asleep in her bed instead of getting up and getting dressed and going home."

"My sister seduced you?" he asked, a touch of anger in his voice.

"It's possible, you know. Have you seen your sister!"

He rolled his eyes. "I'm going to pretend you're not standing out in front of my sister's house, dressed in her robe, in the middle of the night. I'm going to turn around and walk away and pray like hell the memory of you goes away quickly. I'm not going to think about why you're naked, and why my niece found you in her mother's bed. You're my best friend, so I'm going to assume you're just simply out for a stroll, naked."

"I am. Dude, I am your very best friend and you know I'd never…"

"Shut up, Truitt."

I pretended to lock my lips and throw away the key. "Not talking."

He sighed. "I'm fucking happy for y'all. I am."

I grinned, but then he held up his hand.

"If you hurt her, I will give you pain like you have never experienced before in your life."

"Understood."

"Now, I'm going home. I was watching a marathon of *Yellowstone* with my father. You're lucky he didn't hear you out here chasing the damn dog."

Ryan turned to leave when I cleared my throat. "Hey, Ryan, you wouldn't happen to want to maybe drive me to the ER, would you?"

He slowly turned and looked at me. "Why?" he asked cautiously.

"I think I might have torn something in my knee when I was chasing the dog."

When he let his eyes wander down my robe-clad body, I knew I was in serious trouble.

"Sure, Truitt. I'll take you to the ER. No problem at all."

Chapter 25

Truitt

WHEN RYAN INSISTED we not go back into the house and wake up Saryn or Liliana, I knew I was about to get my payback. This is what happens when your best friend catches you wearing his sister's robe after you've had your wicked way with her for nearly half the night.

Karma is a bitch.

When Ryan pulled up to the ER and the doors opened to reveal my brother, I knew my perfect night had taken a turn for the worse.

"You called Roger?" I asked, shooting a dirty look at my ex-best friend.

"Fuck yeah, I did. He was my first call."

"Your first call?"

He smiled. I closed my eyes and prayed it wasn't as bad as I thought.

The door to Ryan's truck opened and I heard my brother.

"Truitt, dude, why didn't you tell us you had a fetish for women's clothing?"

Jerking my head around to look at him, I replied, "Fuck you, Roger. Why are you here?"

"Ryan put the call out and said you were hurt. When you're hurt, we're hurt."

"We?" I asked, not wanting to know what he meant by that.

"Yeah, we." He turned and motioned with his hand. Standing outside the doors of the ER were Jack, Paul, and Pete, who clearly wasn't working tonight since he was dressed in shorts and a T-shirt.

"What the fuck?" I mumbled as they all stood there, their phones up, capturing the entire moment.

"Okay, let's get this guy into the ER and see what damage he's done now!" Ryan said, pushing up a wheelchair.

"Need help getting out? We wouldn't want you to flash anyone," Roger said as he tried like hell not to laugh and failed.

"I'm perfectly fine, motherfucker!" I snapped as I got out of the truck and dropped myself into the wheelchair. If it didn't feel like someone had pushed a knife into my knee, I would have walked in on my own.

Ryan pushed the wheelchair past all my other ex-friends as they started placing bets on what the injury would be.

"I've got fifty on a torn meniscus," Paul said.

"Damn it, I was going for that!" Pete said.

"Did you leave a note for Saryn?" I asked Ryan as he stopped us in front of the nurses' station.

"I did. I told her I found you on the ground in the front yard rolling about in pain. That I had to take your sorry ass to the ER and that I'd make sure she got her robe back."

With a groan, I dropped my head down. "I hate you," I softly whispered.

All he did was clasp his hand on my shoulder and said, "Welcome to the family, bro."

Things didn't get much better when Dr. Turner walked into the room. She stopped when she saw me. She took in the robe I was still wearing and looked at Ryan, Roger, Pete, and Paul.

"Do I even want to know?" she asked.

"The good news is, it's not a broken dick this time, doc," Roger said.

I closed my eyes and prayed I could go back in time and wish on a falling star to be an only child.

"Well, that's good news," Dr. Turner said.

"I'm pretty sure it's a torn meniscus," Pete said. After Dr. Turner did an exam, she ordered an MRI. I begged the tech to leave me in the waiting room outside of X-ray and not bring me back to the ER and my so-called friends. She agreed and even brought me a cup of water.

Pete ended up finding me and bringing me back to the ER to talk to the doctor.

"It's a torn meniscus. I recommend arthroscopic total meniscectomy. It's a pretty bad tear," Dr. Turner said. "There's an on-call orthopedic doctor in this evening, and we can do the surgery tonight."

"Tonight?" I asked, looking around the room. No one was laughing or joking, but I was pretty sure I saw Ryan hand Pete money.

The door to the room opened, and Saryn walked in holding Liliana. Her eyes bounced around the room until they landed back on mine. I saw the concern in there and the fear, but it melted away the moment I smiled at her.

Then she saw what I was wearing, and her cheeks turned a bright red.

"He needs surgery for a torn meniscus," Ryan said, most likely hoping to deflect from the fact that I was still wearing her robe.

Before she could say anything, I turned back to the doctor. "How long is the recovery? I'm pretty busy at work."

"You'll be up and moving around in about a week."

"A week!" I nearly shouted.

"The orthopedic doctor can give you a better idea. I've had him paged, and he should be down to talk to you soon. In the meantime, I'm going to have you moved to a room so you're more comfortable. And maybe one of your friends here might be kind enough to go and get you some clothes."

Ryan walked up and took Liliana from Saryn's arms. She was sound asleep. "I take it you woke up and found the note."

She nodded. "I didn't want to wake Mom and Dad so early."

"I'll take her home, don't worry, he'll be fine," Ryan said as he kissed his sister on the cheek.

Before he could leave, Saryn called out to him. "Ryan, once you get Liliana settled, will you take Rus to the vet? He's limping. I called the emergency vet and they told me to bring him in."

Everyone looked at me, then Roger slapped me on the back. "Dude, either your dog has sympathy pains, or he's got your kind of luck."

"How crazy would it be if they had the same injury?" Pete said with a chuckle. Before I knew it, they were all placing bets on that, too.

"You can all go home now," I said, frustration etched in my voice.

"I'll make sure he's checked out, don't worry," Roger said as he squeezed Saryn's arms lightly. "And I'll bring him some clothes to wear home after the surgery."

"Thank you," I said at the same time as Saryn.

When we were finally alone, Saryn took my hand in hers. "When I read the note from Ryan, I panicked. I ran upstairs and grabbed Liliana, and I noticed Rus was limping. I didn't know what to do. It was either come here or try and get him to the vet with Liliana in tow."

"I'm sorry you left the house so late, and with Liliana. You didn't have to do that," I said as I pulled her to me and kissed her.

"I called Ryan, and he told me not to come, but I had to. I needed to make sure you were okay."

"I'm fine."

"What in the world happened, Truitt? And why are you in my robe?"

Laughing, I rolled my eyes. "We fell asleep, obviously. Liliana woke me up and told me she had a bad dream. She wanted me to read her a book. I knew I had to get her back to her room, and I didn't want to wake you up. I figured if you saw your daughter in your room and you knew she had seen me in your bed, you would freak out. So I asked Liliana to bring me your robe and then told her to turn and close her eyes and I slipped it on. I took her back up to bed, read her a story, then took Rus out. He took off after a cat, which made me take off after him. Honestly, I can't believe I didn't wake you up screaming for the bastard to come back."

She giggled and shook her head. "You wore me out, Mr. Carter. I was in a deep, peaceful sleep."

With a wink, I went on talking. "Anyway, I somehow ended up tearing my knee, and Ryan showed up because you know, that would be my luck."

Her hand covered her mouth, and she at least tried not to laugh.

"I'm sorry. Are you sure you want to be with a guy who's so accident prone?"

Saryn wrapped her arms around my neck and gave me the sweetest smile I'd ever seen. If I had been standing, my legs would have wobbled.

"Yes, I'm sure. Besides, look how sexy you are in my robe."

The door to the room opened and Saryn took a step back. The doctor smiled and introduced himself to us, then proceeded to tell me about the surgery, the recovery, and how if I used ice therapy I would most likely be up and walking in a few days.

Before I knew it, I was being taken into surgery with Saryn walking by my side. Before they brought me into the operating room, she leaned down and kissed me.

"I'll see you in a few."

My head felt foggy and I was fighting sleep, but somehow I managed to speak. "See you soon. Love you."

Saryn froze, and before I could say anything else, I closed my eyes.

I didn't remember much of the drive home from the hospital, and when I woke up, I found myself back in a strange bedroom. My head felt clearer, and I looked down to see I had something wrapped around my knee. I reached down and touched it, only to pull my hand back from the cold.

"Ice therapy," I whispered, remembering what the doctor had said.

"Hey, how are you feeling?"

The voice from the door caused me to look up. It was my brother.

"Hey. I feel like I've slept for days."

He laughed. "You haven't slept for days, but you have been out of it since you woke up. Trying to get you out of the hospital and into this room was a challenge."

I glanced around the room. "Where am I?"

"Saryn's guest bedroom. She insisted I bring you back to her house so she could take care of you. I have to say, I think she's sorta into you, bro."

Smiling, I felt my heart rate speed up some. "Yeah, I'm into her, too. A lot."

He nodded and sat down in the chair next to the bed. "You made that clear when you told her you love her."

I stilled, then slowly looked at my brother. "I did what?"

The bastard took a drink of his coffee in an attempt not to show he was smiling. "You told her you love her. Not just once. But twice."

"Twice?"

The memory of being brought into the operating room came rushing back to me. It had felt so right to say it, even though I knew it wasn't the right time. We'd had one date. One. Two if you counted our time in the hospital.

"I remember the first time now. It kind of slipped out."

"Saryn played both times off, said it was the drugs."

With a groan, I dropped my head against the pillow and closed my eyes. "Is she here?"

"No, she had to work. I told her I could stay with you."

"When did I say it the second time? That I love her."

This time he did laugh. "The moment your ass woke up. You opened your eyes, and she was there. You smiled and told her you love her."

I scrubbed my hand over my face. "One time you can overlook, but twice?"

He grinned. "Let me ask you something, Truitt. Do you love her?"

My gaze moved to his. "I think so. I mean, yes. Hell, this is all new to me. I've always liked her, a lot. She's the only woman I've ever pictured having a future with. Being with her makes me happy. She makes me feel...different. I felt my chest ache when she married that fucker."

Roger nodded. "I'm pretty sure that's called love."

"I probably just scared her away."

With a shake of his head, my brother chuckled. "I don't think so. She's been guarding you like a woman protecting her young. She banned her brother from the house when he was trying to place a bet on how long it would take for you to hurt yourself again."

I rolled my eyes.

Roger cleared his throat and looked back toward the door. "I do have a bit of bad news, though."

My heart sank. "What is it?"

"Rus, he, um, well, he tore his meniscus and had to have surgery, too."

I laughed, but when my brother didn't return the laughter, I abruptly stopped. "You're joking, right?"

He shook his head. "I wish I was, dude, but I'm not. Looks like the two of you had a crazy time running around after that cat."

I stared at my brother. "The dog tore his meniscus, too? He had to have surgery, too?"

This time he did smile. "Yep. There's no doubt in my mind that the two of you were meant for each other."

Slowly, I shook my head and closed my eyes. "Only I would have an accident-prone dog."

I heard Roger chuckle, and I couldn't help but smile. "Is he okay? Where is he?"

Roger rubbed the back of his neck and cleared his throat to stop himself from laughing. "Ryan has him. He was the one who took him to the vet. They did the surgery the same day as yours. Ryan thought it'd be easiest to just bring him to his house and take care of him so Saryn didn't have to deal with the both of y'all."

I stared at him, then we both started to laugh.

"Holy shit. I cannot believe my fucking dog has the same injury as me."

"Same surgery and scar, too."

We laughed harder, and soon I had tears streaming down my face. Saryn walked into the room and looked at me, then rushed to my side.

"Are you in pain? Why are you laughing and crying?" she asked, her hand going to my forehead to check my temperature. It had to be something in women to always check for a fever, no matter the situation. My mother did it to Roger and me all the time, even as grown ass men.

You coughed, she put her hand on your forehead. Mentioned you had a sore throat, she was checking for a fever.

"I'm not in pain, sweetheart. Ryan told me about Rus, and I couldn't help but laugh."

She smiled. "It's not funny. The poor baby. I stopped by to see him and he's all laid up with his leg shaved. Don't worry, though, Ryan's spoiling him and taking good care of him. Liliana also gave him a new toy. She told him it was his baby, and I swear he hugged it to him."

"Please don't turn his dog into a pussy," Roger said from the chair.

Saryn turned and shot him a glare. "You're off-duty if you'd like to head on home now."

Roger shrugged. "I'm in no hurry to get home."

This time I was the one who shot him a look of warning.

He stood. "After thinking about it, I should probably stop by our folks' place and let them know how you're doing."

Saryn smiled. "Is your mother back yet?"

"She just got back from Hawaii or Europe. Hell, I don't know. A warning to you, though, the moment my mother finds out about her boy she will want to come over."

I groaned, and Saryn simply nodded and replied, "Of course. Tell them they're more than welcome to stop by anytime. I'm going to have Truitt up and walking here in a bit." She then turned and faced me. "You've slept an awfully long time. I think your body was exhausted and needed to catch up."

With a chuckle, I said, "Most likely. I've been going and blowing for a few weeks. I do need to check on the playhouse, though."

"Jack has it all under control, so don't even think about heading there," Roger quickly added.

"I need to make sure…"

Saryn placed her fingers over my mouth and shook her head. "He has it under control. Right now, the only thing you're going to worry about is resting."

I smiled. "Yes, nurse."

She winked, and then dropped her hand. "I'm going to go change…do you need anything?"

With a raise of my brows I watched as her face flushed.

"And with that I'm out of here before the two of you say or do something I'll never be able to erase from my mind. Call me if you need anything, Saryn," Roger said as he made his way out of the bedroom.

"Thank you for everything!" Saryn called out.

"Later, Roger," I said, not taking my eyes off of the beautiful woman standing next to the bed.

"Later," Roger called out.

The moment we heard the front door close, Saryn leaned down and kissed me. "Are you in any pain?"

I shook my head. "I honestly don't feel a thing, I think this ice thing has frozen my knee."

She grinned. "I've been doing it off and on. It really helps with the swelling and the pain. Since you've been asleep you haven't asked for any pain medicine, and I didn't want you to wake up with it out of control. Let's get you something to eat, and then I think maybe you should at least take one, especially since we'll be getting you up to walk around."

"You're the nurse."

Saryn leaned in and kissed me once more, and this time I placed my hand around her neck and pulled her closer to me. She laughed when she nearly fell over me on the bed.

"Please answer all my prayers and tell me you have a naughty nurse uniform."

Her teeth dug into her lower lip, and I felt my entire body come to life.

"I do not, but I'm sure I can come up with something," she softly said.

"Where's Liliana?" I asked.

"I dropped her off at my folks' place. My mom offered to watch her so I could focus on you."

"I only tore my meniscus, I didn't nearly die," I said.

"Yes, but I want to make sure you're taken care of. Roger told me you tend to not take care of yourself when you get hurt."

With a fake laugh, I replied, "That's because I'm so used to getting hurt."

She smiled softly and sat down on the bed. "I'm so sorry you hurt yourself. I have to say, though, you looked good in my robe."

I returned her smile. "I'm almost positive you look better in it."

"We can compare, Ryan took plenty of pictures and video of you wearing it."

"That bastard!" I growled.

Her hand went to my chest and she let her eyes wander over my body. "Let me go get changed, then we'll get you up."

"I'm sure I can get up on my own, sweetheart."

Saryn's eyes snapped back up and met my gaze. I could see it as clear as day, she was confused about something. Or possibly worried, even afraid.

I reached for her hand. "I'm sorry if I spooked you."

"Spooked me?" she repeated, her voice cracking slightly.

"When I said I loved you."

She chewed nervously on her lip. "You remember that?"

"Roger reminded me. I don't remember saying it the second time, but I do the first."

"It's okay, you were..."

"Wait, let me finish."

With a nod, she said, "Okay."

"It's true, I wouldn't have said those words just yet, but I know in my heart I feel that way. Yes, we literally just started dating, but I will not deny the way I feel for you. How much I care about you and Liliana. And it's because of Liliana that I want to do this right. I want to prove to you that I'm committed to the both of you, and I know that we don't know each other enough for me to say that.

"You may not want a guy who tears his meniscus all the time or who has friends who bet on how often I'll get hurt. I may snore at night or leave a wet towel on the end of the bed, which is something I do often so I'm disclosing that right now. But I sure as hell want to give this everything I've got, because I have fallen for you and for Liliana. I'm pretty sure you captured my heart years ago, and your daughter grabbed onto it day one and she has pulled me in hook, line, and sinker. There isn't anything I wouldn't do for either of you, and even if things don't work out between us, I do not want to lose your friendship."

Saryn stared at me for the longest time before she sniffled, looked down at her hands, and then smiled.

"Where did you come from, Truitt Carter?" she asked in such a low voice I struggled to hear her.

"What do you mean?"

She lifted her eyes and met mine. "I've never met a man like you. You care so deeply, how is it no woman has ever snatched you up?"

I shrugged. "I think it's because the woman I've been waiting for was off on another journey, but I think she's on the right path now."

She giggled and leaned forward, capturing my mouth with hers. The kiss was soft, but it said a million words. She sighed and leaned her head against mine.

"It's going to be a lot harder for me to say the words. I just want to be honest with you. When I close my eyes, I see a future and it has you in it, but at the same time I have Liliana, and I have to guard her heart as much as I have to guard mine. Does that make sense?"

"Yes, of course it makes sense. Saryn, I'm not asking you to marry me or commit the rest of your life to me. I get that this is new. Like I said, I wouldn't have said those words yet. I want to do this right, sweetheart. And I'll do whatever you want, whenever you want, however you want to do it. I just want to be with you and Liliana."

"Oh, Truitt," she said on a whoosh of air. Her mouth was back on mine, and before I knew what was happening, she drew back and looked at me. "If we don't stop I'm going to take advantage of you in your sick bed."

"Hey, you would get zero complaints from me."

She laughed and stood, then reached for a bottle of pills and my water. She took one out and handed it to me. "Here, take a pain pill, then we'll get you out of this bed and find you some food."

I gave her a wink. "Sounds like a plan to me."

Chapter 26

Saryn

EVEN IF I wanted to, there was no way I'd be able to wipe the smile from my face. Truitt's words replayed in my mind as I walked to my room.

"I'll do whatever you want, whenever you want, however you want to do it. I just want to be with you and Liliana."

A burst of happiness filled my entire body as I quickly changed out of my nurse's uniform and jumped into the shower. A sound caught my attention, and I turned to see Truitt standing by the side of the tub.

"What are you doing, Truitt!"

With that boyish smile of his, he stepped into the shower, only limping slightly on his right leg.

"Truitt, no! Your knee."

"Is fine."

With a stern look I put up a hand and shook my head. "No sex. There is no way you can even attempt it."

He grinned wider. "Who said anything about sex? I simply want to feel your body against mine."

I took a step closer to him and let him pull me to him. The moment his arms wrapped around me, a warmth settled over my entire body. I felt so safe in his arms. Everything seemed to slip away, and the only thing that mattered was that moment with him.

"Besides, I feel like I haven't showered in days," he said.

"Let me wash you up," I said as I drew back and reached for the soap. Truitt stood still as I slowly washed his body. I purposely avoided his mid-section and moved gently around his knee.

"How does your knee feel?" I asked, running my hands over his stomach. I'd never seen abs like his before. My fingers trickled over them and caused him to draw in a quick breath. I loved the way his body trembled from my touch. That did something to me and filled me with a confidence I never knew I had.

"It feels sore, but nothing terrible. I actually feel a lot better getting up and moving around."

My hand moved close to his very impressive erection, but I ignored it. Truitt groaned in frustration, and I couldn't help but chuckle.

"I know something else that would make you feel better."

I dropped down, and before he could say anything, I took him into my mouth. Tim had never wanted me to do this to him, and I had eventually grown tired of asking. I had no idea what I was doing, but by the look on Truitt's face he didn't seem to care.

"Saryn. Fuck, that feels so damn good."

With a smile, I grew bolder and reached up to gently play with his balls. Truitt hissed and pushed his fingers into my hair. He moved his hips gently and allowed me to get used to taking him in deeper. I could feel my own sex throbbing. When I took him deeper yet, Truitt groaned and pulled on my wet hair.

"Saryn, if you don't want me coming in your mouth, you need to stop."

I wasn't about to stop, not when I was bringing him close to orgasm. The power I felt was amazing, and I almost reached down and touched myself I was so turned on. I moved my hand faster as I sucked on him harder.

"Christ, I'm going to come. Baby, oh God, I'm coming!"

My body hummed with delight. Then it all changed. The feel of his cum hitting the back of my throat and the taste of it was not what

I had expected, nor was I ready for it. I pulled back in shock, and then gagged until I nearly threw up.

When Truitt attempted to help me, I put my hand out to stop him and took a handful of water to wash out my mouth. Tears ran down my cheeks from gagging so hard. Once I got myself under control, I faced Truitt, who was still standing in the shower.

The moment my eyes met his, I couldn't help but start laughing. Truitt looked horrified. Stunned into silence. I must have looked a fright after all the coughing and gagging and laughing like an idiot. He looked utterly confused as to what he should do or say.

"I've...I've never done that before, and I guess I wasn't sure what to expect when you came."

His mouth opened and closed a few times before he snapped it shut. "Why didn't you tell me? I would have never...oh, shit. Saryn, baby, I'm so sorry."

Truitt pulled me into his arms, and I practically melted against him. Even under the water, I felt the warmth of his body. The way he held me just felt so right.

"I wanted to do that for you, and the last thing I wanted to do was ruin the moment by telling you I'd never given a blowjob before."

I felt his body shake and heard him chuckle.

"Your ex really was an asshole to not appreciate the amazing woman you are."

"He's the last person I want to talk about." Drawing back some, I smiled. "I will be honest with you, though, I think the next time I'll tap out before you come."

Truitt let out a roar of laughter. Then he kissed me with so much passion that I almost wanted to tell him I was falling in love with him. Truth be told, I was in love with him. A part of me always had been, but I had always told myself it was a high school crush.

When he had said it to me not once, but twice, I had to hide the smile that threatened to appear, and the fact that I wanted to say it back. The ease with which he said it—and with which I felt it—scared me, though. This wasn't just the two of us in this situation. Liliana was in the mix, as well.

"We better get you out of here and give your knee a rest," I said, turning off the shower and getting us both out safely.

"Thank you for taking care of me," Truitt said while he dried off his perfectly chiseled body. The way each muscle moved had me fascinated with him even more.

"It was my pleasure. Now, let's go get something to eat."

An hour later I had Truitt sitting in the chair in the living room, the ice pack on his knee and a game of Yahtzee going.

"Okay, seriously, I think we need to switch this to strip poker," Truitt said before he rolled the dice on the table I'd pushed up next to him.

With a chuckle, I gave him a stern look. "No strip poker because that will lead to sex."

Giving me a look of dismay, Truitt said, "You say that like it's a bad thing."

"It's not a bad thing, but I actually enjoy simply being with you."

He smiled. "I do, too. I've been meaning to ask, did you always want to be a nurse?"

"No, not always. I wasn't really sure what I wanted to do, to be honest with you. Business was my original major with a minor in art."

Truitt lifted a brow. "What made you change?"

I let out a long, deep breath. "Honestly, I was bored with business. I told Tim I was going to switch my major to nursing. It just appealed to me. And I knew I wanted to do neonatal."

"Does it ever get sad working in neonatal?"

"Yes," I said with a soft smile. "But there are more happy times than sad ones. Tim didn't like my career change, and I'm pretty sure that's when things really started to go south for us. I'd actually pick up shifts just to be away from home. I know that sounds terrible."

He narrowed his eyes and studied me for a long moment. "If you were unhappy with him, why did you stay?"

I let out a humorless laugh. "I have no idea. Maybe I was afraid to fail. Or afraid to come back and be lonely. A part of me wanted to walk away, and the other part wanted to fight for my relationship. I should have listened to the stronger side."

"The one that said walk away?"

With a nod, I replied, "But then I wouldn't have Liliana and she's the best thing that has ever happened to me."

A wide grin broke out on Truitt's face. "She is. Are you sure she's Tim's? Cause I can't imagine that asshole having anything to do with something so amazing."

I laughed and rolled the dice. "Yahtzee!"

Truitt rolled his eyes and dropped his head back against the propped up pillows. "Ugh, I'm so over this game."

My cell phone rang, and I jumped up to answer it in case it was my folks calling about Liliana. It was Ryan.

"Hey, Ryan, how's it going?"

"Your boyfriend's dog is whining and I think he wants to see Truitt."

I smiled. "Rus is missing you."

When Truitt didn't answer, I looked over to find him fast asleep on the sofa.

"I think Truitt's pain pill kicked in, he's asleep."

"Can I slip Rus an extra one? Seriously, he is not happy."

"Why don't you bring him here? I'm sure Liliana will love helping to take care of him."

Ryan sighed. "Saryn, you have your hands full with Truitt, who by the way is very capable of going home."

"I like having him here, and Rus won't be an issue."

"What about work? You just got moved to L & D the other day?" Ryan asked.

My brother always had a habit of trying to control things around my life. I knew he meant well, but I was almost twenty-nine years old, I didn't need a babysitter.

"It turns out they didn't need a nurse in L & D after all. They told me today they were moving me back to the ER. I told them I was going to have to decline."

"You quit your job?"

"Yes, Ryan. I did. There's a NICU in San Antonio that's hiring for a few positions and they're not night shifts. I'm going to look into applying after the holidays."

He remained silent for a few moments. "I'm sorry, Saryn. I know I tend to interfere in your life sometimes."

"Sometimes?" I asked mockingly.

"Ha. Ha. Listen, are you sure you want the dog there? He has to go out on a leash."

"I'm sure. Truitt can walk him, actually. It's good for him to get up and walk around on his knee."

"You really like him, don't you?" Ryan asked. "Truitt, I mean, not the dog."

I didn't even have to think about my response. "Yes. I really do."

"Y'all hardly know each other, Saryn."

I laughed and shook my head even though he couldn't see it. "He's your best friend, Ryan. I've known him my entire life, practically. Are you telling me you don't want me to date him?"

"Hell no. There's nobody like Truitt and I know he's a good guy. He's one of only a handful of people I would trust with my life, and the only guy I think even remotely comes close to deserving you. I fully support this relationship, I just think y'all are moving fast, that's all."

I slipped out the back door and onto the porch so that I didn't wake up Truitt. "Fair enough. To Truitt's credit, he did want to take things slowly, as did I. But seeing him with Liliana, and having him here...I don't know how to explain it, Ryan. It feels so right."

"Why do I hear a bit of hesitation in your voice, then?"

"I'm scared. What if Liliana and I fall head over heels for him and..." My voice trailed off.

"That's what life is about, sis. Taking chances. Loving someone is a risk. You of all people should know that. Tim wasn't the one. Truitt might be, or he might not be. Do you remember what grandma said to us the day you declared you were going to marry a cowboy and live on a ranch?"

I couldn't help but laugh as I thought back to that day. I had been fifteen and Ryan sixteen. Little did my brother know that the cowboy I had been thinking of was the man asleep on my sofa that very moment.

"She said something about working on love."

He chuckled. "She said you don't stumble onto true love. You build it, master it. Help it grow. Those words are exactly why I knew Miranda wasn't the one. It just took me a bit of time to realize it and accept that it wasn't going to work. Sort of like you did with Tim. Neither of us were ready to build it. To work on it. You stayed with the douche for your reasons, and I stayed with Miranda because I didn't want to admit I'd made a mistake."

I closed my eyes and thought about my sweet, gray-haired grandmother. I missed her so much.

"She was right. It's a partnership and it takes work. I know that now."

"I know you've got Liliana. I also know that Truitt would never hurt you, or her. When they say find one of the good guys, Saryn, he's the mascot for it."

"So are you, sweet brother."

He scoffed. "I'm actually having a bit of fun now that I'm single, so don't judge me."

"Ugh, don't give me any details. Bring Rus over when you get a chance. Liliana and Truitt will be happy to see him."

Ryan laughed.

"What's so funny?" I asked.

"It's just so damn funny that Truitt and his dog had the same surgery done. That guy has the worst luck, I swear."

I peeked into the window and felt my stomach do a somersault at the sight before me. Truitt was sitting up with his leg resting on a pillow propped up on the table, reading a book to Liliana as my mother cleaned up the Yahtzee game.

I didn't even realize they had come over.

With a slow shake of my head, I let out a soft sigh. "He may be unlucky at times, but I've never met a man like him."

"Then he's worth the jump."

With a smile, I replied, "So worth the jump."

Chapter 27

Truitt

"TWUITT?"

The little voice instantly had my eyes snapping open. There, standing over me with a huge smile and those bright blue eyes, was Liliana.

"Hey, pumpkin," I said, sitting up and finding Evie standing there with a grin that said she had just won the lottery. "Hi, Evie."

"Hello there, Truitt. How is the knee doing?" Evie asked with a slight twinkle in her eye.

"It's doing good, thanks to Saryn."

"I'm so glad I suggested she just have you stay here. You can't be all alone after surgery."

My mouth twitched. Evie was playing matchmaker again, and I had no problem with it at all.

"It was a minor surgery, I'm sure I could have stayed at home."

She tsked and shook her head. "Don't be silly. You shouldn't be staying home alone after any sort of surgery."

"Does Will feel the same as you about me being here?" I watched her grab a sofa pillow and motion for me to rest my foot on it while she moved the ice therapy machine.

"The only thing Will and I want is for Saryn to be happy. And we both knew she wasn't with...he who will not ever be named again."

I laughed as I looked down at Liliana, then back up to Evie.

"You know we just started dating."

She nodded. "And she's practically moved you in! I think that's a good sign."

I sighed and then focused back on Liliana. "What do you have there, darlin'?"

Liliana climbed up onto the sofa next to me and looked at my knee. "Does it hurwt?"

"Not really, your mommy is taking care of me."

She smiled a brilliant smile that nearly stole the air from my lungs.

"I take care of you, too!"

Liliana handed me a book, and I promptly opened it and started reading. I caught a glimpse of Saryn standing out on the back porch talking on the phone. As I read to Liliana, Evie put up the Yahtzee game.

"I made roast for dinner and left some in the kitchen for the two of you. Liliana insisted we come over to see you before she went to bed."

"Nothing makes me happier than seeing my favorite girl," I said. Liliana gazed up at me with nothing but love and trust in her eyes. That look reaffirmed my feeling: there wasn't anything I wouldn't do for her or her mother. Moving slow had officially been taken off the shelf, and I was going to spend as much time with the two of them as I could. I went back to reading as Evie headed out of the living room.

The door to the back porch opened and Saryn walked in. Liliana looked up and gave her mother a grin. "Hi, Mommy!"

"Hey, baby girl."

"Liliana wanted to come say goodnight and have a book read to her," I said.

"Where is Wus?" Liliana asked.

"Uncle Ryan is going to bring Rus over so he can stay here and heal with his daddy."

There was no denying that news made me feel even happier. "He is?"

Saryn nodded. "I told him it would be good for both you and Rus to rest together. You two can lie around on the sofa and watch TV all day."

I laughed. "That is never going to happen."

"Twuitt! Wead the book, pwease!"

God, I loved how she made her r and l's sound like w's. "Yes, ma'am."

After reading two books, I walked with Evie, Liliana, and Saryn to the front door.

Before Saryn walked out, she turned to face me. "I'm going to go tuck her in, and then I'll be back. Please don't go running or anything."

I glanced down at my right knee. It felt good not to have anything strapped around it and to be walking again. Saryn insisted I use a cane at least for the first few days, though.

"I'll try not to."

As Saryn, her mother, and Liliana made their way to the main house, I saw Ryan's truck coming down the drive.

I waited on the porch as he walked around to the back passenger side of his truck. He opened the door and lifted Rus out, then gently placed him onto the ground. He had a leash on so that he wouldn't attempt to run. To be honest, he didn't look like he even wanted to walk.

"How is he?" I asked while they made their way to us.

"He's a bit loopy. I gave him a pain pill so he would be a bit more chill when I brought him over."

Rus managed to hop up the few steps and make his way over to me. I took the leash and gave him a good petting.

"Hey, buddy. Looks like we're two peas in a pod."

My dog simply gave me a small whine.

"I've got his dog bed and stopped and bought a water and food bowl. I also bought him some food since I couldn't get into your place."

"Roger should have let you in," I stated.

Ryan shrugged as if it wasn't a big deal. "No worries. I think Rus is just glad to be back around you. I've got a crate as well, if you want it."

"Nah, I think he'll be okay," I said as I extended my hand. "Thank you so much for taking care of him, Ryan. I really appreciate it."

He gave me a firm, quick handshake. "That's what friends are for. You need help getting back in?" he asked with a quick glance over my shoulder and into the house.

"I think we can manage, can't we, boy?"

Ryan nodded then stared at me for a long moment.

"What is it? What's wrong?"

"She really likes you, Truitt. A lot."

I smiled. "I more than like her, Ryan."

"So I heard," he said with a smirk. "Don't you think it's a little early to declare your love after the first date?"

With a chuckle, I answered, "It was the drugs. But I am falling in love with her and Liliana."

"They're easy to love."

His face went blank, and he looked at his folks' house, then back to me. He looked conflicted about something and exhaled loudly. "Listen, Tim is still in town. Guess he was at the Rusty Nail last night talking shit. He's telling people you and Saryn have been hooking up since high school."

"What!" I nearly shouted.

"Yeah. I was hoping he would get his money and leave town, but it doesn't look like that. I'm glad you're here, because I have a feeling he might be trying to stop back by. I told Dad he needs to change the gate code, but he said too many folks have it and it would be a hassle. So, just a heads up."

"What's wrong with this guy? He cheated on her, gave up Liliana. Why can't he leave them alone?"

Ryan rubbed the back of his neck and glanced toward the main house, obviously to make sure Saryn wasn't on her way back.

"Tim had a thing against you in high school, I'm not sure if you knew that or not."

"I'm beginning to see that, but no, I had no idea back then."

"Apparently, last night he got a little too drunk and started spewing out all this shit about you to Shay, who happened to be at the bar. How you were the high school football star. How you had any girl you wanted, but the one you wanted most was out of reach. He told Shay that you swore you were going to take Saryn's virginity and would stop at nothing to do it."

"I never told that fucker that," I quickly said.

"Dude, I know you didn't. Anyway, he went on to tell Shay that he felt it was his duty to protect Saryn. That he never really loved her, just wanted to keep her from you."

"This isn't new information, Ryan."

"Yeah, well this next bit is. He also told her that Liliana is your kid, not his."

I nearly stumbled back and lost my balance. Ryan reached out and steadied me again.

"He said what! Why in the hell would he say that?"

"Because he's an asshole, and I think he's trying to stir up shit about Saryn. Get people talking about y'all, because he's not happy Saryn has adjusted to life without him. Of course, Shay didn't believe him. He doesn't know that you and Shay have..."

"Had," I clarified.

"Right, had. He doesn't know y'all had a friends-with-benefits thing going on. Shay called me this morning to tell me what Tim was saying. She thought you'd want to know."

My hand scrubbed down my face. "What in the fuck is wrong with this guy?"

"Saryn also told me earlier that she left her job because they were moving her back to the ER. That's not true. I called Pete and asked him. Tim showed up at her job today and caused a scene. Saryn was so embarrassed, she simply apologized and stepped down from her position when her boss called her into her office. Pete asked me not to let Saryn know that he told me the truth."

I stood there, unable to say anything.

"Why in the world is he stirring up trouble?" I finally asked.

Ryan lifted a brow. "Do you really need me to answer that?"

"Because she's moved on without his ass?"

He nodded.

I glanced back at the house and saw Saryn making her way toward us. "Are you busy tomorrow morning?"

Ryan shook his head. "Nope. We're not running any dude ranch stuff this month, and I can step away for a few hours in the morning."

"Good. Come by tomorrow morning and pick me up, will you? I need to check on Liliana's playhouse setup, and I think it's time you and I paid a visit to Tim."

A wide smile erupted across Ryan's face. "I agree."

"What do you agree on?" Saryn asked as she bent down and gave Rus some kisses and a gentle hug.

"That Truitt shouldn't be driving with his knee."

Saryn looked up at me. "No, you shouldn't be at all, not until you go back next week for your follow-up."

"I'm going to stop by tomorrow and pick him up so he can check on a few things at work."

One very upset Saryn placed her hands on her hips and glared at me. "You had surgery yesterday on your knee, Truitt. You've been so overworked and exhausted that you slept nearly the whole day away."

"And I feel so much better because of you. I promise I won't be gone long. I only have two things I need to take care of."

She sighed and then looked at her brother. "You'll come get him and make sure he doesn't do too much?"

Ryan crossed his heart with his finger. "I promise. I'll be his wingman."

Our eyes met, and a knowing smile passed over each of our faces.

"Come on, Rus, let's get you inside and settled," Saryn said. "You, too, Truitt."

"Tomorrow morning, around what time?" I asked.

"I've got to ride the north fence line with Dad, but that won't take us long, so I'll come around eight?"

"Sounds good," I said, reaching my hand out once more for Ryan's. "Thanks for having my back."

He nodded. "You know what I want in return," he said as he motioned toward the house.

"I know. You have my word. I have no intentions of hurting either one of them."

Chapter 28

Truitt

AFTER RYAN LEFT, I made my way back into the house using the stupid cane. I hated to admit it, but it helped. I could hear Saryn in the kitchen, so I made my way there. She was heating up her mother's roast.

"Where's Rus?" I asked as I sat down on the barstool.

"He's in my bedroom. I put his dog bed in there with a soft blanket on it. He laid right down and drifted off to sleep. Poor baby. I wish I could put the ice therapy machine on him."

"You seriously thought about it, didn't you?"

She chuckled. "Yes. If I had two, I would. Want some roast?"

"Roast sounds amazing. Need any help?"

"Nope, you just sit there and stay off your knee for a bit."

I did as she said and watched as she moved about the kitchen. Ryan's words replayed in my head. I wasn't sure if I should bring up Tim or not. Saryn looked so happy, and the last thing I wanted to do was ruin the mood by bringing that dickhead into the conversation.

An hour later, I was sitting back on the sofa flipping through the TV while Saryn cleaned up the kitchen. She wouldn't let me help at all. She nearly dragged me back into the living room to sit.

With a smile, I thought about how easy it was to talk to Saryn. During dinner we'd talked about everything from the process I go through to build a playhouse, to our favorite movies and where we saw our lives in ten years.

I felt the electricity in the air change the moment she walked into the room.

"Anything good on?" she asked as she sat on the sofa, tucked her feet under her, and snuggled up next to me.

God, I could really get used to this.

I didn't want to say it felt like we were playing house, but I imagined that life would be pretty much like this if things worked out between us. I already knew I wanted to settle down and start a family.

"I was just flipping through, not really paying attention."

"Oh! The History Channel, can we leave it on this?"

With a smile, I set the remote down and then kissed her on the forehead. "It's your house, sweetheart, we can watch anything you want."

She snuggled in closer, then pulled back some, as if the idea of simply relaxing was foreign to her. "Do you need a pain pill? Maybe we should put the ice back on your knee, you've had it off for a bit."

The dull ache in my knee had been steadily growing, and the thought of ice numbing it sounded pretty damn good.

"No pain pill, but maybe the ice."

Saryn jumped into action, grabbing the ice therapy machine to dump out the melted ice and refill it with fresh ice and water.

"I'm going to check on Rus while I'm up!" she called out.

"Don't let him talk you into a treat with his sad puppy dog eyes!" I cried out.

I was soon sucked into a show about the pharaohs' tombs in Egypt. I hadn't noticed Saryn wasn't back yet until a sharp pain in my knee caused me to stand up and move it about a bit. The last thing I wanted was for my knee to get stiff from not using it.

"Sorry, Rus needed some extra love," she said, coming back into the room.

I snarled my lip at her. "What?"

She attempted to hide her smile and failed. "Poor baby, he can't say when the pain is too much. I gave him some of the roast and then a pain pill and told him to rest for a bit. We need to be sure and take him out before we go to bed."

It wasn't lost on me how normal this all sounded. As if the three of us had lived together for months now.

"I can't believe I'm jealous of my dog right now," I said with a slight pout.

A sexy smile grew across her face. "Do you need some extra special attention, too?"

Even though every ounce of me wanted to be inside her, I also just wanted her to sit down next to me so we could watch The History Channel together.

"How about you snuggle up next to me again and we learn about dead pharaohs?"

"That sounds amazing." Once she was settled next to me and her head was against my arm, I found myself relaxing like I had never relaxed before.

"This is something I could really get used to," she whispered.

I took her hand in mine and laced our fingers together. "I thought the same exact thing a few minutes ago."

She looked up at me as I gazed down at her. Something in her eyes changed and she suddenly looked sad.

After a deep, steady inhale of air, she started to speak. "Tim is causing problems and I'm not even sure where to begin with telling you the lies he's made up about both of us."

I placed my finger on her chin and brought her eyes back up to look into mine. "I don't care what he's said or who he's said it to. If people want to believe the rumors, let them. Liliana is still young enough that it won't affect her, and who knows, maybe someday she actually will be my daughter."

Her eyes grew wide. "You know about what he's been saying?"

With a nod, I leaned over and kissed her on the forehead. "He's an idiot who doesn't deserve to even be called a father to Liliana. Let him get it all out of his system. He's bound to head back to Dallas any day now."

"But, Truitt, if parents hear rumors about you that aren't true, they won't hire you to build their kids' playhouses."

"If people want to act like that, then I don't want to build for them. Saryn, everyone knows you've been in Dallas this whole time and I've been here. When in the hell would we have time to have an affair?"

"I know it's so stupid, but there was a nurse at work who asked me if Liliana was really your baby. She heard it from Tim himself at a mutual friend's holiday party. Why would he tell people such a lie?"

"Attention? Maybe he's upset you've moved on, especially with me."

She nodded and then frowned. "It doesn't make any sense, though. He didn't want to be married to me any more than I wanted to be married to him. Why is he doing this all of a sudden?"

"I don't know. Maybe his single life isn't all he thought it would be."

"Well, I'm just really sorry he's saying all of this. He's already cost me my job. I sort of lied to Ryan about why I left my job. Tim came in and caused a huge scene. I was devastated, and the way the other employees were looking at me, I couldn't stand the thought of staying there. It just feels like I left Dallas to get away from him, and all the drama seems to have followed me here. If we hadn't gone out..."

"Don't say what you're about to say. Don't make what's happening between us seem like a mistake. He's already robbed us of enough time together, he won't get anymore."

She gave me a weak smile. "I don't think it's a mistake at all. I don't know how to explain how I know this so soon, but I know it with all my heart. You're the person I've been searching for this whole time, Truitt."

Moving her body so that she straddled mine, I cupped her face. "Then let's not worry about he whose name shall not be spoken. And maybe we should kiss. A lot."

Her nose crinkled up in the most adorable way. "What happens when we get tired of kissing?"

"Let's see," I said, lifting my eyes up as if in thought. "We could either watch the dead pharaohs, or we take ourselves to your bedroom and get creative with lovemaking."

"I think I have an even better idea. Let's give your knee a few minutes on the ice, then let me take you to bed where I can kiss and make love to you."

A small bark came from the living room entrance. We both turned to see Rus standing there, barely putting any weight on his back right leg.

Saryn nearly threw her body off of me and rushed over to him. "Oh, baby boy! Do you need to go potty?"

Rus's tail wagged slightly, and Saryn rushed to go get his collar.

"Dude, are you trying to cockblock me?" I asked as I gave him a stern look. He whined and looked away.

"Wow. Okay. Next time you're at doggy daycare I'm going to tell them to keep you in the restricted area."

Rus barked.

"Eye for an eye, dude."

"What are you saying?" Saryn asked while she put my dog's collar on and grabbed a flashlight.

"Nothing, Rus and I were just reaching an understanding. Isn't that right, buddy?"

Rus barked and gave me a wag.

"Aww, that's so sweet how much he loves you."

I rolled my eyes and watched as the two of them slowly made their way out the back door. There were only two steps down into the yard, so Rus wouldn't have to climb back up any stairs.

By the time Saryn came back in, the ice had done its job. I didn't feel any pain in my knee.

I took the ice contraption off and grabbed my cane. I could hear Saryn in the bedroom talking to Rus, so I turned off the TV and made my way there.

"Okay, buddy, I've got your food and water in here, and if you need anything you just bark, okay?" Saryn asked.

The thumping of the dog's tail on the dog bed made me smile. Rus had clearly fallen for both Liliana and Saryn just as hard and fast as I had.

I hobbled over to the bed. "He settled?"

"I think so, poor baby. I hate that he's in pain."

My brows pulled in tight as I looked down at my dog who was looking up at me with what I swear was a smirk.

"He's fine," I said, pulling my shirt over my head. Saryn turned and stopped when she saw me.

"Okay, wow. I was not prepared for the deliciousness that is your body."

The way her eyes moved up and down in a hungry way made my cock grow hard.

I laughed and untied my sweatpants. "I think I'm going to need help getting out of these."

Saryn grinned and made her way toward me. "We are not skipping the kisses part. I really like the way you kiss."

Her hands landed on my hips, and when she pushed down my pants, she watched my dick spring out.

"Please tell me this is something you do often." Her eyes looked up to meet mine. "This not wearing any underwear."

I winked. "Every now and then I like to let my boys hang free."

"So what you're saying is..." she said while she pulled her own shirt over her head then pushed her pants down and off her legs, "... that I should wear more dresses, sans panties."

"If you want easy access to my cock, then abso-fucking-lutely."

Her breath hitched before she let out a breathy sigh. "I really do like it when you talk dirty, Mr. Carter."

"Is that so?" I asked.

"Yes."

I got onto the bed and somehow managed to get myself all the way back and against the headboard.

"I'm ready for those kisses, Ms. Night."

Saryn walked over to the end table, opened the drawer, and pulled out a condom. "I bought new ones."

The memory of the condom breaking the other night came back to me. My stomach dropped a little, but then I relaxed. Saryn had said she was on the pill, so even with a broken condom, the chances of her getting pregnant were slim.

"Probably a good idea."

She crawled on top of me and pressed her warmth on my shaft. We both moaned at the connection of our bodies.

"Please try not to move. Let me do all the work."

I laughed. "Yeah, I'm not sure that's going to work, sweetheart."

Her mouth pressed against mine, and we were soon lost to a passionate kiss. Saryn rubbed herself against me, and I could feel how wet and ready she was. I would have given anything to simply slip inside her and feel her warmth.

"You feel so good, Truitt."

My hands gripped her hips, pulling her down harder on me so that I rubbed against her clit. She moaned in pleasure and dropped her head back.

"That's it, baby, make yourself come on me."

"Oh, God," she panted.

I watched her as she moved her hips, her eyes closed. This was something I could watch over and over and never grow tired of. She moved faster, the beginnings of her orgasm in the making. Her eyes opened and locked with mine as she came. It was one of the hottest things I'd ever seen.

For a moment, I had forgotten about the condom and almost pushed inside her.

"I want you, Saryn. I fucking need to be inside you."

"Yes," she panted as she lifted herself off me. She fumbled with the condom before finally handing it to me.

I ripped it open and rolled it on, tossing the wrapper to the floor.

Saryn moved over me and slowly sank down, causing us both to let out a moan.

"I don't want to move. God, I want to stay like this forever," Saryn said before she leaned down and captured my mouth once again. The kiss was slow yet filled with so many unspoken words and feelings. She moved slowly on top of me, and I was positive if she came in that moment I would tumble right along with her.

"Truitt," she whispered against my mouth. "It feels so amazing. You feel so amazing."

"I know, baby. I feel the same way about you."

She pushed back and placed her hands on my chest. Her body stilled, but my cock jumped and twitched inside her. Almost begging her to take him harder and faster.

"What's happening between us?" she asked, her eyes searching mine.

My mouth opened to speak, but I wasn't sure what to say. I wanted to tell her I was falling in love with her and that I didn't care if it was too soon to say it. I fell in love with her when I was sixteen.

"I don't know," I whispered.

She moved up and down slowly, her eyes never leaving mine.

"Truitt."

My name on her lips sounded like heaven. I focused on keeping my right leg still and not moving my hips. Saryn moved faster and harder and I dropped my head against the headboard.

"Fucking hell, baby. God," I ground out.

Her hands went to my shoulders. "Talk to me. Tell me what you want."

My head snapped forward. She was blushing, either from riding me or from the words she'd just said. She wanted me to talk dirty to her and that made me smile.

"I want you to fuck me. Hard and fast until you're screaming my name when you come."

Her brown eyes sparkled with lust and desire, and something else that I only dared to think about.

"Yes. God, yes," she said, her voice panting as she moved faster. "Touch me, please touch me."

I moved my thumb to her clit and pressed it gently.

"Truitt! Yes. Yes. I'm going to come. Oh, God."

The feel of her pussy squeezing my cock made me lose control.

"I'm going to come, baby."

I came so hard, I swore the room went black for a moment. I tried to keep my body still, but my hips jerked as I released into the condom. It felt like my orgasm went on for days, just like Saryn's seemed to be. Her body was still trembling when I finally felt the last of the orgasm slip away.

Saryn stopped moving, and then dropped her head to my chest and attempted to calm her breathing. My hands ran softly over her back, and I loved that she was still connected to me. Me being inside this woman was my new favorite thing.

"That. Was. Unbelievable," she panted into my chest. The warmth of her breath heated my entire body.

"Yeah, it was."

In a barely there whisper, she asked, "When can we do that again?"

Laughing, I dropped my head back against the headboard. "I wish I could tell you he'll be up and ready in a few minutes, but I'm exhausted. You fucked the shit out of me."

Her head lifted, and she narrowed one eye at me while giving me a beautiful smile.

"I owed you one."

She slipped off of me and rolled off the bed. I reached for a Kleenex on the side of the bed and pulled the condom off, wrapping it up.

Saryn took it from me and disappeared into the bathroom. After a few minutes she appeared again, dressed in the same robe I had put on the night I chased Rus around the front yard.

She sat on the bed and gently wiped off my dick, giving it such attention to detail that the bastard started to come up again. Her brows rose as she glanced over to me.

"Already?" she asked with a sexy smirk.

"He may be ready, but the rest of me is exhausted."

"Poor baby," she said, her mouth in a sexy pout. "We don't want to overdo it now, do we?"

I winked. "If you want to ride me again and do all the work, I won't argue."

She giggled and slipped off her robe and then slid under the covers. I wrapped my arm around her and pulled her against my body. I loved the feel of her head resting on my chest.

With a yawn, she said, "Let's just rest our eyes for a bit."

I kissed her on the forehead and held her even closer. "Go to sleep, sweetheart. I'm not going anywhere."

Chapter 29

Saryn

THE SMELL OF bacon had me rolling over and opening my eyes. "If my mother is in the house, I'm going to die," I whispered to myself. Opening one eye, I turned to find an empty bed. I sat up quickly and found Rus was missing, as well. So was his dog bed.

I jumped out of bed and wrapped my robe around my body and made my way to the kitchen. With each step, I couldn't help but notice how my body ached in the most delicious way. I'd woken up around five this morning and crawled back onto Truitt. I had no idea where this new version of me was coming from, but I rather enjoyed her. And honestly, I did know where all of this new confidence came from. It was Truitt who brought it out in me.

When I walked into the kitchen, I came to a stop and backed out to a spot where I could look in and watch. Liliana stood on a small stepstool, mixing something in a bowl while Truitt sprayed cooking spray on a griddle. My mother stood to the other side of Truitt and cooked bacon.

I narrowed my eyes at her. She was probably eating this all up and feeling pretty damn proud of herself. Little did she know the chemistry between Truitt and I had already been sparked years ago.

"Twuitt, how dis?" Liliana asked as she showed Truitt the bowl.

"That is the best pancake mix I have ever seen. Your mommy is going to love these pancakes. Now, let's put in the secret ingredient!"

Liliana clapped widely and then giggled. I turned quickly and made my way back to my bedroom where I changed into jeans and a sweater. I slipped on my Keds and headed back to the kitchen.

"What's going on in here?" I asked, trying not to look like a woman who'd had the most amazing sex of her life only hours ago.

My mother turned and smiled as she looked me over. "You slept in this morning."

"I did. Thank you for watching Liliana." I walked across the kitchen and hugged Liliana, then gave her a kiss on the cheek. "I missed you, pumpkin."

"Missed you, too, Momma."

I finally got the courage to look at Truitt. He wore a wide grin, and when our eyes met, he winked. My stomach did a somersault.

"When did y'all get here?" I asked.

"I saw Truitt out walking with Rus. I figured you were both up, and Liliana had been begging to come see Rus."

"Poor Wus is huwrt, Momma," Liliana said.

"I know, baby. Where is he?" I asked as I looked around the kitchen.

"He's in the living room. All set up with a comfy bed Evie made for him. Y'all are spoiling my dog and he's never going to want to go home," Truitt said.

I felt my face heat, knowing I didn't want Rus or Truitt to leave. He would have been fine at his own place, but the moment the doctor suggested Truitt not be alone, I jumped on it. I'm positive it was painfully obvious to everyone how much I wanted Truitt here.

"If you kids have got it from here, I need to head on out to the store. Truitt, your momma called and invited us all over to dinner on Christmas Eve."

Truitt froze and then slowly looked at my mother, a shocked look on his face. "My mother invited everyone over?"

"Yes. She mentioned how sweet it was of Saryn to take care of you and she wanted to repay her and visit with all of us. I haven't seen your mom in a few months. Last I heard she was in Europe or somewhere."

"Or somewhere," Truitt mumbled.

I frowned as I watched his brow pull in. A sour look crossed his face before he let it quickly fade away. Truitt didn't talk very much about his family. I knew it was just him and Roger, and neither of them had gone into the family business of cattle breeding. From what I could remember, his mother was never around. His daddy would come to the football games and the holiday parties. Never his mom.

"Mom, thank you for keeping Liliana the past few nights. Truitt was able to really rest and so was I."

My mother gave me a look that said she didn't believe for one second we...rested. I felt my cheeks heat at her look. Then she smiled, grabbed her purse and said, "My work here is done."

Truitt and I both watched her ease out of the kitchen like a leaf floating on the breeze.

"Why do I get the feeling she meant that in a totally different way?" Truitt said with a bit of humor in his voice.

"Because she did. She thinks she got us together."

Truitt laughed. "Well, technically, she kind of did."

I leaned against the kitchen counter and watched Truitt put two pancakes on a plate, and then motion to Liliana to sit at the table. Watching the two of them together nearly left me breathless. It felt like a normal thing that happened every day. Truitt in my kitchen making breakfast, and Liliana going on and on about absolutely nothing. When Rus hobbled in and lay down next to Liliana, my heart nearly exploded.

I brought my hand to my mouth as I tried to hold back the onslaught of tears that were threatening to break free. This was what I had always envisioned my family should be. Even when I found out I was pregnant with Liliana, I knew this would never be a scene in our house. With each day that passed, I knew coming back home was the best decision of my life.

Truitt helped Liliana put on her butter and then poured the syrup for her in a separate bowl when she informed him she liked to dip her pancakes in the syrup.

When he looked up at me, his smile faltered. I quickly dropped my hand and gave him the biggest grin I could. His dimples quickly came out on display.

"Truitt, sit down and get off that knee. Let me make you pancakes."

He did as I asked and sat down next to Liliana. I poured the batter my daughter had been so carefully stirring and listened to the two of them talk.

"Does Wus like panacakes?" Liliana asked, her mouth stuffed with a bite.

Truitt chuckled. "Rus likes any kind of food, but we have to be very careful what he feed him, 'cause if he eats too much people food, he'll get a tummy ache."

"Ohhh," Liliana said, concern and worry etched in her little voice.

"Do you know what I'm going to go do today, Liliana?" Truitt asked.

"No. What!"

"I'm going to check on a surprise for you."

She gasped and then clapped her hands. "I wike surpwises!"

"Me, too!" Truitt said.

I flipped the pancake and tried to calm my beating heart. How was it that Truitt seemed to burst into our lives and yet it felt like he had always been here? The thought of him not sitting in my kitchen every morning nearly left me with anxiety.

I placed the pancakes onto a plate and handed them to Truitt. "Want more than two?"

He shook his head. "No, thanks. This is perfect."

A moment later, I heard my brother calling out. "Hello? Who's home?"

"Uncle Wyan!" Liliana cried out.

Ryan came into the kitchen, a wide smile on his face. Rus looked up and gave him a few tail thumps, then focused back on Liliana in hopes some of her pancake would make it to the floor.

"Hey, pumpkin!" Ryan said as he swept over and kissed Liliana on the cheek. Then he kissed me on the cheek. Then he turned and looked at Truitt.

"Don't you look comfortable."

Truitt glanced around and grinned. "I am, thanks."

Ryan rolled his eyes. "Well, you don't have to look so...happy and satisfied."

My eyes widened as my mouth fell open. "Ryan!"

He brushed me off with a wave of his hand. "Please, like we really believed the whole *he can't be alone* excuse. You should have seen the shape he's been in in the past when Roger just dumped his a-s-s off at home. It'd be days before any of us even checked up on him and he survived."

Truitt laughed and that made Liliana laugh, even though she had no idea what she was laughing at.

"I see you're making a new best friend," Ryan stated as he leaned against the counter.

With a wink at Liliana, Truitt replied, "Are you my new best friend, Liliana?"

She nodded and then said around a mouth full of pancake, "Yep!"

"Well, pumpkin," Ryan said, "I need to borrow your new best friend. We need to get a move on."

A look passed between my brother and boyfriend.

I stilled. Boyfriend. Truitt was my...boyfriend. Wasn't he? Of course, he was. We've had sex more in the last few days than I had in the last three years of my marriage. The fact that I had even gotten pregnant with Liliana was a miracle.

Quickly eating the last of his pancakes, Truitt slowly got up.

"Have you used the ice therapy machine this morning at all?" I asked as I reached for the plate.

"Thank you," he said with a smile that made my insides melt. I took the plate and tried not to drool at the sight of this handsome man.

"Ice therapy machine?" I repeated.

He looked sheepishly away.

"Well, have you at least taken a pain pill?"

He downed his water, then pointed at me. "That I have done."

"Just remember, you only had surgery two days ago, Truitt. Please take it easy, will you?"

He leaned in and kissed me on the mouth and then said, "I promise I'll take it easy."

I was stunned by his easy show of emotion in front of Ryan and Liliana. I didn't mind that Liliana saw him kiss me. I wasn't so sure about Ryan. When I chanced a look his way, he wore a goofy smile on his face. I glanced down at Liliana who wore the same silly smile.

Okay, well, it appears my family is happy about this.

"Y'all be careful," I said as I watched Ryan and Truitt walk out of the kitchen. "Your cane, Truitt!" I called out and quickly brought it to him.

He snarled his lip as he looked at it. "Do I really have to?"

"Yes, you really have to."

Reluctantly, he took the cane, even with Ryan chuckling.

"Shut up or I'll hit you over the head with it!" Truitt said in a low voice so that Liliana couldn't hear him.

"Please don't do anything that will hurt you even more," I said.

Ryan lost it laughing. "If you're going to date this man, you better get that thought out of your head, sis."

Truitt glanced over his shoulder at me and smiled once more. It was the type of smile that little girls dream of. The one that says a million different things all at once.

I love you. I'll miss you. I want you. You're mine.

Truitt Carter had officially made me fall in love with him because of pancakes, winks, and smiles.

"See you soon, sweetheart."

I let out a sigh and whispered to myself, "And by calling me sweetheart."

Liliana came up and took my hand in hers.

"I wuv Twuitt, Mommy."

And there ya go. That clinched it.

"Me, too, pumpkin. Me, too."

Chapter 30

Truitt

RYAN AND I drove to Imaginations Unlimited first. Even though I didn't want to use the cane, I did it. I didn't really want to be laid up even longer simply because I was too proud to use a fucking cane.

"Well, if it isn't boss man," Jack said with a huge grin on his face. "Did you get my flowers?"

I shot him a dirty look. "Fuck off. How is everything going? All the finishing work getting done?"

He sighed and shook his head. "Seriously, you trust me so little that you came down here to check up on things? Yes, we are ahead of schedule and will be ready for the delivery on Christmas Eve. Stop worrying."

"I trust you, it's just that I want this to go smoothly. The fact that we're having to use a new trucking company makes me nervous. So, where are we on everything?"

Jack started toward the shop. When we walked into the large room, I took a quick look around. The playhouse was broken up into five large pieces that would be assembled together once we got it delivered. Each piece had to be carefully loaded onto the trucks, then tethered down.

"All the exterior painting is finished, same for the interior. Lee has finished doing all the stenciling Mrs. Night wanted to do on the inside. A few last-minute additions, and then we'll be ready to start loading up the pieces."

"Good, I'm glad we're on track. I'll be back in tomorrow if I can."

Jack rubbed the back of his neck and looked at Ryan, then back to me. "Roger told me that unless it was an absolute emergency, you were not to be bothered. And not to expect you back for at least a week. He said you needed...to heal."

"I needed to heal? My brother said that?"

Jack cleared his throat. "Something along those lines."

This time I looked at Ryan who wore a smug expression. I couldn't figure out why in the hell my brother would interfere in my job. I would have never told his staff not to bother him. I made a note to myself to talk to him later today.

Ryan lifted his hands up in defense. "Listen, I'm staying out of this. It's bad enough I have a mother who is..."

"Scheming," Jack quickly added.

I rolled my eyes. "It was never lost on me what your mother was up to, Ryan. But, she also wants a playhouse for her granddaughter, and I would really like to finish this job, so..." I looked at Jack. "Can we please get back to the subject at hand?"

He nodded, then cleared his throat. "Right, it's all good to go, Truitt. I've checked and rechecked everything. We will be ready for the move."

"Christmas Eve is in two weeks," I said more to myself than anyone else.

"It's all going to be fine," Ryan said this time. "I'm pretty sure my mother's main objective with this playhouse was to get you and Saryn together. Mission accomplished."

I smiled. "She had me fooled in the beginning, until your sister stormed into my office ready to fire me."

Ryan and Jack both laughed.

"I'm just glad your mother had already signed the contract and put a deposit down," I mused.

With a smirk, Ryan said, "The woman is smart, I'm telling you."

I looked back over the pieces. "I just want Liliana to love this playhouse and for it to be a good Christmas for both of them back home in Boerne."

Ryan placed his hand on my shoulder and squeezed it. "Liliana is going to be over the moon, but I'm pretty sure that's not going to be her best gift."

Facing, him, I lifted a brow. "What will be?"

He let out a soft chuckle. "You, Truitt."

"Me?" I asked in a surprised voice.

"Dude, if you can't see the way my niece and sister look at you, then you aren't paying enough attention."

A loud bang had the three of us turning and looking at the last playhouse piece.

"Shit!" Jack and I said at the same time as we made our way over to the piece.

"Well, that can't be good," Ryan mumbled from behind us.

"It's okay! It's just a piece of wood that was leaning against the wall. It dropped!" Jack said.

I let out a sigh of relief.

"Truitt, we need to take off if you don't want to miss your opportunity," Ryan quietly said when he walked up next to me.

"Right, let's do this. Jack, you're in charge."

He rolled his eyes and then saluted me. "Just get out of here and take it easy, will you?"

"I have one more thing to take care of, and then I plan to take it easy the rest of the day."

Ryan and I barely spoke two words as we drove to the Bevy Hotel to pay a visit to Tim. I finally broke the silence.

"Why is he staying at a hotel and not his folks' place?" I asked.

With a shrug, Ryan replied, "Probably because he's been keeping late hours, getting drunk out of his mind, and spending a lot of that newfound money he came into."

I shook my head in disgust. "Asshole."

"Always thought he was."

"What in the hell did your sister see in him?"

When Ryan didn't answer for a while, I looked at him and asked, "What's wrong?"

He gripped the steering wheel. "It's my fault she ended up with him."

"What do you mean?"

"If I had just been open with you and told you I knew you liked her and that I was okay with you asking her out, she would have never ended up with him. It's just, I wasn't sure at the time if I really *was* okay with you asking her out. She's my sister and I worried that she'd get hurt when you left for college, or that she'd follow you and not do her own thing. It turns out she ended up following an asshole who lied to her from day one."

"The past is the past, Ryan. If she hadn't married him, Liliana wouldn't be here."

He let out an exasperated sigh. "I know and I'm thankful for her. I am."

We pulled up to the hotel and parked. "I hate this motherfucker; I'm going to be upfront with you. It's not good enough that he cheated on my sister, gave up his daughter, and is trying to make Saryn's life miserable, but now he won't go the fuck away."

"I'm not a fan of him either. What room is he in?"

"Third floor, Room 2020."

I opened the door to the truck and got out. I left the cane behind, even though my knee had started to ache pretty good. But I wasn't about to show any signs of weakness.

Ryan knocked on the door. When it opened and Tim saw us, he went to shut it again. Ryan's boot kept him from doing that. I grabbed Tim by the shirt and pushed him back into his room.

"What in the hell are you two doing? Get out of my room," Tim shouted.

I gave him a good push that caused him to stumble back and then sit on the end of his bed.

"You're telling stories, Tim," I said as I pulled the desk chair out, spun it around, and sat down.

He looked down at my knees.

"Aww, don't worry about me, I'm healing up just fine. I've got a personal nurse looking after me."

Tim looked over to Ryan, almost expecting him to go after me for my comment.

"Listen, I don't know what you think you're doing," Tim said, "but you don't scare me, Truitt. You never have."

I raised a brow. "I didn't realize you thought I was trying to scare you. I'm not trying to do anything. I'm simply here to tell you that if you don't stop spreading rumors around about Saryn and Liliana, I will hurt you so bad that you won't be able to walk or talk for weeks."

He let out a humorless laugh. "You realize you're threatening me bodily harm, don't you?"

With a shrug, I replied, "I have a good lawyer if I need one. And I have a lot of money to pay for legal help if needed."

He narrowed his eyes at me. "You know that's the only reason she's with you. Money."

My jaw clenched. "She would have been with me a long time ago if you hadn't fed her a bunch of lies."

He scoffed. "You could have had any girl in school, yet you had your eyes on her. It's not my fault you were too afraid of Ryan to make a move."

I glared at him.

"We both know you would have had sex with her and then moved on. I beat you to it. And Saryn being Saryn thought she owed something to me. You know, the guy who took her virginity and all."

Ryan moved across the room.

"Ryan," I called out. "Don't."

He stopped and flexed his hands into fists as he said, "You little prick. You never deserved her. You lied to get her to even go out with you."

Tim shrugged and then looked back at me. "The only good thing that came out of my stupid marriage to her was that I had something you wanted."

Heat flared over my skin. "What is your fucking deal with me?"

He growled. "Oh, please, like you don't know."

"Dude, I honestly don't. The only thing I know for sure is it's taking every ounce of energy I have not to beat the living shit out of you."

Tim gave me a look that was filled with nothing but hatred. "Don't act like you don't know what we are to each other. You got everything, and I was forgotten like yesterday's leftovers."

I gave him a questioning look.

"You got the family, the fancy house, the ranch to run that both you and your brother fucking walked away from. You're the town football hero, the guy who every girl in high school wanted to be with. And then you had to catch her eye. The one and only girl who actually was kind to me and talked to me. No, you couldn't stand that, could you? So you plotted to take her away from me."

Ryan and I exchanged a quick look. What in the hell was this guy talking about?

"I heard you that day. You and Nolan were talking in the study room in the library."

I stilled, the memory of that very day coming back at me in flash. It was the day I told Nolan how much I liked Saryn. How I was going to ask her out. I was a senior and she was a junior and I worried about leaving for college without telling her how I felt about her. Nolan had told me I needed to tell her how I felt first, then deal with Ryan.

Tim laughed. "Don't look so surprised. I was in the study room next to yours, and I heard every single word the two of you said. How you had always liked Saryn but never wanted to tell Ryan. How you fell hard for her your sophomore year. How you were worried that Ryan would be upset, but that you couldn't stop thinking about her. There was no fucking way I was going to let that happen. I left the library and waited for Saryn after school that day. I told her how you were bragging about how you were going to ask her out and then sleep with her. That you wanted to be the one to punch the hole in her V-card. Needless to say, she was pissed, upset, hurt. I was there for her, though. Don't worry, I took care of her."

I had to force myself to stay calm. That night I had gone over to Ryan and Saryn's house with the intent of asking her out. She answered the door and I will never forget the look she gave me. My mind drifted back to the moment.

The door opened and Saryn stood there. At first, she smiled when she saw me, then the smile slowly faded.

"Ryan isn't here, I'm not sure where he is."

I grinned. "I didn't come to see Ryan. I was hoping to talk to you."

Her entire body went rigid. "Why?"

I felt my heart pound rapidly in my chest, and before I could answer, she spoke again.

"Unless it's something important, do you think we can talk tomorrow, maybe? I'm actually getting ready to go out on a date."

"A date?" I asked, confused.

Her smile looked forced. "Yeah, I'm going out with Tim."

"Tim?"

"Ackerman. Tim Ackerman."

"So does that mean...I mean...I was going to see if you might want to go out, but..."

My voice trailed off and something I couldn't read passed over her face. It looked like a mix of regret and anger. She straightened her shoulders and swallowed hard. Neither of us said a word. I wanted to tell her all the reasons she shouldn't go out with a dirtbag like Tim Ackerman.

But the way she looked at me said I was the last person she would even think of going out with. Had I misread all the looks between us? The way she smiled at me or how her cheeks turned pink when I talked to her? I had it all wrong. In that moment I felt the walls go up around my heart.

The sound of Ryan's old pickup came up the gravel drive. I shook my head and took a step back.

"Sorry to bother you, Saryn." I turned and walked toward the truck. I never looked back at her; I was too afraid to see the look in her eyes or, worse yet, for her to see the pain in mine.

I rubbed the back of my neck as the memory faded away. "That explains why she treated me so coldly that night when I went to ask her out."

"Is that why you were there?" Ryan asked.

I simply nodded. Ryan glared at Tim and looked ready to pounce on him.

"Listen, Tim, so you liked Saryn, fine. Why did you have to play a game, why not just let her pick who she wanted to be with?" I asked.

"Are you listening to anything I'm saying, Carter? Are you that stupid? Do you really not get it?"

I stood, pushed the chair out of my way, and grabbed Tim so fast he didn't even have time to react. I pushed him against the wall, all the while ignoring the throbbing in my knee.

"I'm sick of playing this fucking game with you. You took her away from me once, you're not doing it again. And Liliana is not some sort of toy you get to toss around and tell stories about. You signed your parental rights away, and you know damn well there's no way I could be her father."

An evil look passed over his face. "You don't know. Holy shit. I hate to break this to you, Truitt, but you are indeed related to Liliana."

I frowned and then pushed him harder against the wall. "Stop talking bullshit. Have you lost your damn mind?"

He laughed, and the pure coldness of it made my skin crawl.

"You are related to her. You're her uncle."

My grip on him eased up.

"What?" Ryan and I both said at the same time.

"God, this gives me such great pleasure to tell you this. Your father is also my daddy. Turns out he wasn't so happy in his marriage with your momma and he slept with my mother. My father didn't find out until a few years later. When he found out, he beat my mother and me. Told me I would never be his son. I was five at the time."

I let him go and took a few steps back. Nothing would come out of my mouth.

"Before you ask, your daddy knew. So did your momma. They knew, and they let me stay in that toxic fucking house all those years.

Beaten by a man who couldn't even stand to look at me because I wasn't his flesh and blood."

"And you never thought to ask Roger and me if we knew? If we had known we would have—"

"You wouldn't have done a damn thing. The two of you acted like the princes of Boerne. The sons of the great Nick Carter. The man everyone in town loved, and still fucking does. If people found out he had a bastard son, his whole life would have changed. He couldn't have people thinking ill about him or his homecoming queen wife."

I grabbed him by the shirt again. "That's enough."

"Fuck you, Truitt."

Before I could stop myself, I punched him. He dropped down to the floor and grabbed his jaw.

"I'm telling you right now, take your fucking money you got from your little inheritance and crawl back to Dallas. Saryn and Liliana are no longer your concern, and no one wants you here."

"You gonna take care of them now?" he asked.

"Yes. Because I happen to love them both."

He let out a roar of laughter. "You love them both? How sweet is that. The forbidden lovers have finally found their way to each other. The two of you deserve one another. As far as Liliana goes, I plan on getting a lawyer to recant my..."

I stepped closer to him, causing his words to fade away.

"You gave up your daughter, Tim. Listen to that closely. You. Gave. Her. Up. I will stop at nothing to make sure she never sees you again. And that little bit of money you came into, I can promise you this, I've got a lot more of it and can afford better lawyers."

His eyes flared.

"If you spread one more rumor or even attempt to go near either one of my girls, you will regret it until the day you die."

"Your girls?" he repeated, venom dripping from each word.

"That's right. *Mine.* Since you brought him up, I'm sure you remember Nolan. He has ways of making people...pay for things."

I gave Tim's chest a good push, causing his back to hit the door of his hotel room.

"Do we understand each other?" I asked.

For the longest moment he simply stared at me, then smiled and rubbed his chin. "You can have Saryn. Enjoy my sloppy seconds, brother."

Before I had a chance to go after him, Ryan did. I stood by and let Ryan get in about three good punches before I pulled him off.

"Let it go. He's not worth it, Ryan," I said.

Ryan pointed to Tim. "You ever step foot on our family's ranch and I will personally shoot you dead."

Tim swallowed hard, got up, and attempted to straighten his clothes, then opened the door.

"Get out of my room. Now."

As we made our way out of the hotel and back to Ryan's truck, I worked at calming myself down. We got into the truck, and Ryan looked at me.

"Nolan has ways of making people pay for things? Dude, he's a test pilot in the Air Force!"

I scoffed. "Tim doesn't know that. And that's what you got from that? Did you hear the whole part about him being my half-brother?"

Ryan nodded. "I was trying to forget that part."

We both laughed, and Ryan shook his right hand out. "Fucker has a steel jaw."

Flexing my own hand, I found myself suddenly needing to see Saryn and Liliana. "Let's get out of here."

Without a word, Ryan started the truck and we drove back to Saryn's house in silence. The first thing I needed to do after I saw Saryn and Liliana was talk to Roger about the bomb Tim had dropped on me.

Then we needed to talk to our father.

Chapter 31

Saryn

TRUITT HADN'T ACTED the same since he and Ryan came back to my house yesterday. It wasn't that he was distant, but something felt off. Even Ryan seemed to be taken aback by something. I decided I'd let it go, for now. If Truitt needed to talk to me about something, he would.

I slipped the French toast I had made onto the plate and put a little bit of butter on it. Liliana smiled as she waited for me to cut it into strips for her to dip.

"Two days in a row with the sweet breakfast," I said.

Liliana smiled. "Yummy!"

I glanced out the kitchen window. I could see Truitt standing outside, Rus sitting next to him. He looked lost.

The back door opened, and my mom walked in. "Good morning! I've come to see if I could take this little one off your hands for a few hours and take her to work with me. Santa is going to be visiting the stores and giving out goodies."

Liliana's eyes went wide. "Santa!"

My mother looked so proud of herself in that moment. Santa shopping on Main had been her idea a few years ago, and it had been a huge success.

"Sure, I'll probably swing by, if you can give me a heads up on what time he'll be there."

She nodded and then wiped Liliana's face. "He's slated to be at the store at one."

That gave me the whole morning with Truitt. I knew he was going stir crazy, and I needed to get him out of the house.

"Perfect."

My mother glanced down at Liliana. "You ready to go, sweet pea?"

"Yes! May I get Muke?"

"Of course! The more the merrier!" my mother exclaimed as she took my daughter's hand in hers and they made their way out of the kitchen and upstairs.

The back door opened, and I heard Truitt walk in. He was using his cane and that made me so happy.

"How's the knee?" I asked.

"Actually, it's doing pretty good. Listen, I need to run to my house and grab some more stuff if I'm going to stay here, or maybe I should just plan on heading home?"

He looked at me with an expression that seemed so unsure.

"I vote for you packing up some stuff and staying here."

A beautiful smile spread across his face. "That one gets my vote, as well."

Liliana and my mother came back into the kitchen. Mom was carrying her coat and a bag she must have packed up quickly.

"We are all set," Mom said. "You two enjoy the morning and I'll see you in a few hours."

I kissed Liliana goodbye. "I love you, be good for Grammy."

"I will, Mommy!" Liliana said, her arms wrapped tightly around my neck. When she let me go, she made her way over to Truitt. She carefully hugged his left side. "I see you, Twuitt. Miss you!"

My mother and I both sighed as we watched the exchange and saw Truitt light up.

"I'll miss you, too, pumpkin." Truitt looked up at me, confused.

"She's going to the store with Mom, and we'll meet them there in a bit," I said.

He nodded.

"Behave, kids!" my mother called out and then laughed.

I shook my head. "She's going to forever say she brought us together."

Truitt chuckled, and then walked over to me. "She did."

With a roll of my eyes, I groaned. "Yes, but don't let her know we think that."

He leaned down and kissed me. "You need to do anything, or should we leave now?"

"I can do the dishes later, they're not going anywhere. I'm dying to see your house!"

Truitt laughed and looked at Rus. "What about him?"

We both looked down at the dog passed out on the floor. "I think he's fine. You just took him out, and I gave him a pain pill right before that. I think he's out for a bit."

"Then let's head to my place."

The drive to Truitt's house was filled with light conversation and a few laughs. Truitt still hadn't told me what was weighing on his heart, but I wasn't going to push him.

"So, you don't live on your folks' ranch?" I asked as he pulled up to a large black gate. It wasn't anything over the top. I loved that he had Christmas decorations on it, though.

"No, I wanted my own place. Something that I earned myself, if that makes sense."

"Perfect sense," I replied.

The gate opened and we headed down a winding drive that was flanked with a four-plank fence. It was lined with beautiful oak trees that gave it such a romantic feel.

"Truitt, this is a stunning driveway!" I said.

He smiled. "Thank you."

I glanced out at the empty pastures as we made our way to the house.

"No cows or horses?"

"I've got a few horses, but I had to hire a ranch hand to help out. I've been so busy lately I haven't been able to keep up with it all. Mack, the ranch hand, lives on the property with his wife in a small one-story house that was the original ranch. She teaches riding lessons, so my horses at least get ridden."

My heart raced at the idea of riding. "I need to get Liliana on horses more often. I want her to learn to ride and soon."

Truitt reached for my hand and squeezed it. "Y'all can come ride any time you want. I've got five horses, for right now. I'd like to eventually get a few more."

"Five! That sounds like a dream already."

"Hell, if I knew I could win you over with the horses I would have brought you here sooner."

I laughed and then fell silent as Truitt pulled up to the house. It wasn't just any house. It was a large, ranch-style, one-story house. And it was beautiful. The sandstone rock looked like each piece had been hand-cut, and it gave the house a very classic look, yet it was rustic at the same time.

"This is your house?"

"This is my house."

I slowly got out of his truck. Looking to the right, I saw an equally impressive barn.

"The barn is almost as big as the house!"

Truitt laughed. "Not really, it just looks like it. I've got a covered arena, as well, where Mack's wife gives most of her lessons."

I turned and faced him. "Marry me. Right now!"

He laughed again and put his arm around my waist. "Come on, let's head on in."

The moment we stepped into the house, I fell in love. The space was wide open with a massive, double-sided stone fireplace in the middle of room. The kitchen sat to the right of the fireplace with a living area to the left of it.

"And you really want to stay at my place?" I asked as I walked toward the kitchen.

Rustic white cabinets lined two walls and a beautiful gray stone countertop added to the beauty of the kitchen. A large island sat between the kitchen and the fireplace. A round table with four chairs was off to the side in a nook that was all windows from floor to ceiling. I turned and saw a line of glass doors that led out to the backyard. The doors carried all the way through the living room, letting the outside in.

"Okay, how did I not notice the doors when we walked in?"

Truitt shrugged. "Most people see the fireplace and then get distracted by the kitchen, just like you did."

He smiled and I shook my head. "Come on," he said. "I'll show you around."

We walked through the kitchen into what looked like a butler's pantry...and what that led to nearly had me fainting. It was a room filled from floor to ceiling with wine and every kind of liquor you could think of.

"My version of a formal dining room," Truitt said.

"I like your version. How big is the house?"

His cheeks turned an almost bright red. "It's big."

"Tell me!" I said with a slight nudge on his upper shoulder.

"Six thousand, give or take a few hundred."

"Six. Thousand. Square. Feet?"

He nodded.

"Keep going."

We walked into another room that looked like his office. Rich dark wood covered the walls and ceilings with intricate trim and carvings that gave it such an elegant feel. I was so excited about the walls that I almost missed the small fireplace.

"I love this room," I whispered.

"Good, then it's yours. I hate this room. It's not me, my mother designed it."

"I'll take it!" I said with a slight laugh.

We looked at three bedrooms before we made it to the master bedroom.

A king-size bed occupied the large room. It had a white down comforter and two side tables that matched the rustic brown bedframe. A set of French doors were opposite the bed. On one of the doors was a set of bookshelves with an oversized chair, and the other side had a more masculine chair with a reading lamp and more bookshelves. I could totally see myself curled up in the chair reading a book.

Truitt opened the French doors to reveal the back porch. It was a large covered porch that overlooked a swimming pool, the stables, and the most breathtaking view of the Hill Country I'd ever seen.

Truitt told me there was also a media center, a workout room, another room he had envisioned as a playroom if there was ever a need for one, and a game room above the garage.

"I don't think I should see the bathroom," I whispered.

"Why not?"

"I won't ever want to leave."

He walked up behind me and leaned down to speak into my ear. "I have a huge walk-in shower where I could do all kinds of naughty things to you."

My knees wobbled, and Truitt turned me around to face him.

"I think we need to break the house in, what do you say?" He motioned to the large king bed.

I stepped back inside, and the moment after he had shut the doors and lowered the blinds, I found myself on the bed, naked, being kissed senseless.

"Truitt," I gasped as he moved his lips down my neck and took one of my nipples into his mouth. "Yes. Oh, God."

"I don't think I can be on top yet," he whispered against my skin.

When his hot breath hit between my legs, all thought vanished. "Okay. Just...just...touch me."

I heard a chuckle and then felt his mouth right where I needed it.

My body arched and I gripped the down comforter, moans and soft cries coming out as Truitt brought me to the most amazing orgasm ever.

The rest of the morning was spent in his bed.

The house was a dream. This was a dream. I soon found myself being woken up by kisses all over my face.

"Rise and shine, sweetheart," Truitt said. "We need to get

dressed and head into town."

I rolled over onto my stomach and moaned in protest. "No. I want to stay like this forever. Naked in your bed with your hands on me."

Truitt chuckled. "Hell, as amazing as that sounds, I don't think we can do it."

He kissed along my back and then slapped my bare ass.

"Time to get back to the real world."

When I rolled over, I looked at him. He had showered, shaved, and gotten dressed in jeans, a long-sleeve shirt that hugged his upper body in the most delicious way, and Lord help me...he had on his cowboy hat.

I swallowed hard, then sat up. There was a small suitcase by the door. I looked at it and then smiled.

"Going slow is for losers," I whispered as I jumped up and got myself ready.

Chapter 32

Saryn

"TONIGHT, SANTA WILL be coming. Are you ready?" I asked as I buttered my toast and took a bit of scrambled eggs.

Liliana nodded in excitement. "Where is Twuitt?"

I smiled. "He's outside with Granddaddy and Grams."

"Pwaying?"

"No, pumpkin, he's helping them with a surprise!"

Her eyes got wide. "For who?"

With the tip of my finger, I tapped her nose. "A surprise for you."

"For me!" she exclaimed.

The back door opened, and my mother walked in. "Good morning to my two favorite girls!"

Liliana slid out of her chair and rushed over to my mom. "Gwammy!"

"Oh, hello, my sweet baby girl."

They hugged, and I couldn't help but feel my chest squeeze. The decision to leave Dallas and come home proved itself right over and over again. Especially when I saw Liliana with my parents. I was glad that Tim's folks had never showed any interest in Liliana whatsoever. It was their loss as far as I was concerned.

"Okay, sweet pea, go on up to your room and grab Muke, 'cause Grammy is going to take you shopping today and we only have a few hours before Santa comes!"

"Okay!"

The moment Liliana raced upstairs, my mother took my arm.

"Sweetheart, is there something going on with Truitt and his parents? This morning he told me he didn't think it was a good idea to go over to his folks' house tonight. He said he didn't want to interrupt any Christmas Eve plans we had, and I told him it was perfectly fine."

"He hasn't mentioned anything, but I'm not sure how close he is with his family. I get the feeling not very close."

"I always got the impression the boys were a lot closer to their father than to Janet. She started traveling a lot when the boys were younger. I remember some holidays she wasn't even there. Sad, really." My mother frowned as if remembering something.

My chest ached, thinking about a younger Truitt and Roger without their mom on Christmas.

"Why did she leave them so much?"

With a shrug, Mom replied, "I have no idea. Nick and Janet always seemed like a happy couple until they weren't. A part of me wonders if things went south, and they simply stayed together for the sake of the boys."

"It's happened before," I said with a sigh.

Liliana came back down the steps with not just Muke, but two other stuffed animals.

"Well, looks like I'm going to have my hands full watching all four of y'all," I said.

My daughter giggled and then ran over to the mudroom to slip her shoes on. I reached for her jacket and slipped it on her, then stuffed her hat into the pocket of her coat. It was chilly outside, but nothing too terrible.

"You have fun with Grammy and be a good girl, okay?"

With a very excited nod, Liliana wrapped her arms around my neck and whispered, "I wuv you, Mommy. Be good today."

I laughed and kissed her quickly on the cheek.

"Have fun, Mom. Thank you for doing this. All of it."

Her brow rose. "All of it?"

I let out a breath and shook my head. "Yes."

She reached out, took my hand in hers, and gave it a squeeze. "You know, even if I hadn't arranged for Truitt to build this, I'm almost positive the two of you would have found your way to each other. Saryn, the way that man looks at you makes me swoon, and I'm your mother!"

My cheeks heated and I placed my hands over them. "Oh, Mom. I feel like we're moving at super warp speed, yet at the same time it feels like he's been in my world forever."

"In a way he has."

I tilted my head and regarded her. "Did you know we liked each other back in high school? Is that why you set this whole thing up?"

She laughed as she headed out the door, me following while holding Liliana's hand. As I opened the back door of my mother's car, I looked at her, waiting for her to answer me.

"I didn't know that at first. When I found out you were coming back I was at a bunko game. Margaret Bloom mentioned that Truitt had built her granddaughter a playground to beat all playgrounds. She showed us pictures, and I knew Liliana had to have one."

I tried not to roll my eyes at my mother's somewhat unhealthy keeping-up-with-the-Joneses attitude.

"Anyway, I made an appointment to meet with Truitt. It wasn't like I didn't know him. He probably spent more time at our house than his own when you kids were back in high school."

"Mom, get to how you found out."

She looked away sheepishly as I finished buckling in Liliana.

"Mom, how did you find out?"

"Fine! Fine! I might have looked through some of the things you had stored in your old bedroom. I was trying to find a picture you drew once when you were little. It was of your dream princess castle."

My eyes widened in shock. "I knew it! I knew that playhouse looked familiar!"

"What pwayhouse?" Liliana asked.

"Um, one at Truitt's office, pumpkin," I quickly said.

My mother smiled. "I was wondering when you would figure it out. You were only about seven or eight when you drew it. By the way, you were very talented at drawing."

"I still am," I said with a wink.

She smiled. "In my search, I stumbled upon a book. It fell and opened, and when I picked it up the writing caught my eye."

My stomach dropped. "My journal? Mom, you read my journal?"

"No! I mean, yes. I mean, only that one page. I'm so sorry! But when a mother sees the words, *I think I love him*, well hell, she's bound to stop and read."

I didn't have anything to say to that. If it was me and Liliana, I'd probably do the same.

"What else did you read?"

She shook her head. "I swear to you just that page. I had a feeling I didn't want to read what was next."

I shut the door and walked around to stand in front of my mother.

"Truitt and I have talked about our past. We both know that we felt something for one another, and it appears Tim had a hand in keeping us apart. He lied to me about Truitt. I believed him and it broke my heart, because I truly did think at the time that I was in love with Truitt."

My mother placed her hand on my cheek and gave me a sweet smile. "I really would like to rip that boy's balls off."

I laughed. "Me, too."

"Okay, let me get going with Liliana, keep me up to date on the delivery."

"Will do," I said as I kissed her on the cheek.

"Sweetheart, I am sorry I read part of your journal. And even though all I had planned was the playhouse in the beginning, I did have other ideas after I saw your confession."

I shook my head and kissed her once more. "It's okay, Momma. Everything turned out as it should. Y'all have fun."

"Oh, we will!" my mother called out as she got into the car. "A-shopping we shall go!"

There was something about watching Truitt work. He was commanding yet kind. He was a perfectionist and wanted everything to be just so. I knew it wasn't simply because this was for Liliana; no, he had to be like this for every playhouse he built.

We stood in front of the giant castle. Truitt's cousin Lee was inside adding all the interior touches. The yellow exterior of the castle was perfect, and Liliana was going to die when she saw it. Off to the side of the playhouse was a swing set with two swings, a seesaw, and monkey bars. I covered my mouth and nearly cried. It was stunning. It was over the top. It was the castle I had drawn when I was a little girl. Truitt had recreated it perfectly.

"You know, if you're looking for a job, I could really use someone who knows how to draw up the designs."

Truitt's voice from behind me caused me to spin around.

"You didn't say anything to me about this design starting with my old drawing," I said.

He laughed. "Your mother asked me not to. The original drawing is in the playhouse. Lee had it framed and is hanging it up in the bedchambers."

I hit him on the chest. "The bedchambers." Looking back at the playhouse, I sighed. "Truitt, is it obnoxious? Too much? I can't believe this is scaled down."

He wrapped his arm around my waist and pulled me to him. "Confession: I didn't really scale it down as much as I told you I would."

"Why am I not surprised?"

"Well, someday it might not just be Liliana playing in it. I tried to keep that in mind."

My stomach did a somersault and I turned to look at him. "I like the idea of filling it with one or two more little ones."

A wide smile grew over his face, and when his dimples came out on display, my knees went weak.

This man...oh, this man.

"I'm glad you like the sound of that." Truitt went to kiss me, but we were interrupted by someone clearing their throat.

Lee gave us a smile that said she knew what she had just walked up on. "The house is done. Ready to see the inside?"

I shook my head. "I want to wait until Liliana sees it for the first time. I want us to see it together."

Lee smiled. "I think that sounds like a great idea. Well, I'm done here, so I'm going to take off. I want to get home and finish wrapping up a few things."

"Oh, Lee, thank you so much for doing all of this and giving up your Christmas Eve," I said as I gave her a hug.

"Don't be silly! Most of it was done. It was just a matter of fixing up things that shifted in the transport and bringing in all the goodies we bought. I already staged it all at the warehouse, so I knew where everything was going. I really do hope Liliana likes it."

I looked back at the castle and then to her. "She is going to love it."

"Great! Listen, I'll talk to y'all later. Let me know if you don't like something, and we can change it around."

I nodded and watched as she walked off toward the driveway.

"I feel so bad that so many people had to work on Christmas Eve to make this happen on time," I said.

Truitt took my hand in his. "Nah, don't. They're all getting holiday pay for today."

I leaned into Truitt's body. "That is sweet of you to do."

"It's not sweet, it's the right thing to do."

My phone beeped, and I pulled it out. I had sent my mother a photo of the finished playhouse, or playcastle if we wanted to get technical. There still needed to be some landscaping around the castle, but Truitt had told everyone that could be done after Christmas.

"It's my mom. She loves it and cannot wait to see it in person."

"What time is the big reveal in the morning? I'd like to be here," Truitt said.

My head jerked up. "Where else would you be?"

Truitt laughed. "Home."

It felt like my heart dropped straight to the pit of my stomach. "Home? You're going home?"

Tilting his head, Truitt studied me. "Saryn, I was only at your place for a limited time."

"What if I don't want you to leave? What if I want you and Rus to stay with us?'

The corners of his mouth twitched with the grin he attempted to hold back. "Are you asking me to move in with you after one date?"

I laughed. "I think we can safely say we've had a few more dates. And I'm not asking you to move in, at least not yet. But it would be nice to have you there tonight and tomorrow morning."

Truitt swallowed hard. "I'd like that, but what about Liliana?"

"Let me ask you something, Truitt. Where do you see us in six months? Our relationship, I mean."

He blew out a breath and looked up before he focused back on me. "Well, I don't want to push my luck, but since we just built this massive playhouse here on your folks' ranch, I see me spending a lot of time here. With you and Liliana. I'd like to see y'all at my place, too. I've already thought about building something for Liliana there. On a much-smaller scale."

I smiled. "Yes, nothing so extravagant like this. Maybe just a normal tree house and some swings."

He nodded.

"But back to the other stuff," I said. "I see that, too. I'm not worried about Liliana, Truitt. She adores you. She loves you, she told me so."

Truitt's eyes widened a bit before filling with wetness. He blinked rapidly to keep from crying.

When he tried to speak, his voice cracked, and I fell more in love with him. Finally, he got his speaking voice back. "I love her, too."

Placing my hand on his chest, I drew in a slow, deep breath then exhaled. "She's not the only one who has fallen in love with you."

Truitt sucked in a breath.

"To hell with all the people who say it's way too fast for me to feel it, let alone say it. I fell in love with the boy who was my brother's best friend, and I don't think I ever stopped loving him."

Truitt cupped my face within his hands and kissed me. Neither one of us cared who was watching, what anyone said, or what rumors might spread. He kissed me like he had been wanting to do it for days. Months. Years.

"I've already fallen, sweetheart."

I wrapped my arms around his neck and kissed him again. This time the kiss caused a few people to whistle and yell for us to get a room.

"Are you done snogging my sister, dude?"

"Snogging?" Truitt repeated as we stepped away from one another. He took my hand in his and I loved how it made my stomach flutter.

"Kissing? Sucking face. Making out with her in front of everyone, including my father who currently looks like he might want to rip your balls off?"

Truitt and I turned to see my dad in a deep conversation with Jack and not paying the least bit of attention to us.

"Asshole, you interrupted a perfectly good kiss," Truitt stated.

"Whatever, just do it when I'm not around to see it. Please."

As Ryan walked away, I glanced up at Truitt. "My mom said you didn't want to go to your folks' house tonight. Is there a reason why?"

His smile instantly dropped, and Ryan stopped walking. He turned and looked at Truitt. Something seemed to pass between them. It was then I remembered a couple of weeks back, when Truitt and Ryan had acted strangely after they went out for a few hours. I had forgotten all about it. Life got so busy with Christmas, it had slipped my mind.

Truitt rubbed the back of his neck as he blew out a long deep breath. "Let me make sure everything is good to go here, and then we need to talk in private. The three of us."

Ryan made his way back over to us as Truitt walked toward Jack. I couldn't help but notice how much he was limping, and I wanted to say something about him not using his cane, but I let it go. For some reason, things just turned very serious. A part of me was scared to hear what Truitt had to say. Did this have anything to do with his strange behavior a few weeks ago?

"Come on, let's walk back to your place," Ryan said as he took me by the elbow.

"What's going on, Ryan?" I asked.

He focused straight ahead. "It's for Truitt to tell you, not me."

Chapter 33

Truitt

RYAN HEADED BACK to Saryn's house with her, giving me a few moments to get my thoughts together.

I knew I had to tell her, I was just figuring out how to do it. After I first found out, I didn't even want to think about everything that Tim had said to me. I was angry about so many things. Angry at Tim for lying to Saryn. Angry at my father for having an affair and leaving Tim to fend for himself. I was even somewhat angry that Saryn believed Tim's accusation when he said I only wanted to sleep with her.

All of it swirled around in my mind and confused me. I had planned on telling Saryn the day we went to my house for the first time, but one thing led to another and we ended up spending a glorious morning in bed together, and I totally let it slip from my mind. That was until Evie had reminded me of the dinner my mother invited everyone to tonight. I'd texted Roger to ask him if Mom had invited him, as well, and he said yes.

A million questions ran through my mind. Did my father really know Tim was his son? Did my mother know? Did Dad know Liliana was his granddaughter? What would Saryn say when she found out?

"Fuck," I mumbled as I made my way up the steps of Saryn's front porch.

When I walked into the living room, I saw Ryan sitting on the sofa and Saryn pacing across the floor.

"Truitt, you went and saw Tim? What were you thinking?" she asked.

My eyes swept over her body. She stood there, hands on her hips and a scowl on her face. My God, she was beautiful.

And she was mine.

"I was thinking he needed to stop hurting you and Liliana. That he needed to take his ass back to Dallas and leave you alone. And it worked."

She smiled slightly. "Is it true you hit him?"

My eyes darted over to Ryan who wore a smug smile.

"Yes, but only once. Unlike Ryan who kept hitting Tim until I pulled him away."

Saryn's eyes widened in horror. "What! Ryan! Why?"

"He said some pretty bad shit about you, Saryn. I'm your brother and that kind of talk isn't going to fly with me."

She rubbed her temples. "Okay, well, what does this have to do with going to your parents' house tonight?"

"You might want to sit down," I said as I motioned for her to sit next to Ryan. When she did, I sat across from her.

"Tim enlightened me on a few things during our...talk," I said.

Her brow rose. "Such as?"

"Well, for one, he told me that he overheard me and Nolan talking in the library my senior year of high school. I told Nolan how much I liked you, and that I was worried what Ryan would think if I asked you out. Nolan talked me into it. That was the same day I came over to your house and ..."

Her face went white. "I told you I was going out with Tim. He told me that day that you..."

"Wanted to take your virginity and brag about it. Yeah, I know. The way you acted makes a hell of a lot more sense now."

"Truitt..."

I held up my hand. "None of that matters now. What matters is this moment. You and me, right now. Tim isn't going to be interfering with us ever again."

"We think," Ryan mumbled.

Dragging in a deep breath, I went on. "Some of the things Tim said that day didn't make any sense to me. He was clearly very jealous of me and made comments about me having everything: a family, girls, popularity. He mentioned he liked you, and when he found out I did, too, he was hellbent on making sure I didn't get to be with you. It didn't make sense why he hated me so much until he dropped a bit of a bomb on me."

Saryn swallowed hard. "What kind of bomb?"

Ryan reached over and took her hand as I somehow managed to say the words.

"He's my half-brother."

If I thought her face was white moments ago, I was wrong. I almost stood up to go to her because I thought she wasn't breathing.

"Wh-what? How?"

"According to him, and I'm not really even sure if he's telling me the truth, but according to Tim, my father had an affair with his mother. His father found out about it, and from that moment on he abused both Tim and his mom."

Saryn closed her eyes and shook her head. "My God. It all makes sense. All of it."

"What do you mean?" Ryan and I asked in chorus.

She looked between us both. "Tim's father has always been... distant. I even remember one time asking Tim where he got his blue eyes from because his father had brown and so did his mother."

Her eyes met mine. "His eyes aren't nearly as blue as yours and Roger's, though. Now I know why Liliana's eyes always seemed so familiar. Tim doesn't look anything like the two of you."

I nodded. "No, he doesn't, but I got to thinking as Ryan and I drove back from his hotel. Tim looks almost identical to my grandfather. I never saw it before, because honestly I never thought to look for it."

"So, he disliked you so much that he only came after me to get back at you. I get that. But why did he keep up the act all through college and ask me to marry him? And when our marriage wasn't working, why did he fight to keep me…oh, my God. He only wanted to keep me from you."

"Look at what happened when you did leave him. What did you do?"

She wrung her hands together and looked at me. "I didn't come back thinking you and I would be together. Honestly, I assumed you would already be with someone. I won't deny that I still had feelings for you, though. I did."

"When Tim came back to town and heard someone say you and I were dating, he lost his shit."

Saryn buried her face in her hands. "Oh, my God. This is insane."

"He played both of y'all and took it as far as he could," Ryan said.

"I don't know if my father really knows about Tim, or if my mother does," I said, "but I'm not sure you and Liliana going over there tonight is a good idea."

Saryn stood. "If we're going to be in a relationship, Truitt, I'm not hiding from your parents."

I smiled. "I don't want you to hide, but I also don't want anything to happen to you."

"What in the world would happen?" she asked.

Ryan coughed. "Oh, let's see. Jealous wife meets her husband's grandchild who is not her grandchild. Flies off the handle, goes into a drunken rage, and Liliana sees it all happening."

"You really do know my mother," I said with a slight chuckle.

Saryn let out a frustrated moan. "Stop it, both of you. If you ask me, I think it all needs to come out in the open. At least with your father."

"I would like to remind you of something, as well," Ryan said. "Truitt is actually Liliana's uncle."

Saryn sat back down on the sofa. She covered her mouth.

"Are you okay?" I asked.

She nodded. "I feel so dizzy all of a sudden."

"Saryn, I am in no way expecting you to have Liliana call me her uncle."

"Oh, God, Truitt, it's not that. I don't care that you're possibly related to her. Actually, it makes your connection with her make more sense. Right now, I'm trying to decide if we tell my parents about this. I think they should know what they could be walking into tonight."

"You still want to go?" I asked.

She looked at me like I was insane. "Yes. We are going and you are going to talk to your father and get this figured out. We're not starting our future with a secret."

I glanced over at Ryan who gave me a look that simply said, *good luck, dude.*

Chapter 34

Truitt

SARYN TOLD HER parents the whole story about Tim, the affair that I still wasn't sure really happened, and how none of us knew if my mother or even my father knew. Of course Evie concluded that my mother did know. She stated that around the time I was two she started to travel more, leaving us behind with our father.

I requested that Roger come and pick me up and used the excuse of my knee acting up. I could drive fine now and had been released to do so. It gave me a chance to get my brother caught up on everything.

He seemed just as surprised and taken aback by Tim's accusation as I was.

"We need to talk to Dad about it," Roger stated.

"I agree. Tonight, before Saryn and her family get there."

He pulled up and parked in front of the large, two-story ranch house. My parents did well for themselves, but they were far from rich. My father earned more money off real estate he owned across Texas, New Mexico, Colorado, and Oklahoma than he did ranching. It was one reason Roger and I never really showed a desire to get into the ranching side of the family business. I enjoyed it, but I was perfectly fine having Billy, our ranch foreman, run the ranch with our father. Roger, of course, kept a close eye on everything to make sure

Billy didn't obtain too much control. Someday I might decide to take a bigger interest, but for now, my life was Imaginations Unlimited and the two woman who owned me heart and soul.

The front door opened, and our mother appeared. She was dressed in a white dress with red accents.

"Merry Christmas Eve!" she said as she held out her arms for each of us to hug her. "I've missed you boys."

Roger leaned closer to me and whispered, "Looks like someone has already been hitting up the eggnog."

I chuckled, then hugged my mother after Roger did.

"When did you get back?" I asked.

"The day before your accident, sweetheart. My goodness, I really had hoped you would grow out of this accident-prone thing."

Roger laughed. "That's how he gets the women, by making them feel sorry for him."

Our mother playfully hit Roger in the chest. "Stop that now. And what about you? When are you going to settle down and give me a grandbaby."

The laugh that came out of Roger nearly made me laugh, too. We walked into the house, and I quickly looked for my father.

"Dad around?"

With a forced smile, she pointed to the study that had always been our father's home office. "He's in there, pouting."

I tried to think back to a time when my mother and father were more loving to each other. The more I thought about it, the more I realized I had never actually seen them show any affection. Maybe the occasional kiss on the cheek or hug, but nothing like what I had seen Evie and Will do. Or Pete's parents, or Paul's. And I had always thought Nolan's parents were a little weird, because they were constantly kissing and hugging.

"I need to talk to Dad about a business deal I'm fixin' to do. Do you mind, Mom?" I asked.

Before she could answer, Roger held out his arm to her. "Come on, let's go make a drink and you can tell me all about your trip to..."

"Italy!"

"Right, Italy," Roger replied as he guided our mother out of the room.

I knocked on my father's office door and waited for him to call out.

"Come in."

His voice sounded cold and distant. When he looked up and saw me, though, he smiled and stood.

"You look better than the last time I saw you at the hospital."

As he walked over to me, I held out my hand. He gave it a shake and then pulled me in for a quick hug.

"You came to the hospital? You hate hospitals, Dad."

"Well, it's not every day my son has surgery. When Roger called, I wanted to be there."

He motioned for me to sit down as he walked over and poured us each a whiskey.

I took the whiskey and said, "You should be used to that from me."

He laughed. "I never told you this, but when I was younger, much younger, I was a bit of klutz."

"You?' I asked before I took a drink.

"Yes, indeed. You remind me a lot of myself when I was younger. I'm glad you followed your dreams, even when I gave you a hard time about it."

That took me by surprise. "Was ranching not your dream?"

He looked at his glass and swirled the brown liquid in it as if deep in thought. He finished it off and then answered me.

"Honestly, no. I wanted to leave Boerne and join the Marines."

"The Marines!" I said with a surprised laugh.

"Yes. Your grandfather told me if I did he would disown me, and I'd never be allowed on this ranch again."

My mouth dropped slightly open. "I didn't realize that, Dad."

He nodded. "He also arranged for me to marry one of his best friend's daughters. Said the match would be good for the two families."

I was pretty sure my heart jumped to my throat.

"You didn't want to marry Mom?" I asked.

He stood and walked over to the bar cart, pouring himself another drink.

"What brings you in here, son?"

He didn't answer my question, and I wasn't sure if he would answer the next one either.

"Dad, I need to know something, and I need you to tell me the truth."

His brows pulled in tight. "I'm always truthful with you boys."

"Did you have an affair that resulted in a baby boy being born?"

My father stared at me with a blank expression for the longest time.

"What did you say?" His voice sounded small, unsure. It wasn't something I was used to. My father always had a strong presence. It was in the way he stood and held himself. And it was in the way he talked with authority and with purpose.

I sighed. "Dad, is Tim Ackerman your son?"

This time he let out a string of curses. "That little bastard told you, didn't he?"

To say I was stunned by his words was an understatement. "If by 'little bastard' you mean Tim, then yes, he told me."

I watched as he pulled in a long, deep breath and then slowly exhaled.

"Yes. It's true."

My eyes closed, and I felt my entire body drop. "Does Mom know?"

"Yes. I told her after Tim was born. I couldn't keep something like that from her."

"That's why she's always traveling?"

My father turned and faced me. "Truitt, when I married your mother, I wasn't in love with her. I tried to fall in love with her, and I grew to care for her deeply. She...she never...oh, hell. She never warmed much to me after our wedding. I had a lot of affairs over the first year of our marriage. It's not something I'm proud of. After I gave up the skirt chasing, your mother and I grew closer. I started to fall for her. After she had you, she fell into a depression and she pulled back. Like her duty of providing me a set of sons had been accomplished. I was lonely and I sought comfort. Tim's mother told me she couldn't get pregnant. That she was unable to have kids. Turns out it was her husband who couldn't have kids and never told her. He knew the moment she ended up pregnant that the baby wasn't his. She tried to blackmail me for money to get rid of the baby. I said that I would take the baby and she practically laughed in my face. After Tim was born, she invited your mother to the hospital; they were friends."

He looked down, shame all over his face. "When your mom held Tim in her arms, that was when Fran told her I was the father. Your mother was so hurt and taken aback, she never could get over it."

"Then why did she invite Saryn and her family over here? I wouldn't think she would want to see Liliana."

"She didn't invite them. I did. I never was allowed to see Tim or have anything to do with him. Fran got a restraining order, said I was stalking her. I thought it best to just pretend Tim wasn't my son. Even as he grew older, I didn't attempt to reach out. Then I heard what a little prick he was, and I was glad I didn't have any contact with him."

That little bit of information felt like a brick in my stomach.

"When I saw Saryn at the hospital that night and saw how she looked at you, I figured you two were together. Then Ryan confirmed it. I told your mother I wanted to meet my granddaughter. She was free to come home or stay in Italy."

"And she wanted to come home? Is she going to do something? Start something?"

He chuckled. "No. I think she regrets never being there for you kids. Maybe she'll look at Liliana as a second chance. I mean, if you two are serious."

I wasn't about to share with my father about my relationship with Saryn.

"If she says or does anything," I said, "we'll leave, and we won't be coming back. I care deeply for Saryn and Liliana."

He raised a brow. "Do you love her?"

"Yes. I do."

I waited for the lecture, the one where he said we hardly knew each other and we should take it slow. Instead, he smiled and drank down his second whiskey.

"Then don't let her go."

There was a knock on the door, and my mother poked her head in. "They're here."

I stood and walked over to my mother. She gave me a knowing look. "I spoke with Roger."

I nodded and kissed her on the cheek. Then I whispered in her ear, "I'm sorry, Mom."

She patted me on the back. "The past is the past. Let's move on and start a new path, shall we?"

"Let's." I wasn't sure how I was supposed to feel after my father's declarations. The fact that he didn't love my mother when they married. How he'd cheated on her. It put my father in a new light, and I wasn't sure how I would deal with it.

Whisking away from me, my mother threw open the door. There was the woman I remembered, the one who loved to throw parties. Always the happiest hostess around. Except this time there was something different. She didn't seem to be playing a part. When she saw Liliana, she bent down and smiled at her.

"Those blue eyes, my goodness. Aren't you a pretty little thing."

Liliana hugged Muke tightly. "Tank you!"

My mother wrapped Liliana up in a hug before standing and giving Saryn a hug and then Evie. Will and Ryan came in and shook my father's hand. Then it was my father's turn to see Liliana. He looked slightly taken aback. Clearly, he'd noticed that Liliana's eyes were the same color blue as his. As mine. As Roger's.

Lifting my gaze from my father, I met Saryn's. She seemed at ease, and not the least bit worried. I was going to have to take lessons from her on how she did that.

"Liliana, I'm Nick Carter, but you can call me Pop if you want."

Liliana smiled that brilliant smile of hers. She tilted her head as she giggled and repeated the word. "Pop."

My father laughed.

Liliana took it all in and then said, "Pop, this is Muke!"

My father shook the small teddy bear's paw and replied, "So very nice to meet you, Muke."

The rest of the evening seemed like a dream. Dinner around my folks' table, laughter, stories, and then hot chocolate and gifts. On the Christmases my mother was home, that was what we did on Christmas Eve. She made hot chocolate, we sat around the fire, and we each got to open one gift.

With Saryn sitting at my side, her hand laced in mine, everything seemed to be in place. I wasn't used to things being in place in my life. Everything I touched seemed to falter somehow. Everything with the exception of Imaginations Unlimited.

But with Saryn, things simply felt right. As a matter of fact, everything seemed to be going perfectly, and that made me want to knock on wood. I felt at ease. I was less stressed than usual. I was happy, truly happy, for the first time in years. I knew it was because of Saryn and Liliana.

I glanced over to see Liliana sitting on the floor with my father, Roger, and Ryan. They were teaching her how to play a game. When I looked up and met Will's eyes, he smiled, then gave me a nod. Evie and my mother were chatting about a charity function, and I heard my mother offering to help out. She even told my mother she'd love to go to the store and see how it all worked behind the scenes.

Before I knew it, my mother was bringing out a large cake with a candle on top.

Saryn smiled and Liliana jumped up. "Cake!"

"I know your birthday isn't for another two days, but we're all together, and I didn't want to miss this opportunity to celebrate."

I stood and walked over to the dining room table. Saryn had one of my hands, while Liliana tugged for me to pick her up. I reached down and picked her up and held her while I closed my eyes and made a wish, hoping that I wasn't dreaming.

Chapter 35

Saryn

LILIANA RUSHED INTO my bedroom just as the sun began to rise and jumped on my bed. Truitt had snuck out only an hour before and headed to the guest room. Once Liliana had me awake, she bounded quickly to Truitt's room.

She calmed down some so that Rus didn't get too excited and hurt his leg more. It had been almost three weeks, and he was getting around a lot better, but I had been a very overprotective doggy mom and still made Truitt use a leash when he took him out. It only took Truitt explaining to Liliana that if Rus got too excited he'd have to have another surgery for her to know she couldn't get him too excited. I looked at him with my brows raised and wanted to say that the same thing went for him.

Liliana climbed carefully up onto the bed, then looked back at me and giggled. I stood in the doorway to the guest room, watching them. Truitt was asleep, his arm over his eyes as he breathed softly.

"Twuitt!" Liliana whispered shouted. "Twuitt! Santa came!"

Truitt and I had been up until almost two in the morning wrapping presents and simply talking. At one point we sat on the back porch, cups of hot chocolate in our hands, lost in conversation. We talked about everything and anything. Truitt even offered me a job with Imaginations Unlimited doing the interior design work, as well as drawing out plans. I'd never thought about doing anything other than nursing, but the idea of doing something different and working alongside Truitt left me feeling giddy and excited. It didn't take me long to tell him yes…I'd take the job.

Liliana nudged Truitt harder. I saw him peek an eye open and then close it.

"Go away, Rudolph, I'm still sleeping."

With her hand clasped over her mouth, Liliana giggled.

"It's not Wudolph! It's me! Liliana!"

Truitt moaned and said, "No, Rudolph, it's too early!"

My daughter fell into a fit of laughter on the bed. When Truitt leapt up and started to tickle her, Rus got up. I bent down and gently pet him to keep him calm.

"Shh, they're only playing, sweet boy. Let's go potty and get something to eat."

I glanced over my shoulder once more and saw Liliana sitting on the bed, crisscross applesauce, as she explained to Truitt how Santa had come in the middle of the night and left presents. His attention was one-hundred percent focused on her.

My heart couldn't have felt fuller. After taking care of Rus, I walked into the living room to find Liliana nearly jumping out of her skin.

"Mommy! Mommy! Pwease!"

I tried not to laugh as I asked her, "Can you find the ones with your name on them?"

"I can!" she declared and promptly set out to find them.

Truitt and I sat on the sofa and watched Liliana open her presents one by one. Every now and then I would drop to the floor and help her with one or explain what something was.

After Liliana opened all her presents, she looked between me and Truitt.

"Did Santa not bwing you any?"

Truitt turned and looked at me, a smile so sweet that it made a warm sensation travel over my skin.

"Your mommy was my present this year," Truitt said before he leaned over and gently kissed me.

Liliana giggled, then asked, "Do you wuv Mommy?"

His eyes sparkled, and even if he didn't answer, I saw it.

My phone rang, interrupting the moment.

"Saved by the ring!" I said with a chuckle.

"Hello?"

"We're dying over here, sweetheart. When are we going to get to show Liliana the playhouse?" my mother pleaded.

"How about right now?"

"Yes!" I could hear my father say in the background.

"Did Ryan stay the night?" I asked.

"He did, and we just finished biscuits and gravy."

Truitt waggled his brows and licked his lips.

"Is there more? We haven't eaten breakfast yet. Liliana was too excited to wait," I said.

"Of course, I can make more up."

"Then we're on our way."

I hit End and looked at Liliana. "We need to go change really quickly, Liliana. Granddad and Grammy said Santa left you something in their backyard!"

Liliana gasped. "What is it?"

Truitt laughed. "Let's all get dressed and go see!"

As we walked toward my folks' house, Truitt carried Liliana, even though I argued against it. I knew his knee was healing nicely, but the man never stopped, and I'd seen the way he limped on his leg last night.

I was relieved when Truitt decided that Rus had to stay, even though Liliana begged. I was impressed he held firm on the rule, yet was gentle about it. There was no doubt he would make an amazing father.

My stomach jumped at the idea of someday having a baby with this man.

"Are your eyes closed?" Truitt asked Liliana.

"Yes!" she squealed in delight as she buried her face into his neck. "I'm not peeking! I pwomise!"

My parents and Ryan were waiting for us at the end of the pathway that led to the house. I was shocked to see that someone had come back and added a few more touches to the outside of the playhouse.

"Who did this?" I asked.

Truitt smiled. "Had to be Jack."

I shook my head and said, "I'm going to have to give him a big hug and kiss."

"Over my dead body!" Truitt stated.

We stopped next to my folks, and Ryan peeked at Liliana over Truitt's shoulder.

"Good morning, pumpkin! Merry Christmas."

"Uncle Wyan!" Liliana exclaimed.

"Okay, Liliana, close your eyes and don't open them until we tell you to!" I said as Truitt set her down and I slowly turned her to face the playhouse castle.

I leaned down and said, "Open your eyes, Princess Liliana."

My daughter let out a scream of delight when she saw the castle. She dashed for the front door before any of us had a chance to even move. My mother and father quickly went after her, followed by Ryan. I turned and faced Truitt, who was watching with a wide grin on his face.

"Thank you," I said.

He looked at me and tilted his head as if confused. "For what?"

I looked at the playhouse and then back at him again. "For agreeing to do the playhouse and not letting me fire you."

He laughed and pulled me against his body. "It's just the beginning, sweetheart."

I nearly swooned in his arms, but my daughter's repeated calls to come look at this or that had me walking into the castle. The attention to detail was beyond amazing. Truitt had taken me to a few other playhouses he had designed, and I knew he was extremely talented. They had really thought of everything. I was beyond proud of him.

"In one tower is a dress-up area and stage to perform little plays," Truitt said from behind me. "The other tower is, of course, Princess Liliana's bedroom with a little place to do art work."

"There's a ballet barre in here!" I gasped as I walked in and saw a small area had been made up as a tiny dance studio. Another area was a little lounge with a small sofa and pillows on the floor. A TV hung from the wall and was flanked by family photos of me, Ryan, and our parents. On one wall was a small bookshelf lined with books that my parents kept in their house for Liliana.

I spun around and watched as Ryan climbed a twisting staircase and followed Liliana and my father up.

Another squeak of delight came from my daughter, followed by one from my father. I looked at Truitt who simply smiled.

"That one is for the older kids. It's a media room."

My mouth dropped open. "A media room?"

I quickly climbed the staircase and stopped at the top. Six chairs faced a wall that had a pull-down screen. My parents must have paid a small fortune for this playhouse. Hell, could you even call it that?

"There's a projector. Holy shit, he put in a projector!" Ryan exclaimed. "I'm totally spending the night more often."

"Think of the football games we can watch up there," my daddy said.

I covered my mouth with my hand and stared in disbelief. My mother walked in and had to grab onto one of the recliner chairs.

"It's your own personal movie theater, Liliana!" my father exclaimed.

"Yay! What's that?" Liliana asked mid-jump.

"It's where you watch movies, pumpkin. But on a really big TV," I answered.

There were two walkable bridges that took you to each tower. Liliana's bedroom was done up in the most adorable way. It was princess-themed with a light shade of yellow for the wall color. My heart soared as I watched Liliana climb up onto the bed. A beautiful net surrounded the bed and could be closed or left open.

"This is too much. Way too much," I mumbled. I faced my mother. "Did you have to take a loan out on this? How in the world did he get this thing built in just a few months?"

She shrugged. "He devoted all his time to it from what I'm told. Paid his employees overtime to get it done by Christmas Eve. He didn't do it for me, he did it for her."

My mother pointed to Liliana who was spinning around the room and laughing.

"I plan on having more grandchildren, so it was a good investment. Truitt said the dress-up room in the other tower can easily be made into another bedchamber, should we need to make one for a boy."

"Yeah, my bedchamber, please," Ryan said as he headed down the winding staircase.

"I can't believe he built this," I said again.

Wrapping her arm around my shoulder, my mother said, "He is one very talented young man. His attention to detail is unbelievable, and I'm not sure how he pulled this off. It's like a small house!"

"It's like you said, he did it for her," I whispered. I faced my mother and our eyes locked. "I love him, Mom."

She gave me a soft smile. "Fate is a funny thing, sweetheart."

I saw Truitt pop up and I gasped. "You cannot be climbing these stairs with your knee, Truitt!"

He laughed. "It's fine. I wanted to see what you thought about her room."

My eyes filled with tears of happiness. "It's perfect."

You're perfect, in every single possible way.

"Truitt, everything is amazing. It's beyond amazing. It's beautiful. Y'all must have killed yourselves getting this done."

He simply shrugged and then gave me one of his famous winks that nearly left me panting with want. I was going to have to find a way to sneak off with him sometime today.

"I'll head back down, meet y'all there," Truitt said.

As my mother followed Truitt back down, I took another look around. Happiness engulfed me, and I placed my fingers on my lips to keep from crying.

With each step down the winding staircase I couldn't shake the feeling that life couldn't possibly be this amazing.

Chapter 36

Truitt

CHRISTMAS, MY BIRTHDAY, and the new year came and went in the blink of an eye, and before I knew it, it was the end of January. Things with Saryn were going strong and steady. I had pretty much moved in with her and Liliana, or it felt like I had. Rus and I spent more time at Saryn's place than we did at my own. Saryn and I had decided I would stop setting my alarm early in the morning and sneaking into the guest room. Most mornings I was up before the girls anyway and going for a run.

Saryn had agreed to come work for Imaginations Unlimited, much to Lee's delight. She was now able to take more time off, and Saryn proved to be a natural at decorating the interior of the playhouses. Yesterday she had come to the office and handed me a drawing she had done of a playhouse we had been asked to design. I stared at it for the longest time before she had asked me if it was terrible.

"The opposite, sweetheart. This looks like our architect drew it."

She simply shrugged. "I love doing it."

I rounded my desk and pulled her into my arms. "And I love having you do it."

Her eyes met mine, and as I moved down to kiss her, she whispered, "I love you, Truitt."

With a smile, I replied, "I love you, too."

When our mouths parted, I looked deep into her eyes and prayed what I was about to say wouldn't spook her. "I'd like to have Liliana pick out a room at my house. Y'all can decorate however you would like."

Her eyes lit up. "Truitt, she would love that!"

"I know we haven't talked about it yet, but I'd love to move you and Liliana into my place sometime in the future. It's a bit more... private."

Saryn laughed. "I think that is a great idea."

"I think we should seal it with a kiss."

And seal it we did.

I pushed open the door to the Rusty Nail and walked in. It had been a long while since I had met up with the guys for a night out. I moved through the crowd and caught my brother walking toward a corner table with a handful of beers.

In the booth sat Ryan. Next to him was Pete, who had called off his wedding to Wendy when he came home early from work one night and found her in bed with another guy. Saryn had also dumped Wendy after they had met for lunch one day, and she began to fill Saryn in on the supposed love affairs I had going on all over town.

Jack sat on the other side of Pete. Since Paul had gotten married last year, he had declined almost every one of our guys' night out invitations. I was pretty sure Roger had stopped inviting him at this point.

"Finally! I didn't think you were going to show up!" Ryan said as Roger handed him a bottle of Bud Light, then passed one to me.

"I told you I'd be here," I said, flipping a chair around and sitting on it.

The four of them looked at me as if waiting for me to say something. I took a drink from my beer, set it down on the table, and then laughed.

"Why in the hell are y'all staring at me?" I asked.

Roger lifted a brow. "Is there something you want to tell us?"

I thought about it for a moment. "No, should there be?"

Ryan frowned. "Are you sure?"

I gave them a hard stare.

"Unless you want to hear about the new playhouse we're fixin' to design, then no, I don't have anything new to tell y'all."

Roger huffed as Ryan shook his head. Pete looked out at the dance floor while Jack stared at me.

"What's the matter with y'all?" I asked.

Jack motioned his beer toward Ryan. "It's your sister, you should be the one."

I started at Ryan. "Should be the one to what?"

With a sigh, Ryan placed his bottle of beer down. "Lucy said that she heard from Ms. Townsend's niece that you were seen coming out of Boerne Jewelers earlier today."

"So?"

"So?" they all said at once.

It didn't take me long to figure out why they were all staring at me like I was keeping something from them.

"The owners are interested in a playhouse for their daughter. They asked me to meet them there since it's close to Valentine's Day and they're busy."

"Thank fuck," Roger mumbled. "My God, I thought you had lost your mind."

I shot him a look. "What do you mean?"

"Lucy hinted that you might have bought Saryn a little something for Valentine's Day," Ryan said.

"A ring. They all thought you were going to ask her to marry you, but I knew better," Roger stated with a smug expression.

I laughed. "I know we moved fast when it came to getting together, but I don't think Saryn is in a rush to walk down the aisle."

When I noticed Pete hadn't said anything, I looked at him.

"You're quiet on the subject."

He looked around the table and then at me. "I need to talk to you."

"Okay."

With a shake of his head, he added, "In private."

"Right now?" I asked with a half-hearted laugh.

"Yes. Right now."

He motioned for me to follow him, so I did. "We'll be right back," I said as I stood and turned to walk behind Pete. He walked down the back hall and then slipped into a back room that was used for private parties. When I followed him into the room, he shut the door.

I faced him. "What's wrong?"

Pete scrubbed his hands down his face and then dropped them to his side.

"I know something, and I probably should just mind my own business but I...I can't."

"What's it about?" I asked.

He gave me a blank look. "Saryn and you."

My stomach lurched, and for a panicked moment I thought he was going to say he'd seen her with another man. I quickly pushed that out of my head. I knew Saryn would never do anything like that.

"Okay, what about us?"

Pete looked serious as all get-out as he said, "How serious is it with y'all, Truitt? I mean, do you see a future with Saryn?"

I chuckled. "I would say it's pretty damn serious. I'm damn near living with her, and I can't imagine my life without her."

He blew out a breath and looked relieved. "Then you might want to rethink the whole asking her to marry you thing, and do it quickly."

I tried to figure out what in the hell was wrong with him.

"Why?"

He shook his head. "God, I want to tell you, but she'll kill me."

"Who?"

"Saryn. And Renee."

"Who's Renee?" I asked, starting to feel slightly frustrated.

"She's someone I started dating a few weeks ago. I picked her up for lunch yesterday and...I saw Saryn leaving the office where Renee works."

"Ooookay. Can you give me a little more information there, Pete?"

He looked nervous. "Renee didn't know I knew Saryn, and she happened to mention something about her that she really shouldn't have...the whole patient privacy thing and all. When she realized I knew who Saryn was, she made me swear I wouldn't say anything."

"You're starting to freak me out, Pete. Is Saryn okay? Where does this Renee work?"

"Northwest Ob/Gyn Associates. She's a nurse there."

I paused for a moment before my heart started to beat rapidly.

"She's been feeling sick the last week, couple of weeks, actually," I mumbled.

"In the mornings?" Pete prodded.

I nodded.

"Throwing up?"

"Yes."

Pete attempted not to smile. "Sooo, morning sickness..."

I took a step back in utter shock. "Saryn's pregnant!"

"She is?"

Confused beyond belief, I pushed Pete. "I don't know!"

"You said it, not me!" Pete said, looking relieved and excited all at once.

I pushed my fingers through my hair. "I don't know if she's pregnant!"

"Oh, well..."

"What in the hell! What are you saying? What did this Renee tell you?"

He held up his hands for me to slow down.

"Take a breath, Truitt. Take a breath."

"I am taking breaths! A lot of them! She can't be pregnant, Pete. She's on the pill. I wear a condom every single time. So it's impossible!"

"Truitt, just take a second to slow down."

I leaned over and placed my hands on my thighs as I dragged in one deep breath after another. Could Saryn be pregnant? How would I feel about that? How would she feel? The moment of panic quickly vanished and was replaced by an excitement I'd never experienced before.

When I finally stood up straight, Pete was staring at me, clearly worried he had fucked up big time.

"I wasn't sure how you would feel about it. I asked Roger what you'd do if Saryn ever got pregnant, and he said you'd freak."

I rolled my eyes. "Don't ever ask Roger anything about relationships. He's going to stay single his entire life."

"Are you okay?"

"It depends, what did Renee say?"

He turned, putting his back toward me. "When Saryn walked out of the building and Renee saw her..."

"Wait. Pete? What in the hell are you doing? Why are you standing with your back to me?"

"I can't tell you directly. I told her I wouldn't, so I'm just sort of talking to myself in the same room as you."

My mouth dropped open. "This is what you're going to tell yourself? That you were talking out loud and I happened to overhear it?"

"Yes."

I shook my head. "How are you a doctor? Seriously? How?"

"Do you want to know or not?"

"Yes, I want to know, you dickhead, but turn and look at me, goddamn it!"

He spun around. "Fine! Renee saw Saryn and laughed. She said that she was a patient of theirs and had just found out she was pregnant, and when the doctor told her, Saryn apparently threw up. All over the doctor. Then I said something like *holy shit, Saryn is pregnant,* and then Renee freaked because I knew her, and the rest is history."

"She threw up on the doctor? Why?" I asked.

Pete shrugged. "Nervous, excited, scared? I don't know. Dude, did y'all ever have sex without a condom?"

"I already said—"

I stopped talking, and Pete raised one brow.

"Shit. The second time we ever had sex the condom broke. Saryn said she was on the pill, so I honestly never thought anything about it."

"Well, neither is a hundred percent accurate, you know."

"No shit, Sherlock."

Pete attempted to hide his smile. "So how do you feel about this? About Saryn being pregnant so early in your relationship?"

I thought about it for a moment or two. Then a strange feeling of warmth settled over me. I looked at Pete, and that happy feeling was replaced by anger.

"How in the hell could you tell me? *Why* would you tell me? It should have been Saryn telling me, not you, dickhead!"

He looked at me, befuddled. "Are you angry because you're going to be a dad, or because I'm the one who told you?"

I balled my fists. "Because you told me, you idiot!"

"Right. I can see that...now that I think about it. Probably wasn't the best thing for me to do."

With a frustrated groan, I turned and headed to the door.

"Where are you going?" Pete asked as he followed me out. I ignored him as we made our way back to the table.

Taking a twenty out of my wallet, I tossed it onto the table. "I'm heading home."

"What happened?" Ryan asked, looking from me to Pete.

"Nothing, I'm just eager to see Saryn, that's all."

Roger laughed. "Dude, I know Ryan is cool with it and all, but I'm pretty sure he doesn't need to know you want to..."

"Shut up, Roger," I said as I looked at Ryan. He appeared amused by me leaving.

"This is why I refuse to settle down with anyone," Jack said. "Once they get their claws in, all the fun is sucked right out of you."

I slapped him on the back and said, "Just wait until you fall in love."

He and Roger both made gagging sounds as Pete and Ryan laughed.

With a wave goodbye to my brother and friends, I quickly headed to my truck and drove straight to Saryn's house.

Chapter 37

Saryn

I PACED THE living room as I thought about how I was going to tell Truitt I was carrying his baby.

Yes, things had been good between us. So good. Great, in fact. But a baby.

A baby.

A surprise baby.

I was over the moon, but how would Truitt feel? He hadn't even mentioned not using condoms anymore. He still put one on every time we had sex, and I assumed it was a double precaution because he wasn't ready for a baby.

I thought back to when I had thrown up on the poor doctor, and then asked her how in the world I had gotten pregnant. I knew it only took one time, one thing going wrong. The condom had broken in the shower. But I had still been on the pill. Then it dawned on me. I'd missed taking my pill back in November for a few days. With everything going on and seeing Truitt again and the move back home, I hadn't given it a second thought.

"Oh, Truitt. How are you going to react?"

I glanced at the clock on the mantel. Liliana was spending the night at my parents' house, and Truitt had texted to tell me he was meeting some of the guys for drinks at the Rusty Nail. I already felt guilty as hell that I'd found out yesterday and hadn't told Truitt yet. I was nervous though. Scared of how he would react and worried he would think I was attempting to trap him.

"He is not going to think that, Saryn," I chastised myself.

I heard someone drive up and park. I looked out the window and saw it was Truitt. Rus barked and ran to the back door.

"No running, Rus!" I called out, still being overprotective, though, he had clearly healed weeks ago.

Why was Truitt back so soon? Had the guys decided not to go out?

Drawing in a deep breath, I closed my eyes and quickly sent up a prayer for the right way to break the news to Truitt.

When I opened my eyes, he was standing there. I smiled when I saw him holding a giant bouquet of roses.

"Those are beautiful," I said as I made my way over to him. Rus jumped up a few times until Truitt told him to sit.

"You're not going to believe what happened to me in HEB when I was buying the flowers."

Knowing this could go any way, I asked, "What happened?"

He rolled his eyes and replied, "I knocked over a huge display of flowers. Don't ask me how, I just did. Water went everywhere, and I'm pretty sure the lady who works in the floral department called me a jackass idiot."

I covered my mouth and tried not to laugh but failed.

"Truitt! How?"

He shrugged and handed me the red roses. "Be careful, there are thorns, and if you're like me, you might have forgotten that. Maybe I never even knew it, but I do now."

He held up a finger; there was a bandage wrapped around it.

Carefully, I took the flowers and walked into the kitchen. I gently put them on the counter, and then took out a vase to fill up with water. I trimmed the roses and placed them in the vase and set it on the middle of the kitchen island.

"What are you doing home, and why did you bring flowers? What happened?" I asked suspiciously.

With a soft chuckle, Truitt walked over to me and picked up my hands. He looked me directly in the eyes.

"Is it true? Are you carrying our baby?"

My stomach dropped, then flipped, then my heart fluttered. I must have opened my mouth a dozen times before I finally asked, "How did you know? Truitt, I only just found out yesterday. How? When?"

He laughed and crushed his mouth to mine. Then he drew my body up against his and deepened the kiss. There was no longer any need to worry about how he would react.

"Right now, it doesn't matter. All I want to do is take you to bed and make love to you, after you promise me something."

I was limp in his arms, relief flooding through my veins, along with a sense of desire. He knew. Truitt knew I was pregnant, and he seemed happy.

"Anything," I whispered to him.

Truitt looked at me and those blue eyes seemed to peer right into the depths of my soul.

"Let me marry you."

My eyes widened and I tried not to, but I laughed at the craziness of his words.

"Marry you! Truitt, we..."

"Are in love. We're having a baby, and you're the only woman I have ever wanted to spend the rest of my life with. I want you to be mine. I want to adopt Liliana and officially make her my daughter. I want us to be a family."

Tears filled my eyes, and I threw my arms around his neck. When he wrapped his arms around me and whispered, "I love you so much," I cried even harder.

Truitt reached down, picked me up, and then carried me to the bedroom. He sat down on the edge of the bed and rested me on his lap.

"Are those happy tears?"

"Yes!" I said, wiping them away.

"Yes, you'll marry me, or yes, they're happy tears?"

"Yes to both!" I exclaimed.

He grinned and then moved to place me on the bed.

"Strip out of your clothes, because I am dying to be inside you with no condom on."

I laughed and leaned up on my elbows. "What?"

He pulled his shirt over his head and tossed it to the side. Then he worked at toeing off his boots and taking off his jeans as I knelt on the bed and began to undress. I'd seen Truitt strip in excitement to have sex before, but this time he was moving at warp speed.

Truitt stood before me in nothing but his boxer briefs. My mouth watered at the sight, and my fingers itched to touch his toned body. With each movement he made, his muscles flexed. My goodness, when would I get used to this man and his beauty, both inside and out?

And I was having his baby.

My stomach fluttered like mad. When he pushed his boxers down and revealed his erection, I instantly felt the wetness between my legs and moaned.

Truitt crawled onto the bed, which caused me to fall back onto it and wait for him to touch me. I practically shook with anticipation.

"The entire drive from HEB to here I kept thinking about how now we can have sex with no condom." His eyes closed for a moment before he looked into mine. "I'm going to warn you now, sweetheart, I may come the moment I slip inside you."

I giggled. "Is this all real?"

He moaned as he kissed along my neck. His lips made their way to my ear where he nibbled on the lobe before he pushed himself barely inside me. We both gasped, then he softly said, "No dream could ever be this amazing. Or make me feel this alive."

My fingers moved slowly over his back, feeling each movement he made.

"Make love to me, Truitt. Please."

His hands moved down my body, and he gripped my ass, tilting my hips up so that he could slide inside of me. This feeling was unlike anything I'd ever experienced before. I'd only ever been with one other man without a condom. I wasn't expecting the connection between me and Truitt to be so intense. So moving. So unbelievably sexy.

Truitt groaned out in satisfaction, then looked into my eyes.

"I want to stay like this forever."

I reached up and placed my hand on the side of his face. "So do I."

His mouth crushed to mine in what started as a sweet kiss, but quickly turned into something so much more passionate.

Our sweet lovemaking quickly turned to more.

So. Much. More.

After hours of making love in bed, mixed with some of the hottest sex I'd ever had in the shower, and on the kitchen island, and on the recliner in the living room, I laid in Truitt's arms with my head resting on his chest. I moved my fingers absentmindedly over his muscles while he breathed, slow and steady.

"Saryn?" he asked, his voice sounding so at ease and carefree.

I moved my head, resting my chin on the back of my hand as I gazed into his beautiful blue eyes.

"Yes?" I responded in an equally relaxed voice. To say I was sexually satisfied would be an understatement.

It was also the first time in the last few weeks I hadn't felt queasy.

A brilliant smile broke out on his face, and I almost sighed at the sight of it.

"Will you do me the honor of becoming my wife?"

Heat radiated through my entire body as my heartbeat picked up from sheer happiness.

"Yes. Nothing would make me happier than becoming your wife."

I hadn't thought it possible, but his smile grew wider and he pulled me farther up his body and kissed me so sweetly I nearly cried. I moved and rolled on top of him. I settled down on his growing erection and rocked slightly.

"When are we going to tell Liliana about the baby?" Truitt asked as he gripped the sides of my hips.

"I don't know. Maybe we should wait until I'm a bit farther along."

He nodded and lifted me slightly up as he moved his hips. With my hands on his chest, I practically purred as I sank down on him and he filled me to the core.

"Fuck," Truitt gasped.

I gave him a saucy grin. I planned on doing exactly that.

Before I could move, he spoke again. "Let's get married as soon as possible."

With a frown, I asked, "Are you worried people will find out we got pregnant out of wedlock?"

He laughed, and I felt him grow slightly inside me. It felt delicious, and I wanted desperately to move, but he held me still.

"Hell no. I don't give two shits about that. But I do want to start our lives together as soon as possible. I want us to move in together and be a family of three before the baby comes."

I nodded. "I think we should move into your house."

Truitt smiled. "Really?"

Rocking my hips slightly to get some sort of friction, Truitt eased his grip on me.

"Yes. As much as I love being near my folks, I want to start our lives with just the three of us."

"Four, if you count Rus."

A small bark came from the side of my bed where Rus was laying in his dog bed.

With a chuckle, I placed my hands on my stomach. "Five, if we're going to get technical about it."

Truitt laughed once more and flipped us over, somehow managing to stay inside me.

"Okay. Then let's plan the wedding and then move you and Liliana in with me and Rus."

My fingers pushed through his brown hair as I watched his deep blue eyes sparkle with happiness.

"I can't believe I'm marrying you...and having your baby," I whispered, utter disbelief mixed with pure happiness.

He withdrew some, then slowly pushed inside of me as he brought his lips to mine. He kissed me softly and whispered, "How did I get so damn lucky in love?"

Chapter 38

Truitt

"MARRIED? ON VALENTINE'S Day?" my mother said, a look of utter shock on her face.

Evie, on the other hand, had a notebook and pen at the ready. "There are so many things to do! We only have two weeks!"

While Evie launched into planning mode, my mother sat perfectly still and silent. Both my father and Will stood and shook my hand and then hugged Saryn.

While Saryn was busy talking to her mother and our fathers, I walked over to my mother. She looked lost in thought.

"Mom?"

Her gaze lifted, and she smiled. It wasn't the distant smile I'd grown up with, yet something was wrong.

"Is everything okay?"

She took in a slow, deep breath, and then exhaled just as slowly. "May we speak, alone?"

"Of course. Back porch?" I asked.

With a nod, I reached out for her and she took my arm. We walked together toward the back of the house.

"We're going to get some fresh air," I called back to everyone.

Saryn smiled and nodded as Evie called, "Don't be long, we have a ton of things to plan!"

My father narrowed his gaze slightly before turning back to the conversation at hand.

We walked through the dining room and into the large open kitchen, then out through the mudroom and onto the back porch that stretched the length of my house.

"This piece of land is so different from the ranch," she mused.

I looked out over the Hill Country and smiled. "It is."

"Truitt, why didn't you build your house on the ranch, like your brother did?"

With a shrug, I replied, "I guess I wanted something that was mine. That I'd earned with my own hands."

She turned and leaned against the wooden railing. Her eyes were focused so intently on me that I found myself wondering if she was about to tell me she was leaving the country again.

"Truitt, are you sure about this? Getting married so quickly? Why the rush for a wedding right now?"

"I love her, I want to marry her. I thought you liked Saryn."

"I do!" she was quick to say. "I adore her, as a matter of fact. And Liliana. It's just, the two of you have had this whirlwind romance, and now barely a few months into being together you want to get married. I'm just worried it's for the wrong reason."

"The wrong reason?"

She turned and looked out over the countryside. "Your father and I barely knew each other when we got married. People around town said my father forced your daddy's father into agreeing to the marriage. Your daddy and I never even had a say in it."

I looked down and gave a small nod. "Dad told me a little bit about it."

Her expression was one of utter sadness. "I wasn't the girl your daddy wanted to marry, but I tried so hard to be the woman he might fall in love with. Rumors flew around town about him stepping out on me, and I looked the other way. I guess I did it because I felt like he had no choice in the matter when it came to marrying me."

I took a step back. "What?"

She gave me a weak smile. "It's silly thinking now, I know that. And your father and I are actually in a really good place. Together. But I can't help but wonder with this rushed wedding and the way you are looking at Saryn...the way you are so protective of her today, well..." She gave a soft laugh. "Once upon a time your father looked at me that way when I was pregnant with your brother."

I swallowed hard, and she took my hands.

"Was this baby planned, Truitt?" She looked almost sick with herself for even asking.

"Saryn didn't trap me, Mom. Um..." I felt my cheeks grow hot as I was about to tell her what happened. "We used protection every time, but once my condom did break. Saryn is on the pill, but things happen."

A wide smile broke out over her face, and she hugged me. "I knew she wasn't that type of girl, but I don't want rumors to follow her around like they have me."

"We're going to announce the pregnancy when she's out of the first trimester, and I don't give two shits if people know that she was pregnant when we got married."

"So, you're happy?" Mom asked as she squeezed my hand.

I returned her smile with one of my own. I knew there was a deeper reason she was asking me all of this. My parents hadn't been happy when they got married. "I've never been happier, Mom. I'm glad you're here to share this with me."

Tears pooled in her eyes and she looked down to regain composure.

Things with my parents seemed to be getting better. After Christmas Eve they insisted we do a family dinner once a week. Roger hated it at first, but eventually he grew to enjoy our dinner nights.

Liliana adored him. She was calling him Uncle Roger now. Her little family was growing by leaps and bounds, and she was thriving.

"Mom, how are things with you and Dad?"

"Like I said, we're in a good place. I'm seeing someone once a week, a therapist."

I lifted my brows in surprise. "Really? That's good."

She nodded. "It is. I realized when I heard you and Saryn were together that I was being selfish. All those years I was so angry at your father for cheating on me. The affair didn't last long, maybe a month or two, but the pain was so real. Maybe it was all the other affairs, as well, that hit me all at once. When Roger took me aside Christmas Eve and asked me if I knew about Tim and Liliana, something inside of me cracked open. I was finally able to talk to you boys about it, and that was such a relief. I took my hurt and anger out on the two of you, and I will never be able to make up for that."

I took her into my arms and rested my chin on top of her head. "Mom, the past is in the past. You're here now, and that is all that matters."

She hugged me tightly before stepping out of my arms.

"So, the baby is a secret for now?"

"Yes."

There was a hint of a smirk at the corners of her mouth. "You do realize that Evie knows."

I jerked my head back in surprise. "How?"

With a wave of her hand, my mother laughed. "Truitt, please. A mother knows these things. It only took one look at that girl tonight to see. She practically lit up the entire room with that glow on her cheeks."

"She is glowing, isn't she?" I said with a smile so big my cheeks hurt.

My mother nodded. "Yes, she is. Now, we better get back in there."

As we walked back into the house, Saryn came down the long hall from the direction of the master bedroom. I could tell instantly she had gotten sick. Apparently, so could my mother. She jumped into action and wet a paper towel for her.

"Sweetheart, put this behind your neck. It used to ease the nausea for me when I was pregnant with the boys."

A look of shock passed over Saryn's face. "You told her?"

Laughing, I answered, "No. She seems to have some weird sense for this kind of thing."

Saryn looked at my mother who promptly hugged her and whispered, "I won't tell a soul."

When they parted and Saryn looked at me, she sighed. "My mother knows, as well. She whispered it in my ear when my parents first walked in. She said I was glowing and told me to tell her later how far along I was."

Mom let out a howl of laughter.

I rolled my eyes and brushed a piece of hair from Saryn's cheek. "Do you want to lie down?"

"No. We have way too much to do." Looking at my mother, Saryn grinned. "Is everything okay?"

Taking Saryn's arm in hers, my mother replied, "Everything is more than okay. I'm going to have the daughter I've always wanted and another grandbaby."

It wasn't lost on me that she said *another*. Saryn must have noticed, too, because she wiped away a tear that had slipped free.

"Thank you, Janet."

My mother gave Saryn a wink. "Come on, let's get back in there. We have a lot of things to plan and only a little time to do it."

When Saryn glanced back to me she mouthed, *I love you*.

"Love you, too," I said as I followed them back into the main living room.

The rest of the evening was spent eating pizza Ryan and Roger had brought over and talking about throwing the best quickie wedding the town of Boerne had ever seen.

Chapter 39

Saryn

L UCY STOOD BEFORE me with her hand over her mouth.
"OH. My. Gawd. How does this dress fit you perfectly?"

"I don't know, but it's like it was made for me," I replied back.

The girl who worked at the dress shop beamed at me. "When I took your measurements I almost died. This dress has been sitting here for three months simply waiting for the right bride."

I smiled and wiped away the tears streaming down my face. Apparently with this baby I was not only going to be sick, I was going to cry all the time. I cried at everything, it seemed like.

Of course, the last two weeks had been a flurry of plans and dress shopping. This was my third time. The first two were with my mother and Janet. My mother had something to say about each dress I put on, while Janet told me I looked beautiful even in the ones that looked like potato sacks on me. I made the decision that Lucy and I were going to Austin, and I was hellbent on finding a dress. If I didn't find one today, then I was wearing jeans and a T-shirt. Especially since the wedding was in one week.

Lucy walked up next to me and stared at the reflection in the mirror. Lucy and I had quickly become the best of friends. So I couldn't help but notice how anytime Roger was around, Lucy became distracted and seemed to drift off. Roger also acted funny around her.

Truitt had a suspicion the two of them liked each other, and Lucy had admitted to me that she and Roger had slept together on New Year's Eve. Roger had thrown the party, and I swear there must have been a hundred girls invited to the twenty-five or so men. But Roger seemed to only have eyes for Lucy that night and since.

"Saryn, it's like it was made especially for you," she whispered. Turning to face the younger girl, Lucy asked, "What's the story behind the dress?"

The girl looked back to make sure no one was listening and took a step closer to us. When she started to speak, she lowered her voice. "The bride who was supposed to wear this caught her future husband-to-be in bed with her sister."

Lucy and I both gasped and said, "No!" in chorus.

The girl nodded. "The dress was completely paid for and in possession of the bride. She was due to get married the next day. She came in here, handed the dress back to the owner, and told her to sell it and donate the money to a charity. So that's what we're doing."

"What charity?" I asked.

"All the money we make from the sale of this dress will go toward Dell Children's NICU. Our owner's daughter spent a number of weeks there, and she'd like to repay them."

"Oh, shit, now you have to buy it, Saryn. It's like a damn sign," Lucy said.

The young girl looked at us, confused. "I was a NICU nurse," I explained.

Her eyes widened in delight. "No! Oh, it is a sign! I mean, there hasn't been another woman who has walked into the salon with the same exact measurements as the other bride. The dress was made for you!"

I looked back at it. The mermaid gown fit me like a glove. It screamed romance with its embroidery and embellishments that created a sexy yet sophisticated look. Beautiful flower designs sat atop the delicate tulle cathedral train and added the perfect touch.

The way the neckline plunged deep on the sequined corset gave the whole dress a dramatic look.

My chest warmed at the sight before me, and I placed my hand on my stomach. This was the dress. I knew it the moment I looked at myself in the mirror.

"How much is it?" I asked.

The young girl paused, and when I met her eyes in the mirror, she sheepishly said, "Three-thousand dollars."

I frowned. I knew that wasn't much in Truitt's eyes. He was paying for the entire wedding, with the exception of the dress. My parents had insisted they were taking care of that expense. My father had given me a budget of five thousand, which I had laughed at considering my first wedding dress cost me less than a thousand. I'd bought the second dress I had tried on, thinking at the time it would do. This time around I had wanted the perfect dress, and I was wearing it.

With a wide smile, I let out a breath and said, "I'll take it."

Lucy and the young girl jumped for joy.

"Let's get it off and steamed up and then you are set!"

One week later, I was staring at myself in the same dress. This time Liliana was standing next to me, and it was my wedding day.

February fourteenth. Valentine's Day.

Liliana was dressed in a white satin and tulle dress that tied in the back with a giant bow. We had stumbled upon it in a little children's boutique store in San Antonio while looking for dresses for my mother and Janet. Janet spied it first, and when I saw it was Liliana's size, we all jumped for joy. It was perfect. Yet another sign.

Everything for the wedding seemed to fall right into place. It was small. Family and close friends only. We were getting married on my parents' ranch in a spot that overlooked the beautiful Texas Hill Country. The reception was being held in one of the barns Ryan and my father had converted into a living area of sorts. Ryan had hosted many a poker game and bachelor party there. Today, though, it had been transformed. The ladies in Mom's book club volunteered to decorate everything for the reception. We kept it simple. They draped tulle so that it rolled across the ceiling in waves. White roses filled Mason jars on the table, with white lanterns hanging down from the rafters. Old wooden chairs my folks had up in the attic were brought down and simple white lace fabric was tied to the back of each chair. Ryan and Truitt had spent the last week making three, twelve-foot-long tables to be used for the reception. At the entrance of the barn, large white panels of fabric had been hung and tied back to give the barn a more elegant look.

Everything was perfect.

A light knock came at the door, and I turned to see who Lucy was talking to. She smiled and nodded. We were getting ready in the small cabin that had once upon a time been used by the hunters, but was now my mother's office.

"Truitt wants you to go to the window, he has something he wants to show you."

I looked at her, stunned. "He wants to see me before the wedding?"

She shook her head. "No, just walk over to the window."

I opened the large wooden shutter doors and the moment I looked out, I gasped. Sitting out front was a carriage. A horse-drawn carriage.

"Because every queen and princess needs a carriage." The voice came from the side of the window and my heart jumped at the sound of it.

"Truitt," I whispered. Liliana was holding my hand, looking at the large princess-cut diamond ring Truitt had slipped on my finger last night when we spent the evening alone having supper and just relaxing. While everyone else was at the rehearsal, we were home in bed, making love and eating leftover barbecue. Once midnight approached, Truitt kissed me goodbye and walked towards my parents' house where he had then stayed the night.

"Are you nervous?" he asked.

I laughed. "No. Are you?"

"Nervous as hell, but happy beyond belief."

His hand came around, and I reached for it. I could hear the photographer behind me snapping picture after picture.

"So pwetty, Mommy," Liliana said, twisting the diamond back and forth on my finger.

"Hey, princess," Truitt called out, causing Liliana to yell out Truitt's name and nearly dive through the window. Luckily, Lucy saw that coming and grabbed her.

"Are you ready to become my wife?" Truitt asked, still holding onto my hand.

"Beyond ready. What about you, ready to give up the bachelor life for an instant family?"

"It's what I've been praying for every night."

My heart jumped, and I clutched my chest. This man knew how to make me weak in the knees and speechless.

"I love you so much," I said as I squeezed his hand.

Truitt stepped in front of the window, a blindfold wrapped around his eyes and a smile on his face.

"Kiss me and prove it."

I laughed and leaned out the window. "You goofy man. Please tell me you're not walking around with that on. You'll break your leg!"

"Don't worry, I've got him covered," Roger said, appearing next to his brother. He looked past me, and his eyes widened in delight when he saw Lucy.

"Wow," he said, unable to tear his gaze away from her.

"Does she look beautiful?" Truitt asked.

Roger nodded. "Most beautiful woman I've ever seen."

I cleared my throat and tilted my head as I regarded Roger. His eyes snapped up to me and a blush hit his cheeks.

"Um, I mean, Saryn looks stunning, yes."

Truitt frowned and spun around. "You better not be checking out my future wife, you asshole."

I covered my mouth and giggled. "He was actually looking at someone else and not me."

"Oh, is that so?" Truitt said, intrigued.

"Shut up or I'll spin you around and tell you to find your own way to the altar."

Truitt laughed and then turned again, his back to me.

"I'll see you in a few minutes?"

Roger sighed. "For the love of Christ, man. Has love made you stupid?" He placed his hands on Truitt and turned him so he was facing me.

I fought to hold back the giggles. "I'll see you in a few."

Before I knew what was happening, I was being handed my bouquet, ushered to the carriage, and driven up to the spot where we were getting married. Everything had to be done down to the minute since we were attempting to time the wedding with the sunset. The day had been beautiful and warm for a Texas winter. The few clouds in the sky meant we would have a brilliant sunset, and I was beside myself with anticipation.

The carriage pulled up and stopped. My father got out and helped Liliana down first. She promptly took Lucy's hand. She was given a basket and told not to throw the petals yet.

My father blocked my view of Truitt and, to be honest, I didn't have the courage to look at him yet. I knew the moment I saw him my knees would most likely buckle and my poor father would have to carry me to him.

I took Daddy's hand and allowed him to help me out of the carriage. He placed his hands on my upper arms and said, "You look so happy."

"I am happy, Daddy. He makes me happy."

He kissed me lightly on the cheek. "I know he does. Let's go get you married to the right guy this time."

With a half laugh, half groan, I nodded. I looked down and waited for him to stand at my side. The music started. That was my cue to walk, and when I looked up, Truitt was turning around to watch me. He must have had his back to us, waiting for the music to start.

When our eyes met, my breath caught in my throat and I stumbled slightly. Daddy held onto me and leaned down to say, "I thought he was the klutz, not you."

I giggled and squeezed his arm. Truitt must have seen me trip, because he laughed slightly and shook his head. My eyes drifted to Liliana skipping down the aisle.

"Mommy's getting hitched!" she cried out as everyone laughed over the music. I quickly searched for Ryan and gave him a stern look. He had taken it upon himself this past week to teach my daughter that when she walked down the aisle she needed to sing a special song. It was supposed to be a surprise for me. He laughed and shrugged.

"Mommy's getting hitched!" Liliana cried out again. Then she saw Truitt and ran to him. He bent down and caught her in his arms, lifted her up, and pointed for her to look at me. He whispered something into her ear, and she nodded and smiled as she waved to me.

"Oh, Daddy," I mumbled at the sight that nearly had me tripping again.

"He's a good man, Saryn. There's no doubt in my mind that he loves you and Liliana. He's going to make an amazing father."

A single tear slipped free, and I didn't even bother to wipe it away.

My father stopped in front of Truitt and gave him my hand. I didn't even hear what the preacher was saying because my gaze was locked on the man I had loved since I knew what love was. The man I had once dreamed would be mine and then thought I'd lost. The man who not only loved me but loved my daughter. Our daughter. And would love the child growing inside me just as fiercely.

He lifted my veil and drew in a sharp breath. His voice cracked slightly as he whispered, "My God. You are so beautiful."

I smiled and felt every nerve ending in my body tingle.

"You look awfully handsome, Mr. Carter."

Truitt leaned down and kissed me. It wasn't a quick kiss.

Roger stepped up and placed his hand on Truitt's shoulder, giving him a slight jerk to get him to stop kissing me. Roger was now holding Liliana in his arms. He looked beyond handsome in his tux, holding his niece. I could only imagine what was going on in Lucy's head right now. The two of them tried to pretend they weren't attracted to one another, but both Truitt and I saw the sparks.

"Um, Truitt, as much as we all love to see you displaying your affection for Saryn, I don't think we're at that part yet, dude."

Truitt winked at me and took a step back.

We hardly took our eyes off each other during the ceremony. And when it finally came time for the kiss, Truitt gave me another searing kiss. Then everyone cheered as we were introduced as Mr. and Mrs. Carter.

Truitt took Liliana from Roger, and we walked down the aisle hand in hand. Our little family of four. No, our family of five. Rus raced past us with his little black tie around his neck and made a beeline for the open field. All that sitting still must have been too much for him.

Truitt placed Liliana in the carriage and then took my hand and helped me up. He sat down next to me and let Liliana crawl onto his lap.

"I don't know how it happened, but God has answered almost every one of my prayers," he said.

With my brows raised, I asked, "You have more requests?"

He nodded and flashed me that smile of his that made me want to strip him down and lose myself in him. "Just one more."

"Now what?" Liliana asked.

I looked down at her and said, "Well, now Mommy and Truitt are married and we're all going to live together in Truitt's house and be a family."

Her eyes lit up, and she turned to face Truitt. Her arms wrapped around his neck, and she cried out in joy, "I wuv you, Daddy."

My heart instantly felt full, and a rush of happiness raced through my body. Truitt seemed utterly shocked at first and didn't move. We hadn't talked to Liliana about her calling Truitt Daddy.

He wrapped his arms around her and I watched as the tears he had been fighting to hold back broke free.

"I love you, too, baby girl. So very much, Liliana."

Truitt reached for my hand and smiled. "*Now* he's answered all of my prayers."

Epilogue

Truitt - Two years later

"**D**ADDY, MAY I ask you a question?"
Turning my attention to my five-year-old daughter, I smiled. "Of course you can, pumpkin. You can always ask me anything."

She grinned. "When can I have my own horse?"

I laughed. "Always in a rush to grow up, aren't you?"

Those blue eyes looked up at me and sparkled. Nearly every day, Liliana and I went for a ride on my gelding, Marco. From the first time Saryn placed her in front of me in the saddle, Liliana had been hooked. It was our thing, and I fucking loved it.

"Get her to fall in love with horses, and she won't be interested in men," Will had told me time and time again.

"I'm a big girl now, you said so."

I nodded. "I did say that. What kind of horse do you want?"

Feeling her almost vibrate with excitement, she answered, "I don't care, as long as she's a girl. It's got to be a girl, Daddy."

"A mare."

She nodded. "I forgot. A mare. I'd like a mare, Daddy. Maybe one like Uncle Ryan's horse."

"A paint. My girl has good taste."

Liliana giggled.

"I've got an idea. I need to swing by the shop today and check out a playhouse, and I'm going to need your expert advice on it."

She nodded and said, "I'm on it!"

Since I'd married Saryn, Liliana had become the official tester for all the playhouses we built. We would send her in when they were almost complete and see what she liked and didn't like. There were many times when we followed her around and she asked where something was; in her little mind there should be a telescope here or a chair to read in there. Liliana was very much like her mother, and I wouldn't be surprised if she ended up working for the business someday. Hell, she'd probably take it over and do better than me. She was a valuable member of the team and even had her own T-shirt with her name on the back of it and the title, *Official Playhouse Tester*.

"How about this. We stop by, check out the playhouse, then stop and pick up a surprise for Mommy and then head home and make Mommy dinner."

"Yes! I love that idea. Can we get a surprise for Nolan, too?"

My heart melted. We had named our son after Nolan, my best friend who had surprised me and came in for the wedding. I knew how hard it was on him to be back in Boerne after the loss of his child and Linnzi leaving him.

When baby Nolan was born, he made the trip back to Boerne again. I was hoping he could come again for Nolan's second birthday party.

"If you want to get a surprise for your brother, we certainly can. That's very sweet of you. You're a great big sister."

Liliana leaned her head back against me and let out a very dramatic sigh. "He can be a pain, Daddy."

"Well, he is only two, or almost two."

Another sigh. "I hope the next baby we have is a girl."

I laughed. "You're ready for another baby, huh?"

"Maybe. I'm not sure. Today I am, but tomorrow, well, I might not want her tomorrow so maybe we should wait."

I kissed her light brown curls and turned the horse toward the barn. To my surprise, waiting for us was Saryn and baby Nolan.

"Hey there!" I called out.

My wife and son both waved in excitement.

I slid off of Marco and helped Liliana down. She ran over to Saryn and hugged her.

"Mommy, I'm going to test a playhouse, then we're going to get you a surprise, it's flowers, then Daddy said I can buy something for Nolan."

Nolan cried out in excitement simply from picking up on Liliana's excitement.

"Sweetheart, when we say the flowers are a surprise, we aren't supposed to tell Mommy that."

Liliana covered her mouth and giggled. "I did it again!"

Saryn chuckled and looked up at me. "Your mom and dad offered to watch the kids tonight."

My entire body jumped at the idea of being with my wife for an entire evening alone.

"Really? Both kids?"

She nodded and wagged her brows. "I wanted to have a date night with my sexy husband."

"I like the sound of that," I stated.

Saryn took Liliana's hand. "Come on, let's go eat an early dinner and then pack up for Grandpa and Grandma's house."

"But what about the playhouse and surprise?" she asked with a concerned expression.

"We'll do it tomorrow," I replied.

"Yay!" Liliana cried out as she nearly dragged Saryn back to the house.

As I walked Marco back into the barn, Saryn called out. "I left you a gift in the barn. It's in a small brown bag."

"Okay!" I called back to her. After taking off Marco's saddle and getting him washed and brushed, I walked him back to his stall to give him some oats. Then I saw the small brown bag sitting on the bench across from Marco's stall. I walked over and picked it up. I opened it and pulled out a long box. It was the kind that you might keep a bracelet or necklace in. I opened it and nearly fell to my knees.

I reached in and took out the pregnancy test, the positive pregnancy test.

"Holy crap," I whispered.

"Hey," came a soft voice from behind me. Turning, I couldn't help but smile when I saw my beautiful wife leaning against the barn door.

"Hey."

Her eyes fell to the test in my hand. "I know how much you love a good surprise, so…"

I moved as fast as I could and took her into my arms. Her laugh was beautiful and carefree as she wrapped her arms around my neck.

"You're pregnant."

"Yep. Are you happy?"

"Happy? Saryn, I'm the luckiest guy in the state of Texas."

Her fingers raked through my hair, and her grin turned to a frown. She moved my head to the side and started to laugh.

"Hold still, you have gum in your hair."

The End

Kelly Elliott is a *New York Times* and *USA Today* bestselling contemporary romance author. Since finishing her bestselling Wanted series, Kelly continues to spread her wings while remaining true to her roots and giving readers stories rich with hot protective men, strong women and beautiful surroundings.

Her bestselling works include, *Wanted, Broken, The Playbook, and Lost Love*, to name a few.

Kelly lives in central Texas with her husband, daughter, two pups, four cats, and endless wildlife creatures. When she's not writing, Kelly enjoys reading and spending time with her family.

To find out more about Kelly and her books, you can find her through her website.

www.kellyelliottauthor.com

Other Books by Kelly Elliott

Stand Alones
The Journey Home
Who We Were*
The Playbook*
Made for You*
*Available on audiobook

Cowboys and Angels Series
Lost Love
Love Profound
Tempting Love
Love Again
Blind Love
This Love
Reckless Love
*Series available on audiobook

Wanted Series
Wanted*
Saved*
Faithful*
Believe
Cherished*
A Forever Love*
The Wanted Short Stories
All They Wanted
*Available on audiobook

Love Wanted in Texas Series
Spin-off series to the WANTED Series
Without You
Saving You

Holding You
Finding You
Chasing You
Loving You
Entire series available on audiobook
*Please note Loving You combines the last book of the Broken and
Love Wanted in Texas series.

Broken Series
Broken*
Broken Dreams*
Broken Promises*
Broken Love
*Available on audiobook

The Journey of Love Series
Unconditional Love
Undeniable Love
Unforgettable Love
*Entire series available on audiobook

With Me Series
Stay With Me
Only With Me
*Series on audiobook

Speed Series
Ignite
Adrenaline

Boston Love Series
Searching for Harmony
Fighting for Love
*Series available on audiobook

Austin Singles Series
Seduce Me
Entice Me
Adore Me
*Series available on audiobook

Southern Bride Series
Love at First Sight
Delicate Promises
Divided Interests
Lucky in Love
Feels Like Home September 2020
Take Me Away (TBD)

Coming Soon
Feels Like Home (Book five in the Southern Bride series)
September 1, 2020
Good Enough (Book three in the Meet Me in Montana series) TBD
Boggy Creek Valley Series 2021

Collaborations
Predestined Hearts (co-written with Kristin Mayer)
Play Me (co-written with Kristin Mayer)
Dangerous Temptations (co-written with Kristin Mayer)

YA Novels written under the pen name Ella Bordeaux
Beautiful
Forever Beautiful

Historical
Predestined Hearts by Kelly Elliott and Kristin Mayer